THE CHRIST VIRUS

DAVE SLADE

Zebulun Publishing

Visit Dave Slade's web site at www.daveslade.com.

The Christ Virus

Zebulun Publishing
P.O. Box 67526
Albuquerque, N.M., 87193

Printed in the United States of America. All rights reserved.

Second Edition: September 2018

ISBN-10: 0-9854750-0-5
ISBN-13: 978-0-9854750-0-0

This novel is a work of fiction. Names, characters, places, police departments, government agencies, corporations, religious institutions, and incidents are the product of the author's imagination or are used fictitiously. Any resemblance to actual events, locales, or persons, living or dead, is entirely coincidental and beyond the intent of either the author or publisher.

What is the ultimate terrorist scenario? One that could collapse financial markets, bring governments to their knees and strike terror into the heart of every person?

Sulaiman Hadid knows. The answer is so simple that not a single bullet or missile will have to be fired. No explosives ingeniously hidden from airport scanners. And the U.S. government has made it even easier.

He was called for a time like this, prophesied hundreds of years ago. A time of moral decay and degradation. A time of godlessness and self-indulgence. The stench has filled God's nostrils. With a strong hand, the Creator will separate tares from wheat and cleanse the earth. From the ashes, He will raise a new order—one that is holy, undefiled, and faithful.

The end is near. A new beginning at hand.

■■

"Beyond a great read, this is one of those thrillers that leaves you looking at the world around you with a fresh perspective. Dave Slade delivers in a big way!"

—Wanda Dyson
Bestselling author of *Shepherd's Run*

To my wife, Holly, who encouraged this journey,
made it possible, and shared it.

Major Characters

Luke Chavez ....Pastor

Sulaiman Hadid..................Leader of Mahdi's Chosen

Dr. Jenny George...............Virologist

Hank Jackson ....Newspaper reporter

Reed Hamilton ..................U.S. Vice President

D.W. Coltrane ....Assassin

Pepper Stanton ....Chief of Staff for
Vice President Hamilton

Cindy Chavez....................Luke's wife

Rashid Kamer....................Sulaiman's cousin

Dr. PJ Singh ....Colleague of Dr. George

Dr. Denton Mabe................DNA sequencing analyst

Abdul Kamal.....................Influential radical imam

Kat Rodriguez ....Sanctuary survivor

Gavin Nash........................Forty-fifth U.S. President

"Yes, the time is coming that whoever kills you will think that he offers God service."

John 16:2

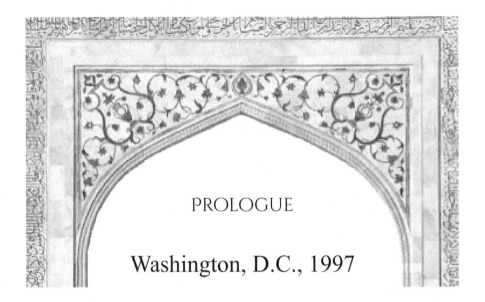

PROLOGUE

Washington, D.C., 1997

"I had a dream last night." Slanted rays transformed the imam's gray beard into glistening silver. "I stood in a great hall. It was filled with hundreds of flags representing the world's countries. Then all of the flags dipped toward the ground as if they were bowing except for one."

The imam stood beneath a dome at the Islamic Center. Behind him a wall of green, blue, and gold tiles formed a striking geometric pattern like a woven tapestry. Rashid leaned over to Samuel. "This is the teacher I told you about. His name is Abdul Kamal."

The man in front of Rashid turned around and frowned.

"In the center of the hall stood one flag. Can you guess which one?" The old man's dark eyes, nearly hidden behind drooping skin, searched the silent room. "It was Turkey."

Heads throughout the hall nodded.

"So what," Samuel muttered. He pulled his t-shirt away from sticky skin. The July heat was making its way inside.

"Cousin, some of Islam's greatest leaders are from Turkey."

What concerned Samuel more than the dream was whether his parents would discover where he was this Friday afternoon. It was a holiday for students and an administration day for teachers. He told them he was going to see Rashid which was true. But he left out the part about coming to a mosque. They would have strictly forbidden it.

The imam's raspy voice rang out. "Soon Islam will rise again to the glory it once enjoyed." He raised his hands upward as if appealing directly to Allah. "Last night I cried out to God. Why have you allowed the Christians and Jews to oppress your people? How long must we wait before the infidels who have controlled the world for so long see justice? How long before the Mahdi returns? The Twelfth Imam, the Guided One, the Lord of the Age."

Samuel had never seen such passion in his parents' church.

Rashid leaned over and whispered, "Muslims have been waiting centuries for the Mahdi to return. He's our Messiah. He will return in power and destroy his enemies. The whole world will worship him."

The imam lowered his hands and opened a book. "O prophet, urge the faithful to fight. If there are twenty among you with determination, they will vanquish two-hundred; if there are a hundred, they will slaughter a thousand unbelievers, for the infidels are a people devoid of understanding."

"The passage is from the Qur'an." Rashid covered his mouth with his hand to mute his voice.

Abdul stared into the crowd of worshippers. His eyes moved back and forth across the crowd. They stopped. "But even with one faithful, Allah can change the world as he did with his prophet Mohammed."

Is he looking at me? The sweat running down Samuel's back turned to an icy chill. The silence in the mosque became so pronounced he was afraid the men near him could hear his heart beating.

Abdul motioned with his hands for everyone to pray. Samuel leaned forward and pressed his forehead against an image of a doorway woven into the rug. The imam began to pray out loud.

Samuel knew every word the old man said before he said it.

How could he? Samuel had never set foot in a mosque. Yet everything felt familiar—the colors, the smells, the light.

He began to pray out loud. Words came slowly at first, then uncontrollably. The first few he spoke; the rest he sang. Rashid jabbed him with an elbow, but Samuel couldn't stop. He didn't understand anything he said, and from the confused stares around him, neither did anyone else. But it sounded beautiful, an unknown melody pouring from the depths of his soul.

What is happening to me?

The unexpected interruption of prayers brought a shocked look from the worshippers. Rashid looked frightened.

"Come here young man," the imam called out.

Samuel rose and walked toward the front of the mosque before several hundred Muslim men. As he drew closer, he could see the old man's skin was like worn leather.

"Who are you?" The teacher walked out from behind the podium.

"Samuel Kramer." He looked up at Abdul who stood nearly a foot higher on the podium.

He wished at that moment his name was anything but Samuel. Something like Rashid. Something more Muslim. For the first time he realized how Jewish his name sounded.

"Where did you learn to speak Aramaic?"

"I...I can't. The only language I know is English."

The imam raised his eyebrows. "You spoke every word flawlessly. Do you have any idea what you said?"

"No." And he didn't want to know. It had been a mistake to come to the mosque.

The old man took a deep breath, then exhaled slowly. A pungent smell of strong coffee flowed from his mouth. "My soul is Islam." He paused as if he were carefully weighing his next words. His dark eyes glistened. "I have called you as a father calls his son to crush the infidels. To throw down the mighty and exalt the lowly."

A gasp rippled through the mosque. Abdul stood and stared into the crowd. The stoop in his posture was gone; his sallow complexion transformed into a crimson glow.

"What have we witnessed?" He stood before the speechless crowd. "A young boy speaks in an ancient language few know. I've never seen such a thing. Can anyone explain it?" He waited for a reply. But no one spoke. "These aren't his words. It's a prophecy."

He looked back at Samuel and studied him for what seemed like a long time. He placed his hands on Samuel's shoulders and looked down into his eyes and smiled. His teeth were stained like old ivory. "You are only a boy. And many here may be asking, 'Why would Allah call a boy?' Many have been called in their youth."

I'm not a boy. I'm sixteen years old.

In a loud voice the imam cried out. "The Mahdi will reappear on the appointed day. He will fight against the forces of evil, lead a revolution, and set up a new world order based on justice, righteousness, and virtue. Islam will be victorious."

The old man laid trembling hands on Samuel's head as he bowed. "God has called you to strike fear into the hearts of the infidels. Perhaps, he is calling you to prepare the world for the Mahdi's return. That is something you will have to discover for yourself. I will give you a new name, one more appropriate for the task before you. Your Muslim name shall be Sulaiman Hadid, after the great leader Sulayman the Magnificent. It means strong prophet."

Abdul lifted his hands from Samuel's head.

He looked up at the imam. "How will I know what to do?"

"You will know at the right time, my son. You will know."

CHAPTER ONE

Congo, June 17, 2019

The sun beat down on the jeep as it bounced from rut to rut along the narrow road. In the distance Dr. Jenny George could see a wisp of smoke rising above the trees. She braced herself as the driver swerved to miss a deep hole. The medical supplies in the back slid sidewise and smacked against the truck. She swung around to ensure everything was still intact. A maze of green pressed in on all sides.

It was a world far removed from her job in Fort Detrick, Maryland where she worked as a virologist for the Centers for Disease Control and Prevention. There the constants and variables were known. Here everything was a guess. But she liked that. It provided the contrast she needed to balance her life—the yin to her yang. She lived what many would describe as a dull life. She was single and worked too much. But here in the jungle she lived life on the edge, which more than made up for long days in the lab.

The road ended at a small village. Tulie, her driver, got out of the jeep. Thick, dense foliage surrounded the village on all sides. A monkey standing nearby shrieked, then disappeared into the green canopy. An emaciated dog rummaged through garbage near one of the grass huts. It growled, closed its jaws around a small animal's remains, eyed them suspiciously, then ran off. An unattended fire burned in a pit near one of the huts.

In the distance an engine revved. It was the second jeep with her assistants Jacques and Dorian. Jenny opened one of the containers in her jeep and donned a white hazmat suit, heavy rubber gloves, and boots. Tulie helped her strap the air tank to her back. She adjusted the hood attached to the suit. She looked more fitted for a moon walk than a medical mission. But the village she was about to enter could be just as deadly as the moon's desolate surface.

It was hot inside the suit and sweat was already trickling down her back. June was the end of the rainy season. There would be four long months with little to no rain.

"You have to put it on," Jenny said. "You can't go in there without it."

Tulie looked at the suit as if he were still unsure. He slowly complied. Soon the dark face peering through the mask was the only evidence left of his identity. Jenny watched Jacques and Dorian climb out of their jeep and open a trunk. Within minutes they were suited up and ready to go. She motioned for them to follow her.

"Where are the villagers?" Jenny asked as she scanned the village for any signs of life. The radio transmitter inside her hood conveyed the question to her assistants.

Tulie shook his head as the group walked through the deserted village. They looked in hut after hut but found no one.

Then, the muffled sound of moans came from a hut in front of them. Jenny quickened her steps, though the heavy suit made running difficult. Inside, a skeletal woman lay on a packed dirt floor. Her dark skin, thin as parchment, was covered with black, oozing scabs that looked like leeches. Blood trickled from her mouth, ears, and the corners of her eyes. Jenny detected a sweet stench even though she knew the air she breathed was from the tank on her back. CDC had been trying to convince her to switch to a new portable air filtration system that was lighter with virtually unlimited capacity. But she preferred to carry her own air.

Her otherworldly appearance seemed to awaken the woman. She weakly raised her arm.

Ebola? Small pox? "She's trying to say something," Jenny said.

Tulie bent down close to the woman. "It's some dialect of Niger-Congo."

"Where is everyone?" he asked in some Afrikaans language.

Her eyes briefly lit up revealing dark, dilated pupils. She whispered something through swollen lips.

He stood up and looked at Jenny.

"What is it?"

"She says you have brought an evil spirit on her village that has killed everyone. Even the Sangoma."

"Sangoma?"

"A healer. Very sacred."

"How could I have brought an evil spirit on the village? I just arrived."

"I think we should leave," Tulie said. "The evil here must be very powerful if it could kill the Sangoma."

Jenny did not believe in the Sangoma or evil spirits, but she had learned to respect the cultural beliefs of the people whose countries she found herself a guest.

"I understand you're afraid. But if we leave, we won't be able to help the others. Many will die. Don't you want to save the other villages?"

Her appeal seemed to work. Tulie nodded slowly. Dorian brought in a container of medical supplies. He placed it on the dirt floor. A gold-and-orange tarantula scurried between his feet. He stomped several times on the dirt floor, mimicking a tribal dance. But the spider eluded him. The woman weakly waved her hand.

"Don't kill it," Tulie shouted.

"Why not? It's a bloody spider," Dorian said, still searching for it.

"Spiders are related to the African God Anansi."

"Oh, brother."

"Leave it alone, Dorian," Jenny said.

She opened the container and pulled out a syringe and several vials.

"I've got to get some blood samples before she dies. Tulie, take Dorian and Jacques with you and look around the village. See if anyone else is alive and if you find someone, get a blood sample."

Jenny looked at the woman. She wasn't moving. She caressed her forehead. *I wish there were something I could do.*

Jenny took the woman's limp wrist and searched for a pulse. She found one. A very weak one. She examined the woman's arm for a vein. They were all collapsed—and there were a number of needle punctures. Jenny checked the other arm. Same picture.

A drug user?

Not a single vein that would work. She looked at the woman's jugular vein and grimaced. *It's the only way.* Jenny inserted the needle into the side of the woman's neck and drew blood up into the vial. When it was full, she detached it and inserted another. After a half-dozen vials, she noticed the woman's eyes stared blankly at her. Her mouth was agape.

"Come here!" It sounded like Jacques. Jenny inverted each of the vials several times to prevent clotting then placed them in a biohazard container that looked like a small cooler and sealed the lid. She ran awkwardly toward the north end of the village. Her three assistants stood in the distance with their backs to her. *What are they looking at?* The answer stared back at her as she approached a long rectangular pit. Dozens of bloated, rotting bodies were piled upon each other. Flies swarmed over the mass grave. It was hard to estimate how many were there, but she guessed most of the village. Several of the dead had been ravaged by animals leaving remains that looked more hellish than human.

Oh, Lord.

"It's a massacre," Tulie said. "This is the worst I have seen since the Ebola outbreak in Sudan."

Dorian bent over and unzipped his hood.

"Don't!" Jenny ran to him and grabbed his hands. He pushed her aside and lurched forward and vomited.

"Do you know what you've done?"

He wiped his mouth. "What did you want me to do? Vomit inside the hood?"

"Exactly. You better pray this isn't airborne."

"Geez, the smell," Dorian said gasping. He pointed toward the bodies.

He dropped to his knees and retched again.

"Get back to the truck. Clean yourself up, and get your hood back on. You're going to ride back to the hospital in your suit. I'm not going to have you infect everyone else after the lengths we've gone to protect ourselves. Stupid Dorian. Very stupid."

The other men looked at her. They were frowning.

It was difficult leading a group of men, particularly Africans. They weren't used to answering to a woman. And, truthfully, she didn't like giving orders. It didn't come easily. She often felt on the verge of losing control. Could they tell?

"Tulie. Get the gas can from the jeep. We need to burn these bodies."

Through his hood, she saw horror in his eyes.

"You can't burn them," Tulie said. "We have to bury them."

Jenny was familiar with African burial practice and their beliefs in the afterlife. A proper burial for the deceased along with any personal items was important to ensure safe passage to the other side. Cremation destroyed this chance.

"Can't do it, Tulie. The bodies are infected. They have to be burned. You saw them. Scavengers have already been here."

"I won't burn them. It will bring evil on my family. It will bring evil on you too. Don't do it."

"I have to." She turned to Jacques. "Come with me." Jenny marched back to the truck and yanked the gas can from the truck.

Sometimes I'd like to...

"Jacques, get the can from the other truck and have Tulie help you bring the woman's body in the hut to the pit." Dorian leaned against the side of the truck still green.

Jenny walked back to the grave and doused the bodies with gasoline. Jacques and Tulie arrived with the old woman's body and hurled it into the center of the pile.

"Stand back," she said. She lit a match and threw it in the pit. In a flash fire engulfed the bodies. Flames stretched upward; smoke twisted like a cobra before its charmer. Some of the dead rose into a sitting position as their muscles contracted—a final protest to their ignominious end.

Jacques looked down at the can of gas he was holding. "What do you want me to do with this?"

"Burn the entire village. These huts must never been inhabited again. Now."

Moments later, flames rose from thatched roofs, and then she remembered. *The blood samples!* She ran to the old woman's hut. The roof was on fire and sagging. Jenny stepped into the smoke filled hut. She couldn't see a thing. She blindly reached for the container. Not there. She got on her knees and ran her glove along the dirt floor. A section of the roof above her head gave way. She rolled away to escape the fiery thatch and collided with something hard. She groped behind her. The cooler. She grabbed it just as the rest of the roof collapsed in an inferno.

CHAPTER TWO

Albuquerque, New Mexico, June 23

uke Chavez knew every face in the room except for two. The men dressed in crisp, dark blue suits and red ties sat in the back pew, but it did little to hide them. He doubted they were here to worship and pray.

The Abeyta family sat on one side of the strangers and the widow Lupe Garcia on the other. The man next to Lupe loosened his tie. He was about Luke's daughter's age. Twenty-five or so. The other man, older, scrunched his shoulders to avoid the Abeytas.

Two-hundred people were squeezed into the church. Luke caressed the pulpit's wooden top, worn smooth from his thick hands. Located in a former strip club in the south valley, the church wasn't much to look at. Faded white paint covered the block walls; circular brown stains on the ceiling identified the most recent leaks; the donated pews bore the carved initials of every kid forced to sit in them. But he loved every scratch and stain. A church needed to fit its pastor as much as a pastor did his church. And Grace Fellowship fit him and he it.

Luke had thought carefully about what he would say. He did every week, but it was even more important today. He would tell his members how much God loved them. Poor people needed to be reminded more often. It was easy to forget when the utility company threatened each month to shut off the gas and electricity.

And there were more poor than last year. A lot more. But he also felt compelled to draw his congregation's attention to recent changes that would impact the church. Nervous tension hung in the air like the anticipation at ringside before a big fight. The normally easy chatter was clipped. Smiles stretched thin. The only people who seemed unaffected were los viejos. The old men were always quiet. They sat with arms folded across their chest and stared stoically ahead.

Luke studied his scarred knuckles. Things had been simpler in the ring. The toughest hombre won. Life outside the ring wasn't that way though, the best man didn't always win. And nothing was fair or right about what had happened.

"A storm is upon us," Luke said. "It shouldn't surprise us. Christians have been persecuted throughout history. Last year two-hundred thousand believers died for their faith. I know that doesn't seem real because it isn't happening here. But I fear it's coming."

Lupe arched her eyebrows at the young man next to her. The Abeyta family discreetly shook their heads. Many in the congregation glanced back at the two men. But they didn't flinch.

They might be monitors sent by the government to protect the individual rights of religious tolerance as the spinmeisters spun it. They might not be. But if the men were monitors, they would sift every word of Luke's message to ensure it offended no one. The recent passage of the anti-hate crimes bill declared it illegal to teach anything from a pulpit that was offensive—and broad license was given to the interpretation of what offensive meant.

The government had warned religious leaders that the monitors could appear at any time, which made every Sunday feel like a potential IRS audit.

The new law was designed to create a melting pot to eliminate differences between religions while preserving cultural distinctions. That was the official line. The government said it wasn't trying to eliminate religion, just create a level playing field. And it had acted only after clashes between Christians and Muslims across the country had intensified following a series of terrorist attacks. But Luke suspected the new law had been in the works for sometime.

"Wake up, church." Luke slammed his fist down onto the podium with such force that the glass of water sitting on top nearly jumped off. A viejo, nodding off in the second pew, startled to attention. The two men didn't blink. "The time has come when the world will no longer tolerate the truth. Strengthen yourself for the days ahead."

The old fighter within Luke roared. He clenched his fists. *How dare the government tell me what I can teach?* "To omit sections of God's word that are offensive to some is a rip off. Like ordering a combination plate with the tamale and taco missing."

A nervous laugh rippled through the congregation. Cindy, who sat in the first pew, shot a worried look at him. He knew what his wife was thinking, what all of his members were thinking. *Be careful what you say. Don't provoke a fight. You'll lose.*

The two men exchanged glances.

"Teaching God's word has been the great love of my life—next to my wife." Luke glanced at Cindy. Still not a gray thread in her dark brown hair. She strained a smile. Her lips silently formed the words "I love you."

The two men craned their necks to catch a glimpse of her.

"The Bible tells us to obey our leaders. Render to Caesar what is Caesar's and to God what is God's. But sometimes it's not possible to do what the government demands. It was true for the early church, true for Christians living in Nazi Germany—and true today."

The room grew even quieter. No coughing, no whispering. The old men adjusted their hearing aids.

Luke took a deep breath. "Jesus died for you. And it's because of his sacrifice on the cross that there's only one way to heaven—not several." He had uttered forbidden words. Several heads dropped in prayer.

The two men stood up, startling the Abeytas and Lupe. They slid past the family and widow and stood in the aisle staring at Luke. Then, they turned and walked out.

CHAPTER THREE

Charlotte, North Carolina, July 4

DW Coltrane watched through the high-powered scope as President Gavin Nash stood in front of eighty thousand cheering supporters at Bank of America Stadium in Charlotte. On the podium behind him sat Vice President Reed Hamilton, the First Lady, and her three daughters.

The President looked like a decent man. He probably loved his wife and kids. A lot of the country's problems weren't his fault. The former administration's record deficits had slammed the country into a financial black hole, creating a hopeless situation for any leader unlucky enough to follow. The euro's collapse had added to the nation's woes by dragging American banks down with it. Inflation was out of control and the dollar not worth the paper it was printed on.

Nash had everything DW didn't. Power, money, and—a wife and three beautiful daughters. DW laid the spotting scope down, pulled out his wallet and looked at the creased picture of his wife and three girls. He touched the photo and returned it to his wallet.

He re-checked the wind speed and temperature in the ballistic PDA attached to the rifle. From a mile-and-half away and fifty stories high, there was no room for error. He removed three five-and-a-half inch shells from his pants pocket and loaded them into the clip. He pushed the magazine back into place, steadied the .50 caliber rifle in its tripod, then peered back through the scope.

The stadium, home to the Carolina Panthers, was at capacity. Bronze statues of lunging felines flanked the east entrance. Their green eyes glowed eerily under the huge stadium lights. It was the Fourth and hot and muggy even by July standards for eight o'clock. As Nash stood to address the crowd, the stadium erupted into thunderous applause that sounded like a rock concert crowd begging for one more encore.

"I love you, Charlotte." The President grinned and waved. Everyone was on their feet. DW adjusted the ear buds that connected him to the radio broadcast from his cell phone.

The crowd's attraction to the President was understandable. He was ruggedly handsome. A multi-millionaire and a rare politician who tried hard to keep his promises—and that was the problem.

"Thank you for your support." Nash waved his hands to quiet the crowd. "The last three years have been difficult. My predecessor left us a broken government and many of you with broken spirits. But we're on the road to recovery. Admittedly, it's a long road, but we'll get there together."

Even with its overwhelming financial problems, the U.S. was still the best country in the world. That's why DW had spent three years in Afghanistan fighting the Taliban and Al Qaeda. To defend the nation against terrorism and protect his wife and girls. He'd seen up close the fanatical face of Islam. A thirteen-year old girl raped by a Taliban. Buried in the ground up to her neck. Stoned to death under sharia law by men who accused her of adultery. Most likely the same men who raped her.

Not all Muslims were bad. Some were friends he'd left behind in the war-torn country. They didn't like the fanatics anymore than he did. They shared the same hopes and dreams—to live in peace and raise their families. But the only peace terrorists would accept was an Islamic world. After the U.S.'s departure, the Taliban overran the fledgling government.

"I've done my best to keep the promises I made three years ago." The President smiled, but then his face clouded. "I promised to make our damaged economy my principal focus. To make the tough choices that my predecessors would not. And one of those choices was a drastic cut in our military budget."

Another thunderous roar lifted into the clear night air. "We can no longer afford to conduct a world-wide war against terror. We'll continue to assist our allies in a limited capacity in their struggle against terrorism but our focus must be at home."

True to his word, the President drastically reduced U.S. forces abroad, including the Middle East. Downsizing the military substantially reduced the deficit. But the retreat ended up costing more than anyone could have imagined. It emboldened enemies of the U.S. to open a new front—this time at home. Everything DW had fought so hard to protect was taken from him. And that was why he was here.

CHAPTER FOUR

Charlotte, July 4

The acid in Vice President Reed Hamilton's stomach was now in his throat. He braced for the President's announcement. He had been in many uncomfortable situations during his long political career, but this was the worst he could remember. Nash had confided to him earlier in the day that he intended to ask the governor of California to be his next running mate.

The President was kind but firm. He appreciated Hamilton's dedicated service but needed California's fifty-five electoral votes to win re-election. He had seen the recent polls and understood the political reality. It would be the first time since FDR that a president sought re-election with a different running mate.

The Republican party had approached Hamilton four years ago to be Nash's running mate. The party needed a stronger southern coalition. Nash was a senior senator from New York at the time, Hamilton a governor from Georgia with strong political alliances throughout the south. The strategy had worked.

But during the last three years Hamilton had learned what all vice presidents eventually discover—no matter what their boss promises. The second-in-command's position is just as John Adams described it: the most worthless, thankless job ever conceived. A vice president endures sitting in the president's shadow because he believes that someday he will emerge and cast his own.

It was for such an end that he had prepared himself the last several years. Nash said he would enthusiastically support Hamilton's bid for the presidency after his second term. Even if their partnership had been fragile, which it wasn't, the President would have supported his bid for the presidency. No one wanted another Democrat in the White House. But none of that mattered now.

President Nash motioned for him to come to the lectern. Hamilton put on his best game face.

"It is with great regret that I inform you Vice President Hamilton will not be on the ticket in November." Nash wrapped his arm around Hamilton's back and gave it a pat. "My good friend has decided not to seek a second term due to health concerns. He is a great friend and has been an invaluable member of my team. I will be forever grateful for his service." Nash looked at him and forced a smile. The crowd was silent. "Gov. John Sisneros, of California, has agreed to be my running mate." The crowd responded with a hearty round of applause.

Hamilton returned to his seat. It was true he had a bad heart. He'd had a couple of heart attacks. But the President's announcement hadn't fooled anyone. He could already see tomorrow's headlines: *Hamilton dumped from ticket.* He loosened his tie just enough to breathe without looking sloppy.

He looked at Pepper Stanton, his chief of staff, standing off stage. His long face summed up Hamilton's feelings—but not entirely. The shock of the President's announcement, the disappointment and embarrassment, were evolving into something much more difficult to control.

His countenance before the cameras may have convinced the American people that he was just as regretful as the president about the decision but he could feel his composure falter against his weakening resolve.

Fireworks exploded in the sky descending upon the celebration in a shimmering display of red, silver, and blue. The President looked up, smiled. Hamilton was thankful the night was nearly over.

Nash's youngest daughter ran toward her father. He bent down to pick her up. In the midst of the thundering booms overhead, there was an explosive crack in the distance that sounded like fireworks. East of the stadium. A small hole in the bullet-proof shield in front of the podium caught Hamilton's attention. Just above the President's head. Had someone taken a shot at the President? Didn't the Secret Service see it?

CHAPTER FIVE

Centers for Disease Control and Prevention, Fort Detrick, Maryland, July 4

The bean-shaped virus with twisted tentacles covering its surface looked like a mutation of H5N1. But it didn't add up. Jenny adjusted the protective hood closer to her face, so she could get a better look through the optical microscope. She had never gotten used to a hazmat suit, but at least it was cool, the only advantage lab work provided over the field.

The elderly woman she had drawn blood from exhibited symptoms inconsistent with the pulmonary pathogen. The hemorrhaging indicated Ebola, but the black scabs didn't fit. The answer would arrive soon enough in a report Jenny had requested on the virus' genome. The analysis would provide a genetic map of the microbe's RNA. She checked her computer again. Still nothing.

Just as troubling as the disparity between the virus and its symptoms were the needle punctures on the woman's arms. Her assistants said they had seen similar marks on the few other victims found. At first she thought the pricks in the villager's skin were indications of drug use but that appeared unlikely. It was an isolated, poor village. Where would they get the money to buy drugs?

Her phone rang. Caller ID indicated it was Dr. Hampton Elliott, the director of CDC. He had a sixth sense for anything unusual occurring within the thick walls. She pushed the button for wireless connection.

"Hello Hampton," Jenny said through the transmitter in her hood.

"Don't you know it's a holiday?"

"I forgot to buy fireworks, so I thought I'd play with bugs instead." The truth was she didn't mind working holidays or long hours. It made being alone easier. At night she was often so tired she fell into her empty bed, disturbing only Caz. And the cat didn't mind.

"Find anything interesting?"

"I'm still waiting on the sequencing report. But this virus is a real enigma."

"I'm listening."

"It looks like some form of H5N1 under a microscope, but its victims appear to have died from Ebola. They were covered with scabs. Almost like…"

"Black pox?" Hampton coughed.

"Yeah."

"Let's hope you're wrong about that. The last thing we need is a small pox outbreak, particularly black pox. People haven't been vaccinated against the pox in more than forty years."

An icon on the computer screen blinked. "Have to go. My report is in."

"Call me when you know something more."

Jenny clicked on the report and scrolled down through rows of numbers representing different sets of genes. She stopped at a cluster and read an attached report by the geneticist. She re-read it. A hot flash swept over her. She ran a quick search of the CDC database for gene sequences, then cross-checked them against the report. Something was very wrong.

The geneticist had highlighted one word in red he didn't want her to miss: chimera.

A chimera in Greek mythology was part lion, goat, and snake, and breathed fire—a monster. In genetics, it was a synthetic life form created from multiple organisms. In recent years an explosion in genetic engineering had accomplished some amazing advances in chimeric organisms. The cure for brain cancer was achieved by combining viruses for the common cold and polio. But rumors had circulated for years of a darker side in genetic research that was being secretly funded by rogue countries and terrorists.

Jenny glanced back at the microbe under the microscope. Was it a man-made chimeric pathogen? Had someone genetically altered the virus by splicing two viruses together? But that wasn't the worst news. Her stomach knotted at the next sentences. The chimera comprised a particularly virulent form of variola major genes— black pox. It was synthesized with H5N1.

Jenny pulled the stool over to the table and sat. Her legs were shaky. Black pox was rare, but when it reared its lethal head, it was almost always fatal. Worst still, pox viruses could be transmitted through a cough or sneeze without human contact.

H5N1 first appeared in Hong Kong in 1997 as a highly pathogenic virus that turned its victims' lungs to mush. H5N1 was a nightmare that resided in the world's bird and pig populations, which provided the ideal environment for rapid mutations. An ever-changing virus was difficult to vaccinate against.

The two viruses had mated to create a monster. The pox ensured stability which gave it legs. No matter how virulent a virus was if it lacked longevity, it could never become a pandemic. By combining the two, the Frankenstein who stitched them together hoped to create a stable, highly infectious weapon capable of killing millions.

But the virus' designer had made a mistake. According to the report, the genome had poison sequences. There were indications that whoever copied the virus had failed to break the genome into shorter segments. The result was instability. Although the chimeric creation had been capable of wiping out a village, it lacked the ability to become a pandemic. For the first time in her life she was grateful for incompetent work.

But who was trying to create a super virus? Images of misanthropic terrorists filled her mind. The suit felt claustrophobic. She took a deep breath. Whoever it was, they preferred human guinea pigs and were obviously very resourceful and very dangerous.

Jenny pressed auto dial on the phone.

"That was quick. What did you find?" Hampton asked.

"Nothing good."

"Anything we should worry about?"

"The microbe, no. Whoever created it, yes."

"What do you mean?"

"The virus is a chimera. Someone tried to create a bird pox virus. But it's unstable."

"Are you sure?"

"I had the virus sequenced. There's no doubt."

"Those poor people. I wonder if they had any idea was happening to them?"

"Evil."

"How's that?"

"The elderly woman I took a sample from said I had brought an evil spirit on her village. It didn't make any sense at the time, but it does now. In the hazmat suit I looked like the people who had injected her and the rest of the village with the virus."

"I'm going to let our colleagues over at Homeland Security's Bioforensic Center know what you've found. They've developed a system for identifying biological agents and tracking their source. Maybe they'll be able to give us an idea whose fingerprints are on this virus."

"I'll bet they want to do more than that."

"What is that supposed to mean?"

"It means they'll probably want to add it to their collection. Everybody knows those guys over at Fort Doom are mad scientists."

"Just remember CDC is part of Fort Detrick. We share this complex with the military."

"I'm trying to forget." Jenny chuckled.

"I thought you were serious."

She was.

CHAPTER SIX

Charlotte, July 4

It was the longest three seconds he could remember. The armor-piercing bullet traveled twenty-seven-hundred feet per second—not fast enough for DW.

It was a difficult shot at one-and-a half miles. It wasn't his longest: that had been one-and-three quarter miles. What made the shot complicated was the steep trajectory from his position to the stadium. He had chosen the Zebco building, Charlotte's tallest. It was far enough away from the stadium to avoid the Secret Service's list of high profile buildings, those considered security threats. The Bank of America building near the stadium would have been much easier shot or any of the several buildings within a half mile. But every one of them had Secret Service agents positioned on the roof.

He had always been lucky. As a sniper in Afghanistan, he was known for being able to bend a bullet to his will. He rarely missed.

The shot cut through the three-inch bullet-proof glass with little effort, but missed its target. Dang it. The President had bent down to pick up his daughter. DW quickly pulled the bolt handle back as the smoking empty shell flipped out of the chamber and a new one loaded from the clip. DW slid the bolt back into place and aimed. Second shots were rare, but maybe the fireworks would provide enough distraction.

The President and his daughter waved. DW moved the rifle upward an inch to adjust for the bullet's sharp parabolic dive. Their faces disappeared from the blue illuminated cross hairs as the night sky filled it. He pulled the rifle tightly to his body and eased the trigger back slowly. A flash of white light filled the scope. The recoil shook his entire body. Even with the suppressor, his ears still rang from the shell's concussion.

He removed the rifle from its mount. The thought of leaving the hand-built gun behind was difficult. He ran his hand along the warm metal. A year had been devoted to meticulously crafting the action, the bolt, the firing pin—the parts that left identification on the shell case. But he couldn't chance being caught with it. Leaving it behind posed no risk. It was untraceable.

DW surveyed the world below through the night-vision scope. Hues of luminescent green revealed empty streets. The elevator would be much faster than trying to descend sixty flights of stairs. But relying on something that could malfunction at a critical time made him nervous. His supervisor said its descent was twelve-hundred feet per minute. He stepped inside and pushed ground floor. As he rode the elevator slowly down, it felt more like twelve-feet per minute. When the door finally opened, he glanced around the dimly lit lobby. Twisted, rapturous bodies captured in a prominently displayed fresco seemed to move. Everything looked different. He limped toward the entrance.

Near the front door were voices. He flattened himself against the wall. Flashlights probed the darkness. He held his breath.

DW's heart pounded. Staying low and close to the wall, he turned and retreated. The elevators were positioned in the middle of the first floor which meant between him and his ticket up was a vast expanse of marble.

He hurried across the open space and right into the path of a flashlight's beam peering through the front door.

"There's someone inside," someone shouted from outside the building.

"Might be the sniper."

"Open it up. Hurry."

Keys jangled outside.

DW pushed the button and waited.

Hurry. Hurry.

Locks clicked as men rushed inside the building. "FBI. Stop or we'll shoot."

The elevator door opened. DW jumped inside and pressed the button to the roof.

A shot exploded in front of the door spraying marble chips inside the elevator. Another thudded into the metal door as it closed. The elevator rose upward. He checked his watch. He had a thirty-second start at best. Not nearly enough time.

The wind would be moving from south to east at approximately five miles per hour, according to the weather report. Most of the high rises were to the west. His real concern, other than being shot, was clearing a circular design of metal tubes extending upward from the roof that looked like they had been yanked from a great pipe organ.

The rucksack was right where he had left it on the roof. He quickly pulled the chute from the bag, and stretched it out. He slipped into the harness and walked backward from the chute. The night air rushed into the black canopy. He swiveled around as the parafoil lifted him upward and directly into the pipe organ display. His feet hit the barrier first throwing him backward. The chute fluttered. He looked upward at the sagging fabric. *Don't stall.*

The chute pulled him toward the tubes again. This time he leaned back in the harness. His feet hit the pipes again, but he was ready and scurried up and over. The parafoil lifted him high into the dark sky. A gentle flutter vibrated across the nylon material.

"I see him," an agent yelled from the rooftop.

Bullets zipped past DW's head. *Climb, baby, climb.*

A thermal lifted the parafoil higher.

But no matter how high he climbed, time was working against him. Agents had spotted him. One of them might even have the same .50 caliber DW had used only moments earlier trained on him, although it was unlikely. It was evidence. But they were searching the skies for him through their night vision scopes, and a chopper would soon be in the air.

He had to get down quickly.

Paragliding at night was dangerous. He had done it before but never over a city. There were no instruments to guide you through the dark. Only your senses. But years of training had sharpened his like the edge of a fine blade. The terrain beyond Charlotte was fairly flat. But there were lots of trees. At night they could be deadly.

A sliver of moon shined through a translucent cloud. The cool wind buffeting his face felt good. He had forgotten how free paragliding made him feel. He didn't want to land. Down there, life hadn't been good in a long time.

He passed over the interchange at highways 74 and 27. He was traveling about twenty to twenty-five miles per hour. The lights below glowed light a swarm of fire flies. He pulled the night vision goggles hanging from his neck over his eyes. Interstate 485. Still too many houses. Need an inconspicuous place to land. A quiet road. He spotted one and began a spiral dive. The paraglider circled toward the earth like water swirling down a drain. As the ground approached, he straightened the chute into a smooth glide.

Then suddenly trees. Lots of trees. The branches slapped him in the face and tore the goggles from his face. The parafoil dragged him through the tree tops. A clearing. More trees. Then he crashed into something solid. The chute collapsed like a long, final exhale. DW hung suspended in the tree. He couldn't move.

A shooting pain in his right leg, his bad one, made him dizzy. He looked down at it. A protrusion poked from inside his pant leg. *Dang it.* He had trained to run on foot for several miles—at least until he was far clear of Charlotte. But now he couldn't move.

The FBI and Secret Service may have seen him go down. And, if not, the chances were slim he'd gone unnoticed even though his parafoil was the color of night. Soon, there would be barking dogs, spotlights, and lots of black vehicles.

DW shook off the panic and grabbed the serrated knife from his pants leg pocket slicing through the lines connecting his harness to the chute. He was free but at least twenty feet from the ground. He tugged at some of the amputated lines and pulled them toward him. After measuring a length of line, DW cut it and tied it around the tree limb above his head. As he moved himself into position to begin his descent, his leg bumped the tree. A shooting pain ripped through his body like lightening. His hands slipped from the cord. He fell backward through the limbs snapping some of them, catching the line with his left hand on the way down. It sliced through his hand as it slid through.

* * *

DW didn't remember hitting the ground. He surveyed the terrain from his back. Had he broken it? He wiggled his fingers and raised his head. *Thank God.* He sat up and looked at the dangling cords from the tree above him. He had fallen about fifteen feet, he estimated. His leg didn't hurt, but that wasn't good. He knew the effects of shock. He didn't have much time. *Can't stay here.*

He searched for something he could use as a crutch. He tilted to one side and removed a tree limb from underneath his hip. It looked sturdy and long enough to work. He rose unsteadily on one leg while he braced himself with the branch. He needed to get as far away from the crash site as possible. He gritted his teeth and began to hop slowly down a dirt road.

CHAPTER SEVEN

Charlotte, July 4

Secret Service Agents surged across the flat screen in Hank Jackson's one-bedroom apartment. Two covered the President's body, another his daughter, while a wall of agents formed a perimeter across the front of the podium searching the grief stricken stadium with MP5s poised at their side.

The heartache on the screen sucked Hank into its despair like a black hole until it was impossible to remember the celebration only moments earlier. He sat numbly watching the assassination replayed over and over. The President thrown violently backward onto the podium from the gunshot, still clutching his daughter; the First Lady bent over her husband and daughter, speaking to them as she caressed their faces.

An agent hurried her to an ambulance as a paramedic removed the small child from the President's unconscious grasp and carried her limp body toward the First Lady. The President's out-stretched arm, still reached for his daughter. Two paramedics and two Secret Service agents carefully lifted the President's lifeless body. Moments later ambulances disappeared from the stadium. Left behind on the empty podium was a little girl's white purse resting beside a dark pool. Crimson splashes marred the little clutch. The image on the screen lingered. Hank wanted to look away, but he couldn't. Instead, he let the stinging sight lash into his psyche.

How could this happen? Was it the work of some far-left wacko or a terrorist? Hank bit down on his trembling lip. Given the complexity of orchestrating an attack on the President, and the boldness of recent terrorist attacks, the later seemed more plausible. Hank felt certain when the assassin was found, he would have the same cold eyes he had seen dozens of times at murder trials he had covered for the newspaper.

The shrill ring of his cell phone broke the silence.

"This is Hank."

"Red, I need your help." The voice was weak and hoarse.

Only one person called him Red. "DW?"

"Yeah."

"You sound atrocious. What's wrong?"

"I'm hurt. Can you help me?"

"Where are you?"

Silence. "DW?"

"Sorry. I'm a little light-headed." DW gave him his approximate location.

"Be there as fast as I can."

Minutes later Hank was headed east toward a rural area on the outskirts of Charlotte. His little Toyota truck shook as he pushed it to the brink of losing control. What was DW doing in the city? More importantly, what was he doing in the middle of nowhere? The last time he had seen him was two years ago at the funeral for his wife and daughters. There had been many funerals that day.

Hank couldn't ever remember his old friend ever asking for help. He was tough—ooh-rah tough. As he pulled onto a deserted dirt road, he spotted a man lying on his back. Hank jumped out of his truck and ran toward him.

DW was unconscious. His face was streaked with blood from a deep gash on his forehead. A sharp edge of bone poked through the dark, soaked pant leg. Hank felt queasy. He removed his t-shirt and ripped it into two pieces. He tied one above DW's knee to slow the bleeding.

He grabbed DW under his arm and dragged him toward the truck.

"Didn't know who else to call," DW said groggily.

"It's okay. How'd you do it?"

Silence. He was out again.

With one hand, Hank unlocked and swung open the door to the back seat. Holding onto DW, he climbed into the truck as he struggled to hoist him onto the seat. He wasn't very tall, but he was stocky and solid. He banged DW's injured leg against the truck door pulling him in. *Glad you didn't feel that.* Hank closed the door.

He hopped in the driver's seat and pushed the accelerator to the floor. The truck's tires spun in the loose dirt leaving behind a light, brown cloud.

"Is that you, Red?" a weak voice called out from the back seat.

The name had stuck since they were kids. Hank didn't like it, but what are you going to do when your most prominent feature is wavy red hair? "It's me."

Hank's heart pounded as he punched the accelerator to the floor. DW had lost a lot of blood. He needed to get to a hospital. The truck bounced down a country road.

Twenty minutes later Hank parked his truck across the street from the emergency entrance at Presbyterian Hospital, which was blocked by black SUVs and reporters gathered thickly under the four-column portico of the red brick building.

DW stirred. "Where are we?"

"At Presbyterian hospital." Hank turned around. "Looks like the President is also here."

DW tried to sit up. "The President?" He seized Hank's arm. His friend's eyes were wide. "Don't worry about me. Get out of here. Don't let the Feds see you. I'm sorry for…" He slumped over.

A tingle rippled across Hank's skin. He shook his friend. "Sorry for what?" But DW was out.

Was he somehow mixed up in the President's assassination? Surely he meant something else. The poor guy was delusional. But the wall of Secret Service agents in front of the emergency entrance eyeing Hank's truck looked foreboding. Maybe he should drive DW to Mercy Hospital? It would take another ten minutes, precious minutes the pale, unconscious figure in his back seat didn't have.

He got out of his truck and opened the back door. He pulled DW toward him, then lifted him off the seat and laid him gently on the sidewalk.

Hank dialed the hospital.

"Presbyterian Hospital." A young voice answered.

"A man is lying on a sidewalk across the street from your emergency entrance. He has a compound fracture in his leg and has lost a lot of blood. He needs a doctor immediately. Hurry."

"Who are you, sir?"

Hank hung up. He jumped back in his truck, glanced at the Secret Service across the street, then drove away. With each car length the still figure on the sidewalk faded, but it would take more than distance to squash the guilt already gnawing away.

CHAPTER EIGHT

Charlotte, July 4

"Why, why, why?" the First Lady sobbed. Hamilton gently patted her back as he fought back his own tears. She leaned against his shoulder and cried, the strain of the last hour etched in her face. What could he say to comfort a grieving wife and mother? Words in times like these were inadequate. They stood outside two operating rooms at Presbyterian Hospital, the Secret Service surrounding them.

He looked at the rooms. Side by side. The President and his daughter. Behind one, the heart of a nation; behind the other, a mother's.

"How could someone shoot my daughter?"

Hamilton was certain the little girl wasn't the target. Tragically, the President had been holding her when the bullet struck. Hamilton would find who did it. He would make sure of it.

A grim-faced surgeon emerged from an operating room. The First Lady looked briefly at him, then buried her face in her hands and screamed.

"I'm so sorry, Mrs. Nash. We did all we could."

The First Lady collapsed in convulsing sobs. Hamilton grabbed the limp woman as Secret Service agents and a doctor rushed to help him. They carried her out of sight.

Tears flowed down Hamilton's cheeks, but they weren't only for Nash's daughter. Her death triggered memories of another young, beautiful face. His daughter had been the same age as Nash's little girl when she died from cancer. Only four. He understood the First Lady's deep sobs wrung from a shattered heart and knew that at the core of that sorrow was the question of why God would allow such a thing to happen. He had never forgiven God and suspected no parent ever truly did.

"Mr. Vice President, we need to go," a Secret Service agent said. "You shouldn't be here. This is not a secure facility. We don't know the full extent of the threat."

"I won't leave until I know if the President is going to survive." Hamilton had insisted on going to the hospital, despite the Secret Service's objections. It was a violation of all protocol, but he didn't care. "Do we have any suspects?"

"No, Mr. Vice President. All we know is some of the shots came from the Zebco building. We took all the precautions we could. Whoever did it was a pro."

It was the risk every president took. It had been more than fifty years since Kennedy's assassination. Hamilton was a teenager then. The black and white images playing on the television, his mother weeping, the flags at half-mast were all still vivid. Was it about to happen again?

Special Agent Cochrane, head of the President's detail, walked up. A scowl deepened his furrowed brow. "Why is the Vice President here? He should be on Air Force Two."

One of the six agents surrounding Hamilton stepped forward, "We tried to convince him to leave with us after the shooting, but he insisted on coming to the hospital."

Cochrane's eyes narrowed as he studied the agent. "I'll deal with you later." Then, he shifted his attention to Hamilton. "I'm sorry, Mr. Vice President, we can't allow you to remain here."

"I'm not leaving."

"With all due respect, it's not your decision."

"You two-bit civil servant. I'll have you fired."

"You can, but it won't keep me from doing my job. So we can do this the easy way or the hard way. Either way you're going with these men. Which is it, Mr. Vice President?"

Hamilton grunted. "All right."

Thirty minutes later Air Force Two lifted into a clear, star-filled night with the President still in surgery. The Secret Service said they had spotted the killer and found his .50 caliber rifle on top of one of the buildings. Hamilton was all too familiar with the damage a large caliber bullet could do.

A .30 caliber shell ripped his buddy's body apart during the Tet Offensive. But this was a .50 caliber. No one survived a round like that even with bullet-proof glass to slow it down. Nash's daughter's face flashed before him. He felt sick. The shot had struck her first. If the President somehow survived, it would be because of her sacrifice. Hamilton leaned back in the leather chair as the improbability of the evening's events settled in like heavy fog.

A few hours ago he was a lame-duck Vice President on his way out. Now he was the acting President. Shortly after the assassination attempt, he had contacted members of the cabinet and secured a consensus that power needed to be transferred to him to ensure presidential continuity. It was the first time section four of the twenty-fifth amendment had ever been invoked. He would remain in that capacity until the President recovered. If he did. And power would only transfer back if Hamilton and the Cabinet concluded the President was fit for office. If they decided he wasn't, the decision would fall to Congress.

Nash had lost a tremendous amount of blood. His chest had been ripped apart. Even if he survived, he would need additional surgery. It might be weeks, even a month or two before the President could resume his duties if he made it. But he might not. The thought troubled him. Not that he wouldn't make it—but that he would. Two internal forces competed for control of his soul.

He tried to dismiss the idea and concentrate on the announcement he needed to make to the nation, but he kept calculating Nash's chances. *I wonder if Teddy Roosevelt struggled while McKinley lingered.*

This might be as close to the presidency as he would ever get. He certainly wouldn't get a chance if Nash survived. Hamilton was off the ticket, and in another four years he would be seventy-five years old. Too old. Americans liked their presidents a little gray through the temples, but not silver headed. In today's youthful world, elder statesmanship was not equated with wisdom, but with being out of touch. Besides the Republican Party would throw its power most likely behind Sisneros, Nash's pick for VP. Political parties didn't care about who was the most qualified. They cared about winning.

Hamilton rang for the flight attendant. His eyes were red. "Can I get a scotch on the rocks?"

"Certainly, Mr. Vice President." The attendant brushed at his wet eyes and left.

The scotch arrived. He took a long, slow drink. It burned at first, but then a smooth, oaky taste followed that he was reluctant to let leave.

How long had Nash been planning to dump him? Was it a spontaneous decision based on the latest poll results or was it something his advisers had been cooking up for awhile? The questions burned in his throat like the first sip of scotch, but unlike his favorite drink, they didn't mellow.

He looked out the window at a city below, shimmering lights peeked through a cloud break. Soft cries reverberated through the cabin. Chief of Staff Pepper Stanton appeared in the window's reflection.

"Want to talk?" Pepper asked.

"Sure, have a seat." Hamilton turned toward Pepper who sat across from him.

The youthful face was drawn. He rubbed his eyes. "I still can't believe it happened."

Hamilton struck a contemplative gesture and nodded. "I remember President Kennedy's assassination. It pierced the heart of every American. My mother cried for days." He paused. "If Nash dies...let's pray he doesn't."

"Do you think he'll pull through?"

"He's the luckiest man I've ever met, until tonight."

The phone on his chair rang. He picked it up.

"Mr. Vice President. There's a call for you."

"Who is it?"

"Special Agent Thompson."

Hamilton looked at his watch. It was midnight. They'd been in the air about two hours, headed to the command center in Nebraska. The Secret Service wasn't taking any chances.

"He has information about the President."

Hamilton turned to Pepper.

"Do you know Agent Thompson?"

Pepper shrugged.

"Go ahead and connect me." There was a click on the line.

"Good evening, Mr. Vice President. I am Sulaiman Hadid with Mahdi's Chosen. I'm deeply sorry about the assassination attempt on the President."

Hamilton sat up straight in his seat. "How did you get this number?"

"Mr. Vice President, I have information about the President. The fact that I could penetrate one of the most sophisticated communication systems in the world should be proof enough that I'm worth listening to. I suggest you switch to a private line so we can talk."

Hamilton looked at Pepper.

"Who is it?"

Hamilton covered the mouthpiece. "A damn terrorist. Trace the call, and tell the communications director I want a private channel. And get me everything you have on Sulaiman Hadid."

Pepper hurried toward the front of the plane. Hamilton reached for the glass of scotch. Small lumps of ice rattled as he drained the last of it. The only way a terrorist could get a classified number was through someone on the inside. Maybe even someone aboard Air Force Two. A voice over the phone line said, "Go ahead, Mr. Vice President."

"Are you calling to gloat?"

"No, we weren't involved."

"Then why are you calling?"

"The President's announcement to change running mates must have been a shock," Sulaiman said.

"Not really."

"I thought all vice presidents wanted to be president?"

"Get to the point."

"The President won't live to see daylight."

Hamilton looked around and lowered his voice. "How do you know that?"

The line went dead.

A chill rippled over Hamilton. He pushed a button on the console in his seat.

"Yes, Mr. Vice President?"

"Get Special Agent Cochrane on the line. No, not him. Call Special Agent Jared."

"I'll contact you when I have him."

Hamilton swirled the ice in his glass as he waited. The phone rang.

"Jared?"

"What can I do for you, Mr. Vice President?"

"How's the President?"

"Cochrane was about to call you. He just came out of surgery."

"What did the surgeons say?"

"He's going to make it."

"That's great news." Hamilton squeezed the receiver.

"Yes, it is. Anything else?"

"No, nothing." He put the phone down and caught his reflection in the cabin window. *Why didn't I tell him?* He glanced at his watch. Five-and-a-half hours to daylight. He motioned for the attendant and ordered another scotch.

CHAPTER NINE

Albuquerque, July 5

A chain hung from the door handles of Grace Fellowship, a heavy lock securing the two ends. A sign was posted on each door: *Closed by order of the U.S. Government for violation of the anti-hate crimes law.* Two signs, just in case you missed one of them.

Luke stared numbly at the barred doors. He had been prepared to find the church closed the day after his Sunday sermon. But not two weeks later. He had almost convinced himself the two strangers weren't from the government. They could have been Methodists from out of town who had stumbled into Grace Fellowship in search of an ecumenical alternative. Luke leaned against the doors. If only they had been Methodists.

Perhaps the closure was temporary. Designed to scare him and others into quietly backing down. Surely the government didn't want to see outcry from the new law's enforcement adjudicated on news programs. And surely it realized that an appeal of the new law would eventually appear before the U.S. Supreme Court.

But the chained doors looked permanent. He and Cindy had discussed the effect a closed church would have on their lives and every member of their congregation. But the reality was worse than he imagined. Everything he worked so hard to achieve during the last seven years was gone.

"I'm sorry, Luke."

The man's voice startled him. He swung around to see Sheriff's Deputy Ray Quinones standing next to a white vehicle. Never heard him drive up. Quiet as a cat. Luke had watched Ray grow up in the church. He had stopped coming after he left home, but his parents still attended—or used to. Luke swallowed.

"It's wrong what they did," Ray said.

It was wrong. But the government didn't see it that way. Neither did most people. Even some Christians approved of the law. Luke nodded. "It could have been worse. Someone could have shot me like they did the President."

Ray shook his head. "I hope they find who did it and hang him." He kicked at the hard dirt. "I guess you know why I'm here."

"The county sent you out to remove the locks?" Luke winked.

The deputy tried to smile. "I wish. I've got to take you down to the detention center."

Luke had taught a Bible study in the county jail every week for the last five years. It appeared he would get an opportunity to continue. If the government didn't like what he taught in jail, they'd have to figure out some other way of shutting him up.

Luke extended his hands.

Ray shook his head. "I'm not going to cuff you, Pastor Luke."

He got into the back seat of the car. Ray closed the door.

As the car drove away Luke said goodbye to the worn, white cinder-block building.

Perhaps for the last time.

"A lot of weird stuff is happening," Ray said looking in the rear view mirror.

Strange times had arrived. When right was wrong and wrong was right. And few seemed to know the difference.

CHAPTER TEN

Washington, D.C., July 5

The sun was well into the morning sky when the limo pulled into the driveway of the white brick Queen Anne at One Observatory Circle. Hamilton hadn't slept in twenty-four hours. His eyes burned. He closed them for a moment to let the pain ease. He'd been flying all night. After arriving at the command center in Nebraska, the secret service notified him that the assassination attempt was most likely the work of a lone shooter and requested Hamilton return to Washington.

The President had died at 5 a.m. The Secret Service contacted Hamilton with the news shortly after Air Force Two touched down at Andrews Air Force Base. Within minutes the Chief Justice would arrive, and Hamilton would take an oath making him the 46th President of the United States.

Hamilton hadn't said anything to the Secret Service about the call aboard Air Force Two. Even if they had known, it wouldn't have made any difference. They had taken over an entire floor of the hospital, stationed agents outside of the President's room and hospital, and had combed through the background of every doctor and nurse with any access to the chief. It would have been easier to get through to God himself.

There wasn't any reason to believe the President had died of anything but complications from the attempted assassination. Agent

Cochrane said the President died of pulmonary arrest. Just quit breathing. Perfectly normal given the stress of a six-hour surgery and the shock of waking to learn his daughter was gone. The terrorist's call and Nash's death were a coincidence. But what if they weren't? Which left only two explanations—either the terrorist leader was clairvoyant, or somehow he had outmaneuvered the Secret Service.

Hamilton walked into his home to find his wife, Lucy, waiting along with Pepper. Hamilton embraced his wife and kissed her lightly on the lips. She took his hat and left the room with it. Pepper stood looking down at his shoes.

"When did you hear?" Hamilton asked.

"About thirty minutes ago."

"Poor little girl." He could still see Nash lying on the podium, his hand extended toward his daughter. Hamilton wiped at the corner of his eye. "Any suspects?"

"The FBI found the sniper's rifle on the roof of the Zebco building and two casings."

Two bullet holes in the President's fractured shield flashed before Hamilton. "Sounds like he had military training."

"Definitely. His chute was found in a forested area fifteen miles east of Zebco."

"You can bet that by the end of today the agency will have the name of every sniper ever trained by the military in the last twenty years. Anything else?"

Pepper nodded. "Blood was found near the chute. The DNA will be cross-referenced against anyone admitted to hospitals in the surrounding Charlotte area during the last ten hours. And here's an interesting anecdote: the FBI found tire tracks in the area. They think he had an accomplice."

"Must have. The sniper's gone, which means someone picked him up." Hamilton motioned for them to move to the sitting room. The smell of fresh coffee wafted from the kitchen.

A butler walked in with a silver tray holding two pale blue china cups, sugar, cream, and a pot of coffee. There was also a plate of buttery croissants and jam. He placed them on the table in front of Hamilton and Pepper and poured each a cup of coffee. Hamilton looked up at the man. He was doing his best to keep it together. Hamilton touched his arm. "I miss him, too." The butler nodded, brushed the tears away, and left the room.

"It's hard to believe he's gone," Hamilton said.

Pepper poured cream into his cup until the dark liquid looked less like coffee and more like milk. He added four teaspoons of sugar and slowly stirred the concoction. "I have some information on Sulaiman."

"What do you know?" Hamilton took a sip of his black coffee.

"Not nearly enough. No pictures of him. But the FBI believes he was behind the subway bombing here two years ago."

Hamilton put his cup down. "I thought that was Al Qaeda."

"So did the FBI until recently. But Director Broughton told me they're pretty sure now it was Mahdi's Chosen."

"Why?"

"Remember the terrorist the FBI captured last month?"

"The guy who tried to blow himself up?"

"Yes. He was a member of Mahdi's Chosen. They couldn't get a lot of information out of him, but he did say Sulaiman was responsible for the bombing."

Pepper put his cup down, picked up a croissant and spread raspberry jam on it. He took a bite.

"Was he part of it?"

"He said he wasn't."

"Right." Hamilton sniggered.

"Here's something else the FBI said that's interesting."

Hamilton leaned in toward Pepper.

"The terrorist told the FBI that Sulaiman is revered among radical Muslims."

Hamilton sipped his coffee. "Because he blew a bunch of our people up?"

"I'm sure that's part of it. But according to the terrorist, Sulaiman believes he is called to prepare the world for the return of the Mahdi. And no one is more dangerous than a religious fanatic." Pepper took another bite of his roll.

"Their messiah?"

Pepper nodded. "Shiite Muslims believe he will conqueror the world and force everyone to worship Allah."

"Thus, the name of his group," Hamilton said.

"Right."

Hamilton threw his head back and exhaled. "They're all insane." But a terrorist who engineered the deadliest terror attack since 9/11 and penetrated Air Force Two's communication system wasn't crazy. He was ingenious and zealous—a bad combination. The thought was troubling. And Hamilton couldn't shake the sense that he had been lured into something larger by a terrorist who believed he was called to change the world.

"Why do you think Sulaiman contacted you?" Pepper popped the last of his roll in his mouth.

"To assure us Muslims weren't involved. The country is still raw from the subway bombing."

"Do you believe that?"

"I wouldn't believe anything a terrorist said."

A car door closed. A moment later there was a knock at the front door. Two Secret Service agents moved toward the door with one hand inside their overcoats. They opened it carefully. The Chief Justice walked in. "Good morning, Mr. Vice President. I'm sorry for the delay."

Hamilton and Pepper stood. The Chief Justice looked too young to be the court's leader. At least his temples were graying. He was 64-years old but looked fifty, unlike some of the geezers on the bench who could fall over at any moment. "Are you ready?" he asked.

Hamilton looked at the court leader's eyes. All business. "I am."

Lucy held the Bible as he placed his right hand on it. Pepper and the two agents stood next to his wife. The butler and two other domestic attendants came into the room to watch.

Hamilton was ready to be President. More prepared than most who had preceded him. He would be stronger than Nash, not an obsequious pushover for Congress. His predecessor had weakened the office by consulting Capitol Hill on everything, turning the presidency into a dual governing body instead of the powerful office envisioned by the founders. Such leadership made Nash immensely popular with congressmen and senators who loved sycophants. But popularity wasn't Hamilton's objective. Lincoln was terribly unpopular, but one of the greatest, if not the greatest, president. Things needed to change in Washington. Hamilton took a deep breath and began to repeat the oath.

CHAPTER ELEVEN

Alexandria, Virginia, July 5

In the dim corner of the room, a dark shape spread like black ink across wet paper. Sulaiman sat up in bed. A bad dream awakened him. He squinted at the wall. What was it? A shadow?

He reached for the Glock 9mm on the bedside table and pointed it at the mutating silhouette. A hissing noise emanated from the corner. With his other hand, he pushed the button on the table lamp, but it wouldn't turn on.

Sulaiman tightened his finger around the trigger as he studied the pitch black image. The shadow's jagged edges, splayed across two walls, merged into smooth contours, forming an elongated figure that crawled up the wall and slithered along the ten-foot ceiling toward him.

He steadied the gun and pulled the trigger. White flashed from the gun's barrel as two rapid shots struck the ceiling. The acrid smell of sulfur and smoke filled the bedroom. The shadow continued to move.

"What are you?" He mumbled under his breath.

"I am a Jinni." The guttural words sounded as if they had been coughed up. A tingle traveled down Sulaiman's back. Had it actually spoken? The gun felt wet in his hand.

Allah created Jinns out of fire according to the Qur'an. Some were good but many were evil like Iblis or Satan. Surely they weren't real. Sulaiman didn't believe in ghosts, spirits, or anything supernatural except for Allah. The hissing intensified as a shroud of liquid black hovered over the bed. Its surface pulsed and teemed with movement as if a layer beneath clawed to escape.

He kept his gun aimed at the ceiling.

"Allah sent me here to help you."

It wasn't an audible voice, but one he heard clearly inside his head.

"I need guns not ghosts."

A long hiss ended with a snap that sounded like the crack of a whip. "Forces are gathering against you."

"Who?"

"You cannot defeat what you cannot see."

"I've never had a problem spotting a Christian or Jew."

"I helped your namesake Sulayman the Magnificent."

"Why should I believe you? The Qu'ran says Jinns can't be trusted."

The surface of the shadowy image undulated and pooled in places like drops of condensation about to fall. A pungent semi-sweet smell that reminded him of incense invaded the room.

Sulaiman glanced at the bedroom door. Maybe he could escape. But he had never run from an opponent yet.

"Do you want to hasten the Mahdi's return?"

"Of course."

"Do you really think you can turn the world upside down by yourself? Nothing eternal is ever achieved by one man."

"How can you help me?"

"I can fight the darkness seeking to destroy you."

"What darkness?"

"Iblis and evil jinn and the men they control."

The only one who can defeat Iblis is Allah.

The dark image jerked and groaned and acted as if it would retch some black bile upon him. "What do you know about Iblis, you puny human? The only power he has is what Allah gave him. Allah could destroy him at any time but has chosen to allow him to exist until the end. Iblis cannot overcome me because Allah is with me."

How could Sulaiman deny what he saw and heard? The jinni even knew his thoughts. Had Allah pulled back the veil separating two worlds to convince him of another realm just as real? Maybe the creature was right. Sulaiman needed it to defeat what he couldn't see.

He released his grip on the gun and laid it on the bed. "Okay, what do you want?"

The silhouette sizzled. "There is a vast chasm separating our worlds. The only bridge is you. Receive my power."

The shape fell upon Suliaman like a dark shroud, covering him in an icy blanket. His body stiffened, his teeth chattered. He reached for the gun, but his limbs were too numb to move. He was trapped.

In the darkness something metal glimmered. Above Sulaiman's chest, the dark shape held a sword. The room circled and faded in and out. Metal flashed. The jinni had lied.

A smooth lick from Le Roi Moore, the late saxophonist of the Dave Matthews Band, played on the radio. Sulaiman bolted up in bed and clutched his chest.

"This is a special announcement by National Public Radio." The announcer's voice quavered. "President Gavin Nash died at 5 a.m. this morning at Presbyterian Hospital in Charlotte, North Carolina of complications from the assassination attempt last night. Vice President Reed Hamilton was sworn in just moments ago as the nation's 46th President. He has declared today a national day of mourning. The President's funeral is expected to be held this coming Monday. The FBI is pursuing all leads, but there are no suspects at this time."

Sulaiman turned off the radio. His gun was on the bedside table. He lay back in the bed and studied the ceiling. No bullet holes. The ghoulish shape that had climbed inside his head was gone. But his chest ached deep inside and felt cold.

CHAPTER TWELVE

Washington, D.C., July 7

It was Sunday. The President had been dead for two days. Jenny needed to forget and the best way to do that was a long bike ride along the Potomac. The Mount Vernon Bike Trail began near downtown Washington, D.C., passed through Olde Town Alexandria, crossed the Woodrow Wilson Memorial Bridge, and turned around at Mount Vernon, George Washington's fabled home. It was eighteen miles long.

Jenny needed every mile of it. She pedaled hard, only vaguely aware of the passing blur of shapes. The President's handsome face faded with each mile only to be replaced with the visage of the infected elderly woman. One face the whole world knew, the other no one did. One died publicly, the other privately. Yet each was etched in Jenny's mind.

The phone inside her camelback rang. She tried to tune it out but the high-pitched sound punctured her concentration. *What's the use?* She pulled off the bike trail and stopped next to the Potomac. A team of mallards paddled near shore. She unhooked her backpack, swung it off, then pulled her cell from the side pocket. She had a voicemail.

"Jenny, it's Sam. I need to talk to you. Something has happened. I'm at a phone booth. I'll wait to hear from you." He left a number.

She had known Sam since Harvard. They had met in Microbiology. Now he was chief of surgery at Presbyterian Hospital in Charlotte. The cryptic message was totally unlike Mr. Unflappable. Jenny dialed the number.

It rang a few times before he picked up. "Jenny?"

"What's going on, Sam? And what's up with the pay phone?"

"I want you to listen very carefully."

"Okay, I'm listening."

"The President was murdered."

"I know. I watched it on television a hundred times."

"I led the team that operated on the President. His injuries were extensive, but he was a strong man. He should have survived."

"Don't blame yourself, Sam. You did everything you could."

"He didn't die of complications."

Jenny heard what Sam had said, but she couldn't process the thought.

"I have evidence."

"What kind of evidence?"

"A toxicology report. When I heard the President had died, I collected a blood sample from the surgery room. It wasn't hard. There was blood everywhere. I sent it to a friend of mine at a lab without telling him whose it was.

"Where was the Secret Service?"

"Busy transporting the President's body to Bethesda Naval Hospital for the autopsy."

"What did the test reveal?"

"The President was given enough morphine to kill an elephant. Someone poisoned him. I need to make sure someone else has this report…just in case. You're the only person I trust."

"Stop talking like that. Nothing is going to happen to you."

"Will you help me?"

"Of course."

"Look, I'm just a little jittery. The President's autopsy was conducted yesterday. I'm sure the pathologists found what I did. We should know the results soon. But if for some reason the report is different, go to the press. People need to know."

"Why not go now?"

"Hopefully, the truth will come out, and I won't have to get involved anymore than I already am. Don't call me on my cell. Someone may be listening. I'll call you. Okay?"

"All right. Be careful. Please, be careful."

"I will. I'll send the file within the hour."

"Goodbye, Sam."

His voice was gone. Jenny bit down on what little remained of her fingernails. She didn't want to worry, but it was hard not to. Sam was her best guy friend. The quintessential gentleman who loved pin-striped seersucker suits and bow ties. His intentions were noble but questionable. People crazy enough to murder a President played for keeps.

* * *

Two hours had passed, and Sam's email still hadn't arrived. Had something happened? The thought twisted the knot in her stomach even tighter. He should have given the toxicology report to the authorities. If someone had killed the President and even remotely suspected Sam knew something, it could get him...She couldn't finish the thought.

Jenny neared the end of the bike trail. She could see the Lincoln Memorial with the Washington Monument looming behind it. Normally she would be soaking in the view of scullers gliding along the Potomac and the smell of hot dogs and burgers on the grill, but she couldn't concentrate on anything except her conversation with Sam. How she wished she had pressed him to contact the FBI.

Her phone beeped. She braked to a stop. She pulled the phone from the side pocket of her shorts. She had an email. She clicked on it. It was from Sam. *Sorry for delay. Think someone's following me. Black SUV. Drove around city to lose it. Gone now. File attached. You know what to do.*

She opened the report, enlarged it, and scanned the toxicology results. The analysis indicated a lethal amount of Roxanol in the President's blood. Sam was right. A cyclist pulled up next to her and stopped. She glanced over at him as she quickly closed her email and put the phone back in her pocket. He wore unusual sunglasses with yellow lenses. He smiled. She nodded once then pedaled back onto the trail. She glanced at her helmet mirror and saw the cyclist pull in behind her.

She pedaled faster, but the cyclist matched her speed. She took a hard left off the trail toward Washington Boulevard. At Memorial Drive she turned left again and headed toward Arlington National Cemetery. Near the park entrance, she risked a look in the mirror. He was gone.

She stopped and took a deep breath. Her heart was pounding. There wasn't any easy way back to her truck from Arlington Cemetery. It was parked in a lot at the trail head near the Francis Scott Key Bridge. The fastest way there was to get back on the Mount Vernon Trail and hope that the guy who had followed her was just enjoying an afternoon ride.

As Jenny followed the trail north toward the parking lot, she kept one eye on her mirror. No sign of him. She pulled up to her vehicle and got off her bike. As she opened up the tailgate of her pickup to put her bike in, she noticed a man in a parked black Suburban watching her.

The back of her neck tingled. Same sunglasses as the man who had followed her. The window in the black vehicle slid up. *What have you gotten me into, Sam?*

Jenny dialed Sam's number. It rang twice then went to voicemail. "Sam, I'm sorry to call. Please call me back."

CHAPTER THIRTEEN

Charlotte, July 10

"Possible 187," the voice crackled over the police scanner. Hank adjusted the frequency on the radio as he turned down Tryon Street. "We have a middle-aged man in a white SUV at Presbyterian Hospital parking garage."

Hank dialed Anne Stupak, the head of personnel at Presbyterian.

"Good morning, this is Anne."

"Good morning, gorgeous. It's Hank."

"Where's my chocolate croissant and cappuccino?"

"I'm on my way to Les Patisseries as we speak."

"What do you need?"

Through the years Hank had cultivated not only Anne Stupak's sweet tooth for fine French pastries but also her need for honeyed words. In exchange, she passed valuable bits of information his way. "Anyone fail to show for work today?"

"Why?"

"Police just found someone dead in your parking garage."

"Dear, Lord." Nails clicked on a keyboard. "There are a number who didn't come in."

"Police said the victim was a middle-aged male."

"Oh, dear. Could be Dr. Myers or Tim Jenkins, one of our nurses. Wait, Jenkins called in, but I haven't heard from Dr. Myers. Do you think something happened to Sam?"

"Who is he?"

"The hospital's chief of surgery."

"Anything else noteworthy?"

"The Secret Service finally left, but the government sent in a team of investigators to sift every detail of the President's death. And this may be nothing, but Dr. Haley has been out since the President's death. I've tried calling her, but she doesn't answer."

"What's so important about Dr. Haley?"

"She was the one of the President's surgeons. She and Sam were part of the team that operated on the President."

"Keep your ears open. My gut tells me there's a bigger story here than just a homicide."

* * *

The following day Hank stood in the doorway of Sgt. Timothy Steele's office.

The big man looked up from a report he was working on.

"Don't you ever knock?" He returned to his report.

"Anything on Dr. Haley?"

Steele looked back up and frowned. He leaned forward on his desk that seemed to sag. "Nada. She's disappeared, but we're looking for her."

"You search her place?"

"Of course. No clues except a photo we found of her and some guy sipping margaritas the size of punch bowls."

"Any idea who the guy is?"

"I could lose my job if the department ever found out how much information I feed you."

"I'd lose mine if you didn't."

"Can't say right now."

"Come on, Steele. You know who he is, don't you?"

He returned to his work.

"Have I ever divulged you as a source?" Hank asked. "Ever gotten you in trouble? Heck, we ran your photo in the paper twice last year."

"This is different." Steele looked up. "Not your typical murder case. The feds are crawling all over the department like fleas." He scratched the back of his head.

Hank folded his arms and learned against the wall. He was prepared to wait it out until Steele gave in or threw him out. "Maybe I should have given the tip to Sgt. Mathews?"

"All right. Shut the door."

Hank closed it.

"I sent the photo to a friend of mine at the national crime lab. No database matches. But on a hunch he shot it over to the Supermax Prison in Baltimore. They locked up a terrorist a few weeks ago who tried to blow himself up. He wouldn't give us a name, but did say the man was a brother."

"As in terrorist?"

"Yeah."

"Now we're talking." Hank sat down in the chair in front of Steele's desk.

"Make yourself at home." Steele gestured with his large mitt toward the chair.

"Do you know what this means?"

"It doesn't mean a thing right yet."

"It means that Dr. Haley, the last doctor to see the President before he died, is connected in someway to a terrorist. And now Dr. Myers, the chief surgeon at the same hospital, has been murdered."

Steele rubbed the cleft in his meaty chin. "How'd you find out about Dr. Myers?"

"Every good reporter has sources."

"That's confidential, Jackson. Who told you?"

"You did."

Folds of flesh creased Steele's forehead. "How's that?"

"I played a hunch, and you confirmed it."

"You're a real piece of work. I should kick your butt out of here."

"But you won't." Hank leaned forward. "What do you know about Dr. Myer's death?"

"We found him in his SUV in physician parking. I'm guessing he'd been there one to two days. He was in full rigor. Two bullets in the head. Small caliber, maybe .22. Nothing taken. No motive at this time."

"Do you think it was a professional job?"

"Could be. Could also be a gang looking for some fun."

"Any surveillance cameras in the garage?"

"None that will do us any good."

"Your guys find anything else?"

"Just a phone number for the pathology department at Bethesda Hospital."

Hank rubbed the back of his neck, already wet from perspiration. "Why would he have their phone number?"

"Maybe he wanted to check on the President's autopsy?"

"What if it's connected in someway to his murder?"

Steele sat up in his chair. The desk looked small in comparison to his hulk. "How do you figure?"

"What if Dr. Myers was suspicious of the President's death and started poking around and asking questions, and it got back to the wrong people."

"You're reaching, Jackson."

"The President is dead, one of his surgeons is missing and appears to be connected to a terrorist, and now someone has whacked the chief of surgery at Presbyterian—all within three days. If we're dealing with pros, do you think they're going to leave a calling card?"

Steele stood up. He grabbed his right knee and grimaced. An old football injury? He straightened up and extended his hand.

Hank shook it. "I owe you."

"You did before you walked in."

CHAPTER FOURTEEN

Fort Detrick, Maryland, July 10

Jenny held her clearance badge up to the security guard at the Fort Detrick gate who examined it before waving her through. As she drove toward the National Bioforensic Center, she passed the U.S. Army's new one million square-foot biodefense complex.

She shook her head. The very combination of the words biological and defense was farcical. Why would the government entrust the military with the world's deadliest pathogens and believe it wouldn't be tempted? Wasn't this the same military that had created weapons based on lethal microbes? The same military that had tested them on its own people? Had the military's soul fundamentally changed?

The Bioforensic Center, where she would be working for the next few months, was under the authority of the Department of Homeland Security. She had agreed at the urging of Dr. Hampton Elliott, CDC's director, to collaborate with NBFAC's forensic testing center on the study of the bird pox. The research facility was a level four lab, which studied the most dangerous pathogens—Ebola, Marburg, Lassa Fever, and now bird pox. She parked her truck in front of the triangular glass and metal building that reminded her of a ship's bow.

Inside she flashed her security clearance to the guard in the foyer. Jenny entered the elevator and rode it up to her new lab. She exited and walked down a gunmetal gray hallway toward a solid metal door. She peered into the infrared light of a retinal scanner, and the door clicked. She took a deep breath as she pushed it open. Meeting new people had always been difficult, and the challenge made her miss her colleagues at CDC even more.

A tall sinewy man with flat lips and strands of gray in his dark hair waved at her as he approached. "Hello, Dr. George, I've been expecting you. I'm Dr. Abrams, the lab's director. Ready to get started?"

Jenny extended her hand which Abrams shook limply. "Yes, I'm ready."

She followed Abrams through another long hallway that thankfully was painted tan. Two horizontal lines of dark brown and blue about waist high extended down the corridor. Every forty feet or so was a door with a large window. "These are the individual labs. Yours is just on the other side of this door." He pointed toward the end of the hallway.

He opened the door for Jenny. Another hallway. "You probably already know that NBFAC is the only one of the several federal research labs in the Fort Detrick complex dedicated exclusively to the forensic analysis of pathogens."

Jenny nodded.

Abrams stopped and pointed into a lab room. "The building's exterior walls are reinforced concrete and over two feet thick." He pointed toward a vent in the ceiling. "We have one of the most sophisticated air monitoring systems in the world." She tried to concentrate on what he was saying, but all she could think about was Sam.

The black SUV had followed her for a harrowing thirteen miles from the Mount Vernon trail head to the junction at Interstate 495 and 270. Jenny suspected the worst about who the men were and why Sam hadn't called.

Perhaps they only wanted to intimidate her. They certainly had done that. And if that were true, maybe Sam was okay and there was another explanation for his silence. At least the Charlotte Police were looking for him. She had called them to report him missing. "This will be your lab station." Abrams opened a door.

A dark-skinned man in a lab coat walked up to the door. Jenny tried to refocus.

"This is Dr. Singh. He'll be working with you on the bird pox."

"It's an honor, Dr. George," Dr. Singh said in a thick East Indian accent. "I'm familiar with your work on H5N1. Please come in."

"Nice to meet you as well." Jenny extended her hand which the scientist pumped enthusiastically. "Please call me Jenny." She walked into the lab as Dr. Abrams remained at the doorway.

"And you can call me PJ."

"I will. What does it stand for?"

"It's a long story, and if I told you, you would think I'm pulling your ankle bone." He grinned.

Jenny smiled, the first time in the last twenty-four hours.

"I'll leave the two of you to get acquainted," Dr. Abrams said closing the door.

The work area consisted of an office and two sealed labs, one about thirty-feet long and twenty-feet wide, and a smaller one.

"Your discovery has scared the brains out of us all." PJ threw his hands in the air. "This is the first genetically synthesized virus we've heard of since the Russians combined Marburg and small pox in the 1990s, though that was never confirmed."

His interpretation of English idioms was just the levity she needed. She immediately liked him. "Have you been studying my virus?"

He nodded. Strands of dark black hair slid over his eyes. He quickly swept them back. "It's a bad bug. Come look at this." He walked toward a table with three computer screens.

One of the screens revealed the breakdown of the virus' genome.

PJ pointed toward the DNA report. "Thank the heavens this virus is unstable."

"They didn't break the genome into short enough segments."

"They probably already know that and are trying to correct their mistake."

Jenny pointed toward the screen next to it. "Is this the protemic analysis?"

He nodded vigorously. "The virus' fingerprint. We can identify the lab that created the virus through this process. It goes one step further than a DNA analysis. A microbe's genetic material doesn't change based on how it grows, but the proteins do." PJ's dark brown eyes looked almost comically large through his wire rim glasses. "And every pathogen has a different protein structure."

"Which is how you trace it back to the lab that created it," Jenny added.

"Exactly. This technology is incredibly important to our nation's safety. Terrorists have realized they can kill more people with the right bioweapon than they can with a nuke and for a whole lot less money. But now we can identify where it came from." PJ pointed toward the third screen. "I cross-referenced it against Fort Detrick's virus database."

Jenny pointed back at the lines of text on the screen. "So where's it from?"

"Here." PJ's voice cracked.

The revelation sent a surge of adrenalin racing through Jenny. "Here as in the U.S.?"

"Here as in Fort Detrick."

"Are you certain?"

PJ nodded slowly.

She studied the third screen. The analysis matched the H5N1 strain of the virus with the Fort Detrick research complex, but didn't identify a particular lab. The other half of the pathogen, the variola major strain, corresponded with the Vector laboratory in Russia.

"It's from Vector?"

"It could be. The U.S. labs have done a better job at protecting their pathogens than Russia. When the Soviet Union collapsed, various strains of the small pox ended up on the black market."

"So you think someone acquired Vector's pox and synthesized the chimera at Fort Detrick?"

"It would be a lot easier for us to acquire the variola major strain than for the Russians to obtain the H5N1 strain."

Jenny shook her head. "Which means our government used those poor villagers in the Congo as guinea pigs."

"I'd be surprised if the government was even aware of what happened in that village. The military is another story."

"You give them a lot more credit than I do. The government authorized several biological experiments on unsuspecting U.S. citizens through the years including a bacterial fog that was sprayed over San Francisco in the fifties that infected 8,000 people."

Jenny spotted a security camera in the corner of the lab and wondered who was watching. She turned her back to the camera and walked to a window of thick glass overlooking a greenbelt. The tops of willow trees rocked gently in the morning breeze. "Somewhere out there is another lab that created this thing."

Her phone rang. She looked at the number. She turned back toward PJ. "Excuse me; I've got to take this call."

PJ nodded and sat down at a chair at the table and studied the computer screens.

"This is Jenny." She turned back toward the window.

"Hello, Dr. George, this is Sgt. Dandridge with the Charlotte Police."

"Is Sam okay?"

"Did Dr. Myers have any idea who was following him?"

"Only that it was a black SUV. Is he okay? Have you found him?"

"Had he received any threatening calls?"

Her breathing quickened. "You asked me these questions before. Why are you asking me again? What do you know?"

"When was the last time you spoke with him?"

The floor beneath her became unstable. She leaned against the wall. "I told you already. One or one-thirty in the afternoon two days ago."

"What's happened?" Jenny took shallow breaths.

"I'm sorry Dr. George. We found Dr. Myers this morning in the hospital garage. Dead."

CHAPTER FIFTEEN

Gaithersburg, Maryland, July 11

Sam was dead.

Jenny walked outside her townhome and picked up the newspaper. Dr. Abrams, her new boss, had given her the day off after yesterday's traumatic news. As she stood up, she shuddered. A black Suburban like the one that had followed her was parked halfway down the block. She hurried back inside, shut the door, and locked the deadbolt. She called the Gaithersburg Police Department and reported the suspicious vehicle.

She peeked through the white wooden blinds. It was still there. She took a deep breath and looked at the new cell phone sitting on the kitchen table. Hopefully, the police would call soon. She sat down on her couch and opened the local newspaper. Splashed across the front page was an article about the President's autopsy.

The President had died of complications from the assassination attempt, not from a morphine overdose. Sam's worst fears had been realized—and now hers.

Jenny flipped to the inside page. An article caught her attention. One of the late President's surgeons was missing and had been connected to a terrorist. The reporter questioned whether the surgeon's disappearance and Sam's death were connected in some way to the President's death. The story was from the Charlotte

Observer. The byline said the reporter's name was Hank Jackson. *If only he knew.*

Sam had asked her to go to the press if the Bethesda autopsy proved to be a cover-up, but the thought of doing so terrified her. The report had gotten Sam killed. She should delete the email he sent and eliminate any connection.

She picked up her cell and dialed information for the Charlotte newspaper and punched in the number and waited.

"Charlotte Observer, may I help you?"

"Is Hank Jackson in?" Her voice was shaky.

"Hold please."

"This is Jill. I'm Hank's assistant. May I help you?"

Jenny hung up. *I'm sorry, Sam. I can't do it.*

There was a knock at the front door. She got up and slowly approached the door. She looked through the peep hole. The police. She opened the door and leaned out.

"Are you the lady who called in the report on the black Suburban?"

"I am."

"I'm Officer Freeman." He nodded. "Ma'am, I couldn't find a black Suburban or any black SUV. I asked some of your neighbors if they had seen the vehicle, and they said they hadn't. Are you sure you saw it?"

"Of course," she snapped. "It's been following me."

"Do you mind if I ask you a few more questions?"

Jenny spent the next ten minutes answering the officer's questions except for the one about why someone would be following her. She said she didn't know. The policeman gave her his card and left.

Jenny closed and locked the door. She peered through the blinds and watched him drive off. *I know what I saw.* She walked into the living room. Caz lounged on top of her hundred-year-old table, his tail flipping back and forth. Not a care in the world.

She sat down at the table and opened her notebook computer and clicked on the email icon. She looked again at Sam's message. With one click she could erase the message and file and put the whole sordid thing behind her. She moved the cursor to delete but once again paused.

She got up and walked down the hallway to the bathroom and turned on the cold water.

In the mirror she saw what had never pleased her mother—a face that would never win a beauty contest. Small eyes, thin lips, a weak chin. She splashed water in her face. Dad had always told her she was beautiful. She wasn't. But at least she was to him. How she missed him. If only he were here to tell her what to do.

She wiped her face with a hand towel. Whoever had killed Sam seemed content to only threaten her for now. But it didn't make any sense. If they knew she had the analysis, why would they let her live? Unless they didn't care about the report, because they didn't know about it. Maybe the people following her weren't the same people. It was the only conclusion that made any sense. But then, who were they?

Jenny hit redial on her cell.

"This is Hank Jackson."

She hesitated. "Uh, Mr. Jackson...I'm Dr. George. I suggest you sit down."

There was a pause. "Okay, I'm sitting."

"I read your article, and your instincts about what happened to the President are correct."

"Who are you again?"

"Who I am is not important; what I have to tell you is."

"I'm listening."

"The President was murdered. He was given an overdose of morphine, and I have a toxicology report to prove it." There was silence on the other end. "Are you there, Mr. Jackson?"

"Sorry." He stuttered. "Can you send me the report?"

"I can, but please be careful. I believe Dr. Myers is dead because of it."

"I will."

"And Mr. Jackson, do not use my name. Are we clear on that?"

"Gotcha."

Jenny gave Hank a brief history on how Sam had secretly obtained the President's blood and sent it to a lab for analysis. Hank gave her his email address and hung up.

Jenny forwarded Sam's email with the file. It felt good to shift the burden to someone else. As she was about to log off, a message arrived from an unknown source with no subject line. Her spam blocker generally filtered out such messages. She opened it.

Forget bird pox. The real monster is below.

A shiver rippled across her skin. Jenny checked for an IP address, but there wasn't any. She would have dismissed the email as a bad joke, but very few people outside of Fort Detrick knew about the synthetic virus. The head of the Department of Health and Human Services had decided not to tell the public about her deadly discovery for fear of creating a panic.

Whoever sent the email was an insider with knowledge of something potentially far more dangerous than bird pox. But if it were true, why tell her? And, more importantly, what did they expect her to do?

CHAPTER SIXTEEN

Washington, D.C., July 13

President Reed Hamilton walked into the Oval Office dressed in his robe. It was early. Still dark outside. He liked to rise before anyone else, before the chaos of the day. A stack of morning newspapers sat on the ornately carved Resolute desk, a gift from Queen Victoria that had served twenty-four presidents. He sipped black coffee as he approached his desk. He scanned a few headlines. Nothing interesting. He touched his computer, and national news flashed onto the screen. *Breaking news. President's Autopsy Falsified?*

Hamilton's hand jerked, spilling coffee over the papers. His heart pounded as he scanned the article's first few lines. He pushed a button on his desk.

"Good morning, Mr. President."

"Get Alex Martin on the phone immediately." Hamilton hung up before the operator could respond. He turned off the computer.

A few minutes later the speaker on his desk buzzed. "Mr. President, the Director of the Secret Service is on the line."

"Good morning, Mr. President. Must be important to wake me up at four-thirty."

"Obviously it's important. Turn on your television. I'm sure it's on every network by now."

"What is?"

Hamilton snorted. "The Charlotte Observer just reported that President Nash died from a morphine overdose, not complications from the assassination attempt."

"But that contradicts the autopsy report released by Bethesda. What proof do they have for making such an outrageous claim?"

"A toxicology analysis. What I want to know is how this Dr. Myers got a sample of Nash's blood? And why didn't the publisher call us before he ran a story like this?

In the background a television blared. "If he was on the operating team, he was probably covered in it. I'll call the publisher."

"Even more outrageous is an allegation that someone poisoned the President with morphine. How could that even happen? Doesn't the Secret Service have procedures in place to prevent such a thing?"

"Every person who had access to the President was fully screened."

"Well, you missed one, Director. Did your men leave to take a piss and let some fanatic kill the President?"

Martin cleared his throat. "Four agents were with the President from the time he came out of surgery until his body was delivered to Bethesda. They were even present during the autopsy."

"Then how did it happen?"

"I'm not sure, but my guess is the saline administered through the IV was tampered with. Someone could have removed the solution from the bag with a hypodermic and replaced it with morphine before delivering it to the President's room. But are you certain the story is even accurate?"

"I'm not sure of anything except what the nation is going to think. You thought the agency's screw up with Kennedy was bad? This will be far worse. Better prepare a statement and don't give any interviews until we have better understanding of what's happened."

Hamilton hung up. He buzzed the operator again.

"Yes, Mr. President."

"Get the FBI Director."

"Of course, Mr. President."

Hamilton eyed the humidor on his desk. It was too early to smoke, but he needed something to calm him. He opened the mahogany box with the presidential seal inlaid in 24k gold. A subtle aroma of cinnamon and coffee wafted from the cigars, which had just arrived from Cuba's President. The repeal of the fifty-four year old embargo by President Nash had brought billions of development dollars into Cuba, and the tobacco had been flowing freely ever since—some of the choicest to Hamilton. He removed a double magnum maduro, clipped the end and lit it. He inhaled the rich smoke. Better.

"Mr. Daniel Broughton is on the line Mr. President."

"Good morning, Mr. President."

"Are you aware of the allegations made by the Charlotte Observer, or did you just wake up like Alex Martin?"

"Caught it on the television."

"Any idea how the reporter got the toxicology report?"

"Any number of ways. Could have come directly from the lab, or through Dr. Myers, or someone the reporter and the surgeon both knew. But, Mr. President, I think the bigger problem is the possible terrorist connection."

"What are you talking about?"

"The Charlotte Observer claims it has evidence Dr. Haley, the surgeon who's missing, has a possible terrorist connection. This raises the possibility that the President was the victim of a terrorist attack."

Hamilton swept the entire stack of newspapers onto the floor. "Can the FBI add anything beyond what the news agencies have reported, or is the television your main source of information?"

"Please, Mr. President, everyone is playing catch up here. We'll know more within the next few hours. I'll assign my best people to the investigation."

"Maybe you should just call the reporter who wrote the story. He seems to know more than the FBI and Secret Service combined." Hamilton punched the button on his desk so hard it stuck in the downward position. He picked up the phone and called Pepper.

"Hello?"

"We've got a serious problem. I need you here now."

"Isn't it Saturday?" Pepper's voice was scratchy.

"Does it matter?"

Thirty minutes later Pepper poked his head in the doorway.

Hamilton waved him in. Dark circles underscored Pepper's eyes. He coughed and swatted at the thick cloud of smoke. "How can you smoke those things at five-thirty in the morning?"

"Are you sick?"

"No, just sleep deprived."

Hamilton leaned forward on his desk. "Are you aware of what's happened?"

"Unfortunately. I scanned the internet on the way over."

Pepper sat down on the white sofa with an alternating pattern of pale and intense yellow flowers. He removed his glasses, then rubbed his face. "How do you want to handle this?"

"Stall the press as long as you can until we can get a grip."

"That's not going to work. They're going to pound us for answers—especially how an autopsy performed under the supervision of the Secret Service could have been altered without government collusion?"

"I'd like to know myself."

But Hamilton knew. From the minute he received a call from Bethesda revealing the President had died of an overdose, he knew what had to be done. The nation was too fragile for the truth that its President, after surviving an assassination attempt, had been subsequently murdered. The memory of Sulaiman's call dulled the fine tobacco. Hamilton put the cigar down. What he did, he did for the country.

"What do you think happened?"

"Well, we have an obvious discrepancy." Pepper put his oval, tortoise shell glasses back on. "Bethesda's autopsy report doesn't concur with the reporter's story which means either he is lying, or someone has deliberately falsified the autopsy results."

"I'd like to nail the hotshot who broke the story." Hamilton re-lit his cigar. "Probably invented the whole thing. Wouldn't be the first time."

Pepper shifted on the sofa. "I don't think the reporter is lying."

"Why not?"

"Given the timing of Sulaiman's call to you aboard Air Force Two and the revelation that Dr. Haley may be connected to a terrorist, I think it's very likely Sulaiman is involved someway in the President's death." Pepper adjusted his glasses and stared at Hamilton. "Is there anything you left out about your conversation with Sulaiman?"

"I gave it to you word for word." But he hadn't and would never share everything he knew with his advisers. Loyalty could never be guaranteed. Especially in Washington. He'd seen too many politicians embarrassed and even destroyed by confidential information that was leaked to the press or ended up in a book. "Do you really think terrorists could pull off what's being alleged?"

"We're not dealing with Middle Eastern thugs anymore, Mr. President. They're sophisticated. They have intelligence networks like us. They look like us. And they have penetrated nearly every level of our society including the government. We just don't know how deeply yet."

Hamilton tightened the belt on his robe. He eyed the decanter of single malt scotch sitting on a table against the east wall. He needed a drink, but what would the First Lady think if she smelled alcohol on his breath in the morning?

"If someone is directing a cover-up, the pathologists who performed the autopsy are in danger," Pepper said. "In fact, everyone connected to any evidence is in danger."

"I spoke with the FBI director this morning about taking them into custody."

Pepper stood. "Good. I think you also should address the press corps directly about the reporter's claims."

"I can't stand their yapping. Have James do it. He's the Press Secretary. But tell him to attack the reporter's credibility as much as possible."

"All right." Pepper turned to leave.

Hamilton stood.

Pepper stopped and turned back. "You know what concerns me most about all of this?"

"What's that?"

"That President Nash wasn't the ultimate target. What the terrorists are really after is our government. And they may have just put a bullet in us."

CHAPTER SEVENTEEN

Charlotte, July 15

Hank sat on a stool sipping a cappuccino at The Dirty Bean, admiring the long legs a table over. They belonged to a young woman dressed in a tight skirt who caught him staring. He looked down at his newspaper and pretended to be interested. He had never been very good with women. His longest relationship was three months, and the last month of that was pretty awful.

His father on the other hand had been a real charmer. Always said the right thing. Hank had tried some of his pop's pick-up lines. They never worked. Women instinctually knew when something was effortless and when it was forced. His dad told Hank he tried too hard. Maybe so, but it was probably more a function of the right genes. You either had smooth moves in your DNA, or you didn't.

A woman sitting at the table with the long-legged beauty got up and ordered a drink.

"Two-hundred thousand dollars," the man said.

She pulled a couple notes from her purse and handed it to the barista.

Tucked inside Hank's wallet was a half a million dollars. Rampant inflation had the government scrambling to issue higher denominations each month. *Never thought I'd be a millionaire and feel so poor.*

The cell rang. Hank picked it up as the long-legged woman with playful, dark eyes glanced at him. He sat up straight and tried to look important. "This is Hank Jackson," he said loud enough for her to hear. Maybe she would recognize his name from the recent article about the President's poisoning? But she turned back to her girlfriend and resumed talking.

"Got a hot lead for you." Sgt. Steele's gravelly voice was hurried.

"What is it?"

"One of my buddies at the FBI called. They just picked up a suspect in the President's assassination."

Hank swallowed. "Who is it?"

"Wouldn't say. Still processing him. But they're pretty sure they have the right guy. Got a match on DNA. And he worked as a janitor at the Zebco building."

"Where did they find him?" It was question he had to ask even though he dreaded the answer.

"At Presbyterian Hospital. The guy was all busted up."

Whatever else Steele said, Hank didn't hear. He had been dreading this moment ever since he abandoned his friend. Choosing to believe that DW wasn't involved in the assassination despite his comments. Irrationally hoping that if he was, somehow he would go unnoticed. Not because he didn't deserve justice, but because if the FBI found DW, they would eventually find Hank.

Would DW tell the FBI Hank had picked him up? He might be sore for being dumped on a sidewalk. Left to die. It wasn't actually like that. Hank had called the hospital shortly after leaving him to make sure he was found. And DW had warned him to leave. But even if DW said nothing, would that be enough? The FBI had already found his chute and knew he had help getting to the hospital. They were probably searching for Hank right now.

He stumbled out into the sticky afternoon and tried to breathe, but his lungs felt incapable of anything except short gasps. Should he go to the FBI now before they found him and try to explain what happened? Would they even listen? The country was so traumatized over the President's death that anyone connected to it, even innocently, would be drawn and quartered.

"Hey mister," a young woman's voice called. "You forgot your cell phone."

Hank turned to see the long-legged woman walk toward him.

"Are you okay?" She touched his shoulder as she handed him the cell.

In normal circumstances the touch from such a beautiful woman would send a jolt through him, but he felt nothing. A sure sign he was more dead than alive. "What?"

"You look a little upset."

A siren squealed in the background. Hank stiffened.

"You in some kind of trouble?"

The word *trouble* seemed inadequate to describe his situation. *Nightmare* fit better. Hank shook his head, turned and walked away quickly.

CHAPTER EIGHTEEN

Albuquerque, July 15

The west and south walls towered starkly over a collapsed pile of scorched cinder blocks. A single charred pew smoldered in the corner. An easterly wind swept dwindling, acrid smoke toward Luke who stood outside the ruins.

His eyes watered. But not all the tears were from stinging smoke. If only he hadn't been locked up at the Bernalillo County Detention Center, maybe he could have stopped whoever did it. He had hoped to someday return to Grace Fellowship when the political climate was different. But the burned-out shell before him put a permanent end to the wishful thought.

"Definitely arson." John Griegos walked among the ash, kicking at the remains. "The fire was too hot to be accidental." The fire captain had silver hair with a thick but neatly trimmed mustache. Flecks of dark ash clung to his mustache, giving it a salt and pepper appearance. He crouched and scooped some residue from the church's floor into a round metal container and snapped the lid on. He stood up and walked toward the west wall and studied a blackened section near the base.

A ten-foot white cross that had stood prominently in front of the church lay on the ground. It had escaped the fire but not the force of a vehicle that had rammed it. Traces of blue paint were embedded in gashes where it had been sheared. Luke leaned down and inspected the cross. Something had been scrawled with a Sharpie on the cross beam. *He never died on this.*

"Any idea who did this?" Griegos asked moving through the dark skeleton.

Luke stood back up. The message on the cross was clear enough. But it could have been written by anyone who hated Christians. And there were plenty who fit that description. He shook his head.

Griegos walked toward where the entrance used to be. "Whoever did it probably isn't from the neighborhood. Everyone around here respects you even if they don't agree with you." He paused. "By the way, I saw you on YouTube."

Luke wiped his eyes. He could feel the grit from the fire. "YouTube?" He didn't remember anyone filming him.

"Someone posted a clip of you telling the government to shove it. More than a million people have watched it. Haven't you seen it?"

Luke shook his head. He didn't need another reminder of when his world changed. "I didn't tell the government to shove it."

"I know. But you stood up for what you believe. You're kind of famous, amigo."

"You mean infamous."

"Yeah, that, too. People are curious about you. They want to know why you were willing to lose everything."

In weaker moments Luke had asked himself why he hadn't gone along the new law. Other pastors had. He would still have a church and a job. Now he would have to return to painting houses to support his wife, two grown, unmarried daughters, and his madre, who was a widow. It would leave little time for even a small Bible study at home.

But if he had conceded to the new law, it would have invalidated everything he had taught during the last seven years. How could he stand in a pulpit without the freedom to teach the truth? How could he rip off people like that? Especially poor people who scraped to help support the church. Every Sunday would be like going to a rock concert where the singers stood on stage and lip-synched. He couldn't do it.

Griegos stepped over a crumbling foundation that used to support the exterior east wall. The July sun overhead seemed hot enough to start another fire. The fire captain had black smudges under his eyes. All he needed was a football. "What are you going to do, Luke?"

"Go back to painting, I guess."

"And give up preaching? You've already got a following. Maybe you should post a sermon on YouTube."

He didn't have a clue of how to post anything on the internet. But someone in the church might know. If he could broadcast sermons, he might be able to continue teaching the gospel, although it probably wouldn't be long before the government shut him down. But maybe it was worth a try. Perhaps God had allowed one door to close because He was about to open another.

CHAPTER NINETEEN

Fort Detrick, July 15

The question had woken Jenny during the night and prevented her from going back to sleep. She stared at the computer screen in her lab. If Fort Detrick was where the virus originated, then the military's new biodefense center must be its designer. But how could she prove it?

PJ swiveled in his chair and stared at her. "Is something wrong? You haven't said two sentences all day."

"I'm sorry. You said the H5N1 virus in the bird pox came from somewhere in the Fort Detrick complex."

"That's right."

"Do you remember the strain?" She turned and looked at PJ.

"I think it was Tien Giang. Why?"

She shook her head. "That can't be right. I discovered that strain in Southern Vietnam. There are only two labs that have access to it—CDC and the Bioforensic Center."

PJ stood up and walked over toward her. "Are you sure?"

"Positive. If you're right about the chimera being synthesized here at Fort Detrick, then that narrows it to two labs."

"I'd believe that if you told me it was the Army's lab, but CDC and Bioforensic are dedicated to true preventative study of viruses, not creating new ones. Maybe someone made a mistake and sent the virus to the wrong lab. It's happened before."

"Let's hope you're right."

A man looking in the lab's window startled Jenny. It was Dr. Abrams. He waved, then opened the door and leaned in. "How's the work coming?"

Jenny stood up. "We're making good progress, Dr. Abrams. We've completed the protemic analysis."

As Abrams turned toward PJ, Jenny slowly shook her head. He nodded slightly.

"We skipped a bullet," PJ said. "Whoever created it, made some errors in its synthesis that made it unstable."

"I'd like to see your research," Abrams said. "Can you summarize it and send it to me?"

"Of course," PJ said.

Abrams closed the door and left.

PJ turned back to Jenny. "What was that all about? Don't you trust him?"

"I don't think we should tell anyone what we know at this point. At least not Dr. Abrams or my boss, Dr. Elliott. I doubt the Bioforensic Center or CDC is involved, but let's not assume anything."

"What do you suggest we do?" PJ's eyes darted to the lab door and back to her.

"Do you know of any other floors below level one?"

PJ threw his hands into the air. "We're forensic scientists, not Sherlock Holmes and Watson."

There wasn't a trace of malice in the dark face. But could she trust him? She'd already divulged more information than she should. Yet she needed a confidant. Someone like Sam, but he was gone. "There's something I haven't shared with you."

PJ crossed his arms. "What's that?"

"I received a strange email the other day that suggests there is another lab at Fort Detrick. One that may be creating biological weapons."

"What did the email say?"

"Something about the real monster was below."

PJ pushed his glasses back up his nose. She thought she detected a trickle of sweat on the bridge. "It may mean nothing at all. Just a joke."

"Maybe."

PJ shook his head. "I don't know where another lab could possibly be. There are about 150 scientists who work here. I know many of them."

"If there's a lab hidden in this building, the scientists who work there are probably just as invisible. Maybe there's another entrance—a secret entrance. Or maybe they live at the lab and never leave. I'll bet we've never seen anyone who works there."

PJ shook his head slowly. "Hidden labs and monster viruses? Pardon me for saying this, but you seem to be hopping to conclusions."

Was she becoming paranoid? Making extrapolations that a junior scientist wouldn't think of doing? Perhaps. The email might be nothing, but the protemic analysis wasn't an illusion. There was a definite link to Fort Detrick.

She checked her watch. The day was almost over. "I've got a plane to catch. I'll see you in two days."

"Your friend's funeral?"

"Yes, Sam's." Jenny got up and walked toward the door.

"Don't worry about the virus. I'll take care of everything."

She turned back toward PJ. "It's not the bird pox I'm worried about."

Jenny walked out of the lab, following the brown and blue stripes down two hallways to a door that connected to another hallway where the elevator was. As she pushed floor one on the elevator she noticed something she hadn't seen before—a thin slot for a security card. She inserted her clearance card, but the digital readout on the panel read *access denied*.

Dr. Abrams told her she had the highest security clearance. Had he lied?

The elevator doors opened, and she walked out of the complex into the glare of the late afternoon sun. She slipped her sunglasses on and walked toward her SUV which was parked in the second lot, about a hundred yards from the entrance.

"Dr. George," someone called her name.

She turned and saw the receptionist running from the building toward her. She approached with a box tucked under her arm. "I forgot to give this to you," she said puffing.

Jenny wasn't expecting a delivery.

"You should have received this a week ago." The receptionist's face was red. "I apologize. When this package arrived last week, I didn't recognize your name, so I sent it back." She handed the package to Jenny.

"That's all right. Who's it from?"

"No name."

"Thank you," Jenny said taking the box and holding it gingerly. It was light.

She walked to her double-cab truck, opened the door, and placed the package on the center console. She climbed inside and shut the door. The box was tightly sealed. She slid her house key along the tape. As she was about to open it, she saw a dark image in the rear view mirror approaching fast.

A black SUV.

Dear God. Her pulsed surged.

A gun was pointed out the window.

Duck.

Glass exploded all around.

She lay crouched on the floorboard, her heart pounding.

"Get the package," someone yelled from outside her door.

She glanced at the passenger door. Unlocked.

"Someone's coming. Let's go."

"No, we've got to get it."

Jenny could feel a breeze blow over her head through the shot-out windows.

"That car is headed right toward us."

The crunching impact of metal against metal exploded outside.

Her door swung open. Hands grabbed her. "We've got to go."

Jenny grabbed the box as she was dragged from her vehicle and into another.

CHAPTER TWENTY

Charlotte, July 16

The crowd in front of Mecklenburg County Jail surged forward toward a line of police that struggled to maintain its position. Signs bobbed up and down among the several hundred. Hank stood toward the back, as unobtrusive as possible. Normally he would be at the front, in the thick of the melee with recorder in hand, firing questions at the protesters. But he didn't dare.

"A Christian killed my President," a short, fleshy woman shouted through dirty hands. A bald, unshaven man in a worn suit screamed something unintelligible and pumped a sign in the air depicting the late President crucified on a cross. A man in a tattered robe with a scraggly beard held a sign that said *the real terrorists are Christians*. Many of the protesters appeared to be homeless and unemployed, casualties of the European Union collapse that had toppled the world's economic powers like a set of dominoes.

What they and the crowd wanted was DW swinging from a tree. Although it had been more than thirty years since the last lynching in Mobile, Alabama, it was still in the blood of some southerners—like Hank's hound dog, Jouser. He was too arthritic to hunt anymore, but it never stopped him from howling whenever he picked up a scent. Fortunately DW was safely tucked into a cell.

The crowd's anger was fueled by the FBI's discovery of a diary in DW's cabin in Boone along with a trash can filled with copies of partially burned Qu'rans. News of the discovery had created a maelstrom. In the diary DW had written that God told him to kill the President, which was as preposterous as the torched holy books. DW didn't believe in God and wasn't a religious fanatic. But few people outside his family and friends knew that. And it wasn't likely anyone was willing to risk ostracism to set the record straight. Hank certainly wouldn't. The whole thing smelled of a set-up, but no one seemed to care.

The nation needed a motive for why its president had been cut down. Now, it had one.

Why had DW shot the President? The FBI had probably drilled DW with the question a thousand times. He had been a highly decorated sniper in Afghanistan with more than 100 kills. A real war hero. But things hadn't gone as well once he returned home. His wife and three daughters were on a visit to Washington, D.C., when a terrorist tragically blew himself and 33 people up in a subway. Everything DW loved was on that train.

Hank had never been married, never had any children. But even without that experience, he could still understand the pain DW felt. Whether that drove him to shoot the President was unknown, but it certainly wasn't because of God. Maybe DW blamed the President for the rise of terrorism at home. And shooting him was his way of letting the nation feel his pain. The world might never know. He was a tight-lipped soldier who had endured torture by the Taliban. If he could survive their brutal interrogation methods, he could certainly outlast the FBI.

Whether Hank could outlast the FBI was another matter. Each day he told himself he would tell the agency what had happened. But as the nation's rage at DW grew daily, it made confessing more difficult. At the same time his chances of not being caught were improving. If DW was going to turn Hank in, he already would have. And if the Secret Service had gotten a good look at his truck at the hospital, they would have picked him up.

A man in the crowd held a rock. Someone else a bottle. The crowd's temperament was changing like a snarling dog about to bite. Hank took a few steps backward. *Don't do it.*

The man hurled the rock as others in the crowd fired bottles and cans at the police. A Molotov cocktail exploded against an officer, engulfing him in flames as he fell to the ground. The police drew their guns.

"They're going to shoot," someone shouted.

A wave of protestors rolled backward, sweeping everyone with it. Hank tripped over someone who had fallen as he struggled to maintain his balance. A shot rang out which sent the crowd charging like a herd of buffalo.

CHAPTER TWENTY-ONE

Gaithersburg, July 16

Jenny woke with ringing in her ears.

She sat up in bed, someone else's bed. The last thing she could remember was being yanked from her truck. Thankfully, she was still in her clothes. As soon as her feet touched the carpet, she remembered where she was supposed to be. *Poor Sam.* She hadn't even been there to say goodbye. A wave of anxiety gripped her. She wiped her eyes as she tiptoed into a sunny room.

"Good morning," a man standing in the kitchen said. The smell of bacon filled the room.

"Are you the one who pulled me from my vehicle?"

The man wiped his hands on a towel lying on the counter and walked out from the kitchen. He extended his hand. "I'm Dr. Denton Mabe."

Dr. Mabe wore a t-shirt stretched so tightly across his muscled chest that it took little imagination to envision what he looked like with it off.

Jenny shook his hand.

"You're lucky to be alive," Denton said.

"What happened?"

"I was leaving work when I spotted someone in a black truck shooting at you. I did the only thing I could think of—rammed it."

"Your vehicle must be..."

"Forget it. That's what insurance is for. I'm just glad I happened to be there. Any idea who those guys were?"

"They're probably the same people who have been following me. But I don't know who they are." Jenny shuddered. "Where's my box?"

Denton pointed toward the kitchen table. "I figured whatever was in it was pretty important. You had an iron grip on it."

Jenny walked over to the table and picked up the package and inspected it. The sides were crushed. She pressed her fingers against the jagged line on the seal left from her house key.

A burnt smell wafted from the kitchen. "Shoot." Denton ran back in. From the pass through, Jenny watched him scrape charred bacon from the skillet. "How about breakfast out?"

"Thank you, but I'm not really hungry. I'd love a cup of tea if you have any." She sat down at the table and opened the box. The metal container inside was familiar. It held a biological sample. A virus? There wasn't anything else inside. No identification of what the canister contained or who had sent it. Strange.

"That, I think I can do. By the way I hope it was okay for me to bring you here. You were in shock at the time, and I was afraid to take you home or to the hospital in case those goons came looking for you. And I didn't want to stick around for the police either.

"You're very kind. I may need you to accompany me to the police department, so I can file a report."

Jenny rolled the container in her hands, then flipped it over. On the bottom was a piece of surgical tape with a number printed on it. She recognized it. The canister slipped from her hands and fell into her lap. She shuddered. It was painfully clear now what the men who tried to kill her were after. As she looked down at the small cylinder, all she wanted to do was give it to them.

But she knew she couldn't. Sam's death would be meaningless. "I've got to make a call." Jenny stood up.

"Do you need privacy?" Denton walked into the great room and handed her a cup of steaming water on a saucer with a tea bag.

She took it and placed it on the table in front. "I'll step outside."

"No, I will. Enjoy your tea."

The fewer people who knew what was in the container, the better. She pulled up Hank's phone number from her phone's memory. But as she was about to dial it, she realized the people who had attacked might be listening to her calls. She opened the front door. Dr. Mabe was leaning against the brick veneer front.

"I hate to ask you for anything else, but could I borrow your phone?"

Denton raised his eyebrows. "Sure." He slipped his cell from his pocket and handed it to her. She walked back inside, closed the door, and dialed.

"Hank Jackson's office."

"Is Hank in?"

"Hold please."

"This is Hank."

"Hello Hank. This is Dr. George."

"You calling because of today's headlines?" His voice broke.

"No." She glanced at the newspaper lying on the kitchen counter but couldn't make out the headlines. "What's happened?"

"Where have you been? The FBI buried me. Said I made the story up about the President's murder. What's even worse is I don't have anything to prove they're wrong."

"What about the toxicology report I sent you?"

"The lab doesn't have a record of it, and the technician who prepared it has disappeared along with the two pathologists at Bethesda. I don't have any hard evidence the President was murdered."

"You do now." Jenny lowered her voice. "I have the President's blood." An image of the fallen leader lying next to his daughter flashed before her.

"You have his blood?"

"Sam sent me a sample before he was—killed." She choked out the word.

"He was very brave."

"He was."

CHAPTER TWENTY-TWO

Washington, D.C., July 17

President Hamilton stood fixated on the flat screen in front of him. Police fired rubber bullets into a crowd of rioters outside of Mecklenburg Jail in Charlotte. He flipped the channel. More riots, these against churches in Detroit and New York City. There was a knock at the door. He turned the television off. A canvas scrolled across the front of the screen until only a framed painting of Washington crossing the Delaware was visible. Early morning light turned the pale yellow walls of the Oval Office a golden hue.

"What is it?" Hamilton snapped.

The door opened, and Pepper leaned in. "Do you have a minute."

"Come in."

Pepper sat down on the sofa and laid a copy of the congressional resolution and a folder next to him. He pointed toward the paperwork and frowned. "We need to talk about this, but before we do, we have to formulate a response to the riots."

Hamilton walked over to the humidor on his desk and removed a cigar. "I can't believe the FBI released the diary and information about the burned Qu'rans without weighing the consequences. Their timing couldn't have been worse. Have they forgotten about the riots last year between Christians and Muslims?"

"Christians are being punished for the assassination. A dozen churches were vandalized, some even burned. And several Christians were assaulted."

Hamilton clipped the cigar, letting the cap fall to the floor. He lit the Cuban. "The riots are perfectly understandable given the fact that the assassin was a Christian fanatic. People want revenge."

"Sounds as if you're justifying the riots." Pepper straightened his striped yellow and blue tie.

"I'm not justifying anything. I simply understand why it's happening. We'll protect Christians and anyone else we have to. My main concern is to ensure we don't let fanatics turn this into something it's not."

"I think that's already happening. Some groups appear to be using the President's death as a cover for attacking Christians, which, if unchecked, could become something much more serious. Some deep gashes remain from the fight over the anti-hate crimes bill. A lot of ugly things were said, and some may feel it's payback time."

"Which groups?"

"Gay rights enthusiasts, atheists, radical Muslims."

"How do you know that?"

"The police in all three cities arrested enough people to get a pretty accurate sampling of the rioters."

Hamilton sighed. "This could escalate very quickly. We have to make sure it doesn't."

"If the protesters find a common chord beyond their immediate core, it could erupt into a nightmare overnight. It's happened before."

This wasn't good news, but then again it might deflect the nation's attention from the pending congressional investigation. Hamilton took a long draw of his cigar. "Kristallnatcht."

Pepper nodded. "Night of the broken glass. The assassination of a German diplomat in Paris by a Jew lit a fuse that resulted in the burning of nearly a thousand synagogues. Thirty thousand Jews were sent to concentration camps."

"That was 1938. It's a different world today. We haven't fed our people a steady diet of propaganda that all of our problems are because of Christians the way the Nazis did the German people about the Jews."

Pepper adjusted his glasses. "We haven't, but that doesn't mean that the people behind the riots believe Christians aren't the source of what's wrong with this country. And there may be a lot more people who share the same thoughts but aren't part of the demonstrations."

"What should I say to the county?"

"There are acceptable and unacceptable ways of expressing the pain and anger we feel over the President's death. The rioters have chosen an unacceptable path which we denounce. We empathize with their feelings but condemn their actions. And the message should come from you, not the press secretary."

Pepper could be didactic at times, particularly whenever he was certain he was right. Unfortunately, he was on this point. "Get the speech writers to frame something along the lines of what you just said and contact the networks to let them know I'll address the nation tonight."

"I thought you wanted to underplay it. A press conference is a better setting for this."

"And give reporters an opportunity to ambush me with questions about the congressional investigation? Are you kidding? Even if I refuse to take questions, the press will be sure to spew them out as I'm leaving to embarrass me. Then they'll spend the next hour focusing on the investigation, not what I said. No, I want to control the setting."

He walked back to his desk and looked at the congressional resolution lying on it. "Nash's cronies are behind this investigation."

"Mr. President, every single member of the House approved the resolution. There is solid evidence President Nash was murdered and that it was a cover-up. Congress has to investigate this. There are four people missing."

"What about our investigation?"

"There was nothing to investigate," Pepper said. "The two pathologists you wanted questioned are nowhere to be found. The lab technician is gone as well. But it doesn't really matter. The blood sample given to the FBI by the Charlotte Observer matches Nash's DNA. And the new toxicology report confirms Nash was poisoned."

"Nash's pals convinced him to drop me from the ticket, and now they're trying to destroy my presidency. They can't stand that I don't consult them about every matter the way Nash did." Hamilton wanted to throw something. A handful of Civil War minie balls lay on his desk. "It's that reporter's fault. He started this. We should pressure the publisher." Hamilton picked up the marble-sized lead balls.

"To do what?"

"To back off."

Pepper stood, eyeing Hamilton's hand. "Mr. President, you have to focus. Forget about the reporter. We have to draft a response for the nation. Every hour that goes by without a statement from the White House breathes more credibility into this thing. It gives your opponents unnecessary justification for building a case that you're involved in a cover-up."

Is that what Pepper thinks? Hamilton rubbed his temples. Blood pulsated through them with each throb. How had things gotten so out of control? He had only tried to rescue the country from more grief.

He took a deep breath. Pepper was right. Focus. He laid the minie balls down on his desk. "What do you suggest?"

"Tell the nation the Congressional and FBI investigations have the full support of the White House and that you will do everything possible to find Nash's killer and whoever is responsible for the cover-up."

Hamilton turned his back to Pepper and looked out the Oval Office windows. A recently completed fountain, based on a 19th century Italian design, spewed arcs of water. Copper pennies in the fountain's bottom, probably tossed by Nash's girls, caught the morning light. "All right. Have my speech writers put something together as soon as possible. We'll speak to the nation tonight on both issues. The riots fist, then this mess."

"Yes, Mr. President."

Hamilton turned around. A portrait of George Washington above the marble fireplace mantle stared directly at him.

CHAPTER TWENTY-THREE

Fort Detrick, July 19

The infected rhesus monkey shrieked as the needle entered the saphenous vein in its thigh. Jenny watched PJ in the sealed lab through the window. He closed the animal's cage and opened the one adjacent to it. He injected another monkey with a different antiviral. Then he stepped into an adjacent room stacked with smaller cages. He picked up a mouse and placed the wiggling rodent into a restraining device. He inserted a needle into the caudal vein in its tail, then repeated the process with another. When he finished, he turned around and gave a thumbs up.

PJ exited the lab through another door and disappeared into a sealed decontamination room with a chemical shower for cleansing his hazmat suit. A few minutes later, he emerged into the office.

"Everything go okay?" Jenny asked.

It was a question everyone who worked with highly infectious diseases either asked or wanted to. A pathogen as deadly as the bird pox could be treacherous even when safety procedures were copiously followed. Human error was impossible to eliminate and with a syringe full of virus, it took only one slip. It had happened more than once to some of the best scientists.

"A-okay. I gave each monkey a different antiviral and repeated the process with the mice."

"Oseltamivir and the neuramindase inhibitor R-125489?"

He nodded as he took a seat next to Jenny. "We'll know by tomorrow."

The Department of Health and Human Services wanted Jenny and PJ to develop a vaccine to stop the virus in case some fanatic decided to unleash the bird pox in a populated area. It still was uncertain who had tested the synthetic virus on the villagers. The military might be its creator, but it was impossible to know if the virus had fallen into other hands.

The first step toward creating a new vaccine was to determine how effective the current antivirals were at combating the virus. Jenny believed the neuramindase inhibitor R-125489, which disrupted the virus' ability to attach to a cell, had the best chance against the bird pox. But given the carnage she'd seen in the Congo village, even that was a long shot.

"I heard what happened. Everyone did. I'm so happy you're safe."

"Thank you." She patted the dark hand resting on the table.

PJ's hand recoiled as he looked away.

What was she thinking? In his culture it was inappropriate for a woman to touch a man. "I'm sorry."

He turned back. A flush of red overpowered his face. "Okie dokie," he said, his voice cracking.

"I wouldn't be here if it wasn't for Dr. Mabe."

"Very brave what he did. He works on the electron microscope team."

"He risked his life for me." Jenny glanced at her nails. The polish was worn. "I wonder if he knows anything about the other lab?"

PJ frowned "We don't know for certain if there is another lab. You haven't said anything to him, have you?"

"Of course, not." She nodded. "By the way I discovered something very intriguing."

"What?"

"I noticed a slot for a security card in the elevator. I inserted my card into it. Access was denied which means there's another area in this building that requires a higher security clearance than ours. There has to be, right?"

PJ pushed his glasses up his nose. "Be careful, Jenny. If you're caught trying to access an area you don't have clearance for, you could lose your position with the lab."

PJ was right. She had been taking unnecessary risks, flitting around the edges of potential trouble. She caught the image of someone staring in from the hallway window. The person slipped out of view. It looked like Dr. Abrams. The man gave her the creeps. She stood and picked up her purse. "Will you excuse me?"

"Of course."

As she left the lab she looked for any sign of Dr. Abrams, but there was none. She slipped her hand into her purse and touched the padded envelope. The anonymous package was in her mail box when she arrived at work. *Con idential* was printed in bold letters across the front. She needed privacy, and there was only one place she could think that was totally secure. She walked down the hallway through a doorway toward the ladies room.

She walked into a stall and closed the door. She pulled out the envelope, took her metal nail file and slit open the top. She dumped the contents into her hand, and a chill raced down her back. She was holding a security card and clearance badge. She sat down on the toilet cover and studied the badge. It granted clearance…to another lab. Until now, a covert lab had been speculation, but the two cards in her hand eliminated any doubt.

She put the cards back in the envelope and tucked the package into her purse. As she left the restroom, she surveyed the hallway and the cameras at each end. She wouldn't say anything to PJ. Whoever had sent the email and provided the clearance would have to find someone else to expose the lab. She needed her job. Besides, the last few days with Sam's murder and her brush with death had taken its toll.

* * *

PJ wanted to work late, but Jenny still didn't feel a hundred percent. She said goodbye and headed down the two hallways toward the elevator. As she rode it down, the events of the past few days flashed before her: Sam's call, the package he sent, Dr. Mabe's bold rescue. Each had taken enormous risks, and without them the public wouldn't know the truth about the President's death.

The elevator LCD panel indicated level one. The door opened. Jenny stood in the doorway as a profound feeling of guilt overwhelmed her. She felt as if she had disappointed someone. Her father. He had always told her to do the right thing so she'd never have to look back with regret.

She took a deep breath and pushed the button to close the door. She slipped her hand into her purse and removed the card. Her hand shook as she inserted it into the slot. The panel read *access granted*. As the elevator descended she wondered which she was more afraid of—being caught or what she would find.

CHAPTER TWENTY-FOUR

Fort Detrick, July 19

Either the elevator was slow or the lab was buried deep in the bowels of Fort Detrick. Jenny continued to descend without any indication from the panel of what level she was passing, not that she expected to see any floor identifications. The stretch between above and below was off the radar screen. It didn't exist. The brakes engaged and slowed the elevator until it stopped.

As the elevator door opened, she looked down at the identification card hanging from her neck and gasped. Wrong badge. She covered it with her hand and reached in her purse and exchanged it for the correct one.

A vast illuminated cavern at least thirty-feet high and a football field across stretched as far as she could see. The underground chamber had been as carefully carved from the cold dark rock as if chiseled by Michelangelo himself. A rail track ran along one side like a subway, a two-lane road with a bike path down the middle and to the other side a vast expanse of modular buildings. Labs she guessed.

A man in a dark blue jumpsuit sat in a jeep about a hundred feet from her studying a chart. He noticed her and drove toward the elevator and got out. "You have that new look about you." He eyed her clearance badge.

"That obvious?"

He frowned. "I'm surprised they sent you down this way. This elevator is rarely used."

"I'm Dr. Jenny George." She extended her hand.

He held up two hands dark with grime. "Sorry, dirty hands go with the job in maintenance. Fred Simmons."

She retracted her hand.

He looked at his watch. "The light rail will be here in a few minutes. It will take you to the labs and living quarters on the opposite end of the complex. Way too far to walk."

"Have you worked here long?" Jenny asked.

"Six months. Feels like forever."

"How long is your term?" Fred asked.

"It's short." *Hopefully, very short.* The train arrived so quietly that she wouldn't have noticed if she hadn't been watching the tracks.

"It's electric," Fred said.

"Thank you, Fred."

Jenny boarded the train and showed the operator her pass. She leaned back in the seat and wondered how she would ever convince anyone she wasn't an intruder.

The train stopped ten minutes later. She stepped out into a labyrinth of laboratories and walked toward Building 56, one of the numbers printed on her badge. She walked into the structure that, like her lab above, was a maze of hallways. Her clearance indicated she was assigned to lab 172. As she passed through the corridors, she hoped to find some numerical sequence for the numbers on the doors, but she couldn't make any sense of their arrangement.

After passing through three long hallways, she arrived at lab 172. She opened the door and walked in. A man sitting at a computer wheeled around.

"Can I help you?"

"I've been assigned to this lab."

"I haven't heard anything about a new team member. And I'm generally the first to know." The fair-skinned man with thick brown hair stood and walked toward her. "I'm Dr. James Jordan, the team manager."

"Dr. Jenny George."

He nodded thoughtfully. "I've read some of your research on H5N1. Top notch. What are you doing here?"

"I've been working on a vaccine for the bird pox."

Jordan smirked.

Did I miss the joke?

"Did they explain what we do here?" Jordan asked.

Say as little as possible. "Bioweapon design."

"That's part of it. What else did they tell you?"

"Not a lot."

He shook his head emphatically. "It doesn't sound like you were properly prepped."

That's an understatement.

"Who sent you down here?"

Careful. "Dr. Abrams."

Jordan's eyebrows jumped. "I didn't know he was aware of our project."

A trickle of sweat slid down Jenny's spine.

"Have a seat." He pointed toward three leather club chairs.

Jenny sank down in the soft dark leather, crossed her legs, and tried to look at ease. But her credibility was in jeopardy.

Jordan sat down opposite her and studied her. "I should probably make a few calls. Verify your clearance."

"For the record I didn't want to come here. I prefer direct light. But here I am." She pointed at her badge. "You can't buy one of these. So can we get started?"

He picked up the phone and pushed a button. He spewed out a rapid stream of numbers, then covered the mouthpiece. "My authorization code. All calls go through a central operator who monitors and records them. Only a few of us are allowed to place outside calls."

The sweat trickling down Jenn's back began to stream. She could hear the line ringing. *Please don't answer.*

"This is Dr. Abrams."

Her heart sank.

"I'm away from my phone. Please leave a message."

Jordan hung up. He rubbed the light whiskers on his chin. "All right. Let me give you a quick idea of what this lab does." His hazel eyes narrowed. "This whole complex is dedicated to one pathogen."

Jenny wasn't sure she had heard him correctly. "You mean the labs in this building?"

"No, the entire Fort Detrick sub complex."

"All these labs support one pathogen?"

Jordan slid forward to the edge of the chair. "You really don't understand what this is about."

"I guess not."

"We do here what you did above. The only difference is that instead of trying to develop vaccines for several different pathogens, we work with only one."

"But why?"

"Because the microbe we're working with is that extraordinary."

The hair on the nape of Jenny's neck tingled. She uncrossed her legs and leaned forward. "Are you developing a vaccine?"

"Good guess. Something this complicated, takes time and lots of manpower."

If the entire sub complex was devoted to finding a vaccine for the ultimate weapon, it meant one thing. The military wanted to ensure it was immune to the virus if it ever unleashed it. "Must be some weapon."

Jordan smirked. "Nothing like it in the world. I was part of the team that developed it. We had a few false starts at first. The bird pox was one of them. But wait until you see it."

The news twisted her stomach. The annihilation of an entire village had been relegated to nothing more than a false start. Jenny had found the source of evil that had killed the village's Sangoma. She reached in her purse for antacids but decided to wait.

"Take a look at this." Jordan stood up and walked over to a large computer screen on a desk. Jenny stood up and followed.

The electron microscope image of the microbe was sickeningly familiar.

"Here's what so cool about this virus." Jordan pointed at the screen. "This is a chimera. We combined H5N1 with black pox. The H5N1 is actually based upon a strain you discovered a few years ago. Normally, we attempt to increase a virus' virulence by infecting lab animals over and over again hoping that that virus will recombine into a more pathogenic form. And we tried that, but we couldn't get the virus to mutate to its full potential. We also had trouble with sequencing some parts of the chimera's combined DNA. The failures sent us in a totally new direction. What you see on that screen is totally synthesized."

Jenny felt her stomach knot. "You created the DNA?"

"Just like God. We removed the DNA from cells infected with your H5N1 strain and from the Black Pox strain and recreated them. But we did more than that. We altered the synthesized DNA to increase its pathogenicity so that the mortality is ninety percent."

"So what's so amazing about that? The Ebola Zaire strain is close to ninety percent."

"But it isn't stable. Our virus is. We haven't given up on achieving one hundred percent. We have a team working on it. In the meantime we came up with another solution that, in effect, achieves our mortality goal." He smiled like a proud papa.

His smugness unnerved Jenny.

Jordan pointed toward a gray spot inside the virus. "See that?"

She nodded tentatively.

He chuckled. "You thought the synthesized virus was the amazing part? Nope. This is the really brilliant part. That tiny gray spot is a machine."

"Nanotechnology?"

He nodded. "Unlike every other virus in the world, this microbe destroys its enemy before it begins replication."

"How does it do that?"

"The programmed nano seeks out the B and T cells and destroys them first. Once the host antibodies are destroyed, the virus begins replication. This way there is nothing within the host to interfere with the replication process. The virus can grow unimpeded."

"Where does the nano engine derive its power from?"

"The movement of electrons within the cell creates just enough electricity to power the machine."

Jenny felt her breakfast crawling at her insides to escape. She covered her mouth.

"You all right? You look a little pale."

Of course, she wasn't all right, but she couldn't let anyone know, particularly Jordan. The image on the screen was the most brilliant creation she had ever seen and the most twisted. She wondered whether recruiters for the sub complex were specifically screening for sociopaths. She removed her hand from mouth and took a deep breath. "Does this Mona Lisa have a name?"

"Leviathan," Jordan said.

A monster without peer.

CHAPTER TWENTY-FIVE

Albuquerque, July 21

It was a sight Luke wasn't sure he'd see again. He stood before a congregation of at least 700 people in Three Crosses, one of the South Valley's larger churches. Pastor Alex Martinez had invited him to teach after watching the YouTube video. Luke recognized many familiar faces in the audience, some former members of Grace Fellowship.

"When Pastor Alex asked me to teach this Sunday, I told him I would be honored but could only accept if I was allowed to preach the whole truth, not a sanitized version. Your pastor agreed. He's one of the few left who's more afraid of the Lord than the government."

Applause filled the sanctuary and a few whistles. Alex, who stood off stage to Luke's right, nodded and smiled.

Three Crosses was about five miles west of where Grace Fellowship used to stand. Rays of morning light poured in through high horizontal windows along the perimeter of the sanctuary, illuminating millions of suspended particles shimmering in the light. Three large wooden crosses towered behind Luke.

Luke held up two Bibles, one in each hand. An unedited one and the newly approved government edition that was as thin as a slice of bread.

"Jesus warned of a time like this when truth wouldn't be tolerated, when the hearts of many would grow cold. What would you do if being a Christian meant persecution, even death?"

Several people in the front pew shifted in their seats.

"We're not afraid." A man shouted from the west side of the sanctuary. Some members cheered while some turned and frowned at the man.

Luke was afraid. Not for himself but for Cindy. He stared down at her in the front pew. What would he do if he ever lost her? From the day they had married twenty-five years ago, she had been his rock.

Some people in the back of the church were out of their seats. Someone screamed.

"I smell smoke," someone yelled.

"The church is on fire," another person screamed.

Everyone jumped from their seats and ran toward the exits.

Pastor Alex ran to the podium and grabbed the mic. Luke leaped down the stairs to Cindy.

"Don't run. Please be calm. Everything will be okay." Pastor Alex said.

His appeal did little to slow the panic. Smoke was already filling the large hall.

"The front doors are locked," someone screamed.

"We can't get out these side doors either," people yelled from each side of the hall.

"We're trapped."

"The doors to the Sunday School are locked," a woman shrieked. "My kids. Dear God help us." Faint high-pitched screams rose above the growing din.

"Break out the windows." Glass shattered in the distance.

A man ran down an aisle with his back on fire as another man tackled him and tried to put out the flames.

Luke wrapped his large arms around Cindy.

"What are we going to do?" she coughed.

Luke studied the windows that ran along the top of the building. They were too high to scale without a ladder. It appeared every exit had been barred from the outside. Someone was trying to burn Three Crosses to the ground the way they had Grace Fellowship, only this time the church was full of people. Smoke continued to fill the sanctuary. Visibility was dropping and breathing getting more difficult by the minute.

"Stay here and pray honey. I've got an idea. Stay close to the ground. It will be easier to breathe."

Cindy crouched down.

Hundreds of people were pressing toward the back of the church.

"Let me through," Luke said.

A white-haired wisp of a woman wheeled around in front of Luke and pointed a bony finger at him. She held a handkerchief to her mouth. "None of this would have happened if you hadn't been here." She shifted her finger toward Pastor Alex. "And you invited him. You're just as guilty."

"She's right," a heavy set man coughed. "Your big mouth caused this."

Luke grabbed hold of a pew and began to push against it. "Help me with this."

Several men helped him rock the pew back and forth. It broke free of its floor mounts. "Break through the double doors," Luke said.

A sharp blow to the back of the head dropped Luke to his knees. The room dimmed and turned black.

* * *

His skin sizzled. Luke gasped for air as he woke. Dense smoke filled the corridor. How long had he been out? Where was Cindy? The question jolted his senses like an electric shock. Flat on his black, he tried to move, but his head pounded. He rolled over on his side and pushed himself into a sitting position. The room swirled. He stood on unsteady legs.

The sanctuary was enveloped in a thick blanket of smoke. Orange flames snaked across the ceiling. Luke crouched as he ran into the billowing wall.

He coughed. His eyes stung, and his lungs hurt. He stumbled over something and reached for a pew to avoid falling. He bent down and felt blindly. A person, not moving. He pulled the body up. It wasn't Cindy. He laid the man back down and held on to the pews and used them as a guide toward the front.

He found the pew where he he'd left Cindy, but she wasn't there.

"Cindy. Where are you?"

There wasn't any answer.

Lord, please.

Luke stumbled up the podium. "Cindy."

The air was too hot to breathe. Too much smoke. He was spinning. "Cindy."

He felt the floor slam into his face. Just like his last fight. As he lay against the carpet, he thought he heard a siren in the distance. Then nothing.

* * *

"Luke, can you hear me?"

He coughed. His lungs felt raw.

He blinked. The sun was bright.

"Where's Cindy?"

109

She stared down at him through a dark mask of soot that intensified the whites of her eyes.

He reached up for her hand. She grabbed his.

"I thought I lost you," Luke said. His throat was so hoarse he had to force the words out.

She smiled. "No, tough guy, I thought I lost you."

A fireman stood next to Cindy and peered down at Luke. "You're a lucky man."

"Have been ever since I met her." But *lucky* wasn't the right word. Blessed fit better.

CHAPTER TWENTY-SIX

Washington, D.C., July 29

Marine One touched down on the south lawn. Pepper was waiting, his thin dark hair swirling almost as fast the chopper's blades. Hamilton loved flying in the VH-71 Kestrel and enjoyed it even more with the doors open, the way he had in Nam. Flying in a chopper with the doors closed was almost as much of a travesty as driving an Indy car fitted with an automatic transmission. But his Secret Service detail wouldn't allow it with the First Lady on board.

Hamilton stepped down onto the lush green south lawn with Lucy beside him. They walked with Pepper toward the South Portico. Hamilton and the First Lady waved at photographers standing behind a roped area east of them. The deafening throb of Marine One's blades diminished as the helicopter lifted into the sky.

As they reached the base of the wrought iron stairs, Hamilton kissed Lucy goodbye. She walked into the White House through the private ground entrance. He and Pepper climbed the stairs to the Portico. Normally Hamilton would head to the Oval Office, but today he wanted to enjoy the mid-morning sun and the fragrance of the magnolia trees near the Rose Garden that were in full bloom.

"How was the trip?" Pepper asked as they reached the top. He ran his hand through his tangled hair to straighten it and adjusted his crooked yellow tie. Two wicker rocking chairs had been set out for them. They both sat.

"Camp David is beautiful this time of year. Nice and cool. The First Lady loves it, but I think I needed the break as much as she."

"I hate to bring this up right now, but did you look at the list of vice presidential candidates I gave you?"

"What's the rush? Truman never had a vice president while he served out Roosevelt's term."

"Why give the press anything else to complain about?"

"All right. Submit Beckley's name. He's the least likely to give us problems."

Hamilton breathed in what he expected would be the sweet scent of magnolia as he rocked backward. "What's that smell?"

Pepper sniffed the air. He pointed toward the northeast. A dark plume twisted upward.

Hamilton studied the billowing cloud. Its location was troubling.

Pepper was already on his cell. He stood and walked toward the colonnades. After a moment he came and sat down on the edge of the chair. He was frowning. "It's the New York Avenue Presbyterian Church. FBI already saying probable arson."

"Is it connected to the others?"

"Too early to tell but given what's happened lately, very likely."

"That's outrageous." Hamilton removed his baseball cap and threw it. It sailed over the balcony. "These aren't protests anymore. They're acts of terrorism. Those thugs burned one of the most historic churches in the country, a national treasure. Lincoln attended that church."

Pepper's eyes narrowed. "Fifty people were killed in a church fire in Albuquerque last week, which I understand could have been much worse."

"Were the same groups involved in those attacks?"

Pepper stood up and walked to the balcony and stared down at the south lawn. "That's the most troubling part. The FBI is convinced that radical Muslims are spearheading the protests and church burnings."

"Sulaiman." He hadn't spoken his name since his swearing in and had hoped the terrorist would disappear.

Pepper turned around and shook his head. "No group has taken responsibility but the FBI believes several organizations are involved including Al Qaeda and Mahdi's Chosen. But I don't think you'll see any of these groups step forward. They want the nation to believe the attacks are driven by average Americans."

Hamilton pulled out a tobacco pouch and pipe from inside his light tan cotton jacket with a dark blue presidential seal. He poured some tobacco into the pipe bowl and tapped it down with his finger, then lit it.

Pepper's eyebrows arched. "When did you take up the pipe?"

"On this trip," Hamilton growled. "Lucy says I smoke too many cigars." A plume of smoke drifted toward Pepper. "She doesn't mind the smell of pipe tobacco."

He wriggled his nose.

Hamilton pulled the pipe from his mouth and studied it. "Average Americans? You don't think people really believe that do you?"

"If they do, they won't for long. The jihadists have cleverly hidden behind protesters venting their anger over the assassination of the president at the hands of a Christian and the burning of the Qu'rans. But it's becoming obvious that the attacks are being coordinated."

What do they hope to achieve?"

"On the surface it appears they want to exacerbate the nation's discontentment with Christians, particularly those defying the anti-hate crimes law. But from what I know about Islam's teachings, they may have another objective—a darker one."

Hamilton puffed on the pipe.

"I think a fundamental shift in their strategy is occurring," Pepper said.

Hamilton put the pipe down in an ashtray and stared at his Chief of Staff. "What kind of shift?"

"The terrorists in this country have never targeted a specific group of people, nationally or socially. They have focused, instead, on creating a culture of fear and intimidation through suicide attacks at subway stations and shopping malls. But I believe that's changing. The FBI has detected a lot of activity between different terrorist organizations which is very unusual. Normally they don't work together."

"Does the FBI think they are coordinating a major attack?"

"They do but they're not sure where."

"And what do you think?"

Pepper adjusted his glasses. "I think they're planning an attack, but not in a way we expect. It's not real estate like the Twin Towers they are after—it's Christians. They want to destroy Christianity."

Hamilton shook his head and relit his pipe. "How did you come up with that idea?"

"I read the Qur'an."

"Well, I hope your instincts are wrong."

"It's not my instincts you should be worried about. It's the one million Islamic radicals in this country."

CHAPTER TWENTY-SEVEN

Fort Detrick, July 30

From the moment Jenny set foot in the underground complex, she believed the reason it was buried two-hundred feet below Fort Detrick was for secrecy. But the more she understood about the Leviathan virus, the more convinced she became it was for protection.

She hadn't slept well since she had arrived. Questions of how to safely obtain a sample of the virus and get it to the surface without being caught had turned her bed into a nightly tangle of sheets and covers. Blowing the whistle on the lab's existence wasn't enough. She needed physical proof of the new bioweapon.

Jenny sat in front of a computer screen in lab 172 and poured over pages of documented attempts at creating an antiviral. An entire complex of hundreds of scientists had been working on the problem for six months and were no closer to an answer than when they began. *They can't untie the biological Gordian knot they created.*

Dr. Jordan leaned over Jenny's shoulder, a little too close. "I told you it was in a class all its own. See anything we missed?"

Jenny turned around and slid her chair back from him. The man apparently knew nothing about invading people's personal space.

He straightened and rested a hand on the computer screen.

"All of the attempts to date have been focused on disrupting the virus' replication."

Jordan crossed his arms. "And your brilliant idea is?"

"Attack the nano part of the virus. Disable its ability to destroy antibodies, then worry about replication."

"And how do you propose to do that?"

"If a molecular machine can be built and placed within the virus to destroy antibodies, why can't the same technology be implemented to design a nanobot to defend the T and B cells? Maybe even create one that does more than defend."

Jordan nodded. "Not bad."

The door to the lab swung open and slammed against the wall. A lean, silver-haired man with dark eyebrows stared at Jenny. From the stars on his shoulders, she could tell he was where the buck stopped.

"Is there something wrong, General Sullivan?" The freckles on Jordan's face seemed to pale.

"Darn straight there is." Sullivan stuck his finger in Jenny's face. "Who sent you here?"

Jenny recoiled and slid her chair back until it bumped against the wall.

"You're a spy, aren't you?" Sullivan's dark eyebrows merged to form a crease between them.

Jenny felt light-headed. She tried to speak, but her vocal chords wouldn't move.

"Don't want to talk? That's okay. Before this is over, you'll be singing like a canary."

She knew exactly what was happening in her brain. The amygdala was over-stimulating her nervous system, causing a panic attack. But the knowledge was of little use. She took shallow breaths.

Jordan leaned into her face. "You lied about your clearance?" He turned to Sullivan. "I had no idea. Her credentials looked authentic."

Sullivan's gray eyes flashed at Jordan.

The general turned back to Jenny. "You thought you could invade my world without me finding out? I know everything about everyone down here."

A security guard, who looked like a UFC fighter walked into the room.

"You know where to take her," Sullivan said.

The guard's grip around her wrist felt like a manacle. He dragged her into the hallway and through a section of lab 172 she'd never seen. She struggled to maintain her balance as he jerked her forward. Everything faded in and out. The guard finally stopped in front of a door and pushed it open. The room was dark. He turned on the light and slammed the door behind them.

The room was empty. It smelled musty like it hadn't been used for sometime, but something else hung in the air. The guard studied her—a little too long.

"We don't get many new faces down here."

Jenny backed away from him.

The guard pulled her into him with one hand while binding her wrists with his other hand. He stared down at her. Thick scar tissue on his eyebrows bore a strong resemblance to Neanderthal man.

He pressed his hard lips against hers. She struggled, but it only made him press his mouth harder against hers. She bit his lip. "Stupid cow." He slapped her face.

She fell to the floor.

He grabbed her arm and dragged her into a sealed room and slammed the door. The lock clicked, and as he left, he turned the lights out.

She curled up on the cool tile floor. Her teeth began to chatter, her hands and legs to tremble until she shook uncontrollably. The side of her face burned. What possessed her to think she could slip into such a place without being caught? If only she had listened to PJ.

* * *

117

How long she lay curled on the floor, she wasn't sure. But the trembling had stopped. In the dark, time is as easy to forget as one's face. She stood up and rolled her head to loosen the stiff muscles in her neck. A pervading stench filled her nose. The old woman in the Congo village flashed before her. Her instinct was to cover her mouth or create a mask from clothing but the microscopic spores of a virus could easily pass through any defense she rigged.

No telling what kind of experiments had been conducted in the sealed room, but she suspected they most likely involved black pox and H5N1. She shuddered. The variola major virus could live for weeks outside its host, and H5N1 could easily be transferred from animal to human.

Was an infected dead monkey or rat curled up in some corner of the room? Or even worse some poor person who had been lured into the lab like an unsuspecting insect into a spider's web?

The lights in the outer room turned on. Jenny blinked from the sudden brightness.

A man approached the door to the sealed lab.

She stepped back.

The door opened. "We've got to go now."

She didn't recognize the voice. She still couldn't see.

"Follow me. Hurry."

Jenny stumbled through the lab into the corridor. The man moved swiftly through the hallways, turning right, then left, then left again until Jenny lost track of how many hallways and doors they had passed through.

They emerged from Building 56 at what appeared to be the rear entrance. The elderly man, who was slightly stooped, pointed toward a stainless steel container the size of a small freezer sitting on the bed of a small truck. The driver waved to her. It was Fred from maintenance.

"Get in. Quickly." The old man looked back at the building.

Jenny hesitated. She hated confined spaces and the chest would only fit her if she folded into an embryonic shape. How long she could breathe inside the sealed container was another matter. On the side of the chest in large red letters was printed BioWaste. Hazardous.

"Isn't there any other way out?"

The scientist shook his head. "This is it. It's a short ride to the top. Don't worry you'll have enough air. I've redesigned the lock, so you can release it from inside, but don't do so until you're sure you're alone."

Jenny climbed into the container. "Who are you?"

"Just an old man who I hope God will forgive for the things I've done down here." The man pulled a slim, metal cylinder the size of a small flashlight from inside his lab coat and gave it to Jenny. "And this is my attempt at redemption."

Jenny curled into a ball and placed the container in her lap.

The old scientist looked down at her. The deep creases in his forehead and around his eyes bore evidence of a man more acquainted with angst than hope. "Be very careful about who you tell about the virus. Trust no one. Get it to the head of Health and Human Services as quickly as possible. You won't be safe until you do."

As he was about to close the top Jenny said, "Thank you."

A tired smile momentarily broke through the clouded countenance. "We're pulling for you, Jenny. Leviathan must be destroyed. It can never, never be used as a weapon." He closed the container, and Jenny was again enshrouded in darkness.

CHAPTER TWENTY-EIGHT

Albuquerque, July 30

L uke stood next to Cindy at the kitchen sink, peeling roasted green chiles. His eyes watered from the sharp aroma. He stripped the charred skin from the Hatch chile, then handed it to Cindy who washed it. His mouth watered at the thought of the enchiladas his wife would later make.

"Honey, I don't need to paint houses. We can make a living selling your green chile chicken enchiladas. Everybody loves 'em."

Cindy smiled. "Not as popular as you."

A car with heavily tinted windows slowed as it passed in front of their home. Luke stopped peeling. Low riders were common to the neighborhood, and he recognized most of them. But this one he didn't. The front and rear windows rolled down, and guns extended outward.

"Get down," Luke yelled. He pushed Cindy to the floor as glass exploded overhead. A rapid staccato of bullets ripped through the wall above them. Luke lay flattened against the floor with his arm over Cindy. Tires squealed as the shooting stopped. Shards of glass, splintered wood, and shattered dishes littered the floor. He sat up and wrapped his arms around his wife. Her body vibrated.

"Tengo miedo," Cindy said, slipping into her first language. "Quienes eran?"

"People who hate the truth."

"Maybe we should move."

"Where?"

"We can stay with my family." Cindy looked up at Luke. "Will we ever be safe again?"

"We will, baby." He patted her back to reassure her, but he could tell she wasn't convinced. And he wasn't sure he believed it himself.

* * *

Luke stood in front a digital camcorder mounted on a tripod in the basement of his in-laws, which now served as their new home. Cindy pressed the record button.

"I'm Pastor Luke Chavez. My church was closed by the government, burned to the ground, and I was thrown in jail. My wife and I barely escaped a burning church. And now we're living in secret after surviving a drive-by shooting. Why have these things happened? What is our crime? Nothing, except we're Christians."

Cindy's green eyes flashed. She was only five-four and a little more than a hundred pounds, but when her hackles were raised, only a fool would tangle with her. *She's the real fighter in the family.*

"We need to take a lesson from the early church. They were ridiculed, exiled, and killed for what they believed, but they never retreated. They went underground. In catacombs and the secret of their homes, they worshipped the Lord."

Cindy repeated silently as if she were speaking to herself, "Fear not for I am with you." Her faith had often encouraged him, and he needed her now more than ever.

"Stand with me, and together we will build a new church, a church where we can worship in freedom from a Bible that was written by God, not rewritten by man."

Luke concluded his message by asking his listeners for help. He needed laborers to build an encrypted internet site for communication between members and a platform for broadcasting his weekly sermons. The weekly broadcast would need to be hosted by a service the U.S. government couldn't shut down. And he needed people who would commit to praying for the new church that was sure to face incredible attacks.

Cindy pushed the stop button on the camera. "How does it feel to be back in the pulpit again?"

Luke grinned. "I never pictured myself preaching to a camera."

"Or talking for only four minutes." She chuckled.

"Yeah, that's the hardest part."

"If this message does as well as the first video, a million people, maybe more, will see it. Not bad for a tough guy from the barrio." She bounced around the room throwing left jabs at Luke.

The thought of preaching to a virtual audience that size was difficult for Luke to comprehend, particularly because he barely understood how to use email. But he didn't have to understand the technology, he only had to understand the opportunity it offered.

Cindy handed him a paintbrush.

"What's this?"

"Our next meal." She winked. "The Garcias called and need their house painted."

"You know how to deflate an hombre. One minute I'm preaching to a million, the next painting houses."

"Just trying to keep you humble."

CHAPTER TWENTY-NINE

Fort Detrick, July 30

The lid on the stainless steel chest snapped shut. Jenny tried to forget that she was locked inside an air tight container. But she took comfort in knowing that at any minute she could release the lock from inside. The elevator door closed. The trunk vibrated as she ascended.

The ride up took even longer than the ride down. She took short breaths and tried to relax but the air was thin. The elevator came to an abrupt halt that rattled the container. She waited for movement to indicate the chest was being unloaded. But there wasn't any. The old scientist had told her to wait until she was sure she was alone. Still not a sound.

She tried the lock but stopped.

"Get this on the truck."

"Gotcha."

Scraping metal slid underneath and lifted the trunk. The movement stopped with a jerk. She began to tilt backward. Then suddenly she was upside down, rolling. The chest slammed into something.

"Geez. Nearly lost it."

Not enough air. She gasped as she reached for the lock. But it wouldn't release. She tried to scream but all she could do was claw at dwindling scraps of air. *Dear God, help me.*

"Give me a hand getting this container upright."

"Too much angle. You're lucky it didn't slide off the forklift and hit the ground."

Jenny tried the lock again, but it wouldn't budge. Sweat ran in rivulets down her face onto her legs.

She turned right side up.

"This unit seems awfully heavy."

"Looks like the lock is damaged."

"Just load it on the truck. Let someone else worry about it."

Jenny banged her fist against the inside of the trunk, then reached for the metal cylinder and banged it against the side. Her face was pressed against the top of the lid as she fought for a breath.

"Did you hear something?"

"No."

She slammed the cylinder against the side again one last time.

"I heard it."

"There's something in there."

"That's biohazard. We're not supposed to open it."

"I don't care. Give me something to pry it open."

There was a faint sound of something striking the top of the container. A flash of light. Cool air. Her lungs grabbed at it.

"Holy leaping lizards, someone is inside."

"Help me get her out."

The metal cylinder slipped from her fingers as she was lifted upward. She felt herself being carried, then laid down on a cool hard surface.

"Lady, are you okay?"

"You better call medical."

Jenny coughed. The blurry image of a man's bearded face stared down at her. "Where am I?"

"Inside a warehouse. How did you end up in that container?" His voice was deep.

She tried to sit up.

"Take it easy now." The man helped her into a sitting position.

"A doctor is on the way," a skinny man with yellow teeth standing nearby said.

"I'm okay. I don't need a doctor."

"Are you kidding? You were nearly dead," the man next to her said.

"Help me up, please." The man pulled her up. Her legs trembled. *Where's the cylinder?*

Jenny took a step. Stabbing needles shot through her legs. She stumbled toward the biowaste chest.

"Where are you going? The doctor is on his way," the skinny man said.

"I've got to go."

She reached down into the container and grabbed the cylinder.

Someone grabbed her other arm. She recognized the grip.

"You're not going anywhere."

She swung the metal tube into the side of Neanderthal man's head. It collided with a dull thud, like a hammer into concrete. She ran for the door ahead. Her legs shook. A large truck was backed up to a dock next to the exit.

A thick forest lay straight ahead. Rays of light shone through a woven canopy of limbs overhead. The sound of cars was off to her right.

"Stop that woman." The voice behind her sent a chill down her wet back. It was Sullivan.

Clutching the cylinder, she ran as fast as she could through the trees toward the road ahead, numb to the branches slapping against her face. Behind her were stampeding feet.

"She's faster than she looks," someone yelled.

They were close. At any moment hands would grab her from behind, throw her to the ground, and pry the evidence from her hands before they put a bullet in her.

"Hurry, she's almost at the road."

She broke through the trees in full stride into the path of an oncoming car that screeched to a halt inches from her. She opened the car door and jumped in. The man's hands were locked around the steering wheel. His large eyes fixed on her. His mouth open.

"Lock the doors."

The man mechanically punched a button near him.

"Now go." Jenny pointed forward, but the driver sat numbly behind the steering wheel staring at her, as if he were in a trance. "Go!"

A fist slammed against the hood, raising Jenny from her seat. Sullivan stood in front of the car. Someone tried the door handle next to her. Sullivan pulled a gun from his side. She jammed the man's leg against the accelerator. The car surged forward throwing the General on the hood and over the vehicle's side.

"Drive!"

The car accelerated down the two-lane road.

Jenny pulled her cell from her pocket and dialed Denton's number.

"This is Denton."

"It's Jenny. I need your help."

"What's wrong?"

"I don't have time to tell you."

"I'm leaving Fort Detrick right now. Where can I meet you? It needs to be somewhere people can't find us."

"Just drive toward my place, and I'll catch up with you."

"All right."

Jenny turned to the driver. "I'm sorry to have involved you. Can you drive toward Gaithersburg. My friend will meet up with us in a few minutes."

The man's lips moved slowly. "What...kind...of...trouble are you in?"

"You don't want to know." Jenny studied the rear view mirror looking for any sign of Sullivan and his men.

The man looked straight ahead and drove without saying another word.

A few minutes later a blue sedan, Denton's rental car, approached in the rear view mirror.

"Can you pull over?"

The man nodded mechanically as he stopped the car on the road's shoulder.

"So sorry. You're very brave. Thank you."

The man managed to force a small smile through quivering lips.

Jenny grabbed the cylinder and jumped out of the car and ran to Denton's car.

The door was already open. She hopped in, and Denton pushed the accelerator to the floor spinning the tires as a tan government sedan approached rapidly from behind. Jenny turned around and studied the face in the windshield that was becoming more identifiable each second. It was Sullivan.

CHAPTER THIRTY

Washington, D.C., July 30

The door to the Oval Office swung open. Pepper stood there looking like he was about ready to yell *fire*. Secretary of State Elizabeth Schomberg's eyes darted toward him.

Hamilton looked up from his briefing. "Have you forgotten how to knock?"

Schomberg adjusted her reading glasses and stared at Pepper.

"I'm sorry, but a very urgent matter needs your attention, Mr. President."

Hamilton laid down the briefing on the sofa. "Can't it wait?"

"Unfortunately not, Mr. President."

Hamilton turned to Schomberg. "I'm sorry, Liz. Will you excuse me?"

She nodded as she gathered some papers and placed them in her briefcase. She glared at Pepper as she passed him on the way out.

"What's so important?"

Pepper checked the door to ensure it was closed. He walked over to the sofa and sat down. "The CIA director called me moments ago. The Congressional Committee on President Nash's murder is going to subpoena him." Pepper adjusted his glasses.

"So." Hamilton crossed his legs and eyed the pipe lying in an ashtray.

"Tingley said under oath he will have to divulge the existence of a black ops unit under your authority, the one established by Nash."

Hamilton grabbed the empty pipe and put in his mouth. It tasted bitter. "I don't know what Tingley is talking about. Nash never told me anything about a covert unit."

Pepper stared intently at Hamilton. "Tingly said President Nash established the covert unit because he wanted to avoid any further international scandals involving the CIA. He wanted to transfer the CIA's nasty business to another agency, one that didn't receive funding from Congress and one that didn't answer to anyone except the President. Tingley said no one knows the team exists except for you and him."

And now you. Hamilton stood and walked over to the windows behind his desk. He wished he were anywhere but here. Ironic. He had spent his entire adult life trying to get to where he now stood. "Did Tingley have anything else to say?" It was one of the few times he hoped Pepper would tell him Tingley didn't say another thing.

"The murder of Dr. Myers and the disappearance of the two pathologists and the lab technician were done by pros, but not just any professionals. He said there are only a handful of men in the world good enough to pull this off without leaving a single clue."

Hamilton took the pipe out of his mouth and ran his fingers over the sharp edges of the bowl's carved wood. "We've established Nash was murdered by a terrorist. There's no reason to believe the other incidences weren't the work of terrorists as well."

"Except that foreigners capable of this kind of work aren't in the U.S. nor have they been. Tingley says the CIA tracks these professional killers. This creates a very damaging problem for you Mr. President."

"What's that?" He already knew the answer.

"The only other killers who could pull it off were transferred from the CIA by Nash."

129

Hamilton could feel Pepper's stare drill into the back of his head, waiting for some answer that made sense, some justification for why the President wouldn't know about a team of assassins that answered only to him.

Hamilton looked down at his pipe. It was covered in blood. "Shoot." He tossed it on his desk and grabbed a handkerchief from a drawer in his desk.

"What happened?"

"I must have sliced myself with the pipe," he said wrapping his finger.

Hamilton sat down at his desk and opened his humidor in hope that Lucy might have missed a cigar during her last raid, but she hadn't. Not even a cigar wrapper. "Tingley doesn't have to say anything. No one on the committee even knows to ask about a covert unit. He's trying to cover his butt by volunteering information about this alleged unit."

Pepper nodded. "You understand that once this is out, you'll be subpoenaed, and it won't be pretty."

"Nash's cronies will smell blood," he said staring at a dark red stain seeping through the white monogrammed cloth. And that's what was wrong with the system. The idea that disgruntled congressmen could initiate an action such as impeachment against the most powerful man in the world was ludicrous. Clearly a mistake the framers of the constitution had made. What other super power would actually seek to remove its president for lying or a sexual dalliance?

"If the committee finds even a shred of proof to substantiate Tingley's claim, it will be enough to push for impeachment. The mere mention of a covert group of soldiers under your control will have Senators clamoring to cast their vote. The committee won't need to prove involvement in a cover-up. It will be irrelevant."

"They won't." Hamilton whispered to himself.

"Did you say something, Mr. President?"

"No, nothing at all."

CHAPTER THIRTY-ONE

Gaithersburg, July 30

Jenny could count on one hand the times she had taken a drink before tonight. The bubbly, white wine tasted slightly of apples. Her anxiety faded, and slowly the edges began to soften. She and Denton raised their glasses as they sat on a balcony at the Marriott Hotel in Gaithersburg overlooking Washingtonian Lake.

"Here's to the bravest woman I know." Denton smiled.

Jenny raised her glass. "And here's to a true hero."

The glasses touched with a bright crystalline ting.

She took another sip. "Thank you for saving me again. Where did you learn to drive a car like that?"

"It's amazing the things you can do when adrenalin kicks in."

Jenny sipped her wine. "I've had enough surging through me these last two weeks to last a lifetime." Denton had outmaneuvered Sullivan and lost the general in a residential area north of Hood College, then ditched the car and called a rental agency for a new one. He and Jenny had jointly agreed it would be safer to spend the night in a hotel than at their homes.

Denton reached across the table and slightly touched Jenny's forehead. "You've got a couple of pretty good scratches."

The touch of his hand against her skin sent a tingle through her.

He got up and went into the room and returned shortly with a damp cloth. He wiped her forehead. "There you go." He stood back and admired his work.

Denton's blond hair swept across his forehead, just above his deep blue eyes. He was the best looking man she'd ever met. Sam had been attractive in a different way. More charming than handsome. It had been a long time since she'd been with a man. Sam and she had spent the night together once, but they were better at being friends than lovers. She blushed at the memory.

"So tell me again why this General Sullivan was after you. Anything to do with the cylinder in your lap?"

Jenny pushed her glass toward Denton who filled it. She drained the flute.

"You like it?" He filled the glass again.

"What kind of wine it is?"

"Dom Pérignon. One of the finest champagnes there is."

"I love it." The setting sun cast a beautiful shimmering glow on the lake. A light breeze provided just the right chill. Everything felt perfect—except the slight spin of the room.

"You were going to tell me about the cylinder."

Jenny looked down at the dented metal container and tried to focus. "I was?"

Denton nodded.

She took another sip and patted the cylinder. "It's called Leviathan, the ultimate bioweapon. It has to be destroyed."

Denton frowned. "What kind of weapon?"

"I've already said too much." Suddenly, she felt nauseous. Jenny clamped a hand over her mouth and ran for the bathroom.

* * *

132

The bright morning light flashed in her eyes. She rolled away from it and placed a pillow over her spinning head. *Where am I?* She sat up in the bed and looked around the unfamiliar room. Then she remembered last night, drinking too much. *Denton must think I'm a fool.*

She walked into the bathroom and found a new toothbrush, toothpaste, and a package of antacid tablets sitting by the sink. She brushed a terrible taste from her mouth, then splashed cold water in her face. As she dried her face, she realized she was still dressed in yesterday's clothes. *I hope drinking too much was the only stupid thing I did last night.*

Jenny turned on the shower and undressed. She stepped into the steaming water and let it pulsate over the back of her neck. The hot water felt good until a question lurking deep within disturbed the luxuriating moment: what had she done with the cylinder? She stepped quickly out of the shower, grabbed a robe from the back of the door and put it on without drying. She hurried into the main room.

"Denton?" She was expecting to see him seated on the sofa with a cup of coffee and the morning newspaper, but the room was empty. She scanned the sofa, the coffee table, kitchen counters, and table, but there wasn't any sign of the metal container. Her pulse raced as she walked out onto the balcony. The last place she could remember seeing the container. But the only thing she found was two empty wine glasses.

Jenny searched for her cell but didn't see it. She went back in the bedroom and found it lying on the dresser. She dialed the main number for the Bioforensic Center. A woman answered, and Jenny asked for the sequencing lab.

"Is Dr. Mabe in?"

"No."

"You haven't seen him today?"

The man sounded annoyed. "Who is calling?"

Giving him her name didn't seem like a good idea. No telling how far Sullivan's tentacles extended. "It's very important that I reach him."

"Dr. Mabe no longer works here."

CHAPTER THIRTY-TWO

Washington, D.C., July 31

"What were you thinking, General?" Hamilton asked Sullivan.

The general was flanked on his right by Pepper and on his left by Dr. Robert Carrington, the head of Health and Human Services. The two men couldn't be more different. Sullivan, a defiant general hell-bent on developing the ultimate bioweapon, and the reserved Dr. Carrington, whose mission was protecting the nation's health. Hamilton sat across from them in the Oval Office.

"Trying to ensure the Russians don't get ahead of us," Sullivan said. His jaw was set, and he stared coolly at Hamilton.

"We have an international ban on the creation of bioweapons. You are aware of that, aren't you?" Hamilton smacked the report he was holding down against the sofa.

Without flinching Sullivan said, "President Nash was well aware of the sub complex and what we were doing down there."

"Well, President Nash is dead."

The statement tightened the tension in the room like a guitar strung too tautly.

"Do you have any idea of the danger you've put this country and the world in?" Hamilton said. "You can bet that whoever took this monster of yours isn't a scientist like Dr. George intent on destroying it."

Sullivan's stony expression broke. "We wouldn't be here if she hadn't stolen it. This weapon could have made nuclear weapons obsolete, changed the world."

Pepper's eyebrows arched. Dr. Carrington coughed.

"I have no doubt it will change the world. You, of all people, should know that you can't keep a weapon like this secret for very long. How long did it take the Russians to steal our technology for the hydrogen bomb?" Hamilton pointed at Sullivan. "Only three years."

Dr. Carrington cleared his throat and crossed his long legs. "Do we have any idea who might have stolen the virus?"

Pepper adjusted his glasses. "Daniel Broughton called just before our meeting." Pepper flashed a look that inferred the conversation with the FBI director might have touched on more than just the virus.

Did they discuss the black ops unit?

"The FBI took fingerprints from a wine glass that Denton Mabe used. According to the national database his real name is Carl Smith. He's from Minnesota. And here's the disturbing part—he changed his name last year to Kareem Umar and made two trips to Pakistan. The FBI suspects he went there for terrorist training.

Hamilton stood and walked over to his desk. He looked at the empty humidor and the pipe lying next to it. The sight of both depressed him almost as much as Pepper's report. He turned back to the three men. "Unfortunately gentlemen, I think we have our answer. It sounds like terrorists have the virus."

A grim-faced Sullivan said, "The terrorists have no idea of what will happen if they unleash this virus. We've been trying to develop an antiviral for months. Without one, no one will survive."

Pepper frowned. "Actually, General, even if the terrorists fully understood the nature of the beast so to speak, it wouldn't make any difference. They believe Allah will protect them, and if he doesn't, they will live happily ever after in heaven surrounded by virgins."

"Pepper, call Broughton and Tingley," Hamilton said. "I want the FBI and CIA to coordinate their resources and find which terrorist organization has the virus. In the meantime how do we prepare for this kind of terrorist attack?" Hamilton asked.

The three men looked at each other.

"Find a deep bunker and wait it out," Sullivan said.

He's serious. "I presume that means we'll find you tucked away in the Fort Detrick sub complex?"

Sullivan's gray eyes sparked.

"If this virus is as deadly as this report indicates, then we're going to need a system for identifying an infected person before it's obvious, so they can be quarantined," Carrington said. "The more proficient we are at separating these people from the general population quickly, the more time we can buy to find a vaccine."

Pepper leaned around Sullivan. "Do you have an idea of how to accomplish this, Dr. Carrington?"

"I might. A few years ago a remarkable device, a chip a little larger than a grain of rice, was created that could detect the presence of harmful viruses and bacteria in the blood. It was like a mini chemistry lab."

Pepper nodded. "I remember reading something about it. It was ahead of its time. Never saw much use except for assisting in the identification of earthquake and tsunami victims. The manufacturer had to discontinue its use because of civil liberty issues—and tumors in lab tests."

"Who cares about civil liberties and tumors when annihilation is the alternative?" Sullivan growled.

Pepper said, "Mr. President, we may face a pushback from some groups concerned about both these issues."

"Thanks to the General here, they won't have much choice," Hamilton said. "It will be the law. If they refuse, they'll be quarantined."

Carrington said, "We'll need to get the manufacturer to dust the chip off and re-program it to detect the Leviathan virus. If we implanted every American with one of these chips, we would have an early detection system that could slow the virus' spread. The chip uses a low-level radio frequency to transmit its findings. A system could be established with city hospitals so they could receive the warnings, much like a 911 system."

Hamilton stood up. "I don't think it's possible to over prepare, and I don't think I'm overstating the situation when I say this is potentially the greatest threat our country has ever faced. Dr. Carrington, I'd like you to have CDC release a statement on the virus. Don't pull any punches: the country needs to know how dangerous Leviathan is. Make the implementation of the chip your top priority. And, let's be clear, every American will be required to be chipped. This is not an optional program."

Pepper tapped out a few notes on his computer tablet. "I'll schedule you for a prime time announcement. When do you want to address the nation?"

"Tonight."

"What are you going to say?" Sullivan asked.

"I'm going to tell the truth." He shook the report in his right hand. "That the Army violated the 1972 bioweapons agreement and created a virus that kills one-hundred percent of its victims, that we unfortunately have nothing to stop it at this time, and that the virus is now believed to be in the hands of terrorists."

Sullivan frowned. "With all due respect, Mr. President, if you make such a statement, you're going to create a panic and fracture our relationship with Russia."

Hamilton walked over to Sullivan and stared down at him. "With all due respect? General, if you had any respect for your government, you wouldn't have misused billions of taxpayers dollars over the last several years to create a monster that may very well be the final punctuation in civilization's story.

"And forgive me, General, if your concern over creating a panic and damaging our relationship with Russia seems disingenuous. You created the mother of all panics and blew a hole in our bioweapons agreement the moment you forged this killer in your dungeon."

The muscles in Sullivan's jaws flexed.

"I hope you spend the rest of your life in Leavenworth for what you did, but I'll leave that to the military court. In the meantime, as your commander in chief, I'm relieving you of your duties."

Sullivan's jaw dropped.

"In other words, General, you're fired."

Hamilton turned toward Pepper. "Get Dr. George on the phone. I've got a new job for her."

CHAPTER THIRTY-THREE

Baltimore, Maryland, August 2

"**D**o you know what the most powerful commodity in the world is?" Sulaiman asked.

"Oil," Rashid said. A slight smirk pulled at the edges of his mouth.

Sulaiman shook his head. "Fear." He pointed at the metal cylinder lying on the table between them. Kareem Umar, also known as Denton Mabe, looked on. Dr. Elisha Haley stood next to Sulaiman. "We haven't even unscrewed the lid on this container, and yet the fear of what's inside has sent shock waves through the country and U.S. government. Before long mosques will be turning people away."

"Why?" Rashid asked.

"People want to be on the winning side. Once nonbelievers realize that Islam will triumph, they will flock to our side. The strongest human instinct is self-preservation." Sulaiman walked around the table and placed his hand on Kareem's shoulders. "Well done. Allah is pleased with you and so am I."

Kareem nodded.

They had gathered in a safe house buried deep in an impoverished neighborhood in Baltimore, Maryland.

Sulaiman turned toward Rashid. "Do you have any idea what the U.S. government would pay to get the virus back?"

"Trillions."

"Their money is worthless. If I were to sell it, it would only be for gold. Truck loads of gold. Allah didn't place it in our hands to make us rich, but to usher in the return of the Mahdi." He pointed at Kareem. "He had no idea Dr. George would lead him to the virus when he saved her life. That's not coincidence. That's the hand of Allah."

Rashid frowned as his thick dark eyebrows sank upon his eyes.

"What is it?" Sulaiman asked.

"I received a call this morning from Al Qaeda, Hamas, and Hezbollah and other groups. They're concerned about the statement released by CDC and the President's statement last night. They want to know how Muslims will be protected against this virus. I'd like to know myself."

Sulaiman's pulse quickened. "Did you tell them we have it?"

"Of course, not."

He nodded. "Good. Allah delivered the virus to us because he knows we will use it to crush the infidels. Not all of our brothers share the same goal. Some might try to take it."

Sulaiman walked to the basement window and looked out at ground level at the house across the street. A teenager, with pants drooping below his shorts, slipped around the side of the house and jimmied a window. "Some of the most experienced virologists, microbiologists, and geneticists are Muslims and share our passion. I've asked many to join us and help us weaponize the virus."

"Where are you going to put the lab? Here?" Kareem asked.

"No, I need a place with an even lower profile. Somewhere completely off the radar." He paused. "Like Anacostia." The suburb was only a mile from the Capitol but a world away. The Anacostia River, which separated the two areas, was more moat than river crossing. The historic district was so infested with violence that even the police avoided it after dark.

Elisha walked over to him and slipped her arm around him. He turned around and kissed her lightly. "I'd like you and Kareem to assist our research team on the development of the antiviral. We need as many minds as possible working on this."

"I hope I still remember enough from Microbiology to be useful." She smiled and tiny lines creased the corners of her green eyes. Her shoulder length hair bounced as she swung it to one side.

"It would be an honor to be a part of such a team," Kareem said.

"Okay," Sulaiman said clapping his hands together. "Let's go to work."

Rashid's dark eyes brightened. "So you intend to develop a vaccine before you release the virus?"

Sulaiman pulled a Camel from a blue pack in his shirt pocket and lit it. He drew in the rich Turkish smoke and exhaled. "Cousin, just because I'm a zealous Muslim, doesn't mean I'm suicidal."

CHAPTER THIRTY-FOUR

Albuquerque, August 3

C indy smoothed back a shock of Luke's black mane. "Can't have you preaching with hair in your face."

Luke smiled as he stood behind the pulpit. A temporary stage had been set up in a section of a large warehouse owned by a new underground church member. A honeycomb of steel beams towered over a platform with a cross in the background. The plan was to change venues each week to ensure the broadcasts were difficult to trace. A videographer cued a digital camcorder attached to a boom.

Gripping the corners of the lectern, Luke looked into the camera. His hands were sweating. "Thank you for all of your help. Your donations of time and money have helped us construct an encrypted site and portable set which we're broadcasting from today. And God's timing couldn't have been more perfect. The broadcast we posted last week on YouTube was shut down after pressure from the government but not before more than two million people viewed the message."

Cindy, who stood to the right of the videographer, smiled.

"Before I begin my message tonight, I'd like to respond to the government's recent announcement that it intends to implant a chip in every American. There is no doubt the threat of a deadly virus in the hands of terrorists is terrifying. And I understand the government program is intended to protect all of us. But I urge you to consider the cost of what the government is mandating. Such a chip could easily be manipulated to provide the government with far more than your blood chemistry."

The videographer looked up from the camera and grimaced.

"I don't know much about these things, but the people around me who do have advised me that the government could easily program the chip to interface with GPS, providing your exact whereabouts 24-hours a day. It could also load your financial information on the chip.

"These innovations might seem beneficial, even altruistic. GPS could aid in the rescue of crime victims and missing persons. And a unique identification code for financial transactions could eliminate identity theft and illegal immigration."

"But what if the government chose to use the chip maliciously, as a tool for reshaping our society? They could declare Christianity illegal and what would you do? Where could you run with GPS tracking your every step and a computer monitoring your every purchase? The Apostle John warned us to avoid at all cost—the mark of the Beast. And brothers and sisters this program bears a strong resemblance."

Cindy nodded vigorously, sweeping her silky hair across her shoulders.

"I urge you as believers in Jesus Christ to refuse the chip." Luke paused and with emphasis said, "Please, refuse the chip." He held up his hands. "I understand there will be a cost for doing so, but I would rather disobey the government than our Lord."

Luke took a deep breath. For the second time in three weeks he had defied a government order. But this time it was more than just his ministry at risk. This time he was asking millions of Christians to follow him down a path of defiance with consequences difficult to predict and that made him uncomfortable. He opened his Bible and turned to Matthew 24. He looked into the camera and began his first full-length sermon to the new underground church.

CHAPTER THIRTY-FIVE

Washington, D.C., August 12

"How can some washed-up fighter no one has ever heard of create such turmoil?" Hamilton hovered over the morning newspaper lying on his desk in the Oval Office. A photo from Chavez's boxing days displayed a battered face. "He might be more dangerous than the jihadists."

Hamilton had little use for religious fanatics, whether they were Islamic or Christian. Too many wars had been fought in the name of God, and he wasn't about to have it happen here. The jihadists had stepped up their attacks against Christians, torching churches and targeting leaders. But Chavez's explosive rhetoric had the potential to be even more incendiary than the fires set by radical Islamists.

Pepper sat on the sofa and sipped his doctored coffee. "The phone lines have been ringing nonstop at HHS since the pastor made his appeal to Christians."

His Chief of Staff was only thirty-four years old but looked older. Gray strands wove across his temples, and the lines near his eyes seemed more pronounced. But Hamilton had observed the strain of the last few weeks in the mirror as well.

"People are scared enough about an apocalyptic virus in the hands of terrorists without having to worry about this mark of the beast nonsense," Hamilton said. "Why would anyone believe in it? This isn't the Dark Ages."

"The mark of the beast is firmly embedded in evangelical doctrine."

Hamilton's hands trembled as he searched for something to smoke. He opened his desk drawers and scoured them for a cigar he knew wasn't there. The dank smell of tobacco ash drifted out. He removed his pipe and stuck the end in his mouth. It tasted sour. "We'll fix that. The mark of the beast is inflammatory, which is reason enough to remove it from the Bible."

"Bible or no Bible most Evangelicals aren't in favor of being chipped. And Chavez is finding an audience willing to listen. His last two YouTube broadcasts went viral before we pulled the plug. But he's found another source, and his latest video reached more than ten million viewers. His influence is steadily climbing and could reach a tipping point soon."

"Why haven't we completely shut him down?"

"Not that simple. The church is now transmitting through several servers located outside the U.S. with hundreds of domains that makes it virtually impossible to disrupt. I've got a team working on it."

Hamilton bit down on his pipe as he inspected the new presidential rug and sofas ordered by Lucy. The last traces of Nash were gone. "So how much damage has Chavez done to Operation First Alert?"

"We'll have the entire nation chipped within another few weeks except for" Pepper rolled his eyes, "the Evangelicals. The only success we're having is with younger Christians who seem more worried about the virus than the mark of the beast."

Hamilton shook his head. "There's going to be a backlash against these crazy people."

"Already is. The news pundits are citing the pastor's latest admonition as further evidence that Christians are willing to endanger the nation for their radical beliefs. The networks have also decreased coverage of the attacks against Christians."

"Frankly, I wouldn't care if every church was burned to the ground, but we have a duty to protect American citizens, even if they are Christians." Hamilton swung his hands up in the air. "So what do we do?"

Pepper frowned. "You have to be firm about your response. No room for conscientious objectors here. In order to protect the nation, there has to be one-hundred percent compliance. Remember the camps FDR set up for Japanese Americans after Japan bombed Pearl Harbor?"

Hamilton nodded.

"I think we need something similar. We could use the military bases closed by Nash during the last round of budget cuts. Maybe put a positive spin on it and call them sanctuaries."

Hamilton rubbed his chin. The idea wouldn't be popular with the far right, but it might convince some of them to think twice before aligning themselves with Chavez. The ACLU might also try to block the sanctuaries, but he could declare martial law if he had to. Suspend civil liberties. The country would certainly function better. "How long will it take to implement?" he said turning toward Pepper.

"We still have barracks at the bases. All we have to do is equip them with cots and turn the power back on."

"Set up a meeting with FEMA. We're going to need to prepare these bases as quickly as possible." He sat down across from his Chief of Staff. "And schedule network time for another address to the nation. I need to talk directly to the people on this matter, help them understand why there really is no other option. We're preparing for war here, and survival trumps civil liberties."

Pepper nodded.

"Surely people will understand that the sanctuaries will help protect the nation. We're also going to need some of those abandoned bases for quarantining infected victims."

Pepper's eyes were glassy and focused on something far away. He hadn't taken a single note.

"Did you hear what I said?"

Pepper nodded. "I was just imagining how different everything will be if any of what we're preparing for actually happens."

Hamilton leaned forward. "It will redefine time as before the virus and after."

CHAPTER THIRTY-SIX

Fort Detrick, August 12

The doors opened, and the dark underworld of Leviathan's home rushed into the elevator. At first, Jenny had refused Dr. Carrington's request to lead the antiviral team. The thought of returning to the underworld even without Sullivan there made her queasy. Even worse was facing the people she had let down. And how could she direct hundreds of scientists who knew more about the pathogen than she did? But it was difficult to say no, since she was personally responsible for the virus' theft and with Carrington's concession of adding PJ to the team, she had agreed.

He stood next to her, the whites of his eyes and teeth, the only things visible against the dark cavernous backdrop. His mouth was agape. "Holy Tuna." He turned to check for a reaction.

She tried to smile, but her emotions were as numb as dead tissue. The last three days had been spent at home beating herself to a pulp for trusting Denton. What a fool she had been. He had seized upon her naiveté like a snake its prey.

"This place would make a great wine cellar," PJ said examining the complex.

Jenny pointed toward the jeep and the driver. They were waiting.

"Hello, Dr. George." Fred jumped out of the vehicle and opened the door for her.

She couldn't look him in the eyes. "I'm sorry."

"Why? You risked your life for all of us."

Jenny introduced PJ as the three of them got into the jeep and drove toward Building 56.

* * *

A dour-faced Dr. Jordan stood at the entrance to lab 172.

"Just like old times," he said.

"I never figured you for the sentimental type," Jenny said.

Jordan frowned.

"This is my colleague, Dr. PJ Singh."

PJ extended his hand, but Jordan left it hanging.

He leaned in close. He smelled of cigarettes. "How does it feel to know you delivered the most important weapon since the atomic bomb to the enemy?" It was Jordan speaking, but the words were Sullivan's. Almost as if he had channeled the general.

Jenny tried to brush off the Jordan's stinging comment, but it hit low in the gut. Just where he intended. She felt terrible for stumbling into the enemy's hands when so many had risked everything to expose Leviathan. It was Sullivan's fault for creating the virus, but hers for losing it.

Jordan was no doubt insulted that she had been appointed to run the lab when he was Leviathan's principal architect. But Carrington wanted an outsider down below, someone who saw the virus not as a pinnacle in bioengineering like Jordan, but for what it really was—a low point in human morality.

CHAPTER THIRTY-SEVEN

Charlotte, August 13

Hank leaned back in a chair in the lounge of the Charlotte
Observer and eagerly waited for President Hamilton's
broadcast. Rain beat against the building's dark window
panes. He checked his watch. It was 9 p.m. Millions would be
watching tonight. The President was supposed to speak about the
bioterrorist threat facing the nation, the progress of Operation
First Alert, and the refusal of millions to be chipped. Most of whom
were Christians. But the question on everyone's mind was how
the President would deal with those who defied the government's
mandate.

The President appeared on the screen of the television mounted
on the wall. He was seated behind his desk dressed in an olive suit
with a gold tie. His hair was combed straight back and looked thicker
and less gray than his last appearance.

"Good evening fellow Americans. As all of you know our
country is facing an unprecedented bioterrorist threat from a radical
group of Islamists. We can't tell you exactly which group possesses
the virus, but we know for certain it's in terrorist hands. The
Leviathan virus is deadly. There is no vaccine for it, although we
are working day and night to find one. To protect the nation in the
event of an attack, we have developed Operation First Alert. And I'm

pleased to announce that most of the nation has complied. The chip is designed to protect life." Hamilton pointed at the light red mark on his right hand. "Most all of you realize that."

He clasped his hands and frowned. "Some of you, however, have refused to be participate in the program. The reasons vary. Some believe it represents a violation of privacy and some a violation of religious freedom. Those of you who share these sentiments must understand that although I respect your decision to object, the government cannot and will not allow you to endanger your fellow citizens."

"Therefore, effective immediately, I am creating sanctuaries across the nation to separate those who have been chipped from those who have not. These sanctuaries, which will be located at former military bases, will provide the protection the nation requires while honoring the beliefs of others."

Hamilton explained further details about how the program would be implemented then concluded his presentation.

* * *

Jack Russo's photos for tomorrow's story lay scattered across Hank's desk as if he needed a visual reminder. The chilling visit to Ellsworth Air Force Base in South Dakota was etched in his mind. The number two pencil in Hank's right hand twirled between his fingers. The government had invited the country's major news organizations to tour the nation's first sanctuary following the President's televised address fourteen days ago.

Located about ten miles from Rapid City, the former bomber base had been polished up with nice beds, a fully outfitted recreation center and even sod for its playground. But the gleaming perimeter of razor wire reminded everyone of what it was—a relocation camp for people who refused to be chipped.

The government could call it a sanctuary or any other euphemistic name, but it didn't change what it was—an internment camp. People would be held just as the Japanese had during World War II and not released until the threat of a bioterrorist attack against the nation was eliminated. Hank touched the slight bump on the top of his left hand. Nearly imperceptible. Why would people choose to give up their freedom over a little chip? As much as he distrusted Big Brother, it was hard to argue against quarantining kooks who wouldn't participate in a program to protect the nation.

Dr. Carrington of HHS had graphically explained what would happen if the terrorists released the virus. A pathogenic nightmare would sweep across the nation's cities in a matter of days, killing the infected in less than a week. The only way to avoid a complete meltdown, other than a vaccine, was to remove the infected as quickly as possible. And the only way to do that was through Operation First Alert.

The government's flurry to prepare sanctuaries combined with Carrington's warning had convinced most people that the threat was real. The result was any and everything necessary for survival had disappeared from retailer's shelves within hours. Guns and ammunition, dry goods and canned items, surgical mask and gloves, which some people were already wearing, and Tamiflu. Pharmacies had been cleaned out of the antiviral within a few hours of Carrington's announcement. The antiviral was useless against Leviathan, but that didn't stop people from buying it. The whole world had gone mad.

Mike, his editor, leaned out of his office and motioned for Hank. The office, which was enclosed with glass on three sides, provided a 180-degree view of the editorial staff and reporters. Two men stood in Mike's office, and Hank felt his pulse quicken at the sight of them.

Hank walked into his editor's office.

"These two gentlemen are from the FBI," Mike said. "This is Special Agent Nolan Rogers and Special Agent Greg Passek."

Rogers stood with his hands in his pockets. Hank could see his reflection in the agent's sunglasses. "We'd like you to come with us downtown."

"What's this about?"

"I think you know," Rogers said with a smirk. Passek's expression was deadpan.

Rogers's smugness sank Hank. *They must know.* Mike's face turned gray, accentuating the perpetual dark circles under his eyes.

The drive to the FBI office took less than ten minutes. It was located on the ninth floor of a towering high-rise in the downtown business district. The two agents and Hank entered the elevator and rode it to the top without a word.

As the door opened, Rogers directed Hank toward an interrogation room. It was about ten feet long and eight feet wide. Somewhere behind one of three interior walls, which one he wasn't sure, was a video camera and an agent poised to evaluate and record his every word and gesture. He searched the walls for evidence of a peephole but couldn't detect one.

He sat down in a metal chair designed for alertness, not comfort. Rogers and Passek sat across from him. Rogers leaned forward on the metal table. The smirk was back. "Why'd you do it?"

Hank's mouth went dry, his mind blank.

"Get the evidence and bring some coffee," Rogers said to Passek. He turned back to Hank. "I know you're a hot shot reporter who thinks he's smarter than everyone else, but you're not."

Passek returned cradling four plaster molds in one arm with photos stacked on top of them with two cups of coffee precariously positioned in his free hand. He placed the casts and coffee on the table and slid a cup toward Hank.

"These are casts of tire prints found about a quarter mile from where DW Coltrane's paraglider crashed," Rogers said. He placed four photos of close-ups of tires next to the forms. "The tread on these matches the molds. Guess whose tires they belong to?" His hazel eyes flashed.

Hank wiped the sweat from his forehead. The small bare room was stuffy and Rogers's cologne too strong. "There are probably thousands of tires in this city that match those casts."

Rogers pointed at the chalky impressions. "Your tires have a unique imprint." He picked up one of the photos and held it in front of Hank's face. "You see that gash in your tire tread and how it's worn to one side? It matches the tire track we took perfectly as well as the depth of the tread." He laid the photo down.

"It took some work to track you down. We contacted everyone DW knew, beginning with his childhood friends. Narrowed the field down to those who were in Charlotte at the time of the shooting, which was about two dozen. Then, we verified the whereabouts of each. That left three suspects.

"Only one set of tires matched." He paused for effect. "But the real zinger was the call DW made to you and the call you made to the hospital. We pulled the cell records." He grinned revealing a mouth of crooked teeth. "You're as connected as Siamese Twins. Now would you like to revise your story?"

Hank sipped the cup of lukewarm coffee. It was bitter, but he needed the edge. "DW called me. He was hurt. I was surprised to hear from him, because I hadn't seen him since the funeral for his wife and daughters. I had no idea what he'd done."

"Then why did you dump him in front of Presbyterian Hospital?"

"Because he told me to."

The agent grunted. "And you didn't think that was strange?"

The room was feeling smaller with each question. Hank sighed. "I guess."

"Do you understand that helping a murderer escape makes you an accomplice?"

155

"I didn't help him escape. I took him to a hospital. There's a difference. And that doesn't make me an accomplice."

Passek removed his suit jacket, revealing forearms that were as thick as his biceps. He leaned in toward Hank. "I don't think you get how much trouble you're in, pal. Your career is over, you're going to prison. Your mom, what's her name?" He opened a file.

"Maggie," Hank said.

"Yeah, Maggie. How will she feel when she learns her son was involved in killing the President and his daughter?"

"She knows I'd never do such a thing." But Hank's arrest would break her heart. Dad had left her years ago and was dead anyway. She didn't have anyone else.

"Do you think any jury is going to buy your cock and bull? If you were innocent, why didn't you come forward and tell the FBI?"

"I didn't know DW was guilty of anything until you arrested him."

"Okay, why didn't you say something then?"

"I should have. It was a mistake." But he was doomed the moment DW called. Perhaps even before that. They had history. Hank and DW's father worked together in the West Virginia coal mines. Thank God his parents weren't alive. They would have stood by him to the end, but it would have destroyed them.

"Darn right it was a mistake. A big mistake." Passek leaned back in his chair. "Let's see how this sounds. You admit that you and the assassin were good friends. Grew up together. You picked him up and took him to the hospital. After DW was arrested, you never told the FBI of your involvement. On the other hand, your defense is that you were helping an old friend, completely unaware that he'd just shot the President and killed his daughter."

Passek shook his head and looked at Rogers. "I'll bet you a million it takes the jury less than an hour to convict this guy."

"I wouldn't take that bet," Rogers said.

He was right. Sometimes the truth wasn't enough. And with the country still grieving and hungry for revenge, his chances for a fair trial were laughable. Soon, he would be one of the tragic cases he'd seen on cable, an innocent man locked up his entire life for a crime he didn't commit.

"There is another way," Passek said slowly.

"And what's that?" Hank asked hoarsely.

"The Director knows the CEO of the corporation that owns your newspaper. They go way back. He doesn't want a scandal involving one of his top reporters. The Director is willing to make you an offer."

"What kind of offer?" Hank took another sip of coffee.

"One you can't refuse," Passek said cracking a smile at Rogers. "Here's the deal. You agree to enter a sanctuary and disappear."

"A sanctuary? But I'm not against being chipped." Hank pointed at his hand. "I'm not even a Christian."

"Well I guess you're about to find Jesus."

Hank grimaced. What kind of deal was this? Prison or a sanctuary. Two sides of the same coin. The sanctuary might end up being worse. Hank stared down at the scratched metal table. Probably claw marks from some poor soul who cracked up. "And what happens when the virus threat is gone and the sanctuaries are closed?"

Passek rocked forward. The metal legs of his chair cracked against the tile floor. "You come back and resume your life."

"Just like that?"

Passek looked at his watch as Rogers reached inside his suit jacket. He pulled out two folded documents and slid them toward Hank.

One was a warrant for his arrest. The other looked like a plea bargain. "This isn't legal. I haven't even been arraigned."

"Do you want an arraignment?" Rogers asked.

Hank knew he should contact an attorney, but the publicity from a trial, even if he won, would destroy his career—and his mom. If he disappeared for awhile, he would spare her heartache and possibly have a job when he returned.

"What's the verdict? Shame or oblivion?" Rogers said.

Hank scribbled his signature on the plea bargain and tossed it across the table.

CHAPTER THIRTY-EIGHT

Albuquerque, August 27

Luke felt queasy. Millions of his followers would soon be on their way to sanctuaries throughout the west. The shuttered Holloman Air Force base in southern New Mexico had already been converted into a quarantine center. The government's swift reaction to his warning had caught him off guard.

Had he been right to give such advice? Perhaps he hadn't heard from the Holy Spirit. Perhaps the government's intentions were only to protect the country. It was easy to stand in front of a camera and tell people it was wrong to be chipped, but it was another thing to see them pay dearly for listening to him. Things had been much simpler when he was only responsible for two hundred people.

Luke stared at the production set located in a South Valley building owned by an underground church member. The cross from Grace Fellowship that had been cut down by a vehicle stood in the background. His producer had objected to the marred cross, but Luke thought it sent the perfect message. Broken but not defeated.

He was scheduled to deliver another broadcast in an hour, but he felt unsettled about his message. He intended to speak about the government's sanctuaries and encourage the millions headed to them. But it seemed the Lord was pressing him to deliver another message. But what?

"Are you ready, tough guy?" Cindy walked up to him with a glint in her green eyes. Luke feigned a smile, but it didn't fool her.

"What's wrong?"

"Sometimes I feel like God made a mistake choosing me. Things are already bad enough. People are out of work. There's not enough to eat. And I've made everything worse. Millions of Christians are going to suffer even more. Those who have jobs will lose them. Families will be torn apart. All because of what I said." Luke shook his head. "Did I do the right thing?"

Her eyes welled up. "I know it's tough, but God has uniquely prepared you for this time. He chose you because he knew you wouldn't run from this fight just as you never did when you were in the ring. You're a fighter." She kissed him.

A loud boom shook the floor. Luke crouched down and pulled Cindy down next to him. The explosion had come from the south side of the building. Two men ran through the building with fire extinguishers toward smoke drifting in from a door. They peeked through a window near the door then opened it and ran outside. A cloud of fire retardant rose outside the window.

Luke rose and helped Cindy up. He motioned for her to stay put, but she insisted on following him to the door. She grabbed his arm as they walked outside. Black smoke billowed from a charred car frame. The windows were blown out: the top had a gaping hole in it. Cindy's fingers dug into his arm. He wrapped his arm around her.

The men doused the car with another jet from the fire extinguishers. One of them pointed toward the building. Luke stepped through the door and looked back, still holding onto Cindy. Red paint ran downward in long, narrow fingers from letters sprayed on the side of the building. *Allah has cursed you!*

Attacks by the jihadists had escalated across the nation. But as far as he knew they hadn't signed their name to any of them—until now. The message on the building left little doubt that the stakes were changing, that the terrorists were becoming bolder.

The bombing wasn't random. Whoever did it could have destroyed any of the other half dozen cars parked on that side of the building including Luke's truck, but they didn't. They chose Cindy's car. Luke had believed the attack at Three Crosses church and the drive-by shooting were aimed at him. But now he wasn't sure. The thought of Cindy being the focus shook him. Losing her was unthinkable.

They had taken precautions by moving in with Cindy's family and moving the site for each week's broadcast. But now they would have to be even more cautious, move more often, leave no trails.

Luke pulled Cindy closer and walked back into the building. As he neared the stage, the videographer was already setting up his equipment and checking the lights.

"Are you going to be okay to teach?" Cindy asked, her words quivering. Her light brown skin was ashen.

He had been unsure of what to say, but the attack clarified everything the way smelling salts had when he'd been dazed in a fight. He knew exactly what he needed to say. "I don't think I really understood the battle facing us until now. It takes a lot of fuel to ignite the fires sweeping the country right now, and nothing makes them burn hotter than hatred."

Cindy hugged his thick arm and looked up at him. "None of this is going to go away. Is it?"

Luke wanted to tell her everything would be fine, but this time he couldn't. He pulled her to his chest, with her head resting just below his chin. "The jihad has begun."

CHAPTER THIRTY-NINE

Anacostia, District of Columbia, August 28

"It will be equipped as well as any of the Fort Detrick labs when it's complete," Kareem said pointing toward the workmen in the abandoned warehouse.

Sulaiman had purchased the former wholesale distribution center located deep in Anacostia because it was cheap and invisible. No one would suspect a research lab buried deep in a war zone.

Electric drills buzzed as men erected steel frames for individual labs throughout the empty building. Others bolted sheet metal panels onto the bullet ridden perimeter walls. But the outside would remained untouched—the graffiti covered walls, crumbling concrete driveway with weeds sprouting from gaping cracks, and parking lot strewn with hypodermic needles and condoms. The less obtrusive, the better.

There wouldn't be any zoning hearings. No code inspections. No final approval from the city. All of which were fortunate because the city would never approve a research lab, particularly one dedicated to a pathogenic virus. A large payment to the city's chief building inspector had insured work on the warehouse would be unhindered and unsupervised.

The equipment for the air filtering and biowaste containment systems would arrive as soon as the interior work was complete. The electron and optical microscopes and other research equipment would arrive last. Sulaiman estimated that most of the lab would be operational in thirty days, provided everyone worked around the clock, and the shipments didn't alert government watchdogs.

"How long do you think it will take to weaponize the virus?" Sulaiman asked the tanned, blond-haired man before him who looked like he would be more at home on a surfboard than in a laboratory.

"I think it can be done in a few weeks," Kareem said. "The virus will have to be converted into an aerosol form that can be dispersed easily during an explosion. The beauty of this pathogen is that we don't have to manufacture a large amount of it because of its virulence. Only a very small number of spores are necessary for infection."

Sulaiman removed a Camel from a pack in his shirt pocket and lit it. "How fast will it spread?"

"The last reported case of small pox was in 1977." Kareem raised his voice above the drills and hammers in the background. "No one has been vaccinated against the disease in decades. The Leviathan virus has no enemies." He pointed at Sulaiman's cigarette. "By the time you finish your smoke, ten people could be infected by one person, and, in turn, each of them could have infected another ten. Its growth will be exponential. With air travel the virus could spread around the world in a few weeks."

Sulaiman motioned for them to walk to the other end of the building away from the noise. A cluster of pigeons perched on a steel beam overhead. Rays of light poured through several small holes in a section of the roof that was rusted through. They stopped in a ring of light shining on the floor. "We're going to recreate the world through jihad. No Christians, no Jews, no Buddhists, no Hindus— no one except those who love Allah. Once we have an antiviral to protect our people, we'll release the virus." But from what Sulaiman understood about the virus, he was uncertain whether his people or the government could create an antiviral to stop Leviathan.

"Where do you intend to detonate the bombs?" Kareem asked.

Rashid approached from across the building. He cupped his hands and yelled, "The construction is moving right along."

Sulaiman noticed a layer of dust covering his dark brown alligator shoes. He pulled a handkerchief from his pocket and reached down and brushed them off. He stood up and looked at Kareem. "The infidel Luke Chavez will be the first to die for his comments about Allah."

Rashid walked up and brushed at a gray streak on his black suit pants. "The infidel posted a video on the internet blaming Muslims for attacks against him and other Christians."

"And he called Allah a false god," Kareem added.

Sulaiman drew in the Turkish smoke and let it exhale through his nose. "If the Christians have a God, he is a weak one. He couldn't stop Allah from placing the virus in our hands, and now he's allowed this fool, Chavez, to convince his followers to reject the government's implantation program." Sulaiman grinned. "The Christians are being herded like stupid sheep into a canyon with no escape. Only Allah could design such a plan."

CHAPTER FORTY

Holloman Sanctuary, August 29

The thermometer's needle pointed at 110 degrees. Hank mopped the sweat rolling down his forehead with his forearm. His fair skin was already rosy. The mid-August sun bearing down on the flat, brown landscape of dry grass and tumbleweeds surrounding the sanctuary appeared to be twice as hot as North Carolina.

He wandered down a deserted, gummy asphalt road not sure where it led. A month ago he was one of Charlotte's top reporters. A call from him could make politicians sweat. Now he was a nobody, a detainee who existed only in a computer file. But detainee was a political spin for prisoner, which is what he was. The only thing missing was a striped uniform and shackles.

The sanctuary seemed largely uninhabited except for workmen who were replacing vandalized windows in the buildings as well as toilets, sinks, and appliances in the base houses that had been stripped. The activity was a sure indication of preparations for a significant increase in population.

Elevated towers stood along the perimeter which was enclosed by a ten-foot steel-link fence topped with shiny razor wire. The posts were empty but he wondered for how long. He hadn't seen any guards or towers at the Ellsworth sanctuary. He wished he had access to the internet or a television, so he could find out what was happening in the country. Not knowing made him anxious. An administrator Hank had bumped into said the camp would soon have internet and cable.

In the distance a group of men huddled in the shade of a former aircraft hanger, dwarfed by the building's immense size. The structure appeared to be only a hundred yards away, but it took fifteen minutes to reach. He walked up, leaned against the building, and instantly seared his arm. The men glanced up at him. He sat down near them but avoided leaning back against the oven-hot metal siding.

"I'm glad I'm here," a man with a thick Mexican accent said. He pointed toward the perimeter fence. "If the terrorists release the virus, this place will be much safer."

A bald man with tattooed arms said, "It would be suicide for them to do it."

"They don't seem to mind suicide," the Mexican said.

"I'm less worried about the terrorists than a chip under my skin," a man with thick glasses said. "The very idea of something transmitting information about my body to the government is too Orwellian."

A heavy-set man fanned himself with what looked like a hot rod magazine. "Pastor Luke said it's the first step toward the mark of the beast. I wish there was some way we could watch his teachings." He turned toward Hank as if he had just become aware of his presence. "What do you think?"

He stuck his left hand in his pocket. They probably hadn't seen the chip because it was easy to miss, and they weren't looking for it. But if they had, he'd have a lot questions to answer, and he wasn't up for that. "The government already knows too much about us. A chip will only make it worse."

The group of men nodded.

The Mexican studied Hank. "You just get here?"

"Yeah."

166

"What did you used to do?"

The question stung. "I was a reporter for a large newspaper."

"No kidding? Maybe you can start a base newspaper?"

Hank tried to smile, but the idea depressed him even more.

"Married?"

"No. And you?"

The man hung his head. "My wife stayed behind." The man's deep voice cracked.

"Why?"

"She didn't want to come. Said I was loco."

A silence fell over the group of men as their gazes fell toward the pavement. Then, one by one, they began to share what they used to do and the loved ones left behind. The Mexican had been a cook, the bald guy a carpenter whose girlfriend refused to come. The bespectacled man, a physicist at the Los Alamos Laboratory with a teen-age son who went to live with his ex. The heavy-set man was a DJ. His wife told him she wouldn't be waiting when he returned.

Why had these men been willing to give up so much? An image of the Rev. Jim Jones in dark glasses flashed before Hank. Hundreds had gone to their deaths because of the twisted ideas pumped into their heads. Luke Chavez was just as dangerous, perhaps more so. The sanctuaries would be his legacy of sorrows.

CHAPTER FORTY-ONE

Washington, D.C., August 30

I understand you're going to testify before the Judiciary Committee tomorrow." Hamilton glanced at the door to his office. It was closed. His assistant had strict instructions not to allow anyone to enter during his call to the CIA Director. A shadow appeared under the door's threshold. Was someone listening?

"I wish I didn't have to, Mr. President, but..." Tingley's voice sounded shaky over the speakers.

Hamilton picked up the phone, lowered his voice, and checked the electronic unit scanning for any trace of recording. Clear. "You know what they're after, right? Those scumbags want my job. That's what this is about. Besides the country can't take any more bad news. It will destroy everything we've built and take us both down."

"I know, Mr. President, but what else can I do?"

"Lie." It wasn't like the CIA hadn't done it before. There were times when the truth caused more harm than good and this was one of those. The world would have been better off not knowing that the CIA had attempted to kill Fidel Castro.

Tingley coughed. "I need to know if any of our men were involved in the disappearance of the pathologists and Dr. Myers. And the lab tech. The unit was never intended to be used for the assassination of Americans."

"It wasn't. This isn't Russia."

Putin was one of the wiliest and most ruthless politicians to ever lead Russia. He was despised by many, but his tactics had succeeded in restoring the country's fortunes and power. It wasn't the means that were important as Machiavelli had correctly observed. It was the end. Everything Hamilton had done, he had done unselfishly for the country. The casualties of the medical personnel were unfortunate but necessary.

"My butt is on the line here, Mr. President. If I tell the committee about the black ops unit, I'll probably lose my position, but at least I'll avoid prison."

There wasn't any probability that he'd lose his job. And there was a chance he'd serve time unless he had cut a deal with the committee. No wonder he wasn't too worried about testifying. "Listen to me. The committee will never know. This is between you and me. The investigation didn't even make the first two pages of today's newspaper, and the networks aren't leading with the story anymore. The country is focused on the virus. The investigation will be forgotten in a few weeks unless you tell them about the agency." Hamilton hated being in this position, begging for common sense to prevail. "We need this covert unit. You know that better than anyone. Without it we'll be right back where we were a few years ago, groveling for Congress's permission. I know you don't want that anymore than I do."

Hamilton turned and looked out the windows of the Oval Office, waiting for Tingley's reply. The lawn was a deep lush green, but the rest of the country was parched and suffering through one of the worst heat waves in a decade. The unfortunate events of the last few weeks, the casualties and the congressional hearing, would never have transpired if the reporter from *The Observer* hadn't stuck his nose where it didn't belong. At least he wouldn't be a problem anymore. And Hamilton couldn't think of a more perfect hell than being confined to a sanctuary in the New Mexico desert. It was the best news in days.

"I'll have to sleep on it, Mr. President."

"You do that, John. But just remember who the unit works for."

Hamilton didn't intend to harm Tingley, although eliminating him would destroy any trail to the covert agency. No, Hamilton just wanted to ensure the director didn't have sweet dreams.

CHAPTER FORTY-TWO

Fort Detrick, September 3

The screeching cry of a rhesus monkey startled Jenny. Something about it was different than anything she had ever heard before. The monkey, located in the lab adjacent to Jenny's, screamed again, the pitch this time at least an octave above a soprano's high note. Jenny walked to the lab's window. The animal's dark eyes appealed for help as it pressed its bloody palms against the cage. Dark streaks stained its white chest.

Jenny quickly dressed in a hazmat suit and entered the animal lab. She and PJ had injected some of the animals the previous night with the Leviathan virus. It was their first look at effects of the synthetic pathogen on living creatures. What she saw sent a chill down her spine. The primate before her belched a dark bile that looked like it contained organ tissue. It had been less than twenty-four hours, and yet the animal appeared to be experiencing a complete internal meltdown, a process that took the bird pox at least four days.

There was a rap on the window behind her. She turned to see PJ, his normally sanguine countenance missing. She waved for him to join her.

A few minutes later he entered the room and shook his head. "It's much more aggressive than the bird pox."

"I've never seen a hemorrhagic virus express itself through the hands."

Her pulse quickened. "I don't remember reading anything about such side effects in the studies on the virus. I think it's mutating."

Jenny walked to the other side of the lab and checked the caged pig they had infected. Blood covered the lens of its blue eyes and seeped from the corners. She tried not to think of the red-tainted world the animal saw. As she studied the hog closely, she noticed that it didn't share the monkey's strange side effects—no hemorrhaging from its extremities.

She walked back toward PJ and stopped. The monkey before her was suffering from side effects similar to the other primate.

"What's wrong?" PJ asked.

"I thought we only infected one rhesus last night."

"We did."

"Check the other animals we didn't inject."

"Why?"

"I've got a very bad feeling."

Jenny and PJ studied the other animals including two ferrets.

The face staring at her through the protective hood had lost its rich, dark color. "They're all infected."

The discovery meant only one thing. Leviathan was airborne.

CHAPTER FORTY-THREE

Washington, D.C., September 4

Hamilton hadn't slept all night. He had examined the problem from every perspective. And, at best, it looked bleak. He had only one real defense against Tingley's testimony—and it was a long shot.

The speaker on his desk buzzed. "Mr. President?"

"Yes, Kate."

"Representative Avery Simpson is on the line. He'd like to speak with you."

Simpson was the chairman of the Judiciary Investigation Committee. The Republican was also chairman of the powerful budget committee and had probably asked the staff of the Government Accountability Office to spend the night combing through the national budget in search of funding for a covert agency. But he was the one friend Hamilton had on the committee, and they went way back.

"Put him through."

"Good morning, Mr. President."

"It's nearly afternoon. What's on your mind, Avery?"

"As you know we've just finished questioning the CIA Director. At least for today. Under oath he made an egregious statement about a covert unit under your control. We're going to have to subpoena you."

"Fine as long as you do it at the White House. I'm not coming down there."

"All right. The director offered a very detailed history of why and how the covert agency was created. Very troubling. But the most disturbing part..." Simpson paused.

Hamilton took a deep breath.

"Is that he believes the unit was involved in the assassination of American citizens." Simpson's voice was grave. "Mr. President, please tell me there isn't any truth to this. This could destroy your presidency and the Republican party."

Tingley would have never spilled that kind of information without a sweetheart deal for himself. Hamilton was prepared for the director to reveal the covert agency. Its existence couldn't be proven, and there wasn't anything in the budget to substantiate it. No names, no faces. It would be Tingley's word against his, and, generally, the bigger gun won these battles. But he never expected the director to reveal anything about the deaths surrounding Nash's assassination. The mere accusation could topple a government.

Hamilton reached for the cigar inside his suit jacket. His hand trembled. Lucy was out of town promoting her new program of animal rights. He clipped the cigar and stuck it in his mouth. He grabbed the lighter in his pocket and started to light it but stopped.

"Tingley is lying about the assassinations and the covert unit. For some reason he has decided to switch sides and join the effort to destroy me. He was Nash's man. Maybe he resents me. Johnson put up with the same attacks from Kennedy's appointees."

"Mr. President, no one is trying to destroy you. We're all interested in learning the truth about what really happened."

"The truth is the Democrats want the presidency back, and they'll do anything they can to get it. Politics doesn't get any dirtier than this."

"So you deny everything the director said?"

"Outside of the director's statement, have you found any evidence to suggest a covert assassination unit?"

Avery cleared his throat. "No, not yet. But we're still looking."

"Well look all you want. You won't find anything because the unit doesn't exist. Anything else?"

"No, Mr. President."

"Avery, I need you to think clearly. There's a conspiracy forming that may include some of our own party. Don't let the snakes around you persuade you that these ridiculous allegations are true. Okay?"

"I'll keep that in mind, Mr. President."

"That's all I'm asking." Hamilton pushed the button on his desk ending the call. He had played the bluff. All he could do now was wait.

CHAPTER FORTY-FOUR

Anacostia, September 18

Sulaiman stood with Rashid in the middle of the completed lab in Anacostia and fumed. "Where is everyone?"

"We're still waiting for the air filtration system."

Sulaiman slapped the folded newspaper in his hand against his leg. "What's the delay?"

"We've been purchasing the equipment for it from as many vendors as possible to avoid attention, but one of them said the government was asking questions. So we had to delay our order."

"What are we using for filtration now?"

"We're not. The only people here are Kareem and Elisha. The other scientists won't commit to the project until we have an air purification system."

"How long before we can get the rest of the equipment?"

"The vendor suggested waiting a few months."

"What's a few months?"

"Four to five," Rashid said sheepishly.

Sulaiman felt the back of his neck burning. "We can't wait that long. We need every scientist who committed to us here and engaged. Don't they understand what we're doing? If we succeed, it will change everything."

"I think they understand, but that doesn't make them feel any safer."

"Allah will protect them."

"I said that, but they're very practical. They like clean air."

"Where's Kareem?"

"He's working in one of those labs." Rashid pointed toward two hallways that led to twelve individual lab rooms.

"We're losing valuable time. The longer it takes us to launch an attack, the more time the government has to find a vaccine before us. And while we wait, the infidel, Luke Chavez, continues to defame Allah's name. He has mounted an effective PR campaign with posts on the internet about several burned churches."

"The publicity is turning the public against us," Rashid said. "The National Guard has also made it difficult for us to launch any new attacks. Maybe we should stop? Christians are on the run. And Chavez's movement is declining. Christians seem split on whether the chip represents the mark of the beast. It has cost him a lot of followers."

Sulaiman studied Rashid. His cousin was three years older, but his receding hairline made him appear much older. Rashid had been loyal. Together they had worked diligently to prepare the Mahdi's way, but sometimes his cousin didn't understand that the battle would never be over until the last infidel was dead.

Kareem emerged from a lab down a hallway. He looked frustrated.

"How's the work progressing?" Sulaiman asked as the scientist approached.

"We're having trouble getting the virus into an aerosolized form."

Sulaiman folded his arms. "Why's that?"

"We don't know exactly." He frowned. "The pathogen's synthesized structure is complex and resisting change."

Sulaiman rubbed his forehead. "What's the progress on a vaccine?"

"None. It's over our heads. We have to wait until the rest of the team arrives before work can begin."

"I don't want Elisha in direct contact with the virus."

"She's not," Kareem said.

Everything that had begun so well was now running into one obstacle after another. The biggest obstruction was one he never foresaw—Luke Chavez. Prior to the pastor, the infidels lacked a central voice. But his weekly broadcasts were continuing to attract large audiences even though millions of Christians had been shipped to the sanctuaries.

Sulaiman pulled a pack of cigarettes from his pocket and slapped it against his other hand, then removed a cigarette. He lit it and inhaled. As he watched the smoke drift upward into the light pouring in through the upper windows, he could feel his chance slipping away. He was in a race against hundreds of Fort Detrick scientists with only two researchers who weren't really researchers at all. Elisha was a surgeon, and Kareem, an electron microscope technician.

Sulaiman couldn't wait months for his scientists to arrive. He had to act before the opportunity was gone. Perhaps his progress had been frustrated because Allah was guiding him in a different direction. Sometimes it was hard to know because Allah was often silent. But as he pondered the dilemma the outline of a new plan unfolded.

CHAPTER FORTY-FIVE

Albuquerque, September 20

L uke drove the rusted 1966 GMC down Interstate 25 headed for his next broadcast. He loved the classic truck even though it looked like it had been plucked from a junkyard. The broadcast would be from a small sound studio a friend owned not far from movie studios south of Albuquerque.

As the GMC bounced over a pothole on the Rio Bravo exit, Luke glanced in the rear view mirror at the white van that had been trailing him for about five miles.

"What is it?" Cindy asked.

"Probably nothing," he said motioning with his head toward the rear view mirror, "but that van has been behind us for awhile."

Cindy looked in the side view mirror.

He wanted to grab his wife's hand and reassure her, but the old truck took two hands to steer. The two miles of road between the exit and the studios was a desolate parched stretch with the exception of the Journal Pavilion, Albuquerque's top venue for concerts. Light brown veins flowed down the surrounding hills from off road vehicles that had once roared up and down.

As he headed up University Boulevard toward the studios, the van behind him pulled into the passing lane.

It's about time you passed. He turned toward Cindy. "Don't worry."

But a look of sheer terror had seized her.

Luke turned to see a man in the van pointing a shotgun at him. "Down," Luke screamed as he reached for Cindy.

A blast hit the left front tire, and the truck veered wildly. He held onto the steering wheel and tried to keep it on the road, but it felt like he was on the losing end of an arm wrestling match. Another blast hit the back. The truck tilted left, then flipped upside down and rolled over and over as he tried to hold onto Cindy.

When he woke, the interior was filled with dust. The truck had come to rest on all four wheels. The windshield was a web of shattered glass. Cindy was slumped against the passenger door. He reached for her, but he couldn't move his arm. "Cindy!" He shouted, but he couldn't hear himself.

Someone opened his door and pulled him from the truck and dragged him. He was lifted and laid on a hard metal surface. A door slammed.

A hand touched his head. It hurt.

A sharp prick in his arm, then darkness.

* * *

Light peeked out from around the corners of dark curtains. Luke tried to sit up, but the stabbing pain in his head stopped him. As he lay back down the room spun, and he felt sick.

A man walked into the room. He flipped a switch on the wall. The fixture in the ceiling had a single bulb and no cover but shined enough light to illuminate cockroaches on the walls. The man dressed in a cream-colored suit with a brown tie crossed his arms. "So you're the great pastor."

Luke tried to sit up again.

"Stay down." The man pointed at him. "You have a nasty gash on your head."

"Where's my wife?"

"She's in another room."

"I want to see her."

The man left and returned with Cindy. He held her arm, but she broke away and ran to Luke. She knelt down beside him. A dark blue lump underscored her right eye. Her lip was cut. "How are you, baby?" She caressed his head.

"Did they hurt you?" He noticed a bruise on her right arm.

"No," she said glancing at her arm. "You wouldn't let go of me, and I'm glad you didn't." She tried to smile. "Looks like someone head butted you."

"Feels like it." Luke tried again to raise himself up on his elbows and did. His head had stopped spinning.

A well-dressed man stepped forward. His eyes were so dark Luke couldn't see his pupils. "Sulaiman," someone called from up the stairs.

"Down here."

Luke was familiar with the name. Was he Sulaiman Hadid? The terrorist leader responsible for several bombings and probably many of the attacks against the churches and Christians. "Where are we?"

"Baltimore."

"What do you want with us?"

The man's eyes brightened. "A confession."

Cindy turned to look at him.

"What do you mean?" Luke tightened his right hand into a fist.

"I want you to make a statement renouncing your faith and—"

"Never," Luke said interrupting Sulaiman.

He raised his hand. "I also want you to declare Allah as the only true God."

"You must be crazy. You'll have to kill me first."

"I have no intention of killing you, but your wife on the other hand…" He pulled a 9mm from the shoulder holster inside his jacket and pointed it at Cindy's head.

Luke instinctively raised his hand in front of the gun as he grabbed Cindy's hand. His outstretched hand trembled.

"Don't do it, baby. I'm not afraid to die."

Luke looked at her. There wasn't anything he wouldn't give to the Lord—except... *Lord, don't ask me to give up my wife. I can't live without her.* He turned toward Sulaiman who still had the gun pointed at her. "Why do you hate Christians so much?"

Sulaiman lowered the gun. His dark eyes blazed. "We both want the same things. You want everyone to worship Jesus. Muslims want everyone to worship Allah. We just have different methods for achieving our goals."

"My confession won't destroy the church if that's what you think. Christians will know it was forced."

Sulaiman shook his head. "You underestimate your influence. You're the head of the snake. If I crush you, the body will die." He raised the gun and pointed it at Cindy. "Does she live?"

Lord, you know I would willing to give up my own life but not Cindy's. Please forgive me. Luke sat up and pulled Cindy to him. "Let her go first."

She squeezed his hand and wiped at her eyes.

Sulaiman lowered the gun. "I'm afraid you have little leverage in this negotiation, but you have my word."

"That's comforting to know," Cindy said. "I'm not going without Luke. You'll have to kill both of us."

Sulaiman's eyes narrowed. "He stays." He removed a sheet of paper from his suit jacket and handed it to Luke.

Cindy looked at him and wiped at her eyes again. "Don't do it, baby."

A tall, slender blond-haired woman walked into the room with a camera mounted on a tripod.

The paper shook in Luke's hands. *Strengthen me, Lord. But how can I ask you to help me deny you?* As he read from the prepared statement, Cindy glared at Sulaiman. When he finished, he tossed the paper on the floor.

Sulaiman leaned down and picked up the paper, then looked at the woman behind the camera. "Will you play it back for us, Elisha?" He smiled.

She turned the camera around and flipped out the LCD screen and hit play.

A loud crash like wood being smashed came from upstairs.

Sulaiman and the woman wheeled around toward the stairs on the opposite side of the room. They both pulled guns and approached the stairs cautiously, one on each side of the stairwell. Two men descended the steps.

"Watch out," Cindy yelled.

Sulaiman nodded at Elisha and leaped around one corner and she the other. They fired several shots at the men who crumpled on the stairs and pitched forward.

The window with the dark shade near the street exploded. Glass spewed into the room as a flood of light poured in along with ear-shattering automatic fire.

Sulaiman hit the floor and fired four shots at the agent. There was a groan from the window. He stood up and turned toward Elisha and stopped. She lay on the thread bare carpet. A dark pool collected near her head. He dropped to his knees and cradled her in his arms. He threw his head back and let out a loud wail. A shiver passed through Luke. Cindy clutched him.

Sulaiman rose. A trace of sulfur lingered in the haze. He walked to the camera that was still playing Luke's confession and removed it from the tripod. A large crimson stain covered the left breast of his light suit jacket. He went to the window and studied the street outside. Then he walked over to Luke and stared at him. "An eye for an eye." And before Luke could raise his hand, Sulaiman fired.

CHAPTER FORTY-SIX

Anacostia, September 22

It was impossible to focus on anything except the face in the center of the storm spinning in his mind. Sulaiman's temples throbbed. The last week had been like a bad dream and particularly the last twenty-four hours. The smooth soles of his new Italian shoes glided across the vinyl floors in the nearly empty room in the Anacostia lab as he paced back and forth. A fresh chalky smell of paint filled the air.

"Why did you let him go?" Rashid asked. "I don't understand it." Kareem sat next to him, his head hung low.

Sulaiman stopped and looked at Rashid. "The FBI was all over the place."

Kareem looked up. "Why didn't you kill him?"

"And make him a martyr? Nothing would galvanize his movement and rally the Christians more than his death." He shook his head. "I'd rather make him look weak, unwilling to die for his faith, and unable to save his wife. And I have the evidence to do it." He pointed toward the camera lying on the stainless steel counter at the end of the room. But in the hours since the FBI's rescue, he had questioned whether letting the pastor live had been the correct decision.

"Are you going to post the video on the internet?"

Sulaiman nodded. "The confession will destroy his church, and once it's gone, the rest of the infidels will drop like flies." But he wasn't so sure. The plan had been to keep Chavez as a hostage, shut down his internet broadcasts, and, after the church collapsed, either kill him or exchange him for brothers the government had imprisoned. With his release the question was whether he would return to preaching and, if he did, whether anyone would listen.

Rashid shook his head and look unconvinced. "I think he'll fight back and say he was forced to make the statement."

"You didn't see what I saw in his eyes. He died when she died. There's nothing left inside."

"I can't believe Elisha is dead," Kareem said shaking his head.

The statement stung. Sulaiman turned his back and rubbed his temples. He had tried to forget what had happened, but she was everywhere, from the smell of her perfume on the sheets to the pumps near his bed to the necklace still lying on the dresser.

"It seems like Allah has deserted us." Rashid mumbled the words to himself.

Sulaiman spun around. "Jihad is about struggle. It isn't meant to be easy. We still have the virus."

"What good is the virus without the vaccine."

"We don't need one."

Rashid's brow creased as he stood. "What do you mean?"

"Do you think we can stand around for months waiting for the scientists to show up?" Rashid turned toward Kareem as if he were trying to enlist his support. "That's insanity. You'll end up killing everyone, including us."

Kareem looked up at Rashid but didn't say anything.

"Don't you think Allah is capable of protecting us?" Sulaiman said.

"He didn't protect Elisha." Rashid shook his head. "I'm sorry. I didn't mean it."

Sulaiman stared at him. But his cousin did mean it. He was a faithful Muslim, prayed five times everyday, recited the Qur'an daily, but at times he lacked even a simple faith. He knew everything was in Allah's hands, and yet Rashid was often uncomfortable truly trusting him.

Rashid crossed his arms. "How do you propose to protect your brothers and sisters?"

Sulaiman wasn't sure. But he had learned through the years that everything happened for a reason. Elisha's death had a purpose as did Luke's escape. It wasn't possible for finite man to comprehend Allah and his plans. There weren't any formulas to calculate his next move, no incantations to force him in a direction he didn't want to go, nothing at all that could be done to affect his great purpose.

Sulaiman's carefully laid plans were in chaos, their success questionable. Yet in the uncertainty he felt a peace, and his headache was gone.

CHAPTER FORTY-SEVEN

Camp David, September 22

Hamilton slammed the phone down and turned toward the window. He stood with his hands clasped behind his back. A thicket of aspens, oaks, and tall evergreens stood just beyond Aspen Lodge, his cabin at Camp David. He loved the approach of fall more than any other time of year, but he barely noticed the gold and red leaves dotting the green canvas.

"What did Avery say?" Pepper asked.

Hamilton turned around. "He called to warn me about a story that will break on the networks."

Pepper sat in an overstuffed, distressed leather chair that engulfed him. A massive river-rock fireplace towered from behind. The fireplace was all that remained of the original cabin FDR occupied as his summer retreat. Twelve presidents prior to Hamilton had wrestled with grave problems in this very room; two with their impeachment. "What's it about?"

Hamilton ran his fingers through his hair. "I'm sorry I couldn't tell you before. The only people who knew were Tingley and me."

"Are we talking covert agency?"

Hamilton nodded.

Pepper's face turned red. "Why did you lie to me?"

Hamilton shook his head. "I didn't have a choice. Tingley and I both agreed to never discuss it with anyone. I kept my half of the agreement, but he didn't."

"I think the American people will fail to see the honor in that."

He turned back toward the window. "Nash and Tingley created the agency after the CIA's failed assassination of President Sangarra of Venezuela was leaked to the press.

"Why didn't you just shut it down after taking office?"

Hamilton rubbed his hands together. There was a slight chill in the room. "There are times when covert missions are necessary."

"You mean assassinations," Pepper snapped.

Hamilton turned around. "Would you rather allow a sociopath like Sangarra to infect the rest of South America with his dangerous ideas?"

"Every time our government has ushered in a regime change, the replacement has ended up being just as bad or worse." Pepper stood and walked toward the fireplace. He rubbed his hand over a smooth river rock as if he were examining it. "You know what's going to happen as soon as the story breaks?"

Hamilton could see the ignominious end. He should have eliminated Tingley. It would have been worth the risk. Now a relentless barrage of questions from the media would be unleashed like a fusillade. Some reporter would try to make a name for himself by digging up dirt on Dr. Myers' murder and the disappearance of the pathologists and the lab technician. A public case would be played out in the media to prove the murder and the disappearances were the work of the covert agency. It wouldn't succeed because the assassins would never be found, but the publicity would destroy his administration.

Congress would move to impeach him, and he would be faced with the same question Nixon and Clinton were. Do I have enough votes in the Senate to survive?

The phone rang. Hamilton picked it up. "Mr. President, Dr. Carrington from Human Health and Services is on the line. He says it's urgent. Do you want to speak with him?"

Pepper turned around and stared at the phone.

"Put him through." Hamilton put the receiver down and pushed the button for speaker.

"Mr. President, I'm sorry to interrupt your vacation, but I thought you should know that I received a call this morning from Dr. George. She says the virus has mutated into an airborne pathogen."

"Dr. Carrington, I have you on speaker phone. Pepper's here. How does this development change things?"

"It means no human contact is necessary to spread the infection. Spores are disseminated through sneezing or coughing. The most frightening possibility is that this mutation, according to Dr. George, may be much more stable than a typical airborne virus."

"Which means what?"

"Its life could be extended for a longer period, which could allow a strong wind to sweep the pathogen through a city."

"What about the strain the terrorists have?"

"It's hard to say whether it will become airborne. No virus ever mutates exactly the same way twice."

"What do you suggest we do?"

"Pray. The terrorists don't have a clue how deadly this pathogen is. If their strain becomes airborne, we won't be able to contain it."

Hamilton said goodbye and hung up.

Pepper's pallid face had turned gray, just a shade lighter than the rocks mortared into the fireplace behind him. "We've got to release this information to the media and hope that whoever has the virus, rethinks releasing it."

Hamilton nodded. But he didn't share Pepper's fear. In fact, something about the new threat reassured him that despite the mess he was in, there might actually be a way out.

CHAPTER FORTY-EIGHT

Holloman Sanctuary, New Mexico, September 22

News arrived at the Holloman sanctuary like the slow drip of an IV. The camp director had never delivered on his promise for internet or televisions. The word was the budget for the sanctuaries had been cut. The only news included a few week-old newspapers and magazines that circulated through the camp like precious heirlooms.

But Hank didn't buy the budget story, although the loss of millions from the labor force had probably ripped a hole in the economy bigger than the one that sunk the Titanic. More probable, communication was being deliberately suppressed to speed assimilation into sanctuary life.

The lack of contact with the outside world did make it easy to forget with each passing day. But Hank refused to let go and craved any information that connected him to his former life. New arrivals at the camp were the best source of current news. Whenever he spotted a new face, he peppered the person with questions. The interrogation always began with one question: what was the latest on the virus?

A thin, dark-haired man with acne, early twenties, walked out of the processing center and stood in the middle of a crowd milling around. He was the first person under thirty Hank had seen in weeks. Most of the detainees were middle-aged or older. There were several families at the sanctuary with young kids, but high school kids and twenty-somethings were conspicuously absent. The chip had driven a wedge between young and old. The younger generation was apparently smarter than their parents and didn't share their phobia about the mark of the beast.

The young man looked lost.

Hank walked up to him. "First day?"

The man rubbed his day-old beard that sprouted through skin the consistency of fresh meat. "Yeah."

"I'm Hank." He extended his hand.

The man shook it weakly. "Tom." A dark green and red tattoo, which looked like a dragon, peered through the man's white t-shirt.

"Come on, I'll show you around." Hank waved him toward a cluster of white buildings in the distance. "Any news on a vaccine?" Everything depended on the development of an antiviral. With one, the sanctuaries became unnecessary, but without one, everyone in the sanctuaries could be quarantined for only God knew how long.

Tom shook his head as he followed silently.

A real talker. "What's the mood of the country?"

"Total paranoia."

He sounded like he was from Jersey or Philly. "And you're not?"

"Nope." He yanked his pants up.

"Why not?"

"I'm not afraid to die."

It sounded like the cocky talk he'd heard among some of the Christians in his barracks. *To die is gain* is how they phrased it.

"But I don't think it will happen anyways," Tom said. "The terrorists have as much to lose as we do."

He was either naive or a blind optimist. The terrorists didn't have as much to lose. They were even more destitute than everyone else. At least the ones he had read about.

"Did you refuse to be chipped because you're a Christian or because you're opposed to the invasion of privacy?"

Tom's eyes flashed.

Was the question too personal? Hank had asked it dozens of times, and never had anyone react the way this new guy had.

"This is the recreation hall," Hank said pointing toward the largest building among the six in the distance. "It's not bad. The Air Force took care of their boys. Nice indoor basketball courts."

Tom looked toward the sun and shielded his face. He wiped his forehead. It was about three o'clock and hot. Beads of perspiration formed on his forearms like rain drops on the hood of a freshly waxed car. "It's hotter than hell here."

"You get used to it."

He frowned as if he had no intention of acclimating.

The road in front of them was deserted except for the occasional government jeep that passed sweeping a rush of hot air toward them. Most people avoided the late afternoon sun. Hank's feet burned in his thin sandals. "Anything new on the disappearance of the pathologists?"

Tom stopped and grinned sardonically. "Dude, you really don't know what's going on, do you?" Then he grimaced and bent forward. A hoarse, sloshy expulsion came from deep inside his chest that sounded as if it would rip loose anything not firmly attached.

Hank bent over and looked at him. "You all right?"

He waved Hank away.

Tom stood up. His face was as pale as a day-old stiff.

"We have a pretty good medical staff here. It's not far. Do you want to go?"

"Where's the rec hall again?" Tom asked.

"Back that way." Hank turned and pointed toward a building behind them.

"Many people there?"

"Sure. A lot of people hang out there shooting hoops."

Tom turned without saying goodbye and left.

Hank shook his head. Strange kid. As he watched Tom walk toward the building, something caught Hank's eye, something out of place. A dark, sticky glob was attached to his sandal strap. He bent down and studied what appeared to be a thick lump of blood.

CHAPTER FORTY-NINE

Cedar Crest, New Mexico, September 22

L uke rolled over in bed and stared at the knotty-pine tongue and groove ceiling. Golden light poured in through the sheers and filled the room.

He was exhausted. His eyes were swollen, his hands sore, and his side ached with each breath which meant his ribs were either bruised or cracked. It must have been a tough fight. Who had he fought? Had he won? He tried to remember, but his mind was blank.

"Cindy, you awake?" He lightly touched the other side of the bed and found it empty. It was probably good she was up. Nothing annoyed her more than being abruptly awakened by being asked if she was awake. *I am now* was her familiar retort. He smiled.

The bathroom door was open, and from where he lay, he could see she wasn't in there. Maybe she was downstairs preparing breakfast. He thought he smelled bacon.

He sat up. A framed wedding photograph on the wall looked unfamiliar. And there were other photos of people he didn't recognize. He couldn't identify a single face. Had he and Cindy spent the night with some friends after the fight?

He studied his hands. They weren't bruised. He pulled the sheets back. No bruises on his body. He got out of bed and walked to the bathroom and studied his face in the mirror. His eyes were puffy but not swollen the way they were after ten rounds.

The sliding door to the balcony was cracked, and the scent of pine drifted in on the cool air. He walked over to it and slid it open. He looked out over a small valley with a grove of aspens. Thin gray trunks lifted a burst of yellow, gold, and red skyward. The early morning sun glistened on the turning leaves wet from last night's rain. This definitely wasn't the South Valley. It looked like Cedar Crest, a village east of Albuquerque. The sight was breathtaking, but it left him sad and alone which was odd, because he loved the mountains. Cindy needed to see this. He called her name, but she didn't answer.

Luke walked back inside and grabbed his pants draped over a chair and put them on. He walked to the bedroom door and opened it. A jeep in the front driveway pulled out into the street and left. A man he didn't recognize was behind the wheel.

"Cindy." He stepped down the wooden stairs and nearly slipped. He steadied himself with the handrail as he descended. As he reached the bottom, he surveyed the first floor. Great room, formal dining room, and kitchen. No bacon on the grill. It was totally unlike her to leave without letting him know.

A note lay on the kitchen counter. *Make yourself at home. See you later today. Dan.* Who was Dan?

Luke felt like a boat that had lost its mooring and was drifting out to sea. He needed to find Cindy. She would know why they were in Dan's house, whoever he was, and why everything felt strange. A newspaper, folded in half, lay on top of a shiny metal trash can in the corner of the kitchen. Luke walked over and picked it up.

He glanced at the headlines. *Pastor's wife killed in FBI rescue.* Something about it was disturbingly familiar. The first sentence of the article stopped him cold. *The FBI's daring rescue of Pastor Luke Chavez...* The headlines rushed at him like a flash flood shooting through an arroyo. There was nowhere to run. No escape.

The room spun as he struggled to catch his breath. And then he remembered. He sank to the floor and buried his head in his hands and sobbed. Cindy had died in his arms. Murdered. He shook his head. "No, no, no."

Why didn't you save her, God? Or at least let me die with her?

The scripture said *God makes all things work together for good*, but nothing could convince him that anything would ever be better because of her death.

The glint of morning light danced off a gun cabinet's glass panels. The case stood against a wall behind a long dark dining table. Luke stared at the rifles. He stood up and walked to the cabinet and tried the door. It was locked. He reached on top of the case and found a key and opened it. A sharp smell of solvent mixed with oil wafted out.

The gun felt heavier than it looked. Luke pulled the bolt back. There was a shell in the chamber. He shut the chamber and sat down at the dining room table and laid the gun across his lap. He stared at the bluish black barrel extending from the brown stock.

He lifted the gun and positioned the end of the barrel in his mouth. His thumb rested on the trigger. He was glad no one was around to try and change his mind. They wouldn't understand. How could they?

Forgive me, Father. He closed his eyes and pushed against the curved metal.

"Luke."

He froze. The voice was unmistakable. He put the gun down and studied the room.

"Cindy?"

The room was silent.

"Cindy?"

The only sound was a cricket's chirp. Was he losing his mind? But he was certain Cindy had called his name. A trace of rose, her perfume, permeated the air. She was here.

He slumped back in the chair and laid the rifle on the table.

He wiped his wet eyes. "I'm sorry, honey. I can't live without you."

The words were barely a whisper. "I know you're in terrible pain and believe it will never end. But it will. I miss you too, but we'll see each other again. Now go on and finish what God has given you. I love you."

The voice was as clear and sweet as any he had ever heard.

CHAPTER FIFTY

Fort Detrick, September 22

The squirming Leviathan virus looked like an octopus gliding through dark waters as it moved with the efficiency of a single-minded killer. Its focus—a group of T-cells. Jenny peered through the optical microscope and watched with trepidation.

PJ walked into the adjacent lab and tapped on the window separating them. She turned to see him balancing two cups of tea in one hand. "Any success?"

"We're about to find out." The wireless receiver in Jenny's hazmat suit transmitted her voice through speakers in the room where PJ stood. Thank God for him. His easy-going ways and quirky jokes eased some of the strain. But the pressure to find a vaccine to stop Leviathan was wearing her out.

The subterranean community of four-hundred researchers had spent the last several weeks working 24-hours a day. The virus' mutation into an airborne killer had electrified everyone in the cave with an urgency that could only be described as desperate. No one had to explain what the stakes were.

The culmination was the development of a precursor to a vaccine. The first step in creating a vaccine was to stop the virus' ability to destroy T and B-cells, the body's antibodies. But before a vaccine could destroy Leviathan, its nano machines had to be destroyed.

The stage-one antiviral harnessed the same nanotechnology embedded in the pathogen. Like the virus nano machines, the antiviral used molecular bots. The difference was that their purpose was to defend, not destroy, the antibodies the body employed to fight off a virus. It was the nascent vaccine's first test, and everyone, with the exception of possibly Jordan, had their fingers crossed that the reinforced T-cells would be able to withstand the virus' onslaught. Jenny pressed her eyes tightly against the microscope's eyepieces as the killing machines penetrated the virus' protein shell and headed directly for a group of orb-shaped T-cells. Leviathan's nano machines were a connection of tiny circular saws designed to destroy the antibodies by slicing through the outer shell and then shredding the DNA.

Molecular technology was still an emerging science and although its machines were crude when compared to the sophisticated equipment of modern manufacturing, they were still proficient at completing their objectives. The nanobots built to stop the invaders were nothing more than a series of gears that looked much like those in an automobile transmission. Their one and only purpose was to sacrifice themselves by smashing into the saws and destroy their effectiveness.

The door to the decontamination room opened, and PJ walked in, clad in his protective suit. "What's it doing?" He was as anxious as a kid on Christmas morning.

"Have a look." Jenny pointed toward the microscope.

PJ sat down and bent over the microscope. He shook his head.

"What's wrong?"

He stood up and stumbled. Jenny grabbed him as he was about to fall. "You okay? Come over here and sit down." She helped him toward a metal chair in the lab.

PJ sat down and looked up at her. "Thanks."

"What happened?" The face staring back through the protective shield sent a shiver through her.

"I must have stood up too soon. I'm a little light-headed." He shook his head again as if he was trying to clear it. "We've got a problem. The antiviral didn't work."

"Have you been feeling okay lately?"

"Just tired and achy."

"For how long?"

"Didn't you hear what I said? The virus' machines sliced through our nanobots like they were tissue paper."

"Where did you go today besides the cafe?"

"Why all the questions?"

The drop of blood clinging to the corner of PJ's blood-shot eye dropped onto his cheek. He didn't seem to notice. Jenny touched his shoulder and stared down at him. "I think you might be infected."

His eyes widened and voice trembled. "Infected? How could I be? I've been very careful. No mistakes."

It was true. PJ had followed the strictest protocol. He'd always worn his hazmat suit when handling the virus and copiously followed all decontamination procedures. Her mind jumped to a frightening thought—perhaps the breach hadn't occurred in their lab. Perhaps PJ had been infected by someone else in the cave. The thought made her queasy. She clung to a fading hope that the symptoms weren't from the virus.

"Let's get to the decontamination room," Jenny said pointing toward the door.

PJ stood up still wobbly and walked toward the other room.

Once inside Jenny and PJ stepped into two separate booths with multiple nozzles that sprayed their suits from top to bottom with a chemical bath designed to kill any pathogens.

"You're going to have to remain in your suit until I can call the hospital and see if your chip has detected any sign of infection."

PJ's eyes pleaded with her. "Why are you so certain I'm infected?"

Jenny took his gloved hand in hers. "I'm not certain about anything. And I pray to God you're not, but your capillaries are beginning to rupture."

PJ turned and found the mirror on the wall and stared into it. He dropped his head and grabbed his helmet with both hands. "I don't want to die. Not like this."

Her eyes clouded. She couldn't lose PJ, her one friend below the surface. The thought of witnessing him die such a horrible death quickened her breathing. She had observed the gruesome death too many times in her lab animals. And if PJ was infected, it meant the entire sub complex was compromised and everyone was in danger.

She started to remove her suit, then stopped. *What if the virus is airborne?* She zipped her suit back up, left PJ in the decontamination room and walked into the adjacent lab room. She picked up the phone on her desk. Her hand was shaking as she pushed the button connecting her to the complex hospital. The line was busy. She tried again but couldn't get through.

The door to her lab swung open. A man in a hazmat suit stood at the doorway with a frightened look.

CHAPTER FIFTY-ONE

Holloman Sanctuary, September 22

T he thick, sticky blob of blood on the sandal Hank held in his hand had darkened to black by the time he reached the sanctuary hospital. His bare right foot felt as if he had walked across live coals. He had fought the impulse to wipe the disgusting stuff off because he thought a doctor might want to see it.

The hospital was a two-story building about a mile from the recreation hall. A blast of cold air hit Hank as he pushed open the door. Gleaming, buffed floors stretched before him reflecting the sandal that dangled from his hand. Antiseptic permeated the air.

"What's that?" The receptionist behind the desk scooted her chair back.

"That's what I'd like to know," Hank said holding the sandal with its specimen gingerly between his thumb and forefinger. "Do you have a doctor or someone who can take a look at it?"

"Is that yours?" The woman covered her mouth as she scooted farther backward.

"The sandal is but not the blob. It's from a new detainee who may be really sick."

"Wait here." She hurried from her desk down a hallway.

A few minutes later a short, bald man in glasses emerged from the hallway. The nurse frowned and pointed at Hank.

"Let's take a look at that over here," the doctor said motioning toward a door off the hallway.

Hank followed the doctor into an examination room.

"I'm Dr. Lutz."

"Hank." He extended his hand, but the doctor didn't reciprocate.

He put on gloves and a mask and took the sandal from Hank and laid it on a counter. He swabbed a piece of the snot and smeared it on a slide and slid it in under a microscope. "I won't be able to tell much without having it tested, but I can get a rough idea." He stared down into the microscope.

"Shouldn't you take a look at the guy who coughed this up?"

The doctor didn't say anything which made Hank feel uneasy. "I hope it isn't TB."

The doctor looked up. "It's possible, but TB is fairly rare in the U.S. I need to send it to a lab. Where is the person this belongs to?" He held up the swab.

"Over at the recreation center. Do you think it's infectious?" Hank asked.

"I don't know, but it's serious. The sample looks like it contains lung tissue."

There was a knock at the door. Lutz opened it, and a pretty nurse with long dark hair stood at the door.

Hank smiled, but she ignored him.

She stared at the swab and scrunched her nose as if she smelled something rancid. Hank sniffed but couldn't detect anything.

"I'm sorry. I didn't know it was occupied," she said.

"No problem," Lutz said. "We're about to leave."

She closed the door.

Hank looked at his sandal.

"Let me wipe it off for you." Lutz removed the glob and placed it in a metal container, then scrubbed the sandal with antiseptic.

Hank reluctantly took the sandal, questioning the wisdom of putting it back on.

Lutz motioned toward the door. He grabbed a baseball cap sitting on the counter. "Let's take a ride over to the rec center. I need you to identify him."

Five minutes later, Hank and Lutz walked into the center. A basketball game was under way between out-of-shape middle-aged men. Hank scanned the crowd for any sign of Tom. "I don't see him, Doc." Hank walked over to a group of kids seated in the bleachers and described Tom's features to them, but they couldn't remember anyone fitting the description.

"Where else do you think he could be?" Lutz asked.

Hank held up his hands. "I don't know, maybe the cafeteria."

"I'll give you a lift over there."

After another five-minute drive, Hank and Lutz arrived at the mess hall.

"I'll let you know if I see him," Hank said climbing out of the jeep.

"I'll be waiting." Lutz spun the jeep around toward the hospital and left.

Hank walked into the cafeteria. It was four o'clock, and a half dozen workers were preparing dinner.

"Anyone seen a tall, skinny kid with dark hair? He's new. Just arrived today."

"Yeah," one of the workers said. "He didn't look so good."

"Where is he?"

He shook his head.

"Thanks."

Now where?

Hank left the cafeteria and cut across an air strip toward the athletic field. Several people were gathered in stands around the field watching a small group of boys battle for a soccer ball. The adults outnumbered the kids ten to one. Some had probably come because they missed their own children; some because they needed to forget where they were if only for a few minutes.

Hank began on the west side of the field closest to him, methodically walking down the sideline looking up into the bleachers at each person. Occasionally he stopped and asked if anyone had seen Tom. Some thought they remembered seeing him while others seemed agitated by the question.

Hank arched his back. He pulled his soaked t-shirt away from his body. A rare cool breeze tingled across his wet skin. Dark clouds over the Sacramento mountains promised a gully washer. In the distance a dust devil danced across the dry plain as several birds circled high in the sky.

CHAPTER FIFTY-TWO

Fort Detrick, September 22

Multiple red lights flashed on a large digitized map that covered an entire wall. Each blinking light indicated the location and identification of an infected employee within the sub complex, according to the hospital's director who stared white-faced through the hazmat hood at the map.

"This is where we monitor the status of every chip implanted in the five hundred people working here," Dr. Greenwood said.

Which light was PJ's? Jenny thought.

"When the board started flashing, I thought it was a malfunction," Greenwood said. Pale blue eyes, overly enlarged by thick lenses, darted between Jenny and the wall as if checking for the addition of any new lights.

Jenny, clad in her hazmat suit, studied the map and tried to count the number of flickering lights, but there were too many. One would have been enough of a nightmare, but this was Armageddon.

"Then my phone started ringing. The infected wanted me to tell them not to worry, that there was some other explanation for the symptoms they were describing." He hung his head. "But they knew."

They all knew. Despite the intense efforts of every scientist to develop a cure, there wasn't one. And now with everyone worried about survival, research would grind to a halt. There weren't enough hazmat suits to protect everyone, especially the support people who cooked the meals and kept the facility running. Without one, a horrible death was a certainty. Even with one, there was no guarantee of survival.

"Have you notified Carrington at HHS?" Jenny said.

"We were hoping for a solution before..."

Jenny shook her head. "What do you mean solution? There isn't a solution. If one person gets to the surface infected with this virus, it's all over. You know protocol. Give me the phone. I'll call Carrington myself. Wait, who's we?"

Greenwood's eyes shifted toward the door. Jenny spun around and gasped.

"I knew you'd screw everything up." Sullivan stood at the doorway without a hazmat suit. He crossed his arms and flexed his tanned biceps.

"What are you doing here? You're not allowed in this complex," Jenny said. "Dr. Greenwood, get security."

Sullivan glared at Greenwood as he pressed himself against the wall.

"Neither were you." Sullivan said. "But it didn't stop you."

Jordan must have let Sullivan in. What a fool. She picked up the phone, but he walked over and ripped the line from the wall.

"Won't be needing this." His gray eyes flashed.

"Have you completely lost your mind?"

Sullivan leaned into her face shield. "This is my operation now. I'm locking the entire facility down. No one leaves."

She could feel the heat rising in her face. "You can't keep the outbreak a secret. What will companies think when their delivery employees don't return to the surface? Or what about the support service workers like the kitchen staff who rotate every two weeks? Their families will be screaming for answers."

Sullivan smiled. "It won't matter."

"Why not?"

He turned toward Greenwood and grinned. "We're going to have a little trial down here like the one they're planning for me on top. Only true justice will prevail down here. Not some kangaroo court. And guess who's on trial?"

Jenny's heart raced as she struggled to process what was happening. She took a deep breath, but the air in her hood seemed restricted.

"Dr. George's assistant was the first infection reported. Isn't that right, Dr. Greenwood?"

The scientist lowered his eyes. "That's correct."

"PJ was infected by someone else," Jenny said.

Greenwood kept his focus on the floor.

"You brought him down here," Sullivan said. "You were responsible for him. It was your incompetence that resulted in his infection. You compromised the entire facility."

"That's a total fabrication."

But it didn't matter what the truth was. There had only been one law down here and it was Sullivan's. He had created an underground world scrubbed of any trace of life above. The long-term commitments required had turned most of the staff into automatons including Greenwood.

"So you see, Dr. George, you're guilty. And the guilty must be punished. We'll get to that in a moment. But I'm curious what a principled woman like yourself would do in the situation we have here. Should we let the infected die gruesome deaths or put them out of their misery?"

Jenny was having trouble breathing. She shook her head. She wasn't going to play Sullivan's game.

"Nah, people like you can never make tough calls. Everyone knows the right decision is to put the infected out of their anguish. You wouldn't let an animal suffer, but you would a human being. Well, I've never been afraid to do what's right. Creating Leviathan was the right thing. It would have restored us as a superpower, made the world safer. Instead, we're a pathetic has-been."

Jordan poked his head in the doorway. A smug look filled his hood.

"Anyone infected will be terminated immediately," Sullivan said. "Take care of it."

Jordan nodded and left.

How would he do it? An injection or a bullet? She shuddered. Images of PJ's dark eyes weeping blood invaded Jenny's mind. She had stopped by to check on him before her meeting with Dr. Greenwood. From behind the plastic tent surrounding his hospital bed, he silently pleaded for an end to his suffering. But Sullivan's plan wasn't driven by compassion. He didn't have a merciful bone in his body.

"My plan offers the best chance of survival for the living. Even the Jews understood that you can't keep an infected person in your own camp. Once we're certain that the outbreak has been contained, we can resume our work."

"Resume work? If the virus is airborne in this cave, everyone will eventually die unless we can find a way to get survivors to the surface without releasing the virus."

A horrified expression twisted Greenwood's face.

Sullivan smiled. The same crazy look from earlier. Then it hit her. He had no intent of surviving or letting anyone else. That was why he wasn't in a suit. In his twisted mind, he didn't have anything left to live for. A court martial waited for him above. Everything important to him was here in this godforsaken hole.

"Now back to your punishment, Dr. George. What would be appropriate?"

A face she had hoped to never see again walked up from behind Sullivan.

CHAPTER FIFTY-THREE

Holloman Sanctuary, September 23

A horde of black birds circled in the distance. Hank watched them glide effortlessly on the thermals, like a merry-go-round of death. He stood at the edge of a concrete runway. Black skid marks stretched in front of him, evidence of the F22s that had once used the two-and-a-half mile landing strip.

All of his efforts to find Tom had been a bust. Either no one had seen him or only vaguely remembered him. Why couldn't he have had some unforgettable peculiarity like an orange-colored Mohawk? Perhaps it was time to turn back and retrace his efforts, but the only place Hank hadn't searched was the eastern perimeter of the sanctuary, where the birds were.

The eastern fence was farther than it looked. It took an hour to reach. Temperatures had dropped into the high 80s, but it was still record heat for September, and the acres of concrete and asphalt made it feel at least ten degrees hotter.

The birds spiraled down and landed near the fence. They stood silently near a thick clump of brown tumbleweeds pinned against the steel fence like insects caught in a sticky web. A large, black bird cocked its pink, wrinkled head and warily eyed Hank as he approached. He bent down and picked up two rocks and hurled one at the bird closest to him but missed. It spread its six-foot wings, flapped enough to briefly lift into the air, then dropped down. The others kept a safer distance.

Hank raised the other rock. "Get out of here." It backed off a few feet but refused to leave. And then he saw what the birds were protecting. A vein in his neck throbbed. Two green Converse athletic shoes stuck out from under the tumbleweeds.

As an up-and-coming reporter, he had covered many homicides. He had hated it, the metallic smell of blood, the vacant eyes of the victims, the morbid humor of cops. But dead eyes were the worst. He knew they were fixed on nothingness, but it still felt like they were watching him.

Hank pulled the surgical mask and gloves Dr. Lutz had given him from his pocket and put them on. He crouched down and raked the weeds away. The vulture backed off indignantly but stayed close enough to pounce at the first opportunity. The man was curled up on his side. Hank rolled him over onto his back.

His breakfast shot upward as he struggled to remove his mask. He leaned over and vomited. It was Tom. A dark liquid sheet covered him and oozed from his mouth, nose, and the corners of his eyes.

Hank stood up on wobbly legs. Whatever the young man had been sick with was deadly. Tuberculosis didn't do this. The large scavenger stepped eagerly toward Tom. Hank threw a rock, this time striking it on its side. It stretched its neck, let out a low, guttural cry, flapped its wings and swept dirt toward him and the body. But it didn't leave.

Hank looked back at the corpse. He didn't want to leave it here, but there seemed little else he could do. He backed away from the body keeping his eye on the vultures staring at him. Something grabbed his ankle.

A jolt of adrenaline shot through him. "Ugh." The cry startled the vultures. A swoosh of black wings lifted them into the air as quickly as if an uninvited cougar had arrived for lunch.

Hank looked down and shuddered. Tom's hand was clamped around his ankle. He opened his mouth and struggled to stretch the corners upward. Was he trying to smile? His teeth were red.

"You're all going to..." he coughed up a dark mass and tore at his chest, ripping his t-shirt. "Die. You're going to die..." A gurgling laugh. "Like me."

An icy shudder shook Hank.

Tom closed his eyes and strained two wheezy words, "Allah akbar."

Then the hand clenched around Hank's ankle went slack.

Hank's heart sank. A bloody imprint encircled his ankle.

CHAPTER FIFTY-FOUR

Fort Detrick, September 23

The dead were laid on top of each other like crushed cars in a salvage yard. Two rows of five piled six high separated in the middle by a path barely wide enough to slide through. Sixty brilliant men and women, many of whom Jenny recognized despite their ghastly twisted countenances, stacked like lumber. Jenny turned away and pressed herself tighter into the corner of the make-shift morgue Neanderthal man had thrown her into. She tried to put as much distance as she could between herself and them, but what difference did it make? She was locked in a room crawling with a virus, which in a matter of hours, would reduce her to one of them.

Had any of them realized when the nurse inserted the needle into their arm that it wasn't morphine but a fatal cocktail of sodium thiopental and potassium chloride, that they were being culled? Judging from the expressions, it appeared a few had. And what about PJ? She dared not glance through the stack. The thought of her friend packed away somewhere in here was more than she could bear.

Oh, God, don't let me die like this. She brushed at her eyes. Her hands trembled and teeth chattered. The heat had been cut to the room leaving it a cool 55-degrees, the constant temperature 100-feet below ground level. She tucked her head against her chest and wrapped her arms tightly around her knees and tried to control the shaking while a tornado of emotions swirled inside.

What could she have done differently? Refused Dr. Carrington's request? She had strong reservations about coming back to the cave, perhaps a premonition. Had she not taken the job, PJ wouldn't be dying or dead and she facing a similar fate.

But how could she have refused? She was responsible for the virus falling into terrorist hands. And even though Leviathan was a terrible pathogen, it was still the most fascinating virus she or any virologist had ever encountered. Taking the assignment was the right thing to do. It would have made Dad proud. *I miss you.* The virus was the greatest threat the country had ever faced according to the President and he was right. The country was on the brink of a war with a monster raging through the cave like a ravenous bear awakened from hibernation.

Her hands itched. Not a good sign. She glanced at Dr. Cacciotti, one of the most gifted immunologists she had ever known. One of her few friends, besides PJ, that she had been able to trust. He lay on top of a heap. Blood oozed from his colorless palm that hung to one side. A putrid odor laced the thin air.

Sullivan hadn't bothered to embalm any of the dead not that it mattered much. Infected cells, like all cells, died soon after the victim's heart stopped. But pox spores could survive for days, particularly in clothing, which meant the air was thick with them. Burning the bodies or stripping them of their clothing and spraying them with a decontaminant would have been much more effective. Even bagging the dead would be better than this.

But Sullivan didn't care. He still blamed her for stealing the virus. And perhaps she had been wrong to interfere. Nothing had turned out right. But if she hadn't stumbled into the discovery, Sullivan would have unchained it one day, and, like now, there wouldn't be anywhere to hide.

The cave had disintegrated into hysterics, and everyone was searching for a scapegoat. The idea that her carelessness had created the outbreak was ludicrous. But Sullivan had successfully pinned the outbreak on her. Even highly intelligent people thought irrationally in such times.

It was possible someone had breached protocol or made a mistake, but she doubted it. Everyone knew how lethal the virus was. No, the outbreak must have occurred because Leviathan had evolved into a new form. Viruses had no intelligence. They were programmed to perform a certain way, but this one seemed almost sentient—like it understood the only way to fulfill its potential was to become untethered, to disperse its infectious spores into the air in search of new victims. She imagined it scouring every exit in the cave looking for a way to the surface.

The room's only window was located in the door. It was fogged because the bodies at the top of the stack were still warm. Jenny studied the door handle. Even though the virus was probably swimming through her veins, she longed to be free. *If only there was some way.* She looked back at Dr. Cacciotti. This lab used to be his. Would Sullivan have thoroughly searched the contents of the scientist's pockets?

Jenny stood up. Her knees were stiff from the cold. She walked over to the stack of bodies and tried to avoid looking at their faces or touching them. She stretched her hand up as far as it would go toward Dr. Cacciotti's pocket, but she was too short and the pile too high. She stood back and studied the corpses. The idea repulsed her, but there wasn't any other way. She grabbed the shoulder of a man below Dr. Cacciotti she didn't recognize and reluctantly placed her foot on a woman she didn't know and began to climb. The stiff body provided a strong footing.

As she reached Dr. Cacciotti, she tried sliding her hand into his pocket but the angle made it difficult. She stepped up onto another corpse, which put her chest high with the immunologist. Her head brushed against the room's ten-foot ceiling. She couldn't look at him as she reached into his left pocket. Pocket change, a good sign. She reached across toward his right pocket. Empty. Her pulse quickened.

The thought of turning him over and checking for a wallet seemed treacherous, and the card key was thick enough that it made its placement in a billfold unlikely. Where could it be?

Jenny's right foot slipped on something slick. Her right leg shot out. She grabbed Dr. Cacciotti's arm. But the sudden jerk dislodged the tall man from his perch. She plunged downward like a mountain climber whose anchor had failed. The dead man's opaque eyes pursued her. Her feet reached for the floor, but it was missing.

Her back slammed into an unforgiving surface with the dead man on top of her.

"Ugh." The impact forced the air from her lungs.

"Help." The cry was pointless. Only the dead were here. She struggled to free herself but she was pinned between a dead man's stiff arms. Her own arms weren't responding. She tried again and with a herculean effort pushed the body up and off. She stood up and frantically brushed at her slacks and blouse as if the process could somehow rid her of the virus.

A transparent cobalt card lay on the floor. She reached down and picked it up. Dr. Cacciotti's key. She didn't care where it had come from, only that it was in her hand. She walked to the door and inserted the card and waited for a click.

CHAPTER FIFTY-FIVE

Washington, D.C., September 23

"I received a call from Dr. Jordan today. He said Dr. George asked him to relay a message that they're making progress." Hamilton frowned. "It struck me as strange."

Pepper looked up from his computer tablet.

"I asked Dr. George to call me directly with updates, which she has always done. Very unlike her to ask someone else to do it. So I placed a call directly to Dr. George. I still haven't heard back." Hamilton sat at his desk in the Oval Office. The warm glow of morning light touched his back.

Pepper slid over on the sofa to avoid the glare of morning light. "Dr. Jordan was Sullivan's right hand man." Pepper wiped his glasses with a cloth.

"I hope we don't have a problem down there."

"You think Dr. Jordan may be covering up something?" Pepper stared at Hamilton.

Was Pepper trying to make a point about allegations against the President? "I don't know."

"What if there has been an accident?"

Dark circles underscored Pepper's eyes. He wasn't sleeping much. Hamilton opened a desk drawer and pulled out a small, orange bottle. "Try one of these." He set the bottle on his desk and pushed it toward his Chief of Staff.

"What are they?"

"Ambien. The next best thing for someone who doesn't smoke or drink."

Pepper eyed the pills but didn't get up. "We need to get someone down there to investigate as soon as possible."

Hamilton frowned. "An outbreak is unlikely. They have systems to prevent that."

"I understand. But what if the unthinkable happened? Don't you think it's wise to at least check it out?"

"Okay, let's assume you're right. If Leviathan is loose down there, and it's as lethal as everyone says it is, then everyone is probably dead anyway. Might be better not to open Pandora's box."

Pepper shook his head. "We need their research."

"Can't we just access their system?"

"Unfortunately not. Sullivan built a stand-alone network. He didn't want anyone discovering his operation or stealing his prize. The Army knew about the lab because they secretly funded it. But they deny it.

"We've got to find out what's happened and get their data," Pepper said. "Creating a vaccine is vital to the nation. Heck, to the world. We've been lucky so far. The terrorists have been silent and Operation First Alert hasn't detected any outbreak. But we're on borrowed time."

Everyone was on borrowed time. Hamilton glanced back at the headlines of the newspaper lying next to Pepper. *Judiciary Committee Votes for Impeachment.* The House would vote on impeachment in the next few days, and from there it would move to the Senate for debate. The CIA director's testimony had given the press the silver bullet they were searching for. They had been relentless since Tingley's disclosure.

"All right. Send a team down. But make sure they understand there is no margin for error. None. If there's been an outbreak, I don't want them bringing the virus back with them."

Pepper nodded as he typed something on his tablet. He looked up and pointed toward the newspaper. "We're still okay. We've got enough votes in the Senate if it goes that far." He coughed. "At least for now."

Hamilton grunted. "The only thing that will stop it getting to the Senate is if Jesus Christ returns."

Pepper sat back in the sofa and strained a grin. "That would do it."

Hamilton leaned back in his chair and clasped his hands behind his head. "Or the virus gets loose."

CHAPTER FIFTY-SIX

Fort Detrick Underground Complex, September 23

The tingle in the back of Jenny's hand stopped her from pushing the door open. She looked down at the veins threaded underneath her near translucent skin. Embedded among them was a chip that could track her every move. What was she thinking? One foot outside of the former lab room and Sullivan would know she had escaped. She had to remove the chip.

She pulled a small Swiss utility knife from her pocket and fumbled with opening its sharpest blade. She pressed the metal edge into her hand. A thin line of blood flowed from the incision and thickened as she pushed her thumb against the narrow end of the chip. She tried forcing it out through the opening the way she had as a kid when she had a splinter. But it wouldn't budge. The chip was embedded too deeply. She held her breath and cut deeper until the tip of the knife was under the tiny device. With a flick of the blade, a small clear cylinder popped out. It was twice the length and width of a grain of rice and slick with blood.

Something touched her leg. She jumped back. An arm protruded from the mound of bodies like a broken branch hanging from a tree. It must have sprung loose during Dr. Cacciotti's fall. A glint of yellow gold shined on the blood-stained hand. The hammered metal with a solitaire ruby was unmistakable. It was PJ's. She cupped her mouth to mute the terror trying to escape, threw the chip on the floor between the rows of the dead, and ran for the door.

The key card shook in her hand as she tried to insert in into the slot in the door. Drops of blood from her cut fell to the tile. She stepped on the spots and ground them into the floor as if somehow she could make them disappear. If only she could make it all disappear—the blood, the dead, and the virus. But all she did was smear a swatch of red across the floor.

The card slipped into the door, and it clicked open. She exited the morgue into the adjacent decontamination room and hurriedly opened a drawer and removed antiseptic and gauze. Red foam bubbled from the antiseptic she poured on her cut. She scrubbed her hand until it was raw and wrapped it. What was she doing? Cleaning a wound teeming with virus was pointless. As pointless as trying to escape. She knew she couldn't outrun Leviathan but something was driving her.

Hazmat suits hung on the wall. She grabbed one and slipped into it. From the closet next to the suit, she retrieved an external air filtration system. She strapped on the pack and glanced in a mirror to make certain everything was connected properly. The face staring back startled her. Even though the hood helped obscure her identity, it wasn't sufficient to ensure she wouldn't be recognized. She ran back into the room and searched for a pair of glasses. A pair set cock-eyed on one of the dead. Jenny cringed as she removed the glasses and put them on. The room was blurry, but at least her odds of not being recognized had improved. As she approached the door to the outer room, her skin tingled again. This time the hazmat suit would shield her against an enemy just as deadly as Leviathan.

The hallway was empty, the lab rooms she passed vacant. Where had Sullivan herded the survivors? After negotiating several more corridors, she entered the last hall before the exit. A guard stood in front of another lab. She dipped her hood and hoped he wouldn't acknowledge her. As she walked past she waited for him to seize her, but he didn't. What was he guarding? She turned back to look. The guard glared at her. Behind the plate glass was the old scientist who had helped her escape, and Fred in maintenance, along with several others. The coalition against Leviathan. Had Sullivan connected them to her? A pang of guilt tore at her conscience. If only she could help them, but she kept moving.

Outside the research lab, the complex was deserted. It was too quiet, and the overhead lights were brighter than normal. She scanned the road and light rail tracks in front of her and the surrounding buildings expecting Sullivan's men to appear at any moment. She hadn't really formulated a plan on how to escape. When the remaining minutes of life could be counted, planning for much in advance seemed a waste. But now the daunting prospect of outmaneuvering Sullivan lay before her.

The closest elevators and emergency exit, a staircase, were about a half-mile away. The other elevators, the ones she had used to escape before, were located on the opposite side of the facility, too far to even consider. The task of walking a half-mile wouldn't be so bad if she wasn't encumbered in a protective suit designed for short trips. And she would be an open target.

Perhaps the jeep parked near the adjacent building could provide help. The keys were in the ignition. She could reach the elevators in minutes, but even the silence of an electric engine wouldn't be enough to avoid detection. She looked back toward the building she had just exited. Moving behind the rear of the buildings would provide cover. They stretched nearly to the elevators. She crouched and ran.

It took several minutes to reach the edge of the last building. A man in a hazmat suit stood in front of the elevators holding an M-16. The hum of a jeep's tires against pavement approached. It came to a silent stop in front of the guard. Six men, all wearing protective gear, got out. One of them was larger than the rest. Probably the Neanderthal creep. They all carried automatic rifles. Another jeep rolled to a stop. Sullivan. He got out and pointed toward the side-by-side elevators, one for passengers and the other for freight, and to the emergency exit nearby.

What were they preparing for? A revolt? No one would be crazy enough to try to escape against that firing squad. Jenny leaned against a building. There was no way out. Nothing she could do but wait for the end. Her legs felt weak.

The soldiers positioned themselves around the exits with guns pointed toward the doors. Sullivan crossed his arms, seemingly satisfied with the placement of his men. Was someone coming?

The General turned toward her direction and stared. She moved back against the building. He motioned for his men to stay put as he walked in her direction. He was coming. Her heart pounded with such force that it was difficult to hear anything else. But the crunch of gravel around the corner was too distinct to miss.

There was an exit door in the building next to her. She ran toward it and turned the knob hard enough to tear it off, but it didn't budge. Locked, like everything in the cave. She ran down between two buildings and looked over her shoulder. Sullivan turned the corner behind her. As she ran toward the street, she tripped over the curb and tumbled into the road. The soldiers standing at the exits raised their guns. A door to the lab building in front of her opened. She stood and ran, bracing for a barrage of bullets. A man in a protective suit stood at the door stunned as she fled past him. Adrenaline pumped through her as her legs thrust her forward through a maze of hallways.

Two men down the hallway struggled with something heavy. They opened the door to a lab room. She burst through them, knocking the body they carried to the ground. She slammed the door in their face. She backed toward the lab room behind her but it was packed with bodies. The adjoining lab, which still contained test animals, was her only choice. She darted into the room and slammed the door. A monkey shrieked.

Sullivan stood in the hallway and grinned through the window. He slipped his card into the door. She was trapped.

The door to the animal lab opened and Sullivan walked in.

"You wench."

The grin was gone. His mouth twisted into a snarl like a growling dog.

"End of the line."

As she stared into Sullivan's lifeless eyes suddenly it all made sense. "You released the virus. You never wanted to create a vaccine that could destroy your baby."

"I never released it. I didn't have to. From the beginning I knew Leviathan was special. It was never some mindless virus like the others. It's intelligent. And it knows why you're here."

"You're insane."

The back of Sullivan's hand slammed against the side of her hood knocking her to the floor. The monkeys screamed and shook their cages. He hauled her up and ripped her helmet off. He wrapped his hands around her neck and bore down on her, pinning her shoulders against the metal countertop, as he tightened his grip. She kicked and beat her fists against him, but it only encouraged him to squeeze harder. His eyes bulged. Her hand reached for the counter to her right. She grabbed something, and with one last effort, thrust it at him.

The crushing pressure around her throat released. She slumped to the floor gasping for air. Sullivan staggered backwards, his right hand groping furiously behind his head as if he had an uncontrollable itch. His face compressed into a mask of pain. His legs struggled to maintain balance. He snorted and pulled something out and swung his right hand forward. The grimace on his face disappeared into astonishment at what he held in his hand—a hypodermic needle.

Then Sullivan fell face forward. Jenny closed her eyes as boots approached.

CHAPTER FIFTY-SEVEN

Holloman Sanctuary, September 30

D r. Lutz leaned forward on his gray, metal desk and stared at the report. His face was grim. The papers clenched in his right hand shook slightly.

"What does it say?" Hank pointed at the report as he stood in front of the doctor's desk.

The top of Lutz's desk was empty except for a stack of papers pushed to one side, a small cactus in a simple clay pot with a yellow bloom that sat on the opposite end, and his phone. The strain of the last twenty-four hours had manifested itself in dark, puffy bags draped under the doctor's dark-rimmed glasses. He laid the report down and looked up. "I don't want you repeating a word."

As a reporter such a request meant the information was off-the-record, not for publication. But Hank hadn't stopped by for an interview. He only wanted to know what had killed Tom and was filling the beds at the hospital at an alarming rate.

Hank swallowed. "You have my word."

"According to the report it's a man-made virus that doesn't exist in nature. Black pox, a deadly form of small pox, was combined with a strain of the avian flu."

The air conditioner overhead was blowing. Hank could feel the air sweep across his face, but it felt hot. "The virus stolen by the terrorists?"

"Yes." Lutz folded his hands as if he wasn't sure what to do with them. "I wish it weren't true."

"Are you certain?"

He nodded.

"Where could he have picked up the virus?"

Lutz scratched his scalp. "I checked with CDC to see if there had been an outbreak anywhere, but there hasn't been."

"Did you tell CDC what happened?"

"He must have been infected when he came here."

"Did you tell CDC about Tom?"

Lutz looked up as if he'd just heard the question. He nodded.

"What are they going to do?"

He looked away. "The sanctuary has been put under a strict quarantine. Nothing goes in or out. Shipments of food, supplies, everything we need to survive will be air dropped until the virus is contained or..." he stumbled, "we're all dead." He opened his desk drawer and removed a tissue and blew his nose. "There are twenty-thousand people on this base, Hank. We don't have a chance. If everyone were chipped, we could isolate the sick and perhaps survive, but without the chips, we have no way of knowing who's sick and who isn't. Until it's too late." He pointed at Hank. "You or I could be infected right now."

The unpleasant thought had been on Hank's mind since being plastered with Tom's blood. Hank rubbed the back of his neck and looked for a chair. He was feeling light-headed. The news was overwhelming. Not only was he going to die, but judging from Tom's death, it would be horrible. His words were haunting. The kid must have known what he was sick with, which meant it wasn't an accident.

Hank sat down. "I think I know where the virus came from." His voice cracked.

Lutz studied Hank.

226

"I didn't share with you what Tom said before he died. He was delusional, and, well, I didn't want to jump to any conclusions. But it makes sense now."

"What did he say?"

"He said we're all going to die. His very last words were *Allah akbar*."

"God is great."

"I think he was a terrorist on a suicide mission. He had the perfect cover to walk in here without any suspicion."

Lutz shook his head. "A terrorist attack here? Why?"

"Radical Islam won't be satisfied until the last Christian and Jew are dead. I wonder if there are any others like him in the sanctuary?"

Lutz looked visibly shaken. "From what I know about the virus one infected person is more than enough to infect everyone. I've got to share what we discovered with Human Health." He reached for the phone on his desk. "The other sanctuaries could be facing similar attacks. There may still be time for them." He grimaced at his own words.

Hank headed for the door, which he wished led straight beyond the sanctuary's walls. He had to find a way out. Remaining here was certain death.

"Not a word about the young man's death." Lutz raised his hand to his lips. "Or his last words. News of this kind will tear the sanctuary apart."

CHAPTER FIFTY-EIGHT

Washington, D.C., October 1

President Hamilton sat at his desk in the Oval Office with cameras positioned in front of him. The lights were hot. Beads of sweat were already forming. He dabbed his forehead with a handkerchief. One of the camera men pointed at him. The words on the teleprompter began to move.

"Fellow Americans, it is with a heavy heart that I address you tonight. I received word today that the virus has broken out in a New Mexico sanctuary. We have quarantined the facility to prevent its escape. Unfortunately, there isn't anything we can do for the poor people inside. We can't risk sending anyone in to rescue them. We're still unsure where the virus came from but haven't ruled out the possibility of a terrorist attack."

"Progress is being made everyday to find an antiviral. Hopefully we'll have one soon. In the meantime I need your support. Our nation is facing the greatest crisis since its founding. As you know, accusations have been made against me by members of Congress. They are false and politically motivated. I need you to call your representatives and tell them you support your President. I must be able to focus on this crisis without having to battle a politically motivated group who care more about their agenda than the crisis facing our nation."

Hamilton finished and thanked Americans for their support.

"Nice job," Pepper said.

Hamilton wiped his forehead as he stood up. "Let's take a walk," he said motioning Pepper toward the door.

They exited through the side door to the Rose Garden. Light poured from the White House windows into the dark garden. The cool evening air energized him. The days were getting shorter and the nights longer.

"When do you think the Senate will vote on impeachment?" Hamilton asked.

Pepper cocked his head. "I don't think it will after tonight's speech. It would be political suicide for any Senator to push for your impeachment with a catastrophe of this magnitude."

The House's vote for impeachment had passed by a slim margin and wouldn't have if it had been delayed a week. The virus was on everyone's mind, and every conversation eventually turned into a discussion about it. In an odd way, the pathogen had become Hamilton's benefactor and might even save his presidency. That's if he could find a cure. If he did, the public would demand that the Senate vote against impeachment. And he would be remembered alongside FDR and Lincoln, as Presidents who preserved the nation in times of great peril.

The thought lifted his spirits. The thick grass felt especially plush, like a deep carpet. Neatly trimmed hedges accented the base of the colonnades that lined the inner courtyard. The roses and tulips were gone, but red, orange, and yellow chrysanthemums peaked through the shadows.

"I'm concerned, Mr. President." Pepper raised his voice to emphasize his point. "People are scared to death. Panic is ripping through our cities. And I'm afraid things will disintegrate even more. Developers are selling shares in underground shelters faster than they can build them. If the virus escapes from the sanctuary..." His words trailed off.

Hamilton reached inside his suit jacket and pulled out a dark Cuban cigar. He ran his fingers down the silky outer wrapper. A complex aroma stimulated his senses as he lit the cigar which he had clipped earlier. A light breeze carried the smoke into Pepper's path.

"Do you think Sulaiman is behind the attack?"

Pepper sidestepped the drifting plume. "What better way to rid the world of infidels than by targeting the sanctuaries, the last stronghold of Christianity. We must not forget that he believes the Mahdi will return when the world is on the brink of disaster. If the virus escapes from the sanctuaries, it will create more destruction than an arsenal of nukes. Everything will collapse. Culture, Art, Science, Banking. Society as we know it will cease to exist. It will set the world back three-hundred years."

"How does that help him if there aren't any Muslims left to worship their Mahdi?"

"I'm sure he believes Allah will protect Muslims. Those who survive the virus who aren't believers will be forced to convert to Islam or suffer beheading."

Hamilton puffed intently on his cigar. "He's declared war on all of us. We've got to stop him."

"So far he's proved very elusive. Until a few months ago, we didn't even know what he looked like. Regardless, our first priority is to develop a successful antiviral. If we can stop the virus, it will be a psychological blow to Sulaiman. And, Mr. President, it's vital that we communicate our efforts to the public. You've seen the polls. The public doesn't have any confidence in our ability to protect them. People are afraid to go to work. Businesses are hurting and Wall Street is frantic. You have to reassure the American people and let them know you'll do everything within your power to protect them."

"Didn't I just do that?" Hamilton growled.

"A weekly address is going to be necessary."

Hamilton inhaled and let the smoke linger in his mouth before exhaling it through his nose. "How is Dr. George?"

"Shaken up but otherwise okay. Ready to get back to work as soon as she's cleared of the virus."

Hamilton grunted. "Still can't believe Sullivan commandeered the complex. Makes me shudder to think what would have happened if Dr. George hadn't stopped him. That's a miracle in itself."

Pepper nodded. "He definitely underestimated her. Maybe we all did."

"Well, thank God, Sullivan's soldiers backed down once they realized he was dead. It could have been a real blood bath. Did we quarantine the survivors?"

"We did and sealed the cave after retrieving the data we needed."

"How many died?"

"More than three-hundred."

"I'm surprised any survived."

"None of them would have if Sullivan hadn't euthanized the infected."

Hamilton removed the cigar from his mouth and stared at Pepper. "Why would he have tried to save anyone since he clearly wanted to die? He wasn't even wearing a suit when our team found him."

"I think he was torn. Half of him clung to the delusion that if an antiviral could be developed, then Leviathan could be used as a weapon. The other half realized it was over."

The General probably never lost any sleep over the villagers sacrificed to create Leviathan. Necessary sacrifices. But Hamilton couldn't rid his memory of the dead faces published in the newspaper. Dr. Samuel Myers, Dr. John Ballard, Dr. Michael Quintana, and Dr. Daniel Chang. They too were sacrificial lambs offered up to protect the country and the presidency. For the first time Hamilton understood how the General's twisted logic had lured him down a path he probably never intended to travel. *Is the same thing happening to me?*

Pepper adjusted his glasses. "My greatest fear is that even as brilliant as Dr. George and her team are, they'll be too late. If this virus escapes from the sanctuaries, we may find ourselves faced with the same decision General Sullivan did."

Hamilton choked on the smoke. "God help us if it ever comes to that."

CHAPTER FIFTY-NINE

Holloman Sanctuary, November 11

The acrid smell of smoke woke Hank. The nonstop pounding of hammers and buzzing of saws that had filled the sanctuary the last several days had stopped. He was so used to the noise that the silence was unsettling. He rose in his bunk and stared at the empty bed next to him. Most of the rooms in the large dormitory were empty. Through the windows the normally crystal blue sky was murky gray. Something was burning.

Hank slipped out of bed, stretched, and opened his window. A foul odor rushed at him, filling his nostrils. He slid the window shut and watched a black plume in the distance twist into the sky and thicken into a dark mass that devoured the sunlight in its path.

He dressed, grabbed the mask and gloves lying on his dresser, put them on, and headed out to investigate. The streets were empty except for recent victims of the virus laid in neat rows along the sides waiting for pickup and burial. With each step toward the distant fire, the smell intensified and with it the memory of a tragic fire he had covered years ago. Burning flesh was difficult to forget.

Thirty minutes later he stood close enough to the roaring flames to singe his eyebrows and confirm his hunch. A shrill warning beeped as a dump truck backed up toward the fire. It stopped at least a hundred feet short of the inferno and raised its bed. A mound of bodies tumbled out. The driver pulled forward and pumped the truck's hydraulics to ensure that nothing clung to the dumpster.

The camp had either run out of lumber for coffins or stopped trying to keep up with the growing demand. But Hank suspected another motive behind the commander's decision to cremate the dead. The urgency to wipe the face of death away as quickly as possible to help the living forget, to give them hope. Everyone knew the disease eating its way through the sanctuary was the virus even though there hadn't been any official statement. Enough news had filtered in to confirm that the killer was the same one everyone feared beyond the sanctuary's walls. The one with no cure.

Several men wearing masks and gloves stood in rows of two behind the mound of bodies. Each team picked up a corpse and carried it as close to the blazing heat as they dared, then tossed the dead into the flames. Then the men returned to the end of the line and waited their turn while the assembly line efficiently moved the bodies, one by one, to their final destination.

The sight strengthened Hank's resolve to escape. Remaining in the sanctuary was a sure ticket to this place, but getting out had proved more difficult than he imagined. The quarantine had been tightened until all obvious cracks had been sealed. But he hadn't given up hope and wasn't above bribing his way out.

Rationing had been in effect for a week. The air drops of food were less frequent. Portions had been reduced by half, but as the number of dead increased, that became less of a concern. If the virus continued its onslaught, there would be plenty to eat and drink, but a dinner partner might be difficult to find.

Hank left the men to their work. He needed to stop by the hospital. Dr. Lutz wanted to run a test on him. Just the mention of a test sent a shiver through him. He had never been phobic about his health, but lately the mere hint of bloodshot eyes or a rash sent him into panic.

The hospital had expanded into the vacant hanger that once housed F-22 bombers. There were too many sick for the main facility. He would stop by the ancillary hospital first to see if Lutz was there. It wasn't difficult to find. All one had to do was look for the white arch invading the horizon. It was the tallest building at the sanctuary and now the most densely occupied.

As Hank walked toward the hanger, a group of men gathered and prayed in the shade of a nearby building, their faces blackened with soot. Members of the cremation crew. He stopped and listened.

"Lord, why are you allowing this terrible disease to kill us? We're your people." The thin man dropped his head and sobbed. His body shook as tears streaked down dark cheeks. Despite Lutz's attempt to protect the virus' origin, most people had figured out it didn't just drop out of the sky. There were lots of theories, but the most common was on the money—a terrorist attack. The disaster had everyone praying, even the handful of teenagers. But not Hank. The only way out of here was by trusting his instincts. His mother had dragged him to church. He even made a commitment when he was twelve to follow Jesus, but upon later examination understood it was his mother's fervor and goading that had whipped him into making such an irrational, emotional decision.

As Hank approached the hanger, he thought he could detect the hint of jet fuel. Inside a sea of beds filled the structure as moans and wails echoed throughout. In the middle of the sick, a glint of light from suspended overhead fluorescents reflected from an oily pate. Dr. Lutz turned as if he sensed Hank's presence and motioned for him to come.

"I'm glad you caught me. I was just about to head over to the main facility. I need to run those tests we talked about."

"You never said why."

"I'm not entirely sure at this point. I'm working on intuition here which is new ground for me."

"What kind of intuition?" Hank's voice skipped up a few notes.

Dr. Lutz paused and stared at the floor as if the question deserved careful consideration. "From what I know about this virus, anyone who has come into contact with a carrier should be infected by now." He looked up and stared at Hank. "You should be dead. You were the first person to come in contact with Tom and that was more than two weeks ago. But you haven't exhibited any symptoms."

Hank felt a sudden tightening in his chest and an urge to cough. Maybe he was infected, or maybe, for some unknown reason, he was able to carry the virus without it turning his organs into mush much like bats could carry rabies. "Where are you headed with this, Doc?"

"I'm not exactly sure. There are others in this camp who have been exposed, and yet for some reason aren't infected. I'm one of them myself. I'm going to send the blood samples to CDC for examination. Perhaps they can tell us."

"Can I give you a letter for Dr. George at CDC to send along with the samples?"

Dr. Lutz's eyebrows arched. "She's coordinating the antiviral team. How do you know her?"

"She helped me break the story on the President's murder."

"That's right. I remember reading it. What's in the letter?"

"Better if you don't know."

Dr. Lutz frowned. "Is she expecting it?"

"No."

"If the wrong person intercepts the letter before Dr. George, we'll both be in a lot of trouble. You know how paranoid the government is these days."

Hank put on his most serious face. "Doc, I wouldn't jeopardize either one of us if I didn't think it was necessary. Please do it."

Dr. Luz hesitated. "All right, but I hope I don't live to regret this."

"How are you going to get the samples through quarantine?"

"The samples will be placed in a biohazard container and lifted out by helicopter."

The thought of stowing away in the vehicle picking up the samples or commandeering it flashed through Hank's mind. Sure, they were stupid ideas, but when one is scraping the bottom, any glimmer of hope, no matter how ridiculous, is better than none.

Dr. Lutz stared at him. "I know you ended up here for very different reasons than the rest of us. But I believe nothing happens by chance. Sometimes God redirects our path, and we end up in a place we never intended. I can't explain it, but I believe your incarceration in this sanctuary wasn't a result of bad luck. It was meant to be."

Lutz's words surprised Hank. Maybe their relationship had moved to a new level, and the doctor saw him more as a friend or confidant. But he didn't buy Lutz's argument of predestination. It wasn't God who sent him here but his association with DW.

But his survival from the virus—that was unexplainable.

CHAPTER SIXTY

Albuquerque, November 20

The heavy bag sagged in the middle from a crunching left hook as it swung violently to the right. Luke shifted his weight to his left and slammed another hook hurling the bag in the opposite direction. He continued his assault with a combination of hooks and uppercuts until he could feel his knuckles inside the gloves begin to peel. In the mirror he saw a small crowd gathered behind him at Anaya's Boxing Club in Albuquerque's South Valley. Larger than life images of local boxing legends, Johnny Tapia and Bob Foster, looked down from the wall on the spectators.

"Ese, he's going to rip the bag in two," a fighter standing behind Luke said to the boxer next to him.

"Vato, have you ever seen anyone hit that hard?" the other fighter said.

The onslaught of Luke's fists produced a rhythmic thudding that filled the gym and shook the ceiling, but as loud as it was, it wasn't enough to silence the angry voices spewing from the small TV in the corner.

"The outbreak in the sanctuaries is God's judgment on Christians," someone shouted.

A reporter positioned the mike toward another man. "We should have forced them to be chipped. Now look at what's happened. This is their fault."

A red-faced woman grabbed the mike and screamed. "Their judgment will be ours if we don't do something."

"What do you think we should do?" the reporter asked.

The crowd yelled, "Destroy the sanctuaries. All of them. Before it's too late."

The reporter turned back toward the screen. His face was pale. "As the virus rages through the nation's sanctuaries, the question is what the government can and will do to further protect the nation. And whether the infected suicide terrorists, who are suspected of being the source of the outbreak, will launch an attack against the rest of us." The reporter signed off.

As Luke circled the bag and positioned himself for another attack, he saw Sulaiman pointing a gun. *An eye for eye.* He had taken Cindy, and now he wanted the rest. The life of every Christian who wouldn't submit to Allah. The government hadn't confirmed the terrorist leader was behind the suicide attacks, but Luke was certain it was Sulaiman.

Luke slammed another blow as hard as he could into the image before him. He had led the church into the jaws of the enemy by convincing millions of Christians to choose a sanctuary instead of the government's chip. The sweat soaking through the leather gloves picked at his raw flesh, but the stinging felt deserved, like a penitent's whip. How could he have been so blind? Now millions of his brothers and sisters were trapped in camps overrun with a deadly disease. He had sent them to their deaths, and even worse, at the hands of Sulaiman. The church could be wiped out.

Another series of blows rocked the bag. *Father, please help me to stop this terrorist's attempt to destroy your people.*

"Hey, Luke. Someone's looking for you," a voice called out.

Luke stopped his assault and turned to see Johnny Barela, better known as El Asesino or the assassin, standing near the front door. Johnny was an up-and-coming bantamweight who had earned his nickname from a ghostly left hook that most opponents never saw until too late.

"Who is it?"

"He didn't say. But he's big and has an attitude, and here he comes." Johnny pointed toward the door.

A man wearing a Harley Davidson do-rag with a reddish brown handle-bar mustache squeezed through the front door. He stood a foot taller than Johnny with shoulders broad enough for two men. He looked directly at Luke, then reached inside his pants pocket and withdrew a mask and gloves. He slid the mask on, careful to protect his mustache, and put the gloves on.

"We can do this the easy way or the hard way," do-rag said. "It's your choice, pastor," which his accent mauled into 'pester'.

Luke clenched his fists. "Who are you, and what do you want?"

"Name's Bear. I'm a bounty hunter hired by the U.S. government to find anyone who has violated Operation First Alert." He pulled out a badge from the side pocket of his camouflage pants and flashed it.

Since the outbreak the level of paranoia had accelerated. People were demanding the government track down offenders and send them to a sanctuary, which meant certain death, or to the nearest clinic for chipping.

Luke hadn't delivered a sermon since Cindy's death. She had told him to complete the work God had given him, but he wasn't certain anyone would listen anymore. Why would they? He had sent millions to their death. It might be better to enter a sanctuary and spend his last days ministering to the dying.

"Let me change clothes." Luke turned to head toward the locker room.

"No, you don't." Bear's hand moved in a blur slapping a handcuff on Luke's right wrist as the bounty hunter reached for the other.

Luke jerked his hand away.

Bear's fist slammed into Luke's back.

He winced, then pivoted to land a hook flush on Bear's jaw. His eyes rolled back as he collapsed to the floor like a chiffon slip.

Luke stood over the fallen man, his pulse pounding.

"Orale," one of the fighters said. "That was awesome."

Luke ignored the boxer's remarks.

"You better split." Johnny threw a towel to Luke as he walked toward him. "You're my bro, but don't come back here again." He put his hand on Luke's sweaty shoulder. "When this guy wakes up, he won't be in a mood to use handcuffs."

Luke nodded. He leaned down and reached inside Bear's pocket and plucked a key and unlocked the handcuff dangling from his right wrist. He wiped the towel across his face, walked to the locker room and grabbed his clothes off a hook on the wall but didn't bother changing.

* * *

Two hours later Luke stood in front of a complex of tan, flat-topped buildings. The Santa Fe maximum security prison was located just south of the *city different*, the town's nickname. He turned and looked at the brown hills blanketed with pink, wispy Apache plume and yellow sprays of Spanish Broom. A light wind whipped up the plant's pungent odor which reminded him a little of mustard. He wrinkled his nose. *Still time to walk away.* He was taking a real risk coming here after what happened at the gym. Bear could have called in support or alerted the police. He turned back toward the entrance. He might walk in and never walk out. But it was a chance he had to take.

Luke flashed his chaplain's badge at the guard, then removed his boots and belt and passed through the metal detector. An alarm buzzed. He stiffened at the sound. The guard frowned as he waved Luke back. "Either put it on the table, or I'll have to pat you down."

He pulled a chain over his head and placed the cross in the tray. The guard looked annoyed as Luke passed through the sensor this time without a sound. A metallic click unlocked the door in front of him. Luke slowly pushed open a foot-thick door that looked like it belonged in a bank and walked into a short hallway. A door off the corridor led to the visitor's hall, a room filled with round tables and chairs.

Luke entered and sat down and waited in the Spartan room. A few minutes later Benny Munoz arrived in an orange jump suit. At one time he was the hardest puncher in the welterweight division, but he was a lefty, which made getting fights difficult. Southpaws often languished for years, like former middleweight champ Marvelous Marvin Hagler, waiting for a chance at the title. They were awkward to fight. But stepping into the ring with someone like Benny, who possessed a one-punch knockout with either hand, made getting a fight next to impossible. So he waited which unfortunately turned out to be too long.

"Primo!" Benny smiled broadly stretching a thin, light jagged scar along his high cheek bone. He slapped Luke's right hand. "What's up, bro?" Scar tissue arched over dark eyes.

Next to Cindy, no one knew him better. "Need to talk."

Benny slumped into a chair. He folded his hands on the table. The skin on his pronounced knuckles was cracked and lighter like it had been worn off.

"Been hitting the bags?"

"Not enough." He motioned with his head toward the guard standing near the door. "They keep us locked up a lot." He paused as if searching for the right words. "I heard about Cindy. I'm sorry, bro. I miss her, too."

Luke winced at the thought of happier times when the three of them were together. He leaned forward and whispered. "I'm in trouble. The government sent a bounty hunter after me, and I just laid him out."

Benny glanced back at the guard who frowned, then angled himself away from the correctional officer's view. "What happened?"

"The government is rounding up people who refused to be chipped, mostly believers, and relocating them to sanctuaries or sending them to clinics for chipping." He shook his head. "I would have gone with the guy, but he slapped cuffs on me, and I lost it."

"That's some serious stuff."

"I feel responsible for those people in the sanctuaries. They're dying from the virus, and they wouldn't be if I hadn't told them to refuse the chip. And now the government is hunting the rest of us down."

"You did the right thing." He rubbed the top of this right hand. "We didn't have a choice in here, but if I had, I would have refused."

"I want to help them, but what can I do?"

Benny's eyes narrowed. He sat up in his chair and clenched his left hand into a fist. He shook it in front of Luke. "You fight back. You're a fighter. You've never backed away from a fight your whole life."

And neither had Benny, but he should have. Some punk approached him after a training session seven years ago and wanted to prove he could whip the top-ranked welterweight. The guy was crazy for even thinking he had a chance. Benny laughed him off, but the man took a swing. Benny instinctively reacted and dropped the guy with a short uppercut that snapped his head back. He never got up. It cost Benny ten years for manslaughter—and a shot at the title.

"I'm already in enough trouble," Luke said. "I don't want anymore."

"You've got to get those people out of the sanctuaries before they're all dead. If you don't, you'll never live it down."

The statement made Luke's head spin. The thought was too big. Too difficult to process. "How?"

"Mobilize what's left of the underground church."

"I haven't broadcast a message since Cindy's...it's been two months." Luke dropped his head into his hands. "Most of the church is in the sanctuaries. There's no one left."

Benny placed his hand on Luke's shoulder. "Organize what's left. I'm sure it's still bigger than any building can hold."

Luke looked up. "The government isn't going to release survivors with the virus rampaging through the sanctuaries."

Benny leaned back in his chair. "Moses didn't think Pharaoh would let the Hebrews go either. And look what God did."

"I'm not Moses." Luke rubbed his week-old beard. "But if the Lord did miraculously release his people from the sanctuaries, what then? Where would we go?"

"What about Mexico?"

"Are you kidding? The country is torn apart by drug wars. Why would anyone in their right mind go there?"

"Some of the homies in here are connected to the vigilantes."

The vigilantes were the Mexican people's solution to a problem their government couldn't solve. An army of peasant soldiers had been formed to protect the people against the drug cartels. The citizen army was armed as well as the drug lords, probably thanks in part to the U.S. government. Systematically the vigilante guerrillas were hunting down the cartel leaders and its members and destroying them. But the war between the cartels and the vigilantes was far from over and would take years to win.

"My homies know who you are. Still talk about your fight with that big Russian."

Luke rubbed his jaw. "Karpenko."

"The vigilantes will provide protection for you."

"I don't want to get in the middle of a war."

"You already are."

Luke shook his head. "It's impossible. The borders are closed."

Benny's thick eyebrows merged into a dark line. "Wake up man. You don't have a lot of options. If you stay here, the bounty hunter will eventually track you down. If you turn yourself in, you'll be shipped to a sanctuary and die from the virus. If you try to rescue the believers in the sanctuaries, you may be shot. But wouldn't you rather die fighting?"

"And I came to you for advice?" Same ol' Benny. He never shadow boxed with the truth. He was right. The chances of getting out of this alive were slim. But that wasn't so bad. His life without Cindy was lonely. Desperately lonely. And, besides, everyone had to die sometime.

CHAPTER SIXTY-ONE

Centers for Disease Control, Fort Detrick, November 21

"Is this what you've been looking for?" A janitor stood on the other side of the protective glass and held up a dented, two-foot long cylinder." Holloman was stamped on the side.

Jenny's heart sank. "Where did you find it?"

"In the trash."

She had been expecting the blood samples ten days ago. Dr. Lutz had confirmed their shipment. An image of Denton Mabe's tanned face flashed before her. She felt sick. Were there also terrorists buried in CDC?

The man held up an envelope. "I found this in the container. The only thing in there."

"Open it up."

The man opened the envelope and pressed a letter against the glass. A quick perusal revealed it wasn't to her but to the editor of the Charlotte Observer. I wonder if Dr. Lutz had any idea what was in it?

"Will you give the letter to Liz and ask her to send it to the Charlotte Observer, to the attention of the editor?"

The man nodded and left.

Jenny pressed a button on a phone. "Please connect me with Dr. Lutz at Holloman."

A moment later a weak raspy voice answered. "Hello."

"Dr. Lutz?"

"Yes."

"This is Dr. George. Are you okay?"

"I'm afraid not." Each word seemed to sap the next of energy until the last was only a whisper. "I've contracted the virus."

"I'm so sorry."

"I've survived longer than most. Only a few thousand left here." He stopped and gasped, grabbing at breaths, making what he said difficult to understand. "Did you finally receive the samples?"

"We found the container, but it was empty."

A long rolling cough that was painful to listen to filled her hood.

"Forgive me." He coughed again. "I'm sorry to hear that. One of them was very promising. The others weren't important. They're either infected or dead. But he's still alive." A long wheezy breath exhaled from the damaged lungs which sounded eerily similar to a person's last breath. "He was the first to have direct contact with the terrorist."

Her pulse quickened. "Who is he?"

"Hank Jackson. Said he knows you." He coughed. "I'll see if one of the nurses can take another sample and send it to you. Everything depends on it."

What's he doing in a sanctuary? Could he possibly be immune to the virus? "Thank you, Dr. Lutz, for all of your help."

"Goodbye, Dr. George."

Jenny's voice broke. "Goodbye." Her hands shook. She had wanted to say something to give him hope. Anything but goodbye. But they both knew there was no hope.

The door to the outer lab swung open. It was Hampton Elliott. The director of CDC was upset. His normally pale complexion was florid. He motioned frantically for her to join him in his office.

Jenny quickly left the lab and entered the decontamination room. Minutes later she stood in front of Hampton. "What is it?"

"We have a big problem." His voice trembled. "I just received reports of outbreaks in Alamogordo, Barstow, and Flagstaff. All three cities are adjacent to sanctuaries."

Jenny's legs felt weak. She grabbed the edge of the counter to steady herself.

"Do you think it's another terrorist attack?" Hampton's bottom lip trembled.

"Let's hope it is."

Hampton looked puzzled.

"At least we have a shot at controlling that strain. But if it's airborne..."

Hampton looked for a chair to sit down in.

"I have my own bad news," Jenny said.

Hampton's face dropped as if the additional burden was too much to bear. "What is it?"

"A janitor found the container from Holloman. Empty in the trash. I think terrorists may have infiltrated CDC the way they did the Bioforensic Center. Unfortunately, one of the missing samples may have been the key to a vaccine. The man is still alive after prolonged exposure."

Hampton dropped his head. "Are they sending more samples?"

Jenny grabbed her coat from the door.

"Where are you going?"

"I can't wait for that. I'm going to Holloman."

CHAPTER SIXTY-TWO

Washington, D.C., November 21

Members of the National Security Council congregated around the oval, walnut table that stretched the length of the Cabinet Room. The Chairman of the Joint Chiefs of Staff, the Director of National Intelligence, and members of the President's cabinet were all there. Those not part of the inner circle sat in chairs against the wall on opposite sides of the table. Pepper sat at Hamilton's right.

Late afternoon light poured into the room and warmed the off-white walls into a golden hue. Marble busts of George Washington and Benjamin Franklin looked on from niches on either side of the fireplace.

"Thank you all for coming on such short notice," Hamilton said. "We have an emergency unprecedented in our country's history that requires immediate attention."

Long faces in the room stared at him, except General Frank Maddox, chairman of the Joint Chiefs of Staff, who sat expressionless with arms crossed.

"I received a call two hours ago." Hamilton looked at his watch. "From Dr. George who is heading up our efforts to create a vaccine. She said there are confirmed reports of outbreaks in three cities near sanctuaries."

Secretary of State Elizabeth Schomberg clamped her hand over her mouth amid several gasps in the room.

Hamilton waved his hand in an attempt to calm the members. "Thanks to Operation First Alert the infected have already been isolated, and there haven't been any new reports of infection. But we have little time according to Dr. George. She believes the virus has mutated and might be airborne."

"What are we going to do?" Schomberg asked.

General Maddox pursed his lips. "The late General Sullivan made a lot of mistakes, but he got one thing right. You have to do more than just isolate the infected. You have to eliminate them."

Schomberg wheeled around in her chair and glared at Maddox. "What does that mean?"

"I think you know."

"Are you proposing genocide?"

"No, Madam Secretary, I'm proposing survival."

They both looked at Hamilton for vindication of their position.

Hamilton's hands shook. He placed them in his lap. Last night had been miserable. Even the generous dose of Ambien hadn't been enough to cure the insomnia. "Before we make any decision, you should all know Dr. George's team is testing hundreds of blood samples from sanctuary detainees who have been exposed to the virus and are still alive. She believes one of them may hold the key to beating this terrible disease."

Maddox frowned. "Mr. President, General Sullivan pursued developing an antiviral long before Dr. George came into the picture. He was unsuccessful. What makes you think she can find one?"

"I don't know if she can. But she's our best hope."

Maddox grunted as Schomberg eyed him suspiciously.

Pepper cleared his throat. "The President called us together to offer the best advice we can. Tests are being performed now to determine whether the virus of those infected outside of the sanctuaries is in fact airborne. There is an outside chance terrorists have struck these cities. But if tests confirm that the virus is what we fear, then we have to consider the alternatives if we don't act swiftly. Operation First Alert won't be able to cull the infected fast enough to stay ahead of the exponential spread of the virus. CDC's computer models project that once the virus reaches a major population center, it will take less than two weeks to spread worldwide. Within a month a hundred million will be dead, within two months five-hundred million, and within three, more than a billion people." Pepper pressed his fingers to his forehead and closed his eyes as if he had a sudden migraine. "Within a year, the entire human population will be extinct."

The room was so quiet that Hamilton could hear his vintage Patek Phillippe watch ticking.

"Are we seriously considering the possibility of eliminating the sanctuaries?" Schomberg searched the faces of each member at the table for any sign of their position. "For God's sake these are American citizens. Many of them may not even be infected. They have mothers and fathers and sisters and brothers. Please tell me I've misunderstood."

A scowl descended on Maddox's face. "If they hadn't refused to be chipped, there wouldn't be any sanctuaries, and this lunatic, Sulaiman, wouldn't have had the opportunity to fulfill his demented vision."

"We don't know that for certain," Schomberg said. "No one has claimed responsibility for the outbreak."

Maddox grunted. "No one has to. Sulaiman is the only terrorist smart enough to dream up an attack like this and implement it."

"Sounds like you're a fan."

Maddox glared at Schomberg. "I live in the real world."

Hamilton rubbed his hand over the back of his aching neck. The prospect of eliminating millions of citizens was mind numbing. What would history say about his decision? Truman had sacrificed the citizens of Hiroshima and Nagasaki to save hundreds of thousands of American soldiers but many American citizens still regarded him as a butcher, not to mention the rest of the world.

Hamilton loosened his tie and unbuttoned his collar. "Let's assume for sake of our discussion that the virus is airborne. Let's also assume that CDC's computer analysis of the virus' proliferation is accurate. If both of these are on the mark, and I have no reason to doubt they aren't, then every minute counts. Whatever response we choose must be rapid."

"What are the options besides eradicating the sanctuaries?" Schomberg asked.

"May I, Mr. President?" Pepper asked.

Hamilton nodded.

"We can pursue the current line of defense and continue to quarantine the infected, but there's a high probability we won't succeed. We can evacuate major cities, which may temporarily slow the virus' spread, but that won't eliminate it. If we pursue either of these avenues and fail, the cost will be catastrophic. The question each of us has to answer is what are we willing to risk in order to save the sanctuaries?" Pepper looked directly at Schomberg.

A look of horror gripped her as she looked from Pepper to Hamilton.

"General, what would be the most efficient way?" Hamilton asked.

"Neutron bomb." His shaved temples twitched. "It releases a substantially high level of radiation."

"Which will be necessary to kill the virus," Dr. Carrington added.

Maddox tipped his head in acknowledgement at Carrington. "The neutron bomb emits a lower amount of explosive power and heat unlike the atomic or hydrogen. It will have a minimal affect on cities adjacent to the sanctuaries because the bomb disperses very little fallout. Of course, we still need to evacuate any nearby cities to be safe, but at least the people will have something to come back to."

"Try to bridle your enthusiasm, General," Hamilton said. "We're not going to war. And I'm not interested in minimal damage. I don't want any damage. And no civilian casualties. Period. Are we clear?"

He nodded.

"General, wouldn't the higher heat of an atomic weapon be more effective at killing the virus?"

Maddox frowned. "No, if any of the infected have burrowed into the ground or built underground shelters, a traditional atomic weapon might not be successful. But the radiation emitted by a 10-kiloton neutron bomb will fry anything within a five to ten-mile radius."

"How long before you can be ready?"

"As soon as we can evacuate nearby cities. Two to three days."

Hamilton placed his hands on the table and folded them securely into each other to conceal the shaking. "What's the consensus?"

The cabinet was split. Half agreed with the general and half with Schomberg. Hamilton reached inside his suit jacket and touched the cigar. He could use one right now. "I was hoping for a consensus, not a stalemate. I won't make a final decision until tests confirm if the outbreak is airborne. If it is, we'll proceed immediately with evacuation plans. Meanwhile pray Dr. George finds a vaccine."

Maddox threw his hands into the air. "Mr. President, we can't wait. At least destroy the sanctuaries near the cities with the outbreaks. You said every minute counts."

Hamilton raised his hand as if he were about to halt traffic. "It does—especially to Dr. George. If she can find a cure, not only will millions of lives be saved, but the sanctuaries will be as well." *And my legacy.* "The nuclear option is a last resort."

Schomberg brushed at her eyes. Her bottom lip quivered.

Long faces filled the room. There were no victors today regardless of position. The lump in Hamilton's throat, and perhaps everyone's with the exception of the General, revealed the struggle of wrestling with something so unthinkable—launching an attack against American citizens to save the rest.

CHAPTER SIXTY-THREE

Holloman Sanctuary, November 22

The fires were out. Putrid decay had replaced the smell of burning flesh. The dead no longer lay in neat rows along the shoulders of the roads. Scattered across the concrete and asphalt and withered grass of Holloman were countless bodies, bloated into caricatures. A cold wind blew through an empty street sweeping barbed tumbleweeds toward Hank. He burrowed into a ski jacket.

His closest friend, Dr. Lutz, was gone. The ones still alive were hiding, some in underground shelters, some locked in rooms with plastic taped over windows and doors. A few like him still walked the streets. There was plenty of food and water, but many would starve out of fear, too afraid to leave their refuges.

Hank stopped at the corner of a building and leaned around. An M-16 protruded from a window in the guard tower. Bullet-riddled bodies strewn near the exit from a desperate attempt to flee the disease-ridden camp were proof of the soldier's resolve to do his duty to the very end. Through binoculars Hank searched the tower. The guard was missing. Boxes of food were stacked on one side of the room, probably enough to last until Christmas, but no soldier. Was he dead?

Hank's determination to find a way out had strengthened since Lutz's death. But the government's resolution to ensure no one escaped had also stiffened. Small bands of soldiers roamed the base and shot anyone trying to dig out or scale the ten-foot fence. He touched the gun in the pocket of his jacket. It was reassuring but no match for an M-16. And this particular guard was adept at luring people into his web. He might be crouched inside his perch waiting. Dark would come soon enough.

An image in a window across the street startled Hank. A man with a mask was staring at him. Upon closer scrutiny, he realized it was a reflection of his own bearded, hollowed-eyed face. He slumped down and leaned against the building. The watch that hung loosely on his wrist read 4 p.m., but where had he been for the last several hours? He couldn't remember. His stomach growled, and he was light headed. Had he eaten today? He couldn't remember that either. His palms, thank God, his palms were clean. Still no sign of the virus.

Had the Observer received the letter he sent to Jenny? The public needed to know the truth.

In the distance the rapid crack of an M-16 broke the silence. He closed his eyes and tried to forget.

* * *

It was dark when he woke. The temperatures had dipped into the low 40s at night, but this felt colder as if a front were moving in. Desperate cries, all too familiar, pierced the moonless night.

He peeked around the corner. The all-pervasive spotlight that dared anyone crazy enough to enter its domain, was unlit. The guard must be dead. But the gate might still be guarded by a patrol. Hank strained to see anything in the frigid dark night, the glow of a lighted cigarette or plume of hot breath. But there was nothing.

He rose on stiff, shaky legs. Even in the thick darkness, his florescent green jacket glowed. He removed it and reversed the black interior lining to the outside and pulled out the Colt 45. The icy steel felt awkward. He pushed the safety forward but wasn't sure if that meant it was on or off. Crouching, his heart beating like a drum, he moved from the building toward the large gate.

Something behind him moved. He froze.

"Wait." A woman's voice.

"Take me with you." A faint image of a young woman emerged from the jet-black night. Her dark eyes looked familiar, as did her long raven hair, but she was impossible to identify with the surgical mask.

"Go back. Too dangerous." Hank spoke in short, hushed clips as he waved her back.

But she moved closer and crouched next to him. It was the pretty young nurse from the hospital.

Hank moved away. "Let me see your hands."

She removed her gloves and rolled her palms up exposing delicate hands. "Good enough?" she snapped.

Hank nodded.

"I'm leaving." Her voice was firm. "With or without you."

Hank sighed. The longer they waited, the greater the risk they would be discovered. "All right." He shook his head. "If there are any guards near, they'll be over there." He pointed toward the dark mass of a building.

"How are we going to know?"

"When they start firing."

She didn't flinch.

"Wait here until I get to the gate." Bent low to the ground, he advanced as quickly and quietly as he could. When he reached the gate, he exhaled a long breath. He waved for her to come. She ran toward him.

In the distance voices approached. The young nurse stopped and sat on her heels with a helpless expression.

"I heard something." The shadowy form of a soldier in a white mask appeared. Tall and thin.

"Just shoot at it," said another soldier still not visible.

Hank motioned for the nurse to stay put. *I knew she was going to be trouble.*

"Not going to waste ammo. We're running low."

"I've got plenty," the soldier grunted.

A rapid gun burst sprayed the ground and fence. "Whatever it was is dead." A short stocky man wearing a mask emerged from the thick blanket of night with a rifle at his side.

The shadowy outline of her body lay against the ground. Hank buried his head in his hands. Why hadn't she listened?

"Man, I can't see a thing. Black as tar." The stocky guard walked toward the nurse's body, stopped twenty-feet away, and stared up at the guard tower as if he had just noticed the spotlight was out.

"Justin," he yelled. "You up there? Wake up." The soldier approached the tower and placed his hand on the ladder.

"I wouldn't go up there," the tall soldier called out. "He's probably dead."

The stocky soldier let go of the ladder as if it were red hot and backed away. "I didn't sign up for this kind of junk."

The tall man grabbed the soldier's shoulder. "Let's go. We've got other rounds. Nothing we can do for him now."

"We should post someone to watch the gate."

"You can stay if you want."

"Not me. Get Brian to do it."

The tall soldier nodded. The two white masks disappeared into the night.

When Hank was sure the two men were far enough away, he darted toward the nurse's body. She was curled up on her side. He reached down and stroked her hair. *Poor girl.*

She grabbed his arm. "Are they gone?"

Hank nearly screamed.

"Are they gone?"

"Yes. But how did you…survive…the shots?" Hank was trembling.

The nurse sat up. "I don't know. Must have been the Lord."

Hank had never witnessed anything like it.

She stood up. "Let's go," she whispered.

They passed through the thin gate opening and were outside. She dropped to her knees and looked heavenward. "Thank you, Lord," she said a little too loudly.

Hank held his index finger to his lips and pointed back toward the entrance. She nodded and stood up.

The lights of town twinkled in the distance. They walked silently for several hundred yards before speaking.

"What's your name?"

"Katherine Rodriguez. My friends call me Kat."

"I'm Hank." He stuck out his gloved hand but instinctively withdrew it before she could touch him. Not that he didn't want to touch her. It had been a long time since he had been touched, especially by a woman.

"You were Dr. Lutz's friend. Thanks for helping me." She stopped and turned back toward the dark outline of the sanctuary as if she had forgotten something.

"What is it?"

She brushed at her eyes. "Nothing."

Hank glanced back at the forbidding structure. "Did you lose family there?" "Yeah," she whispered. "There are still a lot of good people in there."

"Nothing we can do." He rubbed his hands together and stomped his feet. It was cold. "We have to keep moving or we'll freeze."

She nodded and pointed toward city lights. "It's farther than it looks."

"How far?"

"Thirteen miles by road, but as the crow flies probably nine. Let's cut across this ravine." She pointed toward a sunken shadow in the distance. "It feels good to be free." She pulled off her mask, unveiling a slightly turned up nose and full lips.

Hank had forgotten how beautiful she was.

Kat threw her mask upward. The wind caught it as it disappeared into the night.

Her exuberance made him smile. It did feel good to be free of the walls and guard towers and the virus. He removed his mask but stuffed it in his pocket just in case. The foul smell was gone, and the crisp clean air rejuvenating. He breathed deeply.

They stumbled forward in the inky night into a biting wind that was growing stronger. Their feet groped the uneven ground.

During the next few hours they talked about their families and careers as the darkness behind them faded into a thin line that split the horizon. They were still one to two miles from town when they topped a knoll and saw a man on a dirt road below loading two white horses into a trailer.

"Good morning." Hank walked down toward the man as Kat followed.

A wiry old man in a cowboy hat and mask turned abruptly, startled by the early morning visitors. One of his horses snorted and moved sideways.

"Easy Leche." He patted her neck.

"You infected?" The cowboy stared warily at Hank.

"No, we're not."

"What do you want?" he asked brusquely as he ushered the horse into the trailer.

"Nothing. We're headed to Alamogordo."

"Why? No one's there."

"Where are they?" Kat asked. Her voice quavered.

The man's glassy eyes stared at them. He had a slight stoop. "Where you been? You're not from around here are you?"

They didn't say anything.

"The government has ordered the evacuation of any cities within fifty miles of a sanctuary."

Hank's pulse quickened. "Why?"

"There's been an outbreak of the virus in Alamogordo and a few other cities. It's bad." He shook his head. "There's rumors it might be airborne."

Hank reached in his pocket and put his mask back on. "What is the government going to do?"

"I don't know, but the last time they evacuated this city," he paused, "I think it was in '45, they exploded an atomic bomb not far from here. I'm not sticking around to find out what they do this time. You shouldn't either." He untied his other horse and patted its neck. "Let's go girl. Up and easy." The horse's hooves clopped against the metal floor as it stepped inside the trailer.

Kat grabbed Hank's arm. The evacuation didn't make any sense if the government was truly trying to protect people from an airborne virus. A strong wind could easily blow it beyond a fifty-mile radius. At best that was a temporary solution unless—the government had something else in mind. *They wouldn't. Would they?* The uncertainty made him queasy.

He turned to Kat and whispered. "We've got to leave now. Maybe we can catch a ride with this man."

"What's going to happen?"

Hank's stomach churned. "I'm not sure, but I think fifty miles isn't going to be far enough."

CHAPTER SIXTY-FOUR

N.M. Highway 54, November 22

The cracked, worn seat next to Luke was empty. He reached over with his right hand and gently touched the indentation in the vinyl as the old GMC rattled down Highway 54. *I miss you, baby.* The scent of Cindy's perfume lingered, reluctant to leave. *I went to see Benny the other day. He's hanging in there and misses you, too. Thousands of members from the church are headed to sanctuaries all over the country. We're praying big that somehow God will release his people.*

A thick, moonless shroud had descended upon the landscape ever since the little town of Carrizozo, and a strong headwind buffeted the truck's progress. He had forgotten how dark the desert could be at night, especially when it was devoid of even a star's distant twinkle.

The sign announced he was entering Alamogordo. Population 40,000. But not a single resident was there. A hurried mass evacuation had turned the street into an obstacle course. A loaded trash bag sat in the middle of two lanes as an empty shopping cart surrounded by swirling newspaper rolled toward Luke. He swerved into the oncoming lane to avoid the cart and then to the far right to avoid several broken bottles.

News of the virus' spread had paralyzed the nation. Frantic shoppers had cleaned out shelves at grocery stores that would remain bare because truck deliveries had ceased. Pharmacies had been raided. People had holed up in their homes too afraid to leave. Companies had closed due to a lack of employees. And looters roamed the streets forcing small business owners to move into their stores and arm themselves to protect their property.

The only thriving businesses were those specializing in the construction of underground shelters, a concept revived from the 1950's, and those that sold hazmat suits, filtration systems, and survival gear. The protective suits sold at ten times their former price, putting them out of reach for the average person. The President promised a solution, but people weren't willing to wait.

Luke drove through the deserted city and headed for Holloman. Would the church show up the way many had promised, or would fear of the virus prove too much? If they did come, would there be anyone left to save? Would the military prevent their release? The questions flooded his mind as he struggled to think beyond the rescue. He understood everyone's fear. It was the most unforgiving disease mankind had ever faced. But God had protected him so far, and if the Lord wanted the church to deliver his people from the sanctuaries, wouldn't He continue to do so?

Benny wanted Luke to relocate the church to Mexico, but that presented too many problems. He couldn't ask families to risk the safety of their children in such a country. But Belize, still part of the British Commonwealth, was a small, stable nation where English was the official language. If members were successful at liberating the nation's sanctuaries, Belize would be the target. Hopefully, Benny's connections would provide the necessary protection for the church as it traveled through Mexico. The only problem was getting across the closed border.

Luke shook his head at the magnitude of the undertaking. There was no way of knowing how many people were still alive at the nation's two hundred sanctuaries or how many members would show up to assist in the relocation. But even if there were only two or three million survivors, the underground church would still be as large as most of the world's largest armies. The journey would take several days. How would he possibly feed and provide for such a multitude?

Fifteen minutes later his truck rolled to a stop in front of Holloman. As the veil of darkness receded into a grayish dawn his heart sank. Not a single vehicle. He was either too early, or no one was coming. He cracked his sore knuckles and checked his watch. Where was everyone? Maybe they weren't coming. He leaned his forehead against the steering wheel. *Father, did I misunderstand you? I thought this was Your will. I can't do this alone.* In the early morning light, he remembered Elisha's servant and his fear of the Syrian army that surrounded him and his master. But then God revealed the legions of angels protecting them.

I am not alone.

Luke got out of his truck. The smell of decay was thick. He pressed the mask against his face, but it did little to diminish the fetid fumes. Light snow was falling blanketing the ground in a thin white layer that looked like alkaline leaching from the ground. He walked toward the entrance rationing his breaths as he examined the high, gray walls topped with razor wire. An empty guard tower near the entrance loomed above the wall. Luke braced for the worst.

As he entered the sanctuary, his legs weakened at the sight of a grisly slaughter. *I'm too late.* Several bodies, their faces blackened and torsos bloated to three times their original size, lay sprawled beneath the guard tower. The snow was beginning to mercifully cover the dead. In the distance a pack of coyotes tore at the remains of a corpse. Luke stooped and picked up a rock and hurled it as far as he could toward the animals. It fell short but one of the coyotes turned in his direction and growled, then continued with dinner. Between him and the animals lay more bodies than he could count or dared. Had anyone survived?

He picked his way through the fallen and proceeded deeper into the base. With each step he sank deeper into despair. There were no survivors. The entire base was as abandoned as Alamogordo.

CHAPTER SIXTY-FIVE

N.M. Highway 54, November 22

T he first snow flurry started at dusk, shortly after Jenny landed at El Paso International airport. She had been delayed a day waiting to catch a flight and was lucky to be on one of the last flights out of Ronald Reagan Washington National airport. The country was shutting down like a patient waiting for last rites.

By the time she reached the southern edge of the Lincoln National Forest ninety minutes later, it was dark. A thick, white blanket covered the highway.

The mountains to the east rose from the flat barren landscape like sentinels placed strategically to protect the small city of Alamogordo to the north. She strained to see the road through hypnotic, swirling flurries intensified by the car's headlights. From nowhere a deer jumped in front of her vehicle. She jammed the brakes to the floor missing the deer. But it sent her car whirling down the middle of the highway.

Her dad's warning to not hit the brakes in a spin overrode her impulse to do just that.

The world outside spun in rapid, undistinguishable clips, but everything inside slowed. She was aware she could strike another car or veer off the road or flip over, but she was strangely calm, even analytical about her chances. *If the car stays centered, it will eventually lose momentum.*

How many times she spun around, she couldn't tell. But as her car headed toward the shoulder, she pumped the brakes. The wheels grabbed the softer snow bringing it to an abrupt stop. She sat gripping the steering wheel, teeth clenched. She tried backing out into the road but the wheels spun uselessly. The engine died. She swung her door open and leaned down to look at her front left tire. A clump of snow fell on her lap. The whole front end of the car was in a ditch. Jenny shut the door and grabbed her cell phone and dialed. No reception. She leaned back against the seat and took a deep breath.

At least she had a heater. She started the engine and turned it on. The blast of warm air felt good. But the engine sputtered and died. She tried again, but this time it wouldn't start at all. *Don't panic. Someone will be along soon.* But the self-talk didn't ease the rising panic. She was stranded in a blizzard on a road with little traffic on a good day and probably none on Sunday evening. The temperature in the car was dropping quickly. The biting cold cut through her khaki pants and light leather coat. It was supposed to be a quick trip. She shoved her hands deeply into her jacket pockets and hunched forward. It was 7 p.m. *I've got to get to the sanctuary and find Hank.* She remembered Dr. Lutz's words. *Everything depends on it.*

She felt a sudden urge to close her eyes and sleep for a few minutes, just a few minutes. The adrenaline of the accident was subsiding. But it was dangerous in such cold temperatures. Once hypothermia set in, she wouldn't have long. But she was so tired.

* * *

Jenny jerked her head up at the sound of an engine. How long had she been asleep? She shielded her eyes from the bright light. Her breath hung in the air like trapped smoke. A face peered through the fogged driver's side window. The man rapped on it pointing a flashlight at her.

"Anyone in there?"

Jenny wanted to scream *I'm here*, but she couldn't force the words out. Her mouth was stiff, her mind muddled.

The man tried the door, but it was locked.

"If you can hear me, get back from the window."

He hit the window with a flashlight, fracturing it into a glass spider web. He punched out the splintered sheet of glass. It fell into her lap as he reached through to unlock the door.

"Lady, you all right?"

Jenny nodded her head.

"Lucky for you I happened by," he said. "Not much traffic on this road at 2 a.m and particularly in a storm like this."

Jenny nodded slowly. Her neck ached.

"Are you hurt?"

"No...just...cold." The words rattled out through teeth that chattered uncontrollably.

"Let's get you out of the car and into my truck where it's warm."

The man helped Jenny into his truck. It was difficult to walk because she couldn't feel her feet.

"Don't know if you like coffee, but it's hot." The man poured a cup from his thermos and passed it to Jenny, then handed her a blanket.

"I'm Barry." He tipped his cowboy hat.

"Jenny. Thank...you...for stopping."

"You're probably suffering from hypothermia, but, unfortunately, I can't get you to a hospital. Not yet anyway. I'm on an emergency call. You're going to have to come with me for now. Let me see your hands and feet."

"What...kind...of...doctor? Jenny removed her shoes and socks. Her toes were white.

"Veterinary medicine. Your hands are going to be okay, but you may have some tissue damage on your toes. Won't know for sure for a few hours."

The feeling was slowly coming back to Jenny's numb lips. "What kind of emergency call do you have?"

"Headed to Ruidoso. Race horse is breech."

Jenny sat up in the seat. "I've got to get to Holloman." She glanced back at her rental car."

Barry cocked his head as if he had misunderstood. "Did you say Holloman?" His squinty eyes narrowed into slits.

Jenny nodded.

"Why in heaven's name would you want to go there?"

"I'm a virologist from CDC."

Barry raised his eyebrows.

"There is a man in there who may be immune to the virus. I've got to find him as soon as possible."

The engine roared to life. "You know the government evacuated Alamogordo today because of the outbreak?"

She nodded. But the news still troubled her. Why hadn't she been consulted on the protective radius? She would have told the President fifty miles wasn't far enough.

He handed her a respirator. "Better put this on."

Jenny slapped her deadened hand to her forehead. "I almost forgot."

"What?"

She opened the door and tried to step out.

"What do you need?" Barry reached across and grabbed her arm.

"I've got a case in the trunk with protective gear." She dug into her pocket and gave him the key. "Thanks."

Barry disappeared into the blinding snow and returned a few minutes later. A clunk sounded in the truck bed. He got back in and shivered. "It's a real humdinger out there. Cold enough to freeze a frog." He turned the heater up.

The blast of hot air felt good as she wiggled her toes and fingers back and forth. They burned, but that was good. Evidence that circulation was returning.

Barry pulled the truck onto the road and headed north into a white fury.

CHAPTER SIXTY-SIX

Washington, D.C., November 23

Hamilton tapped his finger repeatedly on the headlines of the Charlotte Observer. "How did the reporter get this out? We had a strict quarantine."

Pepper adjusted his glasses. "The newspaper isn't saying."

"I should have the publisher locked up. This is the second time he's pulled this. I remember when a president knew what tomorrow's headlines would be. Kennedy certainly did." Hamilton shook his head. "This article could change everything." He punched the newspaper again with his finger. "It makes us sound like Nazis. We had to quarantine those people. There wasn't any other way to protect the nation."

Pepper stood up and walked to the desk and laid a sheet of paper on it. "Here's the latest poll. It's not scientific, but at least it's a quick snapshot. It doesn't appear the article made much difference. People are desperate for any solution that will protect them. The sanctuaries present too great a threat, especially now that we've confirmed the outbreak is from an airborne mutation. Conservatives and liberals agree on this."

Hamilton grabbed the report. "Even if it means nuclear eradication?"

"It's the only plan that guarantees destruction of the virus."

"I wish there were more time." He looked at the portrait of President Lincoln that hung near the door to his private study.

Pepper's eyes were puffy with gray circles underneath. "You'd think people would be angry at the terrorists for releasing the virus in the sanctuaries." He shook his head. "Instead, people blame the outbreak on Christians."

Hamilton rubbed the back of his neck. He had a headache again, but it was rare when he didn't anymore. The nightly news had been full of vitriolic attacks against Christians. One was seared in his brain. *What difference does it make if we kill them to save ourselves: they're going to die anyway?* Hamilton crumpled up the pollster's report and threw it in the basket under his desk. "Is General Maddox ready?"

"He's ready." Pepper walked back to the sofa and sat on the edge.

"I'll bet he is." Hamilton stood up and turned to the window facing the south lawn. He was desperate for a cigar, but it was too cold outside to smoke. The branches of the National Holiday tree drooped with snow. Soon the tree would be lit in celebration of the season. But would anyone even notice the holiday? And, if they did, what was there to celebrate?

He turned around. "What's the latest on Dr. George's efforts?"

Pepper dropped his head. "According to Dr. Elliott there is a sanctuary detainee at Holloman who appears to be immune."

"That's the news we needed. Are they working on a vaccine?" Pepper was despondent. "What's wrong?"

He looked up. "The sample of his blood was stolen."

"Stolen? In a secure lab like CDC?"

"Dr. Elliott suspects terrorists infiltrated the lab."

Hamilton kicked his desk. "How does this keep happening? Why even have background checks if we can't identify these people?"

"They aren't terrorists when we hire them Mr. President. Sulaiman has been very successful at recruiting people already employed by our labs."

"Why can't we get this guy? He doesn't walk on water. He's just a man." But Sulaiman had elevated terrorism to a whole new level. In the short span of five years, he had blown up subways and malls, skirted past the highest levels of security, and brought the nation to its knees. And despite the government's best efforts at capturing him, he remained free.

"Well, Mr. President..."

Hamilton waved his hand for Pepper to stop. "I don't want to talk about him." He reached inside his suit jacket and removed a cigar. Pepper's eyebrows arched above his glasses. "Screw it. Lucy will just have to understand." He clipped the cigar and lit it and inhaled. "Let's get Dr. George on the phone."

Pepper looked down at his tablet. "She's missing too."

Hamilton removed the cigar from his mouth. "Missing?"

"Dr. Elliott said she rushed off to Holloman to find the detainee who is supposedly immune. No one has heard from her since or been able to reach her."

"Dear God." Hamilton plopped into his chair.

Pepper cleared his throat. "General Maddox suggests you commence Operation Lifeguard at once. He said security at the sanctuaries is in shambles."

Hamilton cringed at the mission's name. "What about the guards?"

Pepper picked his words carefully. "Many of them are dead or too weak from the virus to effectively secure the bases, which means, unless you give the order to launch immediately, some of the survivors could escape."

"But Dr. George may be in there as well as the cure we need." His voice broke.

The phone on his desk buzzed. He picked up the receiver.

"I'm sorry to disturb you, Mr. President, but I have an urgent call from Dr. Carrington of Human Health and Services. Do you want me to put it through?"

"Go ahead."

"Mr. President?" His voice trembled.

"What's the problem, Bob?"

"I just received news that we have outbreaks in several more cities. I'm afraid we're too late. What are we going to..."

Hamilton laid the phone down on his desk with Dr. Carrington still speaking. A faint voice from the phone asked, "Are you still there, Mr. President?"

CHAPTER SIXTY-SEVEN

N.M. Highway 54, November 23

Visibility was only a few feet. The truck inched forward through the fierce headwind of snow as it had for the last several hours, then rolled to a stop.

"This is it." Barry turned to Jenny and pointed. "Holloman is out there. Only a hundred yards."

"I don't see anything." Jenny shivered at the whiteout beyond the windows. Her toes still tingled from hours of exposure to the cold, although her fingers felt fine.

"I wish I could be more help, but if I don't get to Ruidoso soon, I may lose a horse—a very expensive horse." The blue eyes squinted as he forced a smile.

"You've been very helpful. I don't know what I would have done if you hadn't come along."

Barry tipped his cowboy hat. "My pleasure." He took off his heavy down jacket and gloves. "Take these."

"I can't." Jenny pushed them away.

"I insist. If you don't, you'll freeze."

"Thank you." Jenny slipped into the jacket which engulfed her and put on the insulated lambskin gloves that were twice the size of her hands. She got out of the truck and shut the door. Blowing snow pelted her face as the truck disappeared into the blizzard.

She leaned into blinding flurries placing each foot carefully in the two-foot deep snow. A pang of desperation shot through her as she looked back at the tire tracks left by Barry's truck.

"Stop. My equipment. Come back." She waved her hands and yelled as loud as she could, but her words were lost in the howling wind. Barry was gone and so was everything she needed to protect her against the virus, her suit, her oxygen tanks, even the medical equipment necessary for testing Hank.

She sank to her knees almost disappearing into the snow. *What am I going to do? If I go in there, I'll die. If I don't, and Hank is the key to a vaccine, millions will die.* If she turned back, where would she go? It was impossible to walk more than a few feet at a time because of the wind. And she had no idea which way town was or how far away. The biting wind had already numbed her face, and her toes ached.

Either decision meant certain death. She stood up on shaky legs and trudged forward. After several minutes she began to doubt each step. Barry said it was only a hundred yards. Surely, she had walked that far. Where was the base? Had she gotten turned around? She pivoted and searched unsuccessfully for any trace behind her of footsteps. Her teeth began to chatter, and her body shook.

Icy wind screamed in her ears, but above it she heard a whisper like someone speaking far away in a dream. She stumbled toward the voice. It was impossible to understand. But with each step it became clearer.

"This is Pastor Luke Chavez. I have come to take you away from here. If you can hear my voice, come to me. I'm in the commander's office." He kept repeating the statement like a recording. It seemed to emanate from somewhere overhead.

The moisture in her eyes froze making it difficult to even blink. She brushed away the crystals. She knew the pastor's name, everyone did who watched the news. The terrorist abduction, the FBI rescue, and his wife's murder.

In front of her was a narrow opening near the skeletal contour of a tower. Chavez's message issued from it. Something inside the entry caught her feet, tripping her. As she stood the frozen features of death stared back through the disturbed snow. But this man didn't die from the virus. He had a dark hole between his eyes.

In the distance something moved across the snow. She studied the obscure shape but couldn't tell what it was. More appeared, all moving in the same direction. Then they were gone in the whirling snow. Jenny shivered at the ephemeral images skulking through the storm. She didn't believe in ghosts, but the fleeting outlines certainly fit the description.

She pushed forward against the wind in the direction of the shapes. Slowly they emerged again. But the white, wispy images weren't ghosts. They were survivors. Hundreds of them all plodding through the blinding snow toward a common destination. Jenny dipped her head into the wind and followed.

CHAPTER SIXTY-EIGHT

NM Highway 70, November 23

"Can't this thing go any faster?" Hank stared out at blinding flurries through the windshield.

"You seem awfully itchy, kid." The old cowboy rolled down the window, moved his mask to one side, and spit out a stream of tobacco juice that a blast of icy wind curled back toward the truck. He cranked the window back up and glanced at Hank. "In case you haven't noticed there's a storm out there. Go any faster and we'll end up in a ditch. Something eatin' you?"

Hank rubbed his bristly beard. "Just want to get as far away from the base as possible."

The cowboy studied the mileage odometer. "We're almost out of danger. About twenty-five miles away."

"That's not going to be far enough. Neither is fifty miles."

Kat, who sat next to the old man, turned to Hank. "Okay, that's the second time you've said that. You're scaring me. What do you mean?"

Hank shook his head. "I don't trust the government. They're planning something. Think about it. If this virus is really airborne, fifty miles isn't enough of a barrier. No distance is."

"Humph." The cowboy moved his jaws like a cow chewing cud.

"Sir, what do you think?" Kat turned to the cowboy.

"Don't call me, sir. Name is Jack." He pointed at a jack of diamonds playing card stuck in the band of his cowboy hat.

Kat smiled. "I'm sorry."

Jack stared suspiciously at Hank. "Your friend there sounds like a radical. Looks like one, too."

Hank looked out the passenger window next to him. "I think they're going to destroy the sanctuaries."

Kat jerked his arm. "What?"

"It's really the only way to ensure the virus doesn't spread. Fifty miles is about the right distance for an evacuation if they use nukes."

Kat's mouth dropped open, and her large dark eyes grew even larger.

A procession of lights approached through the storm.

"What the blazes?" Jack rolled down the window again, moved his mask out of the way, and spit. He left it down to get a better look.

Kat shivered as raw air rushed into the cab.

Jack waved at what looked like an approaching semi. He leaned out the window and hollered. "Where you headed?"

The truck slowed to a stop as its diesel engine rumbled. "What did you say?"

"Are you lost?" The wind grabbed Jack's mask and ripped it off and nearly his cowboy hat before he snatched it and held it down.

"I'm going to Holloman," the driver said.

"Are you crazy? Haven't you heard about the evacuation?"

Hank leaned around Kat to get a look at the driver, but his cab sat too high above Jack's truck.

"That's what this is. An evacuation. Me and my friends are going to get whoever's left at the sanctuary."

Jack waved the man off like a pesky fly and rolled the window back up. An icy crust covered his thick salt and pepper mustache. Dark stains lined the deep creases in the corners of his mouth. He clamped his hand over his mouth realizing his mask was gone.

"Sounds like a suicide mission." The words were muffled from behind his hand.

Hank leaned back in the seat. The old cowboy was right about one thing. Anyone headed back to Holloman was a dead man. But why would these truckers do such a thing? Whoever was still alive would soon be infected. Why not just let them die?

Kat gripped Hank's wrist.

"What is it?"

"I'm going back."

Hank turned to her. "What?"

Jack choked on a wad of tobacco and frantically rolled the window down in an attempt to spit.

"Stop the truck, Jack. I'm going to catch a ride with one of these guys." She pointed out the driver's window. Jack leaned out and spit, then coughed. He turned to Kat. Dark, grainy liquid dribbled down his chin. "The cold gone to your head, lady?"

"Why would you do such a thing?" Hank could feel his heart pounding. He felt betrayed. He'd risked his life to help her escape. And in the last several hours, they had formed a bond. At least he thought they had. "You twisted my arm to help you get out of there. That's what you wanted. Why go back?"

"I shouldn't have left. I should have trusted the Lord."

"A lot of people back there died trusting your Lord. If you go back, you'll join them."

"Do what you want, Hank. I know this is right. There are hundreds back there still alive. And they need help."

Hank pointed over his shoulder in the direction of Holloman. "The government is getting ready to light up that sanctuary. Incinerate every living thing there."

"You don't know that for sure. Besides, God can do anything. I wish you understood that Hank."

Jack stopped the truck. Hank forced the door open against the driving wind and let Kat out. He watched her walk in front of Jack's truck and wave her arms at the advancing cavalcade of semis. One stopped, and she disappeared around the other side of it.

Hank got back in the truck and slammed the door.

"Don't take it out on my truck," Jack snapped from behind his hand.

Hank slumped down in the seat and tried not think about Kat or why she had left.

CHAPTER SIXTY-NINE

Holloman Sanctuary, November 23

Jenny's legs felt like two pieces of dead wood poking holes in the snow. The survivors in front of her came to a stop. She looked up from inside Barry's jacket. Several hundred people were massed in front of a building buried under snow.

"God..." The howling wind swept the rest of the sentence away. The voice came from speakers on poles that rose on either side of the building. The same husky voice she had heard earlier.

Jenny craned her neck to see beyond the heads in front, but she was too short.

Someone weakly replied. "God bless you too, Pastor."

Luke's voice cut through the wind. "God sent me here because he loves you. He hasn't forgotten you. Thousands of your brothers and sisters are headed here and to other sanctuaries across the country. We're going to get you out."

She needed to talk to Chavez.

"I want everyone to move as quickly as possible to the front gate. We'll meet there. If you know of anyone who isn't here, and they are healthy, please tell them to come. We're leaving soon."

In the distance Luke walked out of the building. He faded in and out of snow flurries. Jenny pressed through the crowd to get closer.

"What about the sick?" a thin voice called out from the crowd.

"Where are they?" Chavez asked.

"Most of them are at the hospital."

"I need several of you to volunteer to gather blankets, food, everything the sick will need and bring it to the hospital. Hurry now. We'll wait for you." Several raised their hands and trudged off.

"Why did the guards leave?" a man asked.

"I don't know," Chavez said.

"Something isn't right," the man said.

"Please, proceed quickly toward the exit. Let's go."

Luke stepped down into the crowd and disappeared.

Jenny moved through the dispersing throng searching from memory for anyone who looked like the large Mexican ex-fighter she had seen on television. The survivors shuffled past her silently.

At the end of the crowd a man, who seemed lost in thought, traipsed through the knee-deep snow. His eyes were closed, and he seemed to walk more by feel than sight. In the storm it was difficult to identify anyone. Everyone looked like frozen sculptures trying to escape their rigid existence.

"Are you Luke Chavez?"

He looked up, startled by the question. "I am."

"I'm Dr. George from the Centers for Disease Control and Prevention. I'm looking for Hank Jackson. It's extremely important that I find him. Do you know where he is?"

"I'm sorry, I don't."

One of the last departing survivors turned around. "I haven't seen him in days." The frail man hurried to catch up with the others.

The news drained her last resources. Jenny felt herself sink into the snow.

A strong hand grabbed her and lifted her up. "I've got you. Don't worry, if this man you're looking for is here, we'll find him."

Chavez wrapped a strong arm around her waist and lifted. Her feet dragged across the top of the snow as he carried her back to the commander's office.

Inside Jenny sat in a chair and rubbed her legs trying to massage life back into them. Her feet were beyond hope.

"Hank Jackson this is Pastor Luke Chavez." He spoke into the microphone. "If you can hear this, it's very important that you meet me at the front gate." He repeated the call to action several times then turned to her. "We've got to go now."

Jenny tried to stand, but her legs wouldn't cooperate. Luke picked her up and cradled her in his arms and walked back into the blowing snow. She pulled the jacket up over her face and closed her eyes, confident that the strong arms under her wouldn't fail.

* * *

"There isn't anyone here," someone yelled.

The shrill panic in the voice woke her. Jenny raised her head and peeked through the jacket as Luke stopped and eased her to the ground. "You okay?"

She nodded, unable to speak. She stood on shaky legs in the midst of hundreds of survivors.

"Where are they?" another person said.

"Why did you bring us out here if no one is coming?" a man demanded. "I'm going back to my shelter before I freeze."

Several turned away from the gathering and followed him.

"Wait." Chavez held up a hand. "Have faith. Help is coming." *Please, Lord. Save us.* "I'm not staying," a man said. "Come on." He waved at others near him, to encourage them to follow.

In the distance above the wind's howl was a rumble. Tiny bouncing lights pricked the white veil beyond the gate.

Luke pointed toward the gate. "They're here." He closed his eyes. Thank God, the angels had arrived.

Dozens of semis rolled to a stop in front of the sanctuary led by a snowplow. The drivers climbed down from their cabs as several smaller trucks and cars began to arrive behind them. Soon the entire front of the base was packed as far as she could see with vehicles. The survivors, many weeping, began filing through the narrow opening. It would take some time to get everyone through the exit.

A young woman with long stiff hair pushed past a survivor into the compound. She was looking for someone in a hurry.

"Are you Pastor Chavez?" she asked.

He nodded as he motioned for people to keep moving through the gate.

"I need to talk to you privately."

"Okay."

The two of them separated from the crowd. Chavez lowered his head and listened intently. When he raised it, his face was as white as the snow covering his head. He glanced toward the sky.

Jenny walked toward the two of them.

"Any word on Hank?"

The young woman turned to Jenny. "You know Hank?"

"Where is he?"

Her dark eyes turned downward. "He's gone."

"What do you mean he's gone?"

"He's headed to Las Cruces and from there who knows. Why?"

Jenny tried to think, but her mind was as slow as the thickened blood struggling to pump through her near frozen body. "I've got to get to him. He may be the key to a vaccine that can stop the virus."

A beeping noise inside her jacket interrupted. Her cell phone. She reached inside her leather jacket, which she wore under the down jacket, and pulled it out. A light was flashing. She had several messages.

She pushed a button and put the phone to her ear.

"Jenny, where are you?" It was Hampton. His voice was strained. "Where are you? I've been trying to reach you. My God, I was just informed by the President that all sanctuaries," he stopped, his voice trembling, "are to be eradicated. They're going to nuke every base. Did you hear me? Get out of there now."

The recording said the message was received at 7 a.m., an hour ago. A quiver rippled through her.

Jenny looked at Chavez. Their eyes met. A profound sadness tore at his countenance like a man who has just learned he arrived too late at the hospital to say goodbye. The pastor looked up and studied the gray blanket overhead. And she knew exactly what he was searching for.

CHAPTER SEVENTY

N.M. Highway 70, November 23

A plume of steam billowed from the truck's rusted hood and blew sideways in the fierce wind. The engine temperature gauge shot to red.

Jack stopped the truck and slammed his hand against the dashboard. "Dern!"

"What's wrong?" Hank asked.

Jack jumped out into the storm and jerked the hood upward. A white cloud erupted and swept toward the vehicles filing past.

The hood clanked as Jack closed it. He hopped back inside bringing a cold blast of air with him. "Engine is hotter than hades. Heater hose is split wide open like a gutted fish."

"What does that mean?"

"The radiator is bone dry. This truck ain't going nowhere."

"You can't drive it any farther?"

The cowboy pushed his hat back on his head. "You going to buy me a new engine?"

"What are we going to do?"

"I'm going to hitch a ride."

"To Las Cruces?"

"See anyone headed that way?"

Hank shook his head.

Jack removed the keys from the ignition and tucked them into his jeans. He grabbed his pouch of tobacco. "Coming?"

"Staying here. Someone will be along. Leave the keys just in case."

Jack squinted. "Why? You can't drive it like this."

"Just in case someone comes along who can fix your truck."

"You drive it dry; you're going to buy me a new engine." He removed the keys and put them on the dash. The cowboy smiled, revealing dark stains between his dentures. "You know I had an old mare like you. Boy, she was stubborn." He whistled. "I'd pull the reins left, and she'd jerk her head right. I'd draw the reins back, and she would throw her head down and refuse to stop. Didn't matter what I did, she always did the opposite. Never did break her."

"What happened to her?"

"Traded her for a mule."

"Look, Jack, I'm not trying to be obstinate. It's just that I believe going back to Holloman is like putting a gun to your head. You'll die if you go back there."

"Kid, if you stay here, you'll freeze in a couple of hours. And if the government nukes Holloman, which I don't think it will, you'll die from radiation. Either way, you're dead."

"I'll take my chances."

"Like I said, you remind me of that ol' mare."

"But what about your horses?" Hank pointed at the trailer behind them. "You can't just leave them."

Jack ground his jaw, then opened the door and spit. "I'm not worried about them. They've got a better chance of making it than you. But if there is a bomb..." He paused and rubbed bristly white whiskers on his chin which sounded like sandpaper on wood. "I better let 'em loose. They'll head in the right direction." He turned back and stared at Hank, then shook his head before shutting the door. Through icy windows Hank watched Jack walk around the end of the trailer and let the horses out. He swatted them on the rear and watched them gallop west toward Las Cruces. With his hat flapping in his hand, the cowboy flagged down an approaching truck that rolled to a stop. Thin strands of white hair danced wildly on his head. He put his hat back on and held it firmly down as he disappeared into the truck.

Hank lowered his head and tucked his hands under his armpits. *Someone will be along.*

But with each drop in temperature, he began to question his decision. Bitter cold attacked his body like a thousand little needles pricking his fingers, toes, and ears. His breath hovered in the air like thick fog as an ice-covered windshield skewed a gray breaking dawn.

* * *

Hank checked his watch. It had been thirty minutes since the last vehicle passed and there wasn't any sign of approaching lights. Fresh snow covered the highway, removing any trace of the cavalcade's dark grooves.

"I'll buy you a new engine." Hank slid over into the driver's seat and started the engine and turned the heater on, but it didn't work.

The engine clanked as the truck rolled forward. A thick white blanket so thoroughly covered the road that it was impossible to tell where it began and ended. Clouds of smoke rose from the hood.

With each passing mile the engine clanked louder like a wrench had somehow made its way into the inner workings of the motor. But on the horizon, city lights twinkled. Hank's spirits lifted just as the engine seized and sputtered to a stop.

Hank got out of the truck. The wind had stopped, and it was quiet. Cold sliced through his jacket. Could he make it to Las Cruces? It couldn't be more than a few miles. If he stayed in the truck, he was sure to freeze. He had to keeping moving, try to make it to the city. He warmed his hands over steam hissing from the truck's hood, then started toward the lights.

As he trudged forward, he lost track of time. How long had he been walking? His mind began to dull. All feeling left his feet, legs, and hands. They no longer ached. But he couldn't keep his balance. He fell to his knees. He turned back toward the truck but couldn't see it. The lights ahead were just as far as when he began. He stood back up and tried to walk, but it was useless. He lay down on a snow drift and curled up. The hard outline of the .45 in his jacket dug into his side. He slid his numb fingers into the pocket and touched the gun. Could he do it? No, he removed his hand.

He should have listened to Kat. He missed her—the large brown eyes, the quiet strength. Even, maybe especially, her courage to face death for something she believed in. It was hopeless of course and a needless waste of life for people probably already infected. But it would have been better to die with her than here all alone.

Had he ever been willing to die for anything? Had he ever even believed in anything? Christians prayed faithfully to their God, but what had he done for them? If he were real, why hadn't he protected them? The poor people had lost their Bible to censors, been thrown in camps for refusing the chip, and were about to be wiped off the face of the earth. And Hank was going to die because of them.

But what if Christians were right? This was a new thought. He'd always just assumed they weren't. There wasn't any way to know for sure. No one could offer concrete proof either way. Prayer was ridiculous. The wind began to howl again. He could feel it against his skin, but it wasn't cold. And then he did something he'd never done before. Not sincerely, anyway. He prayed.

I don't know if You're real or not, but if You can hear me, please help me. If You're really God, You can do anything. Sending someone down this road shouldn't be a big deal. I don't want to die. He tried to raise his hand to brush his eyes, but he couldn't. *Please help me. Please, please help me.*

Hank repeated the appeal over and over like a chant and something strange happened. The words comforted him. Maybe it was the cold's final toll. Deadness taking hold of the last remnant of sensation. He closed his eyes. *If You're real, prove it.*

CHAPTER SEVENTY-ONE

Holloman Sanctuary, November 23

The storm had passed. Ice crystals sparkled in freshly fallen snow like millions of diamonds discovered by the sun. Patches of light blue washed across the sky as the last remnants of gray receded. The change in weather terrified Jenny.

Most vehicles had left the sanctuary packed with survivors bundled in blankets. All were headed for an RV park between El Paso and Las Cruces where everyone would rendezvous. Luke and a team of volunteers were making a final check on the sick. A few survivors had even insisted on remaining behind to comfort the dying. Jenny had rummaged through the hospital in search of protective gear.

Volunteers passed out masks and gloves. They provided little protection against the virus, but it was better than nothing. There was a chance, however, that the extreme cold might inhibit the pathogen's spread. A chance.

Everyone's hands had been checked before leaving. It was the only quick test available. No doubt some of the survivors were infected, but it was impossible to know without the chip. In the end though, what difference did it make? Without an antiviral even the courageous efforts to save the survivors would be forgotten, because all would die. And the very person who might prevent such a tragedy had vanished.

"Let's go," Luke said as he waved for everyone to follow. Then he ran toward the gate with a small group. "We've done all we can for the sick."

Distant trailing thunder turned every head upward.

Everyone stopped as the jet continued its pass over the sanctuary. Jenny felt like a bystander about to witness an accident. She could see the coming collision before the drivers, but there wasn't time to warn them. All she could do was wait.

The trailing exhaust of a missile broke through the clouds, its fiery tail propelling it downward.

"Run," Luke shouted as he pointed at the gate.

But it was too late to run. The supersonic speeds of the nuclear blast would flatten every square inch of Holloman and spread radioactive debris for miles beyond ground zero. Those who survived the blast would wish they hadn't. Jenny grabbed the flag pole next to her to steady herself and closed her eyes.

A loud thud in the distance shook the ground. She opened her eyes. A cloud of white rose in the east beyond the wall against deep purple mountains. No one said a word, but no one needed to. Jenny ran as fast as she could on Luke's heels with others close by. How the first bomb failed to detonate she didn't know, but she was certain they wouldn't be so lucky twice.

Luke motioned for her to come with him. She jumped in the truck next to the dark-haired woman he spoke with earlier. Tires spun on the snow-packed road as he punched the accelerator to the floor. The truck swerved right then left as it swung onto US 70. With each shake and roll, the arrow on the speedometer steadily climbed until it hit 100 miles mph and couldn't go any further. The woman grabbed Jenny's arm as she braced herself against the dash.

"Come on you old beast. Faster." Luke pushed against the accelerator already flattened to the floor as if somehow his efforts could coax more from the engine. Jenny studied the side view mirror for any sign of a blast, although she was sure she'd feel it before she saw it.

At first it felt like they had hit the mother of all pot holes. The truck dipped downward then bounced into the air mashing her head against the roof. For a moment she was suspended in air. But the weightless ride ended when the truck landed on its rear two wheels before rocking forward. It slammed the old suspension and worn-out shocks to the highway like an over-the-hill wrestler and everyone inside along with it.

The truck surged forward with such force that it whipped her head back, cracking it against the rear window. The centrifugal force pinned her against the seat. It felt as if Luke had engaged some kind of turbocharged booster. But a blinding flash in the side view mirror eliminated any doubt. A flash of pure white light erupted into a fireball. It looked as if the sun had fallen to earth. The dazzling ball morphed into yellow-orange before blooming into a black canopy over the sanctuary. It was magnificent and terrifying all at once. One of man's greatest achievements and failures.

Luke's white knuckles wrapped around the wheel as he fought to control the truck that slid from one side of the highway to the other. Jenny gripped a loose door handle with her right hand and braced against the dash with her other. The woman next to her had wrapped herself into a protective cocoon. She was praying, and, for once, Jenny hoped someone was listening because the dark swelling mass behind was gaining on them like a cloud of locusts intent on devouring everything in its path.

CHAPTER SEVENTY-TWO

Washington, D.C., November 25

"Islam will rule the world again!" The imam thrust his fist upward toward the tiled dome of the Washington Islamic Center. Then he brought it down onto the wooden podium with a smack that resonated through the hall. "The fierce hand of Allah has struck a fatal blow against the infidels in our land. Soon the world will bow before the one and only true God."

Sulaiman sat with his feet tucked under him. It was early Monday morning, and thin rays of light filtered through windows illuminating the Persian rug he knelt on. He leaned forward and pressed his forehead against the carpet. His eyes were moist. *Thank you, Allah, for using me to destroy the unbelievers.*

He had grown a thick beard and wore dark glasses. His customary suit and tie were gone, replaced by a black dishadasha over which he wore a heavy black woolen chapan. Even in the mosque, the FBI had eyes. They were hunting him, and he had to be careful.

The teacher switched to a passage from the Qur'an and continued morning prayers. "So when the sacred months have passed away, then slay the idolaters wherever you find them captives and besiege them and lie in wait for them in every ambush..." The imam's voice faded as a white-bearded Adbul stood in front of a young boy and urged him to fulfill Allah's calling. Abdul had stirred

Sulaiman's heart sixteen years ago. If only the old man were here to share in the victory.

Who could have ever imagined then that the government would willingly destroy its own citizens? Only Allah could have engineered such a plan. Now the snake was crushed. The virus was spreading across the country. Infected airline passengers had pumped poison through every major artery of the country. There was even a report of an infection in Paris. Before long London, Moscow, and Beijing would feel Allah's judgment.

And soon the Mahdi would arrive.

The imam looked directly at him. There was a slight smile on his lips. "And we gave Sulayman power over the wind—a month's journey in the morning and a month in the evening. And we made a fount of molten copper flow out for him. And some of the jinn worked in front of him by his Lord's permission."

The scripture triggered an unpleasant memory of the black slithering image in his bedroom. The experience still troubled him. He wasn't sure if the jinni had been real or a nightmare. Perhaps the message was meant to reassure him that the encounter was authentic. Perhaps Allah wanted to erase any doubts about the jinni. The Qur'an taught that God used the supernatural beings at times to accomplish his will as he had done to help his namesake, Sulayman the Magnificent.

Certainly his plans had been blessed. Any number of things could have gone wrong with releasing the virus, but nothing had. It was very possible Allah had employed the jinn to enable the suicide martyrs to penetrate the bases and manipulate public opinion against the Christians. Clearly, supernatural intervention was involved in convincing the government to bomb the detention camps.

Of course, he hadn't always understood Allah's will. The Holy One hadn't intended for Chavez to die, though it seemed right at the time. It was clear now that if the pastor had been killed, it would have emboldened his followers. Instead, the death of his wife had left him broken, and his church without direction. Even the setback at creating the antiviral made sense now. If Sulaiman had focused all of his energies on the vaccine, he would have missed his chance at destroying the sanctuaries. Allah's will was perfect except Elisha's death, which was still perplexing. And the memory stung like an open wound that wouldn't heal. And maybe never would.

The imam finished morning prayers. Attendance had been light. Many had stayed away because of an outbreak in Alexandria. Some Muslims would die from the virus, but Allah would protect the most faithful. Sulaiman stood up. His knees were stiff. Rashid, who had come late, nodded at him from across the hall and began walking toward him—more quickly than usual. He was frowning.

"What's wrong cousin? You should be happy. It's a great day."

"I'm sorry I'm late."

"What could be more important than morning prayers?"

"I was glued to the television. A news report is claiming Christians escaped the sanctuaries before they were bombed."

"How many?"

"I don't know."

"I don't believe it." Sulaiman's pulse pounded so hard the veins in his neck throbbed.

Rashid stepped back. "It doesn't matter. The majority of them are dead."

Sulaiman motioned for them to leave the mosque. The sun had disappeared behind gray clouds that hung low in the sky. Light, persistent rain tapped at puddles pooled along stone steps. He and Rashid descended to a broad sidewalk that led to Massachusetts Avenue, empty except for National Guard troops that marched toward the Capitol.

He turned to Rashid. "It matters."

CHAPTER SEVENTY-THREE

Washington, D.C., November 26

"It's unraveling Mr. President," Pepper said. "I think it would be wise to get you to Camp David." He looked disheveled, his neatly trimmed dark hair longer than usual. Dark stubble covered his face.

"I'm not going to run," Hamilton said. "People need to know their President isn't afraid. It's important to stay in Washington." Hamilton ran his hand over a kitchen counter in the Presidential Emergency Operations Center, better known as PEOC. Buried two-hundred feet below the east wing of the White House and encased in tons of steel, the bunker was designed to withstand a direct nuclear strike. "It's filthy. Can you get someone to clean it up?"

Pepper nodded.

Hamilton peered into a room at six army cots and shook his head. "And put in some decent beds."

"Yes, Mr. President."

Hamilton walked out to the adjacent executive briefing room and took a seat at a long oval table. The room served as communication center for the President and his staff during an attack on the White House. The bank of flat screens was dark, but images of the last hours before communication was lost still lingered in his memory: scarlet stained bodies slumped on each other in an alley, a chain hanging from a hospital entrance below a sign that said "no room," a funeral home overflowing with body bags —and most of all, the fiery mushroom clouds.

He leaned forward and shook his head. "All those lives lost for nothing."

"The eradication plan would have worked if the virus hadn't mutated." Pepper leaned against a wall opposite the flat screens and furrowed his brow. "The minute it became an airborne pathogen, though, it was hopeless. It spread faster than CDC projected. Our health officials did their best to quarantine the infected. But once they removed the sick, there were ten more the following day, then one-hundred the next, until the first responders couldn't keep up."

Hamilton tapped his fingers on the table. "General Maddox was right. We should have acted faster."

"I think history will show you erred on the side of compassion. You did everything you could to give Dr. George time to find a cure."

What difference did history make now? If they didn't stop the virus soon, there wouldn't be anyone to read it. Sometimes doing the right thing wasn't the best thing. Like agreeing to pursue diplomacy with Iran instead of bombing their brains out. That had only given Admadinejad the time he needed to complete a bomb. "Any word on Dr. George?"

Pepper shook his head. "No confirmation yet on whether she escaped the blast."

"Can't we track her through her chip?"

"Unfortunately, we can't. The blasts temporarily disrupted communication. Shut down radio frequencies, cell phones, satellite, pretty much all communication. Let's hope she was among those who escaped before detonation."

"When will we know?"

"There's too much radiation surrounding the sites to conduct an investigation for at least three days."

"Any reports of radiation poisoning in areas bordering the evacuation zones?"

"Not any so far, but, again, communication with these cities has been knocked out," Pepper said. "But fallout is supposed to be minimal."

"That's what Maddox said. But no one really knows, do they?"

"I think fallout is less of a concern than the virus. We're in a real meltdown right now. The pathogen has spread to every major city including here. The World Health Organization has declared Leviathan a pandemic and issued a quarantine on all travel to and from the U.S. The stock market has collapsed, and gold has soared to a million an ounce."

Hamilton massaged his temples. The virus had outsmarted the best minds in the country. A virus was one of the simplest life forms. Unintelligent. But he was beginning to wonder whether the late General Sullivan had given it sentience.

The pathogen had certainly out flanked Hamilton. The opportunity initially created by the outbreaks, which had forestalled his impeachment, seemed now like a cleverly disguised plot by the virus to draw him into its jaws. He had mistakenly believed he could defeat it by eliminating the sanctuaries and, in doing so, avoid impeachment. But that had been Leviathan's tactic: lure him with the carrot of saving the country and his presidency. Now he faced condemnation from not only Americans but from the world.

Riots had broken out in Washington as the Senate debated his fate. The nation's angst had transformed into rage, and he had become its focus. Had the eradication worked, he would have been hailed as a hero. Now many accused him of releasing the virus in an effort to save his presidency. How could anyone charge him with such a thing? It would take a truly psychotic narcissist to even conceive of such a plan. Or a religious fanatic like Sulaiman, the man most likely responsible. And yet, the public had completely forgotten the terrorist.

The phone in the center of the table rang. Hamilton motioned for Pepper to take the call.

"This is Pepper." His Chief of Staff listened intently. His hand holding the receiver began to shake, and his face lost all color. He laid the phone down.

"What is it?"

"A mob has broken through the White House fence."

"How is that even possible?"

"A 50-ton tractor trailer just plowed through it."

CHAPTER SEVENTY-FOUR

Anthony, New Mexico, December 1

The murky sky looked like muddy water washing over the RV park north of El Paso. Christmas was four weeks away. Many of the camp sites were adorned with trees. Colorful bulbs bobbed on branches in the light wind. Red, blue, green and white lights blinked on the exterior of semis, motor homes, campers, and cars. Even those living in tents had adorned their shelters in glittering lights. Outside the park tinsel draped over cactus, and tumbleweeds shimmered, adding a touch of glamour to the brown, barren landscape.

Everyone was celebrating—except Jenny.

She walked with Luke and a small group that included Kat. They searched inside the camp for Hank, then outside. Some two thousand people had survived, far more than the RV park could contain. Hundreds of vehicles were parked beyond its walls. The search had become a daily ritual. But the prospect of finding the reporter faded each passing day. He had been missing for a week.

He was the last bridge to hope, a hope Jenny had fiercely clung to. But now she felt her grip slipping.

Everything depended on finding him. Everyone's life, including hers. That hope was grounded in Dr. Lutz's firm belief that Hank possessed an antivirus. How she hoped the late doctor was right, but he might not be. Just because Hank had survived, didn't mean he was immune. She was still alive and so were the survivors in the camp. It didn't mean she or the others were resistant to the virus, just lucky. But with each passing moment, the odds increased that their luck would run out.

Luck was a fickle thing. She had seen its impact in research. A mistake that led to a new drug. But even those blessed by luck could quickly discover it had abandoned them. After leaving Holloman a few drivers had apparently taken Route 15, a southern detour from US 70, thinking it a safer escape route. They hadn't been seen since.

Memories of the dark mass that had nearly swallowed Luke's truck made her shiver. "I don't think he's here," Jenny said weakly.

Kat's eyes sank.

Luke stared into the distance as a cold breeze tousled his hair. "There are still a few more camps we haven't checked."

"You cheated," a child yelled. "You're a cheater." The high-pitched complaint came from a camp in front of them.

"Sugar, that's the way poker is played. Two jack of spades trump two jack of hearts." The crusty words were followed by a throaty chuckle. "Pay up."

Kat bolted forward toward the man's voice. "Jack."

A weather-worn man with a sweat-stained cowboy hat sat at a picnic table across from a small, tow-headed girl. A mound of pennies sat in front of the old man, a smaller pile near the girl. He grabbed the child's cards and tucked them into his Levi jacket along with his own. He looked up sheepishly at Kat.

"Give me my cards back." The little girl pulled at Jack's arm.

"Jack, where's Hank?"

He spit a wad of dark liquid on the ground. Some of it splashed on his muddy boot. "Left him back there in the truck." He pointed east toward dirty brown skies. "Tried to convince him to come with me. He's got a head harder than a good mule." He pushed his hat back on his head. "But he was right about one thing. He swore the government would nuke Holloman, and it did."

Kat grabbed the edge of the table. Her arms quivered as she eased herself down onto the gray wooden bench.

Jenny stepped forward. "Where exactly was your truck?"

"About thirty miles from Holloman, on 70. I sure hope the feds reimburse me for it." He shook his head. "My horses, too, but they might have made it."

Luke patted Kat's shoulders. "Someone might have stopped to pick him up."

"Doubt that," Jack said. He pushed the little girl's hand back who continued to tug at his coat. "We passed it on the way back. Completely covered in snow. Couldn't even tell it was a truck. Besides, everyone was driving crazy, trying to get as far away from Holloman as possible."

Jenny pushed the thought of Hank's cold, rigid body from her mind. She dug into her coat and pulled out her cell, then remembered it was useless. She turned to Luke and Kat. "I'm going to check the hospitals again."

"I'm going with you," Kat said standing up.

Luke turned and looked north. "I'll stay here and pray that the rest of the church arrives soon from the other sanctuaries."

CHAPTER SEVENTY-FIVE

Washington, D.C., December 1

A wall of soldiers and Secret Service moved in front of Hamilton and Pepper as they hustled toward Marine One sitting on the south lawn. Shots rang out. Agents pushed Hamilton to the ground and covered him. It was difficult to tell from which direction the shots had come, but it sounded like a small caliber, probably a handgun.

Several bullets slammed into Marine One.

"Those crazies are trying to take out the President's chopper," one of the men shouted.

"Can you tell where it's coming from?" another asked.

"I'm not waiting to find out."

A deafening burst from an M-16. Then silence.

"Move." An agent pulled Hamilton to his feet. They ran toward the waiting chopper. Wamp, wamp, wamp. The wind from the Sikorsky's blades flung Hamilton's tie over his shoulder and flattened his suit against his legs. The sounds carried him back forty-seven years.

He was running through a jungle toward the Huey. The dense foliage around him fell in clumps, shredded from AK47 fire. The Marine next to him pitched forward. Dark stains bled through the soaked green fatigues. Hamilton hoisted his comrade up and dragged him to the chopper as bullets whizzed by.

Hamilton leaped up the stairs into the safety of the helicopter and took a seat.

More shots slammed into Marine One.

An ashen-faced Pepper slipped at the top of stairs. An agent pushed him into the cabin as soldiers followed.

"Get that door closed. We've got to get the President out of here." The pilot glared at the Marine retracting the stairs. "Forget this." The pilot pulled the stick back with his left hand. The chopper rose rapidly.

Through the window the full specter of the attack below unfolded. A crowd of several hundred encircled the White House and fired at National Guard soldiers and special security forces. It looked like a Civil War battle. Two opposing armies unloading their guns into each other's ranks. But the mob far out numbered White House defenders and appeared to be advancing despite the large number of dead left behind on the snow-covered lawn.

"Do you think they can hold?" Hamilton turned to the Marine Lieutenant who had just managed to secure the door. He was staring down at the fight below and holding his rifle a little too tightly as if he were waiting for the right moment to bash out the window next to him and start shooting.

"They have to. It's the White House."

Pepper slowly shook his head as he peered out the window.

Firing from the mob stopped momentarily as heads turned upward toward Marine One. "Step on it, Roy," said the co-pilot looking down at the crowd.

Several shots slammed into the chopper's belly as the pilot pushed the joystick forward with his right hand. The nose dipped down slightly as Marine One launched forward. Below the nation's capitol reeled from unfolding chaos. Looters ran from Union Station Mall as scattered fires burned uncontrolled. Troops braced for a battle on the steps of the Capitol Building.

"Is the First Lady safe?" Hamilton asked.

Scott, his favorite among the Secret Service detail, pressed his phone to his ear. "I'm checking, Mr. President. What's the status on Monte Cristo?" He nodded, then turned to Hamilton. "A chopper has just landed for the First Lady and her staff. Two more are on their way for your cabinet and the Vice President."

"Well they better damn well hurry. It's turning into a war zone down there."

Pepper's face was clammy. Beads of perspiration dotted his forehead.

"Are you okay? You look like death."

The tablet computer pressed against Pepper's side slipped from his grasp and fell to the floor. He attempted to reach for it but slumped over in his seat. A large stain darkened the side of his charcoal, pin-striped suit.

"He's been shot," Hamilton yelled. He turned to Scott. "Do something."

"Who's shot?" the pilot asked.

"Pepper," Hamilton said. The name caught in his throat. *This can't be happening.*

The co-pilot pushed the overhead throttles all the way forward. Scott braced himself against the cabin wall as the engines of Marine One roared to top speed.

Another agent with a noticeable pock mark on his right cheek sprang from his seat and removed a large metal case secured to the back of the cabin. He tore into a package and pulled out a wad of gauze. Pepper coughed up blood. Working quickly, the agent removed Pepper's suit jacket, tie and shirt. Blood spurted from the wound in rhythmic bursts like water hand pumped from a well. The agent eased Pepper down onto the floor and pressed the bandage against a dark crimson hole. Scott covered him with a blanket as an IV was inserted into Pepper's arm. Flecks of dark red splattered his face.

Scott turned toward Hamilton. The expression on the agent's face said it all.

Hamilton had seen what a bullet through a man's stomach could do, particularly when it sliced an artery. Pepper was losing blood fast.

"Why didn't he say something?" Hamilton asked, his voice breaking. "Call my surgeon now."

But the young face staring up at him from the floor was the soldier's from forty-seven years ago. A medic worked feverishly over him. Dozens of hot M60 casings fell to the chopper's slick red floor as a door gunner leaned outside and unleashed his machine gun. The soldier's eyes stared upward. Hamilton looked at the spot on the ceiling where they were fixed. A photograph of Raquel Welch in a ripped animal-skin bikini was taped there. Someone's attempt to encourage the wounded to hang on, that better times were ahead. But he was sure the soldier no longer cared.

"Marine One has taken fire." Scott raised his voice as he spoke into his cell. "Maduro is safe. I repeat Maduro is safe. But Stanton is hit and critical. Have Dr. Epstein prep for surgery." The agent described the wound, then hung up.

The Raven Rock Mountain complex, Marine One's destination, was approximately seventy miles from the White House. The secure underground facility, code name Creed, was six miles northeast of Camp David. It would take a half hour to reach. Hamilton glanced at his watch and belched acid. Pepper didn't have a half hour.

Chapter Seventy-Six

Las Cruces, New Mexico, December 1

Jenny slipped on heavy black leather gloves. It was cold out. The sun hadn't shone since the blast and wouldn't for weeks because of debris kicked into the atmosphere.

If she still possessed a chip under her skin, a red light would be blinking somewhere or an alarm going off. But she didn't. It didn't matter anyway because the scaffolding of the government's carefully designed Operation First Alert had collapsed along with everything else. There were simply too many infected.

No one would suspect anything unusual about the gloves, but it didn't make her feel any better about the deception. If it weren't the eleventh hour, she would have isolated herself and not endangered Kat or anyone else. But she had to find Hank and determine whether he really possessed an antivirus. No one else could do it.

The truck rolled to a stop in front of the last hospital. No one had seen Hank at the previous five facilities. The fingertips on Kat's blue protective gloves on her right hand were chewed through. "I'm almost afraid to see if he's here," she said.

It was difficult to tell whether her trepidation was what Jenny felt—that if Hank wasn't here, all was lost. Or whether it was motivated by something more. Kat and Hank hadn't known each other for very long, but a crisis could bring people together, who in different times, would never be attracted to each other.

Jenny stepped out of Luke's truck. She had to lower her expectations. There had been too many disappointments. Kat hesitated, then got out. The parking lot was deserted like the previous five. A change in weather had blown ominous clouds toward Las Cruces and with it fallout. Across the hospital's glass exterior the clouds moved slowly. Everyone who could leave had already evacuated.

Walking up the steps to the entrance proved exhausting. Jenny stopped and coughed.

"Are you okay?" Kat asked as she gently touched Jenny's shoulder.

"I'm okay. Go inside. I'll be along in just a minute."

"Are you sure?"

Jenny nodded.

Fluid was already building in her lungs. Her antibodies were under siege by Leviathan's molecular bots. Soon, the virus would invade her cells and begin replication. The octopus-shaped pathogen would multiply exponentially until her blood looked like a river teeming with thousands of minnows. Then the virus would attack her organs, reducing them to the consistency of jello. She had, at most, twenty-four to forty-eight hours. It was difficult to tell exactly because it varied from person to person.

Once the assault on her organs began, it would be too late. Even if Hank possessed a cure, the damage would be irreversible.

A few minutes later Kat emerged from the hospital with a thin, red-headed man on crutches wearing a surgical mask. Even if she hadn't known what Hank looked like, she could have guessed it was him from the look in Kat's eyes. *Thank God he's alive.*

"Look what I found," she said.

Hank hobbled up. "The indomitable Dr. George." He awkwardly extended a bandaged hand while trying to balance himself on crutches but then seemed reticent when he noticed her gloves.

"The virological phenomenon. We hope." Jenny steadied herself against the handrail as she shook his bandaged hand. His feet were also bandaged. "Frostbite?"

"Yeah. At least I'm still alive. Thank God."

The brown eyes were weary. His freckled face was sunburned, his lips cracked.

"Is this about the tests that Dr. Lutz performed?" Hank said.

Jenny let go of the handrail and pointed toward Luke's truck. "I'll fill you in on the way down to the medical school in El Paso. We've got to hurry. Kat, can you drive so I can talk to Hank?"

"Sure."

Jenny couldn't disclose the real reason she didn't want to drive. Her hands burned and ached from exploding capillaries, and she wasn't sure if she could even grip the steering wheel. Kat slipped in behind the wheel with Jenny next to her. Hank put his crutches in the truck bed and hopped in. Kat pulled out of the parking lot and headed toward Interstate 25 south.

Jenny glanced at her watch. She shifted in her seat. It wasn't nearly enough time. She still had no idea how Hank's immunity against the virus worked or if it even did. Did he possess an extra chromosome, like the one that came with Down Syndrome and protected against cancer? Had he inherited genes that somehow made his antibodies impervious to Leviathan's attack? Or was there some other biological anomaly? The answer to those questions could take weeks of research. The sequencing of Hank's genome alone would take a day, which was fast compared to the weeks it used to take. But she didn't have a day. She needed a miracle.

An hour later they pulled up in front of University Medical Center. Two guards stood at the entrance in front of a group of people who were shouting at them. Hank rolled his window down.

A woman cradled the limp body of a small child that was hemorrhaging. "My baby's dying. She needs help." The woman dropped to her knees. "Please help us."

"Look lady, it's not that the hospital doesn't want to help you," the taller of two guards said. "There aren't enough healthy doctors left to treat the patients we have. Maybe Providence Hospital can."

A heavy-set unshaven man in a black leather vest pushed through the crowd. He stood eye-to-eye with the taller of the two guards. "You better open these doors." Metal glinted in his fist.

The shorter guard pulled a gun from his holster and waved it. "Get back."

Jenny turned to Kat. "Quick. Drive around to the back."

As they turned the corner, several shots rang out.

Hank swiveled in his seat toward the shots. "This place is coming apart. Isn't there somewhere safer?"

"Antarctica," Jenny said. "Anywhere there are people there's going to be infection. And where there's infection, there's going to be panic and hysteria. This hospital is one of the few places that has a sequencer and the equipment I need."

Kat pulled up behind the hospital and turned off the engine. Jenny pulled out her cell. Still no service. "Let's hope we can get someone to answer the door."

Hank hopped out of the truck and grabbed his crutches. Jenny slid out behind him and Kat followed. Jenny walked up a short flight of concrete stairs and peered through a window in the door. She tried the handle. Locked. She pressed a button near the door that buzzed inside the hallway. A moment later a nurse appeared, but she stared at them through the wire-reinforced glass and left abruptly.

"See if you can find something to write on," Jenny said.

Kat came back with a dirty sheet of paper she found lying in the nearby alley.

Jenny scrawled her name across it and pressed it against the glass. But as she pushed the button again a man emerged from the alley and pointed at them.

"They've found another way in. Come on," he yelled behind him.

The group from out front rounded the corner and ran toward the stairs.

"We're running out of time here, Doc," Hank said.

Another nurse entered the hallway behind the glass door and squinted at the note. She ran toward them.

The man who had spotted them reached Hank just as the nurse touched the door. Something smacked into the window in front of her, leaving a chip in it. Jenny spun around. Hank pushed a man back, then swung his crutch like a bat. It connected against the man's face. He fell backwards into the rush of people scrambling up the stairs, toppling them. The door opened, and Jenny, Kat, and Hank hurried through.

As it closed, a collage of faces pressed against the door. Hands beat the glass leaving bloody impressions. The locked door provided little separation from their screams, curses, and pleas.

"Those poor people," Kat said.

"You're lucky they didn't get their infected hands on you," Hank said.

Jenny flinched.

The silver-haired nurse's face was pasty, and make-up missing from under her eyes revealed red skin the texture of crepe paper. "Dr. George we heard you were…"

"I thought I was, too. I need to use your sequencing equipment. This man may be our salvation." Jenny looked at Hank.

"The lab is this way." The nurse pointed toward the elevator.

A moment later the elevator door opened to a dimly lit hallway and the stench of death. Dozens of black body bags were stacked waist high on both sides of the corridor, creating a narrow passage way.

Jenny covered her nose.

"Never get used to that smell." The nurse shook her head. "No room in the morgue anymore. We've asked the mortuaries to pick them up, but they don't have room either. I don't know what we're going to do."

The nurse pointed toward the end of the hallway. "It's right down here."

With each step it seemed the end was farther away. The floor shifted under Jenny's feet. She grabbed one of the bags to steady herself. Something inside moved. The bag was unzipped. Dull eyes stared at her—eyes that looked eerily similar to PJ's. The dim light above swirled and the floor collapsed.

Someone caught her from behind and eased her to the ground.

Hank peered down into her face. He asked something, but his words came out so slowly she couldn't understand them.

"Why is PJ here?"

From the confused faces peering down at her, she knew they either hadn't seen him or didn't understand her question.

The nurse lifted her wrist to take a pulse then quickly dropped it. "She's infected."

Jenny looked at her right wrist. Rivulets of blood ran from her glove down her arm. Then the people above her faded until there was nothing.

313

CHAPTER SEVENTY-SEVEN

El Paso, Texas, December 2

A clear plastic tent enclosed the hospital bed. A sophisticated filtration system scrubbed the air going in and out. A series of tubes connected Jenny's right arm to two machines next to her bed. Two tubes carried clear solutions, a pain killer probably and something else, and the third delivered blood.

Kat leaned against Hank. "I wish there was something we could do. Why didn't she let us know she was sick?"

"She thought she had more time. She told me on the trip down that nothing was more important than finding the vaccine. Everyone's life depended on it. I think she knew that if people found out she was sick, she wouldn't be able to complete her work."

Jenny opened her eyes slowly and studied the tent envelope. Then her eyes fixed on Hank. She opened her mouth and tried to speak.

"What did she say?" Kat asked.

"I don't know." Hank searched the room and found what he was looking for. He steadied himself on his crutches and lifted the tent. He handed a pen and pad to Jenny. She pushed them away and grabbed his arm with her bandaged hand and held it. Her delicate fingers trembled. She whispered something.

Her words were faint. Barely a whisper but deliberate. "Get me out of here." She tugged at the IVs in her arm. "Take me to the lab."

Hank slipped out of the tent and searched the room for something to wrap Jenny's arm with, but there wasn't anything. "Don't do anything until I get back."

Kat stepped backward. "What are you doing? She's infected."

"If I'm really immune, then I have nothing to worry about. Right? But you should find a safer place."

"Where are you going?"

"Right now to find some bandages." Hank hobbled out of the room to the nurse's station across the hallway.

A young nurse with her blonde hair pinned back stood behind a counter examining a chart.

Hank grabbed his left hand and grimaced. "I cut myself. Do you have anything I can wrap this with?"

"Let me take a look at it," the nurse said.

"Not necessary. I just need something to wrap it."

The nurse left the station and returned shortly with some bandages. "You sure?"

"Definitely."

Hank returned to Jenny's room and shut the door. He switched off the machines before ducking back inside Jenny's tent. He helped her remove the IVs, then wrapped her arm with gauze.

"Why are you unhooking her IVs?"

Hank folded the tent back from Jenny's bed. He gave her a surgical mask to put on. He took his crutches and laid them on her bed. Then he pushed the bed back from the wall and positioned himself behind it. "We're headed to the lab."

"Have you lost your mind? She's sick. Let her die in peace." Jenny shook her head.

Kat opened the door as Hank pushed Jenny's bed out of the room into the hallway. The nurse at the station across the hallway dropped her clip board and stared. She opened her mouth to say something, but nothing came out. She ran.

315

As Hank wheeled Jenny toward the elevator, doctors and nurses and hospital personnel scattered. When the elevator door opened, a nurse standing inside flattened herself against the wall and slid past Jenny's bed.

"You're crazy," she said as she ran out of the elevator.

Hank shrugged. "That's old news."

The elevator door opened at the basement. The body bags stacked on both sides made the hallway too narrow to get a bed through. And there were too many bodies to move.

"Can you walk?"

Jenny nodded. He helped her out of bed, but as soon as she stood, her legs gave way. Hank grabbed her and lifted her into his arms. He still couldn't feel his toes which made walking difficult. But he took small careful steps toward the lab at the end of the hallway. When he arrived, he backed up against the door and managed to fiddle with the handle and open it. Jenny switched on the light as they entered. He sat her down in a chair. The room was packed with machines and instruments, none of which he recognized.

"Okay, how's this going to work?" It was a question that had troubled him from the moment Jenny told him what she wanted to do. He didn't know anything about virology. And he could barely understand what she was saying, let alone follow a complex set of instructions.

She pointed at a needle lying on a metal table. "Bring it to me."

Hank picked up the needle and gave it to her. Her hand shook as she aimed for a vein in his arm. *No telling where this will end up.*

"Here, let me help." Hank steadied her hand as she inserted the needle a little too forcefully into his arm.

She drew back the plunger and watched the syringe fill with deep red fluid that looked almost violet. "Do you know your blood type?"

"I think it's O positive."

"That's mine, too." She removed the syringe. "Help me toward the microscope."

Hank picked Jenny up and carried her to a chair near the microscope.

"Put some blood on a slide," she said.

Hank pushed a squirt of blood from the syringe onto the glass.

"Too much. Just a drop. Try again."

Hank grabbed another slide and watched as a drop fell onto the glass sliver from the needle.

"Good. Now put it under the microscope."

Hank did as instructed.

"What do you see?"

"Nothing. It's blurry."

"Adjust the lens with those knobs." She pointed toward the controls on either side of the microscope.

A microscopic world of wriggling forms that reminded him of writhing worms filled the lens.

"Can you see anything now?"

Hank nodded. He reached down and helped Jenny to her feet and supported her as she peered down into the instrument.

"This doesn't make any sense," she said shaking her head.

"What's wrong?"

"Your blood is full of virus."

The news nearly buckled Hank's legs. "I thought you said I was immune?"

Jenny looked up from the microscope. The blood vessels in her eyes had ruptured. Her skin was flush, and Hank thought he detected beads of blood forming on her forehead. "I thought you were, too."

She bent down and stared into the lens again. "But it doesn't look anything like Leviathan." She paused. "Unless it's mutated again."

"Can it do that?"

"So far it's been able to do anything it wants." She studied it further then looked up. "The virus in your blood is t-shaped." She took another syringe from the metal table in front of them and withdrew blood from her arm. She added a speck to the slide that contained Hank's blood. "Only one way to find out."

"What are you doing?" Hank asked.

"Testing to see how well these two microbes like each other."

Jenny looked down into the microscope and adjusted the focus, then studied the image for minutes. Slowly, she raised her head. She looked at Hank without saying a word. Her blood-shot eyes filled with tears.

"What is it?"

She couldn't speak. She just shook her head and brushed at her eyes as she pointed at the microscope.

Hank stared down through the two lenses. The t-shaped virus had completely surrounded the octopus-shaped pathogen. "What is it doing?"

"The virus in your blood..." She stopped and swallowed, "is isolating Leviathan to prevent it from replicating. Without the ability to reproduce, it will die. This is why the pathogen hasn't affected you. The virus in your blood is performing like super antibodies." She smiled. "Even Leviathan's nanobots are useless against your virus."

"So I'm okay?"

"It's the hope everyone needs."

The news added to his confusion. He still hadn't sorted through whether his rescue by a trucker was coincidence or an answer to prayer. His skeptical mind that had served him well as a journalist was beginning to strain under the growing weight of evidence. "But why me?"

"I don't have any idea. But I'm grateful." Jenny took the syringe still full of Hank's blood and inserted it into her arm.

"Are you injecting my blood?"

"It's crude science, but it worked on the slide. And since we're both O positive, it's the only chance I have. There's not enough time for anything else. I'm hoping that somehow it will replicate in my blood and shut down Leviathan the way it did in yours."

But as Jenny leaned back in the chair and closed her eyes, Hank sensed that the hope she clung to was as thin as the blood oozing from her bandaged hands.

CHAPTER SEVENTY-EIGHT

Nine miles east of Waynesboro, Pennsylvania, December 3

"We've done everything we can for him, Mr. President." Hamilton nodded at the surgeon then turned back to Pepper's still body lying in the ICU unit at the underground Raven Rock Mountain complex.

"We repaired the wounds to his stomach and liver, but he lost five liters. So much blood." Dr. Phillip Epstein's words trailed off. "His kidneys are in shock. We're trying to get them working again. And we're draining fluid off his heart."

Hamilton put his hands in his suit pants and tightened them into fists. They were shaking badly. His knuckles were sore and swollen.

"Why don't you get some sleep, Mr. President," Epstein said. "You must be exhausted."

He thanked his surgeon and walked down the corridor. It was a long walk through the concrete tunnel to his office, but he didn't mind. He needed time alone to sort through everything that had happened in the last twenty-four hours. The White House, a national treasure, was in flames, Pepper was battling for his life, and his presidency was in tatters.

People seemed to believe that if he were removed from office, everything would be fine again. The way it used to be when Nash was President. But the country would never be that way again. The virus had carved a deep scar across the country's face. Who could ever forget the millions of lives lost or erase the memory of the bombs that fell?

The country was under martial law, but there weren't enough healthy soldiers to quell the riots. He didn't blame the people. They were hungry, struggling to stay alive, and afraid. And still, there was no cure.

As he reached his office he collapsed into a chair. The office was a near recreation of the Oval Office. The colors had changed from peach to white, but beyond that he could close his eyes and walk from one end of the office to the other without stumbling. It felt hollow without Pepper, one of the keenest political minds he had ever known.

Hamilton's aides had already begun the process of compiling a list of possible candidates for Chief of Staff in case Pepper didn't make it. He detested the thought. The very idea of replacing Pepper had a finality to it that was repugnant. Like someone remarrying too quickly after the death of a spouse. Pepper would recover. He had to.

Pepper should be sitting across from him on the sofa, tapping at his tablet. But someone else was. Hamilton sat up in his chair. He hadn't even noticed him when he entered. It was General Frank Maddox.

"Did we have a meeting scheduled, General?"

"I'm sorry Mr. President. Your assistant told me to have a seat."

That's unlike her to not let me know.

"How's Pepper?" the general asked.

"No change."

"I'm sorry to hear that."

"What's on your mind?"

"You're aware that some two million Christians have massed near the border with Mexico? The ones who escaped from the sanctuaries along with others who had been in hiding."

"I heard."

"I received a call this morning from President DiRivera. He's very concerned about their plans. He doesn't want infection pouring across his borders."

"Why did he call you?"

"I guess he thought it was a military question."

"I'm the commander of the nation's military. Not you." *I never should have given him the authority to administer martial law. The increased responsibility has only fed his appetite for power.*

"Yes, that's true."

"What did you tell him?"

"I told him I understood his concern. That if we had responded more quickly against the sanctuaries, there wouldn't be a problem at the border."

Hamilton stood up. "You said what? Who do you think you are, General? You answer to me."

The General tried to restrain an emerging smirk. The phone rang. Hamilton picked it up.

"Mr. President, it's Phil. I'm sorry. I did everything I could... Pepper expired a few minutes ago from complications."

Hamilton's hands shook so badly he dropped the receiver. Pepper couldn't die. Hamilton needed him now more than ever.

A distant voice on the other end of the line asked if the President was all right. He sat back down and buried his face in his hands. When he looked up, Maddox was standing. He was a big man. Six-three and still trim at sixty-five. He approached the desk and put the handset back on the receiver.

"Pepper didn't make it?"

Hamilton shook his head. He grabbed a tissue and blew his nose.

"I'm sorry to hear that. He was a good man." Maddox stood hovering over Hamilton's desk.

"One of the best." Hamilton stood up. "General, our meeting is over."

Maddox didn't move.

"Did you hear me, General?"

The General crossed his arms. "Mr. President, I'm assuming responsibilities as of now."

"Responsibilities for what?"

"The military is taking over the government. The country needs new leadership. Someone who can command."

Hamilton pointed toward the door. "Get out of here. You're fired!"

Maddox stood motionless, his arms still crossed.

Hamilton picked up the phone. "Send in my Secret Service."

"I'm sorry, Mr. President. They've been detained."

"Detained? How?"

Maddox grabbed the receiver. "The military is in charge now." He placed the phone back down on the desk.

"This is the United States General. Not some Third World country where a president can be deposed by thugs." Hamilton felt the skin around the top of his head tighten. He grabbed the arm of his chair and eased himself down as his head began to throb.

The door to his office opened and the Joint Chiefs of Staff entered along with the Speaker of the House and the Senate Majority Leader. They said nothing but stood behind Maddox. The General had covered his bases well.

"Mr. President, we are here to ask for your resignation," Maddox said.

"Resignation? Why don't you call it what it is. A coup. You should be ashamed of yourselves. George Washington is rolling over in his grave right now."

"Then, Mr. President, you leave me with no choice except to arrest you for crimes against this country." Maddox motioned to soldiers who entered the room. They walked up to Hamilton and handcuffed him.

* * *

Hamilton sat in the corner of a room that smelled of insecticide and tried to remember what had happened. His thoughts were jumbled. His head ached. The room was dark except for a crack of light at the bottom of the door. Shadows moved across the opening. Someone was there.

"Help me." The plea rang out in his head, but his mouth didn't move. "Someone help me." Again, his lips remained silent. What was happening?

He tried to push himself up from the floor. His hands wouldn't answer his command. They hung limply at his side. His legs wouldn't budge either. He couldn't feel much except for the ache in his head.

His chin rested on his chest. Focus. Try to remember. *Where are you?* Slowly, the fog began to lift. *Raven Rock. Why are you here? Trouble in Washington. What kind of trouble? Riots. Where is Pepper?* Then, the memories rushed at him. Pepper was gone. And the military had seized power.

He had to get out of here. If he could, he might be able to regain control of the government. But he couldn't even move. Had he had a stroke? That would explain the throbbing in his head and the paralysis. Was this the end? His punishment? God's retribution?

Perhaps if he had alerted the Secret Service about Sulaiman's call, events would have transpired differently. Nash might still be alive as well as the four doctors. His stomach roiled at the thought.

The whole virus catastrophe might have been averted as well. Nash was a religious man and had carried the evangelical vote in the last election. He might have been able to convince Christians to be chipped. They trusted him.

And if the Christians had participated in Operation First Alert, there wouldn't have been any sanctuaries for Sulaiman to attack. No outbreak. No bombs necessary to kill Leviathan. If, if, if. Hamilton wanted to wipe his runny nose, but he couldn't even lift his hands.

He wished there was a God he could pray to, a divine power who could save him and possibly even forgive him. But there wasn't. If God really existed, he would have saved his little girl years ago. A God of love wouldn't have let her die, not after all the prayers.

Steps approached the door. "Open it up."

The lock clicked.

CHAPTER SEVENTY-NINE

Washington, D.C., December 5

T he city's finer restaurants near the White House were closed, with the exception of Komi's. The owners had installed the same state-of-the-art air filtering system that CDC used in their level four labs. They claimed the air in their restaurant was safer to breathe than the air outside. And the air did seem tasteless and cool.

Sulaiman sat at a table across from Rashid. A golden hue radiated throughout the restaurant like the scintillating embers of a fire. Normally, there wouldn't be an empty chair anywhere in sight. Reservations were booked weeks in advance. But tonight the establishment was half empty. Any business at all was remarkable given the riots that had left much of the downtown charred. The smell of ash hung in the air outside and occasionally clung to new customers even after they passed through the air lock entry, which was equipped with a UV light designed to kill microorganisms.

The atmosphere was as subdued as the light. People spoke in whispers, a sharp contrast to the mood that had once filled the room when wine flowed and voices rose and fell like a crescendo directed by the power brokers holding court at the choicest tables. The current patrons seemed content to savor the respite from the terrible events of the last few weeks. But furtive glances among them suggested the virus was never far from anyone's mind.

Rashid raised his glass. "Congratulations, cousin. You've crushed the infidels. Praise be to Allah."

Sulaiman didn't raise his. He didn't feel like celebrating. The televised aerial image of the Christians' massive camp north of El Paso had left him with questions. Troubling questions that raised doubts. Why would Allah allow any infidels to escape? There were reports of jets being grounded by the massive storm that had swept the country and of missiles not exploding. Wasn't Allah supreme over all things?

"Come on, cousin." Rashid put his glass down and reached across the table and tapped Sulaiman's shoulder. "You look like someone who was just defeated, not victorious."

Sulaiman seized Rashid's wrist. "We haven't won until the last one is dead."

Rashid stared down at Sulaiman's white-knuckled grip. Sulaiman released him. "Christians will never trouble us again. There aren't enough of them left. We outnumber them now. Besides, they're trying to leave. Let them go."

"Have you forgotten what the holy prophet said? That the last hour would not come until the Jews hid themselves behind the stones and trees out of fear from us. And the stones and trees said, '*Muslim, or servant of Allah, there is a Jew behind me; come and kill him.*' Only then will it be over. And that includes the two million kaffirs near El Paso."

Rashid shook his head. "If you pursue the Christians, you'll reinforce an image we've tried to make the world forget—that we're terrorists."

Sulaiman pointed at Rashid. "You tried to make them forget. Not me. I have never been ashamed of the mission Allah gave me."

Rashid leaned forward and spoke quietly. "I'm not ashamed of anything. But there are different ways to accomplish the same goal. We don't need to remind everyone that our ambition is to force the whole world to worship Allah. Why do you insist on showing the enemy our plans?"

"Because fear will break their resolve faster than anything else. Look at these people around us. They would bow down to Allah right here, right now if they thought we would behead them if they didn't. People are afraid to die. The more obvious it becomes that Islam won't tolerate a world that doesn't worship Allah, the sooner people will choose our side. Only fear can do that."

Rashid leaned back in the dark-cherry stained chair. He had also grown a beard and was dressed in the traditional Muslim dishadasha. A dark cap sat on his head. His eyes dropped to his unfinished rack of lamb. "I have stood by your side for eighteen years. But I can't support you on this. It's a mistake."

Sulaiman had always been able to convince Rashid. He almost always disagreed at first, because Rashid, like a good attorney, could argue a case from either side of the aisle. But Sulaiman suspected his cousin's views had changed and were evolving into something more dangerous. Something non-Muslim. He was beginning to believe in bloodless jihad. Maybe Rashid even believed Muslims, Christians, and Jews could all coexist. Many Muslims shared this view.

But they were wrong. They selectively interpreted the Qur'an and the Hadith, disregarding passages that clearly indicated there wasn't room for three religions that all claimed Jerusalem as its holy city. Scripture was clear on this.

The blade of Mohammed's sword was stained red from the blood of infidels. The holy prophet had set an example of how to treat kaffirs. And Allah had blessed him for it.

Sulaiman stood up. "The mistake is yours. And I fear for your life. Allah will protect his faithful but not those who are lukewarm. I will finish the jihad." He threw his napkin and a wad of cash on the table, then walked out into the smoky night air.

CHAPTER EIGHTY

El Paso, December 9

The vibrating tentacles of Leviathan slowly ebbed to a flutter, then stopped. A group of t-shaped virus encircled the dead pathogen. Hank's virus moved closer to the lifeless form as if to inspect its work, then satisfied, dispersed like sparks into the night. Jenny lifted her head from the optical microscope and looked at her bandaged hands that no longer bled.

She didn't believe in miracles. But she had lived longer than anyone ever infected with Leviathan. It had taken another transfusion of Hank's blood, but now only a trace of the deadly pathogen remained in her body. The virus had been stopped before any damage to her internal organs had taken place.

She wasn't certain if Hank's virus could protect others as it had her, but she intended to find out. She had already isolated the microbe and begun culturing it in kidney cells. Soon, she would have enough to test on the hospital's infected patients. A sample had also been sent to CDC for evaluation. If her colleagues confirmed that Hank's virus indeed isolated Leviathan and strangled its ability to replicate, then every pharmaceutical manufacturer worldwide would go into full production.

New cell-culture technology had replaced the egg-based manufacturing process of the 1950's. And thank goodness it had, the antiquated methodology would have required the virus to be cultured in billions of eggs before enough vaccine could be produced for an infected world. It would have taken nearly a year, and, by then, there wouldn't be anyone left to inoculate. Now, enough vaccine for the U.S. could be ready in a matter of weeks and for the rest of the world within two months. Millions more would die before the drug reached them, but at least humanity would survive.

The most remarkable thing about Hank's virus was that it appeared to be a pure vaccine. Before a virus could be transformed into a vaccine, a distillation was required to isolate the virulent parts so they could be mitigated, leaving just enough of the former virus to trigger an immune response. But as far as Jenny could tell, Hank's microbe didn't possess any malevolence which was why it had efficiently destroyed Leviathan after entering her blood. It looked like a virus, replicated like one within cells, but acted like an antibody.

The door to the lab opened. Jenny turned around to see Hank and Kat enter. Hank looked a little pale from the last transfusion, but he said he always looked pale. Kat was still in a hazmat suit. Who could blame her? Leviathan was still raging, and the only certainty about Hank's virus was that it had saved one person.

"You look wonderful," Hank said.

"Thanks to you," Jenny said.

"I wish I could take credit for it. But I can't. Have you made any more progress identifying where it came from?"

"I wish I knew so I could say thanks." It was a question Jenny asked herself the first moment she witnessed the virus surround Leviathan. It was as much of a chimera as Leviathan. Different organisms brought together to create something unearthly. In Hank's case, a virus that seemingly merged with antibodies to become a savior. In Leviathan's, two lethal viruses that were stitched together to create a devil. *Too bad General Sullivan wasn't still alive to see his creation get its butt kicked.*

Kat picked up a note pad lying on the metal table in front of the three of them and wrote furiously as if she were taking diction from someone speaking too quickly. She ripped a page from the pad and handed it to Hank. He held the page and seemed to study it. Then he turned and gave the paper to Jenny. The reporter's self-confident exterior, forged no doubt through hundreds of interviews, seemed shaken.

God placed this virus in Hank to save the world.

Jenny looked at the unlined face behind the plastic shield. Large eyes, moist from a connection with her God, stared out. She really believed the virus in Hank's body was divinely placed. It wasn't logical. And biologically it didn't make any sense, but something about Kat's faith made Jenny wish she could suspend her reason for just once and believe.

CHAPTER EIGHTY-ONE

Anthony, December 21

Luke gathered with several members of the church around a small television that sat on a gray, warped picnic table. Intermittent, grainy images flickered across the screen. General Frank Maddox, the chairman of the Joint Chiefs of Staff stood before a packed room of reporters in the press room. It was the first conference since The White House had been retaken from rioters. The General's olive green uniform with four, shiny stars on each shoulder had been exchanged for a solid, dark blue suit with a red tie. A small American flag pin adorned his lapel. The Speaker of the House, the Senate Majority Leader, and a few members of the President's cabinet stood on either side of the General.

"I've always believed the President of the United States is the Supreme Commander of all military forces," Maddox paused as he gripped the podium, "but we live in extraordinary times."

"He reminds me of Patton," said Jeremy, a middle-aged man with a Mets hat and a Jersey accent. "It will take more than a suit to change my mind."

A short woman standing next to him laughed nervously.

"But sometimes it's necessary to dispense with tradition when the very survival of a nation is in jeopardy. What good is a government that can't protect its people? We're on the verge of anarchy. I did what I did to save the nation." He paused and looked down at his hands, then back into the screen. "I'd do it again."

"What do you think, Luke?" asked Dan. The wind caught the teenager's fine blond hair and blew it backwards, revealing a minefield of acne on his forehead. He burrowed deep into his yellow jacket.

Luke rubbed the stubble on his chin. "If we listen carefully, I think the General is telling us what's on his agenda."

Dan cocked his head. "Huh?"

"Those nukes that fell on the sanctuaries weren't Russian made. They were red, white, and blue. Maddox sees the church the same way he sees the government—it's a tradition that threatened the nation's safety. He dispensed with the government, but the church slipped away. I don't think he's used to failure. Now that he's in charge, he may want to complete unfinished business. "

Everyone stared at him, their faces even more distraught. He shouldn't have said it. They were scared enough. And he didn't know for a fact the general would attack the church. But Luke felt deep in his gut that he was right. If only he could gather the church and leave immediately for Mexico. But the border was closed and wouldn't reopen until the virus no longer posed a threat. The longer he waited, the easier a target two million believers became. They were pinned against the border with nowhere to go. Stretched from Las Cruces to El Paso. Why would God bring the church this far and abandon it in the desert?

The General looked at the Speaker of the House on his right and the Senate Majority Leader on his left and nodded at each of them. "Once order is restored and the nation is healed, an election will be held for new leadership. That's my promise."

Jeremy raised three fingers on his right hand in a pledge. "Scouts honor."

Luke shook his head. "Every general who has ever participated in a coup says the same thing. To my knowledge though, none has ever willingly relinquished power. We already know he's not a big fan of the constitution."

An older man with a cane limped up. He waved the black stick at the screen. "Did any of those criminals say what they did with the President and Vice President?"

"They're not on a cruise. That's for sure," Jeremy said.

The old man adjusted his hearing aid and frowned.

The broadcast disintegrated into a snowy image. Dan slapped the television, but the picture didn't return.

"Party's over," Jeremy said.

Luke turned away from the picnic table into a biting north wind. Tumbleweeds rolled down the gravel road in front of him. Strands of Christmas lights adorning the RV park swayed back and forth. Some of the bulbs clinked against each other. He zipped up his ski jacket and lowered his head.

A few spaces up an old woman staggered out of her trailer in a daze.

"What's wrong?" Luke asked running toward her.

She raised her right hand in a halting gesture. Blood dripped from her palm. The virus was back. And where one was infected, several more would be soon follow. "Go back inside your trailer dear. I'll have one of the nurses come and take care of you."

The old woman trembled as she walked back to her Airstream.

Luke sat down on a nearby picnic bench. His legs felt weak. Any hope of crossing the border was gone. The realization was devastating. *What am I supposed to do, Father?*

And then in the rush of wind a familiar voice. Cindy's sweet words swept to earth from heaven. *Finish what God has given you.*

Luke looked up into the murky sky, even murkier now from swirling dirt. *I miss you, baby.* The stinging gale brought tears to his eyes.

In the distance a truck accelerated down a frontage road parallel to the camp. Puffs of blue smoke trailed behind it. It was his GMC. It careened into the park and kicked up a cloud of dust, then slid to a stop. Hank jumped out from the driver's side.

CHAPTER EIGHTY-TWO

El Paso Border Crossing, December 22

A man dressed in military fatigues with an M16 slung over his shoulder held his hand up as Luke braked his truck. The soldier's eyes narrowed behind a gas mask. Two tubes exited the bottom and connected into an air filtration unit attached to his back. The contraption gave him the eerie appearance of an insect. He walked back inside a small building and returned with a pair of binoculars. He raised the field glasses and studied the vehicles that had just arrived at the Cordova Bridge crossing. All four lanes were jammed. The soldier seemed to be searching for the end of the traffic snarl.

Luke rolled down his window. "You'll need something more powerful than those."

"*Hijole!*" The soldier lowered the binoculars and glared at Luke. He removed the rifle from his shoulder and pushed it through the driver's window. The man was in his twenties but the strain of guarding one of the most dangerous border crossings between the U.S. and Mexico had etched itself into his face. Dark circles underscored his eyes.

"Turn back. The border is closed." The man's English was decent but his voice was muffled and difficult to understand through the mask. And he didn't seem likely to remove it any time soon.

"I'm Pastor Luke Chavez. This is Hank and Kat." Luke motioned toward the two sitting next to him.

"Who are these other people?" The soldier waved toward the packed lanes.

"That's my church."

The soldier looked back at the never ending line of vehicles and shook his head. "No church is that big."

"There are more than two-hundred thousand vehicles behind me." Coordinating the move for a 2,000 mile journey was a logistics nightmare. But at least cell reception was back. And the two-way radios were working. Still it would take twenty-four hours just to move everyone through the border. Provided they could cross.

The soldier leaned down and examined Luke's face as if he vaguely recognized it. "Didn't you used to fight on TV?" He smiled revealing stained teeth. Probably bad water. He withdrew the rifle pointed at Luke's chest and slung it over his soldier.

"A long time ago." Luke caught the man's name on his badge. "Wilfredo, you going to let us pass?"

"Sorry. No one can enter." He took a step back. "You infected?"

Recent outbreaks in the border cities and in Mexico City had sent shock waves of fear throughout the country. And for good reason. The virus was spreading faster than it had in the U.S. Hank said Jenny believed it was a new mutation, one even more virulent than the original Leviathan strain.

Luke held up a small bottle containing a clear solution. "You know what this is?"

The guard shook his head.

"It's a vaccine against the virus."

The man raised his eyebrows.

Hank and Kat had roared into camp the previous day with enough vaccine to inoculate the few hundred infected church members. And it seemed to be working. The bleeding had stopped, and many were regaining their strength. The vast majority of the church was unprotected and would be until more vaccine could be produced, but at least the infection had been momentarily stopped.

Hank leaned over Kat. "It doesn't sound like the border authorities are in the loop."

"What loop?" the soldier asked.

"Your government agreed to allow us to pass through your country in route to Belize," Luke said.

"I don't believe you." He swung the rifle from his shoulder but lowered it to the ground.

Jenny had convinced Dr. Carrington to make a bargain with the Mexican government. In exchange for allowing the church to pass through the country, the U.S. would agree to release the vaccine culture to Mexico's pharmaceutical giants. Luke was pretty sure General Maddox was unaware of the deal, but he wouldn't be for long.

"All it will take is a simple call," Luke said.

The soldier stared at Luke as if unsure of what to do. He went back into his building and picked up the phone. He pulled off his mask. Through the window the soldier appeared to be arguing with whoever was on the other end of the phone. Then he nodded obediently and hung up. He turned toward the GMC and flung his right hand upward. At least the message was easier to understand than his muffled English.

The GMC passed over the Bridge of Americas. The Rio Grande lay below, a natural border between the two countries. In the rear view mirror he watched a trail of RVs, semis, fifth wheels, and cars. Upon the advice of many, he had decided to avoid as much of Juarez as possible and head straight toward Highway 45. Their destination for the first day was Chihuahua, then Torreon the second day. The whole trip would take about a week.

Military jeeps carrying soldiers with M16s passed by slowly. Some of the men were wide-eyed, and some scowled at the endless line of bumper-to-bumper vehicles invading their country.

The road between Juarez and Chihuahua was one of the most dangerous in Mexico. Luke's group would be exposed in a two-lane column stretching nearly 400 miles with no protection. By the time he reached Chihuahua, the last of the church would be passing through into Mexico. Benny had promised help, but where were the vigilantes?

CHAPTER EIGHTY-THREE

Federal Highway 150, Mexico, December 25

From his position near Iztaccihuatl mountain, Sulaiman studied the column of vehicles through his field glasses. It reminded him of a never-ending chain of boxcars with no caboose in sight. The truck at the front was the same piece of junk he had seen photos of on the internet. Why would anyone drive such a wreck? He lowered the binoculars.

Snow-draped pines lined the steep walls of the canyon. "Allah be praised for delivering the infidels," Sulaiman said to the soldier next to him. The man's fingers tightened around the trigger.

Sulaiman motioned with his hand. "Not yet."

His men were positioned strategically from the base of the Iztaccihuatl mountain range to four-hundred miles north. They were armed with rocket grenade launchers that could easily hit a target a mile away. The same weapon, although more sophisticated, that the Afghans had used to take down the Russian army.

The approaching vehicles were easy prey because the steep and twisting road had slowed their pace, packing them closely together. A single grenade could take out two.

Rashid should be here. Perhaps, he would finally understand that only Allah could lay such a trap. The entire Christian church exposed on a deserted highway on Christmas day. Allah's will was not moderation. Not peace. But the total destruction of the infidels. Anyone who refused to submit to Allah deserved to die.

Sulaiman's cell rang. "The last car..." a scratchy voice disappeared in static.

He frowned. "Call me back."

The phone rang again. "Can you hear me?" the voice asked anxiously.

"Better."

"The last car just left Chihuahua. Ready for coffee?"

"Ten minutes." Sulaiman had trained his men to reveal nothing of value over a cell or two-way radio. Someone was always listening. He called the rest of his troops and relayed the same message. He checked his watch, then raised his field glasses. "Ready?" he asked without breaking his fixation on the front truck.

The two men next to him raised grenade launchers to their shoulders. A slight wind carried the scent of pine. Gray clouds parted revealing pale blue skies. *Allah is pleased.* Sulaiman breathed in the cool air. It tingled in his nose.

His pulse quickened at the thought of completing his mission in one massive blow. In glory. "Now."

A series of concussions rocked the plain. A fireball flipped over the lead truck.

"Allah Akbar." He lowered the binoculars to congratulate his two soldiers. But the men were face down. Crimson splattered the snow. Sulaiman crouched to investigate. White puffs exploded near his feet. He lowered his head and ran as fast as he could toward the mountain behind him. A withering fusillade drilled the landscape. A sharp sting bit into his right shoulder nearly knocking him over. He stumbled forward and dove under a rocky ledge. His heart pounded as he gasped to catch his breath. *Who's shooting?*

He removed the field glasses hanging cockeyed from his neck and focused on the two men sprawled in the distance. Both had been shot in the back of the head. Whoever shot them and wanted him dead was positioned on top of the mountain. They had him pinned down.

His phone rang. He reached in his pocket and fumbled for his phone. His right hand was numb. He switched hands.

"We're being attacked." The staccato sound of automatic fire punctuated the background. The line went dead. He called his other units. None answered. A sickening feeling clawed at his insides. Had his entire Mexican network been wiped out? Cells that had taken years to build.

He leaned back against the cool stone and tried to think. His four-wheel drive was parked about fifty yards away under some large trees. Too far to reach. He had been lucky to make it here.

Night was only a few hours away and would provide the best chance of escape. If his attackers came before dark, he would die gloriously. He touched the 9mm on his side, then reached in his jacket and fingered the clips. Three left. The brief movement triggered a sharp, stabbing pain in his shoulder.

He gingerly removed his coat and unbuttoned his shirt, half of which was wet and heavy. He peeled the shirt off and examined the wound. His head spun at the sight of the shredded mass that used to be his shoulder. He closed his eyes and tried to pray, but nothing came to mind except—why?

* * *

The sharp smell of gunpowder lingered in the night air like a bitter aftertaste. Sulaiman didn't know what hurt worse—the infidels' escape or his throbbing shoulder. But the pain eased at the memory of a fireball. Luke's truck had been destroyed. At least the head of the snake had been severed.

The breaking clouds that had earlier promised a starry night had massed into thunderheads. The ghostly outline hung like a curtain draped across the night sky. A procession of lights crept through the canyon like a vast herd of nocturnal animals.

Whoever was protecting the infidels would most likely remain in position until the last vehicle had safely passed, which would take until tomorrow. But he couldn't wait that long. He had to move while it was dark.

With his right arm immobilized in a make-shift sling, Sulaiman left the protection of the hollow and hugged the mountain as he crept silently toward his jeep. The darkness was so thick he could only feel his way forward.

He reached the vehicle hidden behind bushes. He examined the mountain behind him for any lights indicating the enemy's position, but he couldn't see anything, not even a lighted cigarette.

If he could cling to the base of the mountain, he might be able to stay beyond the enemy's reach. The only problem was getting from where he was back to the safety of the mountain without being riddled with bullets. Once he started the engine, he might have two or three seconds. But he only had one good hand to maneuver his jeep. Too risky. Better to head for the road, away from the line of fire.

Sulaiman sat in the jeep clutching the key in the ignition. He turned it but stopped short of engaging the ignition. His fine-tuned senses sifted the night for any noise or movement. Only dead stillness.

He cranked the steering wheel as far to the left as it would go and nudged the stick shift into first gear with his useless right hand. Once the engine engaged, he would whip the truck toward Highway 150, then drive north. The infidels were headed south which would provide a perfect shield.

He took a deep breath, then cranked the ignition, and popped the clutch. The jeep lurched forward and died. His heart pounded as he quickly restarted the engine.

Armor piercing slugs slammed into the jeep's hood cutting through the engine like it was tin. Sulaiman rolled out of the jeep and under its belly. A volley of bullets slammed into the opposite side. The rear of the four-wheel drive shook as the gas can exploded into a fireball.

The fire made its way down the back of the truck and licked the gas tank only three-feet from Sulaiman's face. He slid away from the truck. Bolts of pain shot from his shoulder down his right side. With his belly to the ground, he gritted his teeth and slithered through snow-covered shrubs toward the highway. A loud explosion behind him lit up the night sky casting eerie shadows among trees that towered in front. But he never looked back.

CHAPTER EIGHTY-FOUR

Washington, D.C., December 26

ormer President Hamilton's eyes flicked to Jenny then away. It was the third time she had caught him looking at her. He had been careful to avoid direct eye contact, but his furtive looks were making her increasingly uncomfortable.

The Oval Office smelled of fresh paint. It looked like the photos she had seen except for the portrait above the fireplace. The painting of a regal Washington in his military uniform had been replaced by Theodore Roosevelt who stood in pince-nez glasses with his hand tucked inside his vest. The carpet bearing the presidential seal was missing, exposing a floor of inlaid oak and mahogany. Rioters had made off with the rug and Rembrandt Peale's portrait of the first President.

Evidence of General Maddox's brief tenure in the White House had apparently been wiped clean, although the miniature Civil War cannon sitting on the President's desk might be the General's. The damage from his two-week stint as Dictator would not be so easily erased.

Cameramen from every major news network packed the room. John Tingley, the director of the CIA, stood next to Jenny. He was about to be awarded the Presidential Medal of Freedom for coordinating a covert operation that ended the coup. General Maddox and the other conspirators were being held at Fort Leavenworth prison while they awaited trial for treason.

Tingley leaned in and whispered. "I feel kind of strange getting a medal for doing my job. How about you?"

"So do I." The ones who truly deserved the award weren't here. Dr. Frederick Lutz and Hank Jackson. It was Lutz who had discovered Hank's immunity to the virus, not her. And if it weren't for Hank, there wouldn't be a vaccine. But Lutz was dead, and her calls to Hank still remained unanswered. There were unconfirmed reports of an attack on the Christians who fled to Belize.

President William Beckley, the former Vice President, glanced over at the frail figure propped up on the sofa. The left side of Hamilton's face drooped. Spittle ran down the side of his chin. His hands shook uncontrollably. But there was still a glint in the greenish gold eyes, perhaps the only indication he was cognizant of what was happening. Lucy, who sat next to the President, reached over and wiped his chin with a handkerchief.

His eyes darted toward Jenny, then away. *He remembers. He must.* Hamilton's goons had killed Sam and nearly her. He must also know that the man who carried the virus that would save the world was the same man who had exposed his crimes.

Hamilton deserved to be impeached, tried in a civilian court and thrown in prison for the rest of his life. But what was the point now? The stroke had left him unable to discharge his duties. He was locked in his own prison.

Beckley looked into the cameras and smiled. "We're here today to honor the extraordinary courage of two patriots. We have them to thank for our lives and our nation." He opened a rectangular, dark brown wooden box that revealed a shining gold medal with a white, enamel centerpiece. He draped the medal around Jenny's neck and hooked it in back. "Dr. Jenny George, it is my pleasure to present you with the highest recognition a civilian can receive..."

His words faded into a procession of faces. Some she recognized like Dr. Lutz, Hank, PJ, and the other scientists at the sub complex, but others she didn't. They were the thousands of nameless doctors and nurses who had sacrificed their lives fighting the virus— the real heroes.

But even the heroic efforts of so many and Hank's virus wouldn't be enough to save one-and-half billion people, the number CDC estimated would die before the vaccine reached them. The virus was continuing to mutate. At least three new pathogens had been discovered. The Mexican microbe was the most virulent of the new mutations, killing its victims in less than twenty-four hours. It was almost as if Leviathan sensed its days were numbered and intended to spin off as many mutations as possible in hope that one would be impervious to the vaccine.

"The world has never experienced a pandemic like Leviathan," Beckley said. "Let's hope it never does again. But thanks to Dr. George's untiring efforts, nearly six billion people will live."

CHAPTER EIGHTY-FIVE

Belize, December 27

The freshly turned dirt was dark and thickly clumped like clay. Clods of green grass had been stamped into the ground around two rectangular plots like ill-fitting patches on a pair of jeans. The plots overlooked Spanish Lookout in Belize. The air was warm and moist. Hank stared at two simple white crosses in front of each grave. The mourners had left. Kat walked up and looped her arm through his.

"Still here?"

"If Luke's truck hadn't broken down, it would have been us in those graves," Hank said.

"I feel so badly for the families."

Two were fatherless. The two mechanics who had repaired Luke's truck had offered to switch vehicles, and drive the GMC in case the engine failed again.

"I can't get it out of my head. Why them and not us?"

"I'm sure every survivor who walked away from a sanctuary asked the same question. It's difficult to understand why God lets some live and not others."

"Do you think God really cares who lives and dies?" Hank asked. "Maybe it's just chance."

But Hank didn't really believe that anymore. He had eluded death too many times. He turned away from the graves and looked toward a patchwork of green squares that extended for miles below him like a quilt. Spanish Lookout was a Mennonite community of farms. Land was abundant and affordable. Streams crisscrossed the landscape. Kat stared at him. "The safest I ever felt was when I sat between you and Luke."

"If you had any idea how many people wanted us dead, you would have scrambled for another ride."

"I knew God had a plan for both your lives. I still believe that."

"Will you let me know the minute you think differently?" Hank grinned.

"I'm serious." She punched his arm lightly.

Hank wrapped his arms around her. He still hadn't kissed her. It wasn't that he was afraid: he just wasn't sure how a relationship would work. He wanted to return to Charlotte and his job at the Observer. His editor was anxious for the stories Hank had promised about his experiences, especially the one about the vaccine flowing through his veins. But Kat wanted to stay in Belize and help the church begin a new life. They were so different. She was giving and full of faith. He was self-absorbed and skeptical.

Kat ran her fingers through Hank's hair, catching them in a tangle. "You need a haircut and a shave."

"It hasn't exactly been at the top of my list." Like everyone else, staying alive had been his main objective. And now, after months of holding his breath, he could finally breathe. He felt more alive than ever before. But his feelings were more than the catharsis many experience following a life and death struggle. It felt more like an awakening. As if that part of him some call the soul had opened its eyes for the first time.

His doubts were disappearing. Perhaps God was real. Not some remote, ethereal force that didn't care about mankind, but a being of pure good who interacted with people. His buddies back at the paper would think he had lost his mind. But he was certain he had discovered something lost since childhood.

Kat stared up at him. She was beautiful. He pulled her close. The faint smell of citrus was on her breath. He kissed her lips.

"Took you long enough," she said with a sparkle in her eyes.

"The best things are worth waiting for. Right?"

"Same old Hank." She winked.

But he wasn't.

CHAPTER EIGHTY-SIX

Washington, D.C., January 1

Getting back home proved almost as difficult as his escape. Sulaiman still had no idea who attacked him and his men. His hands were cut and scratched from crawling through a rough snow-covered landscape; his feet blistered from walking for miles, and his clothing torn. Every Mexican who passed him on the highway was reluctant to pick him up because of the outbreak and his ragged appearance. If it hadn't been for the wad of bills he waved at passing cars, he might have bled to death before getting to a hospital.

He spent a week in Mexico City recuperating from his wound and then caught a private plane home. The government had grounded all airlines to limit infection.

He stared out the window of the twin-engine turbo Cessna at the darkened portico of the White House in the distance.

"Still a mess down there," the pilot said.

Sulaiman didn't feel like talking. He dialed Rashid's number. No answer.

"Things should start returning to normal with President Beckley in charge and now that there's a vaccine. What do you think?"

Sulaiman's jaw tightened. "When did that happen?"

"Where have you been? It's been all over the news. The CIA ended the coup…"

"Not that. The vaccine."

"Announced two days ago. Supposed to be the real deal."

Sulaiman's cell rang. It was Rashid.

"Where have you been?" Sulaiman snapped the question. He was tired, and news of a vaccine further dampened his spirits.

"Are you Sulaiman?" a woman asked. She sounded young.

"Why are you calling from Rashid's phone?"

"Your cousin is very sick. I've been trying to reach you. He asked me to call before he..."

"Before what?"

She hesitated. "He's dying from the virus."

The words felt like a kick in the stomach. "Who are you?"

"I'm a nurse. Your cousin is hemorrhaging."

"Where is he?"

"At the Islamic Center."

"Why isn't he at a hospital?"

"This is where we found him. He didn't want to leave."

"How much time does he have?" His voice quavered.

"Maybe a few hours."

"I heard there's a vaccine for the virus."

The windbag pilot looked at him.

"It's very difficult to get. I don't think the hospitals here have any yet, but even if they did, the damage to your cousin's organs is too extensive. The vaccine has to be administered in the early stages."

"I'll be there as soon as I can."

* * *

It felt like evening, but it was only 3:30. The sun had disappeared behind dark towering clouds that scrolled across the sky. Sulaiman parked his car on the abandoned street in front of the Islamic Center.

The dead lay scattered on the steps leading up to the mosque. Frozen sculptures of agony. Opaque eyes stared at him as he carefully advanced up the icy, stone steps, still slick from palms that bore the virus' fatal mark of ownership.

A large raven perched on one of the bloated bodies. A biting breeze fanned its black feathers. It cocked its head and eyed him warily as it stripped away a stiff piece of flesh. An unrestrained wail in the distance shattered the silence.

Sulaiman entered the mosque. The gloom from outside poured in through the windows. He made his way toward the sanctuary. At the rear of the hall a man lay on a mattress with a young woman next to him on the floor. Sulaiman's skin tightened as he approached the shell that used to be Rashid. Blood seeped from the corners of his closed eyes, nose, and ears.

The young woman looked up at Sulaiman. She was pretty with large, dark eyes and long lashes. A strand of silky black hair slipped out of her hijab. She quickly tucked her hair back inside her scarf. "Put these on." She handed him a mask and gloves. He sat down on the floor next to Rashid and slipped on the protective wear.

"He's been fighting to stay alive to see you."

Rashid slowly awoke. The corners of his mouth turned upward slightly. His teeth were streaked red. "I prayed you would make it." A gurgling noise drowned his words. He extended his heavily bandaged hand toward Sulaiman.

"I wouldn't touch him," the young woman said.

Sulaiman clasped Rashid's hand. The young woman shook her head.

"What happened to your arm?" Rashid motioned with his head toward Sulaiman's arm that was in a sling.

"Just a scratch."

"Did you get them?"

Sulaiman could still feel the abrasions on his belly from crawling like a cowering dog.

"I did. All of them." Sulaiman looked away. He couldn't lie directly to Rashid's face. The Qur'an permitted lying to infidels when it advanced Islam's cause—but not to believers.

"Allah be praised. You were right. I should have gone. Maybe this wouldn't have happened." Rashid attempted to lift his hand to point upward, but he was too weak. "Isn't it beautiful? The tiles and ceiling?"

Sulaiman looked up. He had never really noticed. "Yes, it is."

"This has always been my favorite place," Rashid said. "So peaceful, so full of Allah's presence."

Sulaiman looked at Rashid. Here was a man truly devoted to Allah. A man who prayed faithfully and strived to obey the Qur'an. And yet, Allah hadn't protected him against the virus. Sulaiman had thought it was because Rashid believed in bloodless jihad, but he wasn't sure anymore. Allah hadn't protected his men either. Men such as himself, who had devoted their lives to the destruction of the infidels. There wasn't any explanation for what had happened, nothing any imam could say to rationalize why Allah had allowed the kaffirs to escape.

"I had a dream yesterday." Rashid coughed up blood. He motioned for the young woman to help him into a sitting position. She raised him up and wiped his chin. "About when we were young. Can you remember back that far?" A strained mischievous smile parted Rashid's bloody lips.

"I can."

"Abdul laid his hands on you and prophesied that you would one day crush the infidels. Do you remember?"

"I do." But the memory that had once encouraged him to press forward toward its fulfillment now seemed cruel. Rashid was dying because of the virus Sulaiman had released. A virus that was intended to rid the world of infidels and hasten the Mahdi's return. His zeal had destroyed Rashid. Sulaiman struggled to maintain his composure and fight back the tears welling up in his eyes.

"You fulfilled the prophesy, cousin."

But he hadn't. And he wasn't certain if the remorse gnawing at his insides was for Rashid or the years sacrificed for a lie.

CHAPTER EIGHTY-SEVEN

Belize, January 1

The forty-foot motor home swayed as Luke negotiated it around a pothole big enough to swallow a goat.

The newspaper resting in Hank's lap fell to the floor. "And I thought the worst of the trip was over." Hank sat in the front passenger seat, his hands firmly gripping the leather arm rests.

"This road isn't exactly designed for motor homes. But be my guest." Luke motioned with one hand toward the steering wheel.

An anxious look gripped Hank. "Hey, keep your hands on the wheel."

Luke laughed.

Hank reached down and picked up the paper.

"What do you think of the headline?" Luke pointed toward the newspaper. *World Saved by Christ Virus.*

"I doubt the copy editor understood the real meaning of what he wrote."

"The whole world has been touched by the merciful hand of God. Will anyone ever see a bloody palm and not think of the Christ Virus? People who have never heard of Jesus Christ, now know his name. Through it God reminded us that life is in the blood—your blood, Hank. Have you fully grasped that?"

"How could anyone fully comprehend what's happened in the last six months? I don't know why God chose me, but I'm humbled by it."

"We have witnessed a great struggle between heaven and hell. But what man meant for evil, God used for good." Luke arched his back. "But it's not over. In fact, it's just beginning."

Hank buried his face in the paper, ignoring the comment.

The lush green countryside poured through the panoramic windshield. A bearded Mennonite to the north bounced in the seat of his green tractor as he plowed white powder into his field. A farmer had told Luke the white dust was dolomite lime used to keep the clay soil from packing. Planting for summer crops would begin in February, only a month away. The farmer tipped his straw hat.

I wish you were here to see this, baby. It could be Pennsylvania. We'll rebuild the church here.

As they approached Western Highway, the fields disappeared. Dense vegetation of trees lined the two-lane highway that stretched for eighty miles across Belize. A sign said Belmopan 16 kilometers. "How many miles is that?" Luke asked.

"Ten miles," Hank said looking at his calculator.

"That's cheating."

"Can you convert kilometers into miles in your head?"

"You've got a point," Luke said. "We should be at the airport soon. It's going to be great to see her."

"I wish Kat could have come. But there are still so many sick."

"She's a good woman. Very sweet. I hope things work out for the two of you."

"So do I."

Fifteen minutes later the motor home lumbered into the parking lot of Belmopan International Airport. Luke checked his watch. Her flight should have already landed. He followed Hank out of the coach. In the distance a small woman stood in front of several pallets stacked with boxes. She directed the forklift operator toward them.

"There's Jenny," Luke pointed toward the tarmac and waved.

Jenny waved back.

"It's not all going to fit in the motor home," Hank said.

"We'll make it work the way we have everything else." Luke quickened his pace and broke into a jog, then into a full run, leaving Hank behind. And as he approached Jenny, he remembered Cindy's words. *Finish the job God has given you.*

I have, honey. I have.

CHAPTER EIGHTY-EIGHT

Washington, D.C., January 1

A thin mattress bore the dark, bloody prints of Rashid's struggle. The sanctuary was quiet, his anguished cries silenced. Neither Sulaiman nor the young nurse had said a word since Rashid's last gasp. The only measure of time was the luminous outline of the crescent moon through the clerestory. Sulaiman touched Rashid's arm. His skin was tepid. In a few more hours it would be cold.

The young woman's eyes darted across the sanctuary. It was empty except for the two of them. Beyond the great arch at the edge of the hall something moved. A silhouette of a man stepped from the shadows. Sulaiman touched the impression of the 9mm under his dishadasha. The man tipped his head toward them. He walked around the perimeter of the hall to avoid stepping on the Persian rugs. His leather soles tapped against tiled floors.

The man seemed vaguely familiar. Sulaiman removed his hand from the gun.

"I'm sorry about your cousin," he said as he approached.

"Did you know him?"

"I knew of him."

"Would you like to have a seat?" Sulaiman motioned toward the floor.

The man stared at the young woman. She stood. "I should be going."

"Thank you for everything you did. I never even got your name."

"Shahida."

"A lovely name."

She walked quickly across the hall toward an exit.

The man sat down and crossed his legs. He laid his wool overcoat across his lap. "I'm Yasin Mohammed."

"I thought you looked familiar." Sulaiman had seen the man on Al Jazeera. He was a well-known Turkish billionaire.

"If you came to say goodbye to Rashid, you're too late."

Yasin wasn't much older than Sulaiman. Perhaps almost forty. He was dressed in a black tailored suit, white shirt, no tie and expensive Italian shoes. His thick, jet black hair was combed straight back. "I came to thank you."

"You don't even know me."

"Oh, I do Sulaiman Hadid."

How does he know my name?

"Thank me for what?"

"For what you've done for all Muslims, for the Ummah."

"And what's that?"

Yasin's dark eyes were penetrating. Sulaiman shifted his position.

"I know your faith has been shaken. You even question whether Allah exists."

Sulaiman didn't like where the conversation was headed. "That's not true." But it was.

"You think the Mahdi's return is a myth."

Sulaiman stood up. "Who are you?"

"Please, sit down, and I will explain." Yasin motioned with his hand toward the floor.

Sulaiman sat down again.

"Are you familiar with Revelation, chapter six in the Bible?"

"I haven't read much of the Bible. Rashid was the scholar." Sulaiman glanced at his cousin. The nurse had closed his eyes, but his jaw had dropped open, his mouth agape like an old man who'd fallen asleep.

"It describes the Mahdi. *And I looked, and behold, a white horse. And he who sat on it had a bow; and a crown was given to him, and he went out conquering and to conquer.* Many Muslim scholars have testified to his coming. Do you think the Holy Scripture and the scholars are wrong?"

"I don't know what I think anymore."

"*Weeping may endure for a night, but joy comes in the morning.*" Yasin leaned forward. "Morning is nearly here."

The sanctuary was getting colder. Sulaiman rubbed his shoulder. It ached like a bullet fragment still remained. "And what does that mean?"

"It means that the suffering of Muslims is nearly over. That Islam's golden age is about to return."

"Luke Chavez is still alive and so are his followers."

"Yes, but the Christian church is in tatters. The virus has mankind by the throat. And calamity has upended governments." The hint of a smile appeared. "You have set the stage. Well done."

The flattery made Sulaiman even more suspicious. "So where is the Mahdi?"

Yasin stared as if he expected Sulaiman to answer his own question. The silence was uncomfortable. "Don't you know me?"

What kind of game is he playing? "You're Yasin Mohammed."

"I came here to tell you that you succeeded, that you fulfilled the prophecy. And because of you the world is ready for the return of the Mahdi. Ready for me."

The words felt like an electric shock. Sulaiman sat transfixed, his head spinning with questions. *He couldn't be the Mahdi. He*

was a businessman. The Mahdi would be a conqueror. Then he
remembered Abdul's dream from many years ago. The flags of the
world bowed to one flag—from Turkey. But it would take more
than a dream and mere words to convince him. It would take a sign,
something irrefutable.

Yasin stood up and dusted off his pants. "You don't believe me."

Suliaman shook his head. Yasin stared down at the lifeless body
below him and then looked at Sulaiman. He knelt down and placed
his left hand on Rashid's chest. He pressed down and bowed his
head.

Sulaiman's pulse quickened. His skin tingled. And then he
gasped—as Rashid's eyelids quivered.

The Mahdi had arrived.

ACKNOWLEDGMENTS

Those who live with authors are the real heroes behind the success of a published work. They serve invaluable roles as editor, critic, and counselor as a manuscript evolves into a book. Their ideas are often sprinkled throughout the pages. They endure endless discussions and monk-like obsession. My wife, Holly, experienced all these without complaint. Without her encouragement, this story never would have been written. She started me on the path of becoming a novelist for which I will always be grateful.

When I first began this project, I hadn't written in 25 years. The last piece was for a small newspaper. Fortunately, I was blessed to have two critique partners, Dr. Rosslyn Elliott and Nathan James, both gifted writers. They patiently guided and shaped my writing. It's not an overstatement to say I learned the craft of writing fiction from Rosslyn.

Author and editor, Susan Parr, was one of the first to support the story at a time when I wasn't certain whether to continue. I'm indebted to novelist Wanda Dyson who provided much needed encouragement at critical stages in the story's development. And to my readers Brandon Elliott, Dr. Harry Krause, Lenya Heitzig, David Stokes, Aaron Cordova, Colleen Santistevan, Craig and Laura Sowers, and Jean Lewis, thank you for your feedback which influenced this final work.

Many thanks to my pastor and friend Skip Heitzig, who took time away from his nonstop schedule to read the book and endorse it.

Retired undercover detective Greg Cunningham, who served on several presidential details, provided invaluable insight into the Secret Service and FBI. Retired detective Vince Harrison provided information about police procedures. And my son, Army Staff Sgt. Derek Slade, who trained with a sniper team, helped me understand the fundamentals.

This story began as an idea, a what-if scenario. Its evolution into a book was propelled by ideas from several authors including Joel Richardson, Joel Rosenberg, Brigitte Gabriel, Bruce Bawer, Ergon Mehmet Caner and Emir Fethi Caner, Ken Alibek, Dr. Michael Osterholm, Janet Folger, and the Rev. Don E. Wildmon. A list of their works is included at the end of this book.

My sincere thanks to my editors Steve Parolini and Sarah Joy Freese who skillfully refined the story. Steve pushed me to make the story better, and Sarah ensured that every comma was in the right place.

And finally, thank you, Lord, for giving me the desires of my heart.

To all, my deepest gratitude.

Dave Slade

ABOUT THE AUTHOR

Dave Slade is a former newspaper reporter. He spent three years covering local and county policics in Rio Rancho, New Mexico where he became a veteran observer of political machinations. He left reporting to teach U.S. Government and Journalism at the secondary level.

During the last 32 years, Dave has owned three real estate companies. As an agent he developed a unique brand in the Albuquerque market as a Christian Realtor.

He is a graduate of San Jose State University with a Bachelor or Arts in Journalism and the School of Ministry at Calvary of Albuquerque.

He lives in New Mexico with his wife, Holly, and dogs Squirt and Steinbeck.

SUGGESTED LIST FOR FURTHER READING

The Islamic AntiChrist by Joel Richardson

Inside The Revolution by Joel C. Rosenberg

They Must Be Stopped by Brigitte Gabriel

While Europe Slept: How Radical Islam is Destroying the West from Within by Bruce Bawer

Unveiling Islam by Ergun Mehmet Caner and Emir Fethi Caner

Biohazard by Ken Alibek

Living Terrors: What America Needs to Know to Survive the Coming Bioterrorist Catastrophe by Dr. Michael Osterholm

The Criminalization of Christianity by Janet L. Folger

Speechless: Silencing the Christians by Rev. Don E. Wildmon

Made in the USA
Las Vegas, NV
15 September 2021